IN SPACE
NO ONE CAN
HEAR YOU
SCREAM

BAEN BOOKS
EDITED BY HANK DAVIS
))((((()))))

The Human Edge by Gordon R. Dickson

We the Underpeople by Cordwainer Smith
When the People Fell by Cordwainer Smith

The Technic Civilization Saga
The Van Rijn Method by Poul Anderson
David Falkayn: Star Trader by Poul Anderson
Rise of the Terran Empire by Poul Anderson
Young Flandry by Poul Anderson
Captain Flandry: Defender of the Terran Empire by Poul Anderson
Sir Dominic Flandry: The Last Knight of Terra by Poul Anderson
Flandry's Legacy by Poul Anderson

The Best of the Bolos: Their Finest Hour, created by Keith Laumer

A Cosmic Christmas
A Cosmic Christmas 2 You (forthcoming)

In Space No One Can Hear You Scream

IN SPACE NO ONE CAN HEAR YOU SCREAM

Edited By
HANK DAVIS

IN SPACE NO ONE CAN HEAR YOU SCREAM

A Baen Book

Baen Publishing Enterprises
P.O. Box 1403
Riverdale, NY 10471

ISBN 13: 978-1-4516-3941-4

Cover art by Bob Eggleton

First Baen printing, October 2013

Distributed by Simon & Schuster
1230 Avenue of the Americas
New York, NY 10020

Library of Congress Cataloging-in-Publication Data

In Space No One Can Hear You Scream / edited by Hank Davis.
   pages cm
   ISBN 978-1-4516-3941-4 (pbk.)
1. Science fiction, American. I. Davis, Hank, editor of compilation.
PS648.S3I53 2013
813'.0876208--dc23

                         2013032754

Printed in the United States of America

10 9 8 7 6 5 4 3 2 1

(((((CONTENTS)))))

((((o))))

This one is for my brother, Charles Richard Davis,
known to some as Richard, and to others as Charles,
with whom I watched *Shock Theater* on Saturday nights
in the late 1950s. Golden hours.

((((o))))

((((•))))
ACKNOWLEDGEMENTS

My thanks to all the contributors,
as well as those who helped with advice, permissions,
email addresses, and other kindnesses,
including Andrew and Ann Dibben, Noel Sturgeon,
William Dorman, Moshe Feder, David Drake,
Barry Malzberg, Chris Lotts, Ann Behar,
Russell Galen, Cameron McClure, Katie Shea,
Kay McCauley, Ellen Datlow, Bud Webster,
Nicholas Steers, and Christopher Cifani.
And to Toni Weisskopf, whose idea the whole thing was,
including the title

IN SPACE
NO ONE CAN
HEAR YOU
SCREAM

INTRODUCTION:
IT'S DARK BETWEEN
(((((THE STARS)))))

So, you're here to be scared, eh? No evasions, now. You saw the title. You saw the cover. You read the back cover copy. You knew this book was scary when you bought it. You didn't come in here just to get out of the rain. No fair claiming intellectual curiosity, even if you're in grad school and desperate for a thesis topic. You wanted to come in and get scared. Never mind that afterwards you'll leave, looking over your shoulder on the way home—did something *move* in the shadows over there?—twitching at odd noises, noticing for the first time how dark it is between those unsettlingly wide spaced streetlights (the ones that aren't burned out, that is), and of course when you walk home, it'll be *long* after dark. The whole nine scary yards.

So why are you spending time reading this introduction, then. Introductions aren't scary (though they may border on violence—hi, Harlan®). You should go right to the stories, without delay. Well, after you make sure all the doors are locked, all the lights are on, and there's nothing hiding under the bed or in any of the closets. (Yes, I know I just had you outdoors, walking home in the dark—this is an introduction and doesn't require rigorous consistency of scene, so there!) *Then* (did you look in *all* the closets?), you should go right to the stories.

Still here? An unkind person might think you were a bit scared of reading the stories. And I may be an editor, a contemptible breed

1

known for being as lacking in kindness as lawyers, insurance executives, politicians, journalists, and other such bottom-feeders, but I'd never accuse one of the readers who pays perfectly good money for books of being scared. You haven't read the stories yet—how could you already be scared? (Of course, there was that cover on the book . . .) You're just not in the mood, probably. So let's sit here (yes, all the doors are locked—just ignore that scrabbling at the door as if something wants in—and all the lights are on, and this is an imaginary room with no closets for things to hide in) and have a relaxed discussion about science fiction and horror stories. They're not necessarily the same thing, you know, though some people seem to think so.

In fact, I've long been puzzled by how many people think science fiction is *scary* . . . These are mostly people who don't *read* science fiction, of course. The idea isn't so much wrong, as very incomplete, like other general notions the mass mind has about science fiction, such as that all science fiction is set in space or in the future, or involves dystopias or post-apocalyptic worlds . . . or is intended to frighten. But some of it *is* intended to frighten, and here's a book full of tales by top writers who definitely intend to disturb your equanimity. (Are you sure you wouldn't rather be reading those nifty spine-chillers than listening to me drone on? But it's your choice.)

A friend of mine in college, who had observed my habit of consuming sf by the bushel, once mentioned that she didn't read it because she didn't want to be frightened. As it happens, she had been pushing me to read Agatha Christie, and I thought I'd expand her horizons by getting her to read the absolutely non-scary *Beyond This Horizon* by the Master, himself, Robert A. Heinlein (currently available from Baen Books, incidentally). In return I'd read one of Hercule Poirot's exploits. I held up my part of the deal, but she wimped out on her end, and as far as I know (haven't seen her in decades) she may *still* think sf is scary. (Maybe I shouldn't have mentioned to her how underwhelming I found Christie in comparison with Rex Stout, Raymond Chandler, or Leslie Charteris, but that's an introduction for a different book.) And her attitude was typical of a lot of people.

There might be a number of reasons for that. One might be the science fiction comic books of the 1950s (before the half-wit comedy team of Wertham and Kefauver ruined everything), which often had sf stories with a horror slant. *Weird Science* and *Weird Fantasy* from EC comics were a prime example, and probably the best done.

A more pervasive influence was in the many science fiction movies of the 1950s which were also horror movies. *Destination Moon* and *The Thing from Another World* debuted close together, but I think the latter movie stuck in people's minds more than the Heinlein-Pal flick. Before long, for every movie like *The Day the Earth Stood Still*, which certainly was not a horror movie (even if the alien robot Gort gets a bit scary in spots if you don't say the code words), there were several sf-horror hybrids, such as *Invasion of the Body Snatchers* or *The Creeping Unknown* (originally titled *The Quatermass Xperiment* in England), along with a veritable deluge of giant ants, giant grasshoppers, giant leeches, giant snails (in *The Monster That Challenged the World*, featuring the inimitable Hans Conreid, though he wasn't playing one of the snails), plus regular-sized or larger dinosaurs, as in *The Land Unknown*, *The Beast from 20,000 Fathoms* (which bore little resemblance to "The Foghorn," the Ray Bradbury story that "inspired" it) and the ever-popular *Godzilla* (or *Gojira*, as the big guy is called on his home turf—did you know that Godzilla has a star on the Hollywood Walk of Fame?).

Some of these were very good (the *Body Snatchers* and *Quatermass* movies in particular), and some weren't (the giant grasshopper and giant leech flicks, also in particular), but they all gave the typical movie-goer, who, also typically, wasn't reading the sf books and magazines of the time, the impression that science fiction equals horror.

Even sf movies which weren't constructed as horror often had monsters obligatto, such as a one-eyed amorphous blob in *It Came from Outer Space* (another flick indebted to Ray Bradbury, who had wanted the aliens to remain unseen, ala Val Lewton's *Cat People*), *This Island Earth*. with insect-like humanoids, and *The Incredible Shrinking Man*, with a regular-sized spider menacing a microscopic hero. Other movies felt the need to take a supernatural staple of horror movies and add a shaky science fictional rationale, as was done with two werewolf movies; though of the two only *I Was a Teenage Werewolf* is still remembered.

Nowadays, people are (I hope) more likely to think of science fiction in terms of *Star Trek* and *Star Wars*, which aren't frightening (unless you have a phobia for pointed ears or loud breathing). Since both franchises are more like written science fiction, or at least the written sf of the 1940s and 1950s, than the cinematic variety, the masses (who, remember, *read* little or no sf) may no longer conflate science fiction with horror. But on the other hand, I've noticed that a lot of people think of *The Twilight Zone* (the original) as scary, apparently because of a few episodes which were ("Nightmare at 20,000 Feet" for one, from a story by the late, great Richard Matheson). The wife of a friend of mine will not watch reruns of the show because she thinks it's scary, and mentions "Nightmare at 20,000 Feet," as a case in point. Even though very few installments of *The Twilight Zone* could be called scary, the attitude is widespread: check out the opening of the seriously flawed Spielberg movie clumsily based on the TV show. And then, there's *Alien* and its sequels.

Still here? Those are really neat stories you could be reading, you know? (Well, maybe except for one—something about a shadow.) I'm sure you didn't buy the book so that I could pontificate on old, er, vintage movies and TV shows. But I'll continue.

I may be focusing too strongly on movies and TV, even if most of the population get their impression of the sacred literature from the big and little screens. In the realm of the written word, there were all the covers of paperbacks of the 1950s and 60s, and even some of the hardcover dust jackets, on which anonymous and underpaid copy writers inscribed misleading descriptions. Their favorite word to use, of course, was "prophetic" (though sf is not, of course, prophecy), but the second, third, etc., most popular words with the cover copy writers were "frightening," "terrifying" (that one was on the front cover of an early paperback of Orwell's *1984*), "horrifying," and so on. Maybe those copy writers were seeing the aforementioned movies.

And, let us finally admit, there have been literary crossovers between sf and horror, and this goes back to the beginnings of the genre. *Carmilla* and *Dracula* weren't science fiction, but *Frankenstein* was. Stories about ghosts and werewolves weren't science fiction (at least until Jack Williamson wrote "Wolves of Darkness" and *Darker Than You Think*), but *Strange Case of Dr. Jekyll and Mr. Hyde* was. *The War of the Worlds* can be read as a horror story—certainly, the first appearance of the tentacled Martians is meant to be frightening—and as far as Universal Pictures was concerned, Wells' *The Invisible Man* was definitely a horror story, even if the eponymous character never went on to meet Dracula or the Wolf Man. Almost everyone agrees that John W. Campbell's greatest story is "Who Goes There?"—and it's also one of the greatest horror stories in or out of science fiction. A bit earlier, H. P. Lovecraft, whose influence on the horror genre is incalculable, would introduce his Cthulhu mythos (though I believe he never called it that) in which the universe is a downright terrifying neighborhood, and unspeakable horrors, the very sight of which drives humans insane, have come to Earth from space in the distant past and still drop in unexpectedly, and will someday take the planet away from the pathetic humans who thought they ruled it.

Of course, though Lovecraft's critters came from outside the Earth, Lovecraft himself never set any of his stories off the planet. That left possibilities open for other writers. Instead of waiting for nameless eldritch alien horrors to come to us, why don't we go to them? And many writers sent their characters out to do just that. (What some of those characters might have thought about it is conjectural, of course, particularly with those who were never heard from again.)

So here's a selection of stories old and new, three from the grand old days of the pulp magazines early in the last century, three new ones appearing here for the first time, and an assortment of blood-curdlers from the years in between, waiting for you to read them. You needn't be so apprehensive, since sometimes the Thing from Outer Space doesn't win. On the other hand . . . but you'll have to read them to find out which stories are which. You *are* going to read them, surely . . .

I'm nearly finished now, and there's nothing to keep you from the stories. In summary, science fiction isn't scary all of the time, or even most of the time, but sometimes, as the immortal Mr. Fudd might put it, it's vewwy, vewwy scawwy. John W. Campbell, the legendary science fiction editor, once wrote that science fiction stories are the dreams of a technological society such as ours. He also noted parenthetically that "some dreams are nightmares."

Pleasant dreams.

—Hank Davis

((((Arthur C. Clarke))))

Through his distinguished career in science fiction, Sir Arthur C. Clarke (1917-2008) was known both for writing the hardest of hard science fiction stories and novels and also for visionary far-future stories showing the influence of Olaf Stapledon. But there were more sides to Sir Arthur, as in the humorous stories he collected in *Tales from the White Hart*, and in his being a fan of celebrated horror writer H.P. Lovecraft ("[H]is best stories were masterpieces in their genre," Clarke wrote in a letter to fantasy master Lord Dunsany), which led to his writing, early in his career, "At the Mountains of Murkiness," a Lovecraft parody. "A Walk in the Dark" is definitely *not* a parody, and starts out apparently in Clarke's best hard science vein, but gradually takes a sinister turn. A distinguished science fiction editor once wrote that the first story she read by Clarke, when she was very young, was this one, and it frightened her so much that it was years before she could bring herself to read anything else with his name on it. Of course, the typical reader isn't going to grow up to be an editor, and can probably handle this story. Right after they make sure all the lights are on and check the batteries in their flashlight . . .

Known for being one of the "Big Three" writers of modern science fiction (with Robert A. Heinlein and Isaac Asimov), co-author of and technical advisor for the now-classic movie, *2001: A Space Odyssey*, author of many best-selling novels, commentator on CBS's coverage of the Apollo missions, and winner of numerous awards, Sir Arthur C. Clarke (2017-2008) surely needs no introduction (though I just snuck one in anyway). In a technical paper in 1945, he was first to describe how geosynchronous satellites could relay broadcasts from the ground around the world"., bringing a new era in global communications and television. His novels are too numerous to list here (but I'll plug three of my favorites: *The City and the Stars*, *Childhood's End*, and *Earthlight*), let alone his many short stories. He was equally adept at non-fiction, notably in his *The Exploration of Space* in the early 1950s, his frequently reprinted *Profiles of the Future*, and another bunch of books also too numerous to mention. So, instead of not mentioning them further, I'll just say, go thou and read.

(((((A WALK IN THE DARK)))))

Arthur C. Clarke

Robert Armstrong had walked just over two miles, as far as he could judge, when his torch failed. He stood still for a moment, unable to believe that such a misfortune could really have befallen him. Then, half maddened with rage, he hurled the useless instrument away. It landed somewhere in the darkness, disturbing the silence of this little world. A metallic echo came ringing back from the low hills: then all was quiet again.

This, thought Armstrong, was the ultimate misfortune. Nothing more could happen to him now. He was even able to laugh bitterly at his luck, and resolved never again to imagine that the fickle goddess had ever favored him. Who would have believed that the only tractor at Camp IV would have broken down when he was just setting off for Port Sanderson? He recalled the frenzied repair work, the relief when the second start had been made, and the final debacle when the caterpillar track had jammed.

It was no use then regretting the lateness of his departure: he could not have foreseen these accidents, and it was still a good four hours before the *Canopus* took off. He had to catch her, whatever happened; no other ship would be touching at this world for another month.

Apart from the urgency of his business, four more weeks on this out-of-the-way planet were unthinkable.

There had been only one thing to do. It was lucky that Port Sanderson was little more than six miles from the camp—not a great distance, even on foot. He had had to leave all his equipment behind, but it could follow on the next ship and he could manage without it. The road was poor, merely stamped out of the rock by one of the Board's hundred-ton crushers, but there was no fear of going astray.

Even now, he was in no real danger, though he might well be too late to catch the ship. Progress would be slow, for he dare not risk losing the road in this region of canyons and enigmatic tunnels that had never been explored. It was, of course, pitch-dark. Here at the edge of the Galaxy the stars were so few and scattered that their light was negligible. The strange crimson sun of this lonely world would not rise for many hours, and although five of the little moons were in the sky, they could barely be seen by the unaided eye. Not one of them could even cast a shadow.

Armstrong was not the man to bewail his luck for long. He began to walk slowly along the road, feeling its texture with his feet. It was, he knew, fairly straight except where it wound through Carver's Pass. He wished he had a stick or something to probe the way before him, but he would have to rely for guidance on the feel of the ground.

It was terribly slow at first, until he gained confidence. He had never known how difficult it was to walk in a straight line. Although the feeble stars gave him his bearings, again and again he found himself stumbling among the virgin rocks at the edge of the crude roadway. He was traveling in long zigzags that took him to alternate sides of the road. Then he would stub his toes against the bare rock and grope his way back onto the hard-packed surface once again.

Presently it settled down to a routine. It was impossible to estimate his speed; he could only struggle along and hope for the best. There were four miles to go—four miles and as many hours. It should be easy enough, unless he lost his way. But he dared not think of that.

Once he had mastered the technique he could afford the luxury of thought. He could not pretend that he was enjoying the experience, but he had been in much worse positions before. As long as he remained on the road, he was perfectly safe. He had been hoping that as his eyes became adapted to the starlight he would be able to see the way, but he now knew that the whole journey would be blind. The discovery gave him a vivid sense of his remoteness from the heart of the Galaxy. On a night as clear as this, the skies of almost any other planet would have been blazing with stars. Here at this outpost of the Universe the sky held perhaps a hundred faintly gleaming points of light, as useless as the five ridiculous moons on which no one had ever bothered to land.

A slight change in the road interrupted his thoughts. Was there a curve here, or had he veered off to the right again? He moved very slowly along the invisible and ill-defined border. Yes, there was no mistake: the road was bending to the left. He tried to remember its appearance in the daytime, but he had only seen it once before. Did this mean that he was nearing the Pass? He hoped so, for the journey would then be half-completed.

He peered ahead into the blackness, but the ragged line of the horizon told him nothing. Presently he found that the road had straightened itself again and his spirits sank. The entrance to the Pass must still be some way ahead: there were at least four miles to go.

Four miles—how ridiculous the distance seemed! How long would it take the *Canopus* to travel four miles? He doubted if man could measure so short an interval of time. And how many trillions of miles had he, Robert Armstrong, traveled in his life? It must have reached a staggering total by now, for in the last twenty years he had scarcely stayed more than a month at a time on any single world. This very year, he had twice made the crossing of the Galaxy, and that was a notable journey even in these days of the phantom drive.

He tripped over a loose stone, and the jolt brought him back to reality. It was no use, here, thinking of ships that could eat up the light-years. He was facing Nature, with no weapons but his own strength and skill.

It was strange that it took him so long to identify the real cause of his uneasiness. The last four weeks had been very full, and the rush of his departure, coupled with the annoyance and anxiety caused by the tractor's breakdowns, had driven everything else from his mind. Moreover, he had always prided himself on his hardheadedness and lack of imagination. Until now, he had forgotten all about that first evening at the Base, when the crews had regaled him with the usual tall yarns concocted for the benefit of newcomers.

It was then that the old Base clerk had told the story of his walk by night from Port Sanderson to the camp, and of what had trailed him through Carver's Pass, keeping always beyond the limit of his torchlight. Armstrong, who had heard such tales on a score of worlds, had paid it little attention at the time. This planet, after all, was known to be uninhabited. But logic could not dispose of the matter as easily as that. Suppose, after all, there was some truth in the old man's fantastic tale. . . ?

It was not a pleasant thought, and Armstrong did not intend to brood upon it. But he knew that if he dismissed it out of hand it would continue to prey on his mind. The only way to conquer imaginary fears was to face them boldly; he would have to do that now.

His strongest argument was the complete barrenness of this world and its utter desolation, though against that one could set many counterarguments, as indeed the old clerk had done. Man had only lived on this planet for twenty years, and much of it was still unexplored. No one could deny that the tunnels out in the wasteland were rather puzzling, but everyone believed them to be volcanic vents. Though, of course, life often crept into such places. With a shudder he remembered the giant polyps that had snared the first explorers of Vargon III.

It was all very inconclusive. Suppose, for the sake of argument, one granted the existence of life here. What of that?

The vast majority of life forms in the Universe were completely indifferent to man. Some, of course, like the gas-beings of Alcoran or the roving wave-lattices of Shandaloon, could not even detect him but passed through or around him as if he did not exist. Others were merely inquisitive, some embarrassingly friendly. There were few indeed that would attack unless provoked.

Nevertheless, it was a grim picture that the old stores clerk had painted. Back in the warm, well-lighted smoking room, with the drinks going around, it had been easy enough to laugh at it. But here in the darkness, miles from any human settlement, it was very different.

It was almost a relief when he stumbled off the road again and had to grope with his hands until he found it once more. This seemed a very rough patch, and the road was scarcely distinguishable from the rocks around. In a few minutes, however, he was safely on his way again.

It was unpleasant to see how quickly his thoughts returned to the same disquieting subject. Clearly it was worrying him more than he cared to admit.

He drew consolation from one fact: it had been quite obvious that no one at the Base had believed the old fellow's story. Their questions and banter had proved that. At the time, he had laughed as loudly as any of them. After all, what was the evidence? A dim shape, just seen in the darkness, that might well have been an oddly formed rock. And the curious clicking noise that had so impressed the old man—anyone could imagine such sounds at night if they were sufficiently overwrought. If it had been hostile, why hadn't the creature come any closer? "Because it was afraid of my light," the old chap had said. Well, that was plausible enough: it would explain why nothing had ever been seen in the daylight. Such a creature might live underground, only emerging at night—damn it, why was he taking the old idiot's ravings so seriously! Armstrong got control of his thoughts again. If he went on this way, he told himself angrily, he would soon be seeing and hearing a whole menagerie of monsters.

There was, of course, one factor that disposed of the ridiculous story at once. It was really very simple; he felt sorry he hadn't thought of it before. *What would such a creature live on?* There was not even a trace of vegetation on the whole of the planet. He laughed to think that the bogey could be disposed of so easily—and in the same instant felt annoyed with himself for not laughing aloud. If he was so sure of his reasoning, why not whistle, or sing, or do anything to keep up his spirits? He put the question fairly to himself as a text of his manhood. Half-ashamed, he had to admit that he was still afraid—afraid because "there *might* be something in it after all." But at least his analysis had done him some good.

It would have been better if he had left it there, and remained half-convinced by his argument. But a part of his mind was still trying to break down his careful reasoning. It succeeded only too well, and when he remembered the plant-beings of Zantil Major the shock was so unpleasant that he stopped dead in his tracks.

Now the plant-beings of Xantil were not in any way horrible. They were in fact extremely beautiful creatures. But what made them appear so distressing now was the knowledge that they could live for indefinite periods with no food whatsoever. All the energy they needed for their strange lives they extracted from cosmic radiation—and that was almost as intense here as anywhere else in the universe.

He had scarcely thought of one example before others crowded into his mind and he remembered the life form on Trantor Beta, which was the only one known capable of directly utilizing atomic energy. That too had lived on an utterly barren world, very much like this . . .

Armstrong's mind was rapidly splitting into two distinct portions, each trying to convince the other and neither wholly succeeding. He did not realize how far his morale had gone until he found himself holding his breath lest it conceal any sound from the darkness about him. Angrily, he cleared his mind of the rubbish that had been gathering there and turned once more to the immediate problem.

There was no doubt that the road was slowly rising, and the silhouette of the horizon seemed much higher in the sky. The road began to twist, and suddenly he was aware of great rocks on either side of him. Soon only a narrow ribbon of sky was still visible, and the darkness became, if possible, even more intense.

Somehow, he felt safer with the rock walls surrounding him: it meant that he was protected except in two directions. Also, the road had been leveled more carefully and it was easy to keep it. Best of all, he knew now that the journey was more than half completed.

For a moment his spirits began to rise. Then, with maddening perversity, his mind went back into the old grooves again. He remembered that it was on the far side of Carver's Pass that the old clerk's adventure had taken place—if it had ever happened at all.

In half a mile, he would be out in the open again, out of the protection of these sheltering rocks. The thought seemed doubly horrible now and he already felt a sense of nakedness. He could be attacked from any direction, and he would be utterly helpless . . .

Until now, he had still retained some self-control. Very resolutely he had kept his mind away from the one fact that gave some color to the old man's tale—the single piece of evidence that had stopped the banter in the crowded room back at the camp and brought a sudden hush upon the company. Now, as Armstrong's will weakened, he recalled again the words that had struck a momentary chill even in the warm comfort of the base building.

The little clerk had been very insistent on one point. He had never heard any sound of pursuit from the dim shape sensed, rather than seen, at the limit of his light. There was no scuffling of claws or hoofs on rock, not even the clatter of displaced stones. It was as if, so the old man had declared in that solemn manner of his, "as if the thing that was following could see perfectly in the darkness, and had many small legs or pads so that it could move swiftly and easily over the rock—like a giant caterpillar or one of the carpet-things of Kralkor II."

Yet, although there had been no noise of pursuit, there had been one sound that the old man had caught several times. It was so unusual that its very strangeness made it doubly ominous. It was a faint but horribly persistent *clicking*.

The old fellow had been able to describe it very vividly—much too vividly for Armstrong's liking now.

"Have you ever listened to a large insect crunching its prey?" he said. "Well, it was just like that. I imagine that a crab makes exactly the same noise with its claws when it clashes them together. It was a—what's the word?—a *chitinous* sound."

At this point, Armstrong remembered laughing loudly. (Strange, how it was all coming back to him now.) But no one else had laughed, though they had been quick to do so earlier. Sensing the change of tone, he had sobered at once and asked the old man to continue his story. How he wished now that he had stifled his curiosity!

It had been quickly told. The next day, a party of skeptical technicians had gone into the no-man's land beyond Carver's Pass. They were not skeptical enough to leave their guns behind, but they had no cause to use them for they found no trace of any living thing.

There were the inevitable pits and tunnels, glistening holes down which the light of the torches rebounded endlessly until it was lost in the distance—but the planet was riddled with them.

Though the party found no sign of life, it discovered one thing it did not like at all. Out in the barren and unexplored land beyond the Pass they had come upon an even larger tunnel than the rest. Near the mouth of that tunnel was a massive rock, half embedded in the ground. And the sides of that rock had been worn away *as if it had been used as an enormous whetstone.*

No less than five of those present had seen this disturbing rock. None of them could explain it satisfactorily as a natural formation, but they still refused to accept the old man's story. Armstrong had asked them if they had ever put it to the test. There had been an uncomfortable silence. Then big Andrew Hargraves had said: "Hell, who'd walk out to the Pass at night just for fun!" and had left it at that. Indeed, there was no other record of anyone walking from Port Sanderson to the camp by night, or for that matter by day. During the hours of light, no unprotected human being could live in the open beneath the rays of the enormous, lurid sun that seemed to fill half the sky. And no one would walk six miles, wearing radiation armor, if the tractor was available.

Armstrong felt he was leaving the Pass. The rocks on either side were falling away, and the road was no longer as firm and well packed as it had been. He was coming out into the open plain once more, and somewhere not far away in the darkness was that enigmatic pillar that might have been used for sharpening monstrous fangs or claws. It was not a reassuring thought, but he could not get it out of his mind.

Feeling distinctly worried now, Armstrong made great effort to pull himself together. He would try to be rational again; he would think of business, the work he had done at the camp—anything but this infernal place. For a while he succeeded quite well. But presently, with a maddening persistence, every train of thought came back to the same point. He could not get out of his mind the picture of that inexplicable rock and its appalling possibilities. Over and over again he found himself wondering how far away it was, whether he had already passed it, and whether it was on his right or his left.

The ground was quite flat again, and the road drove on straight as an arrow. There was one gleam of consolation: Port Sanderson could not be much more than two miles away. Armstrong had no idea how long he had been on the road. Unfortunately his watch was not illuminated and he could only guess at the passage of time. With any luck, the *Canopus* should not take off for another two hours at least. But he could not be sure, and now another fear began to enter his mind—the dread that he might see a vast constellation of lights rising swiftly into the sky ahead, and know that all this agony of mind had been in vain.

He was not zigzagging so badly now, and seemed to be able to anticipate the edge of the road before stumbling off it. It was probable, he cheered himself by thinking, that he was traveling almost as fast as if he had a light. If all went well, he might be nearing Port Sanderson in thirty minutes—a ridiculously small space of time. How he would laugh at his fears when he strolled into his already reserved stateroom in the "Canopus," and felt that peculiar quiver as the phantom drive hurled the great ship far out of this system, back to the clustered star-clouds near the center of the Galaxy—back toward Earth itself, which he had not seen for so many years. One day, he told himself, he really must visit Earth again. All his life he had been making the promise, but always there had been the same answer—lack of time. Strange, wasn't it, that such a tiny planet should have played so enormous a part in the development of the Universe, should even have come to dominate worlds far wiser and more intelligent than itself!

Armstrong's thoughts were harmless again, and he felt calmer. The knowledge that he was nearing Port Sanderson was immensely reassuring, and he deliberately kept his mind on familiar, unimportant matters. Carver's Pass was already far behind, and with it that thing he no longer intended to recall. One day, if he ever returned to this world, he would visit the pass in the daytime and laugh at his fears. In twenty minutes now, they would have joined the nightmares of his childhood.

It was almost a shock, though one of the most pleasant he had ever known, when he saw the lights of Port Sanderson come up over the horizon. The curvature of this little world was very deceptive: it did not seem right that a planet with a gravity almost as great as Earth's should have a horizon so close at hand. One day, someone would have to discover what lay at this world's core to give it so great a density. Perhaps the many tunnels would help—it was an unfortunate turn of thought, but the nearness of his goal had robbed it of terror now. Indeed, the thought that he might really be in danger seemed to give his adventure a certain piquancy and heightened interest. Nothing could happen to hims now, with ten minutes to go and the lights of the Port already in sight.

A few minutes later, his feelings changed abruptly when he came to the sudden bend in the road. He had forgotten the chasm that caused his detour, and added half a mile to the journey. Well, what of it? He thought stubbornly. An extra half-mile would make no difference now—another ten minutes, at the most.

It was very disappointing when the lights of the city vanished. Armstrong had not remembered the hill which the road was skirting, perhaps it was only a low ridge, scarcely noticeable in the daytime. But by hiding the lights of the port it had taken away his chief talisman and left him again at the mercy of his fears.

Very unreasonably, his intelligence told him, he began to think how horrible it would be if anything happened now, so near the end of the journey. He kept the worst of his fears at bay for a while, hoping desperately that the lights of the city would soon reappear. But as the minutes dragged on, he realized that the ridge must be longer than he imagined. He tried to cheer himself by the thought that the city would be all the nearer when he saw it again, but somehow logic seemed to have failed him now. For presently he found himself doing something he had not stooped to, even out in the waste by Carver's Pass.

He stopped, turned slowly round, and with bated breath listened until his lungs were nearly bursting.

The silence was uncanny, considering how near he must be to the Port. There was certainly no sound from behind him. Of course there wouldn't be, he told himself angrily. But he was immensely relieved. The thought of that faint and insistent clicking had been haunting him for the last hour.

So friendly and familiar was the noise that did reach him at last that the anticlimax almost made him laugh aloud. Drifting through the still air from a source clearly not more than a mile away came the sound of a landing-field tractor, perhaps one of the machines loading the *Canopus* itself. In a matter of seconds, thought Armstrong, he would be around this ridge with the Port only a few hundred yards ahead. The journey was nearly ended. In a few moments, this evil plain would be no more than a fading nightmare.

It seemed terribly unfair: so little time, such a small fraction of a human life, was all he needed now. But the gods have always been unfair to man, and now there were enjoying their little jest. For there could be no mistaking the rattle of monstrous claws in the darkness *ahead of him.*

(((((Tony Daniel)))))

Here's a tale with a number of twists, with an alien who didn't think she was evil or malevolent, though her preteen prisoner had a different take on the matter. And maybe the alien shouldn't have assumed that kidnapping an adolescent girl was the best and easiest way to bring a specimen back to her home system. Too bad the alien wasn't familiar with human fairytales, and what happened to evil stepmothers in them . . .

Tony Daniel is the author of five science fiction books, the latest of which is *Guardian of Night*, as well as an award-winning short story collection, *the Robot's Twilight Companion*. He also collaborated with David Drake on the novel *The Heretic*, and its forthcoming sequel, *The Savior*, new novels in the popular military science fiction series, The General. His story "Life on the Moon," was a Hugo finalist and also won the *Asimov's* Reader's Choice Award. Daniel's short fiction has been much anthologized and has been collected in multiple year's best anthologies. Daniel has also co-written screen plays for SyFy Channel horror movies, and during the early 2000s was the writer and director of numerous audio dramas for critically-acclaimed SCIFICOM's Seeing Ear theater. Born in Alabama, Daniel has lived in St. Louis, Los Angeles, Seattle, Prague, and New York City. He is now an editor at Baen Books and lives in Wake Forest, North Carolina with his wife and two children.

))(((FROG WATER)))(((

Tony Daniel

The ship soothed my legs with the slop wands. Aleria had ordered it to do so. She thought I was upset about the blisters on my thighs and shins, but the truth was that I was used to those now. I let her keep thinking that was what it was, though. This was something I'd learned to do back home, even though maybe I didn't know I'd learned it at the time: you know, act like something bad that happened is much worse than it actually is until you can figure out your next move.

The wands were wet and gooey. I was holding onto a wall strap and stuck my legs out floating in front of me so the ship could get to them easily. Living in the ship was like living inside a kind of cave, only the stalactites and stalagmites could grow out of the ship wall instantly, and they could be long and thin, or thick and bumpy. They would also be hollow, like a hose. They delivered all kinds of stuff, from fluid to the goo on the slop wands, to the gray stuff I sucked out of one of them that Aleria called food. It must be something close, because it had kept me alive and kicking for over a year.

Anyway, the slop wands were a little different. They were more like sea anemones with swirling little tentaclely brushes. They were coated with this combination of nutrient and lubricating solution for the mechs in my skin.

The goo was kind of rancid to tell the truth. It smelled like that time Dustin found the frog eggs when he was playing at the creek by my old house, and he brought this big mass of eggs home and put them in a bottle of water—one of those plastic bottles that used to be at the grocery stores and they came in a case of twelve or twenty or however many and they were wrapped in that clear wrap like a little squeaky pod. We always got Something *Springs* Water, something like that. I'd forgotten the brand name. It wasn't something I ever thought I'd want to remember, you know?

I used to really like to poke my fingers in the plastic wrap of those cases, because it would give a lot without breaking and make these kind of dorky dimples that looked funny, before finally it would break. Da yelled at me for wasting my time doing it once.

"But it feels good, Da," I would say, and he would smile and say, "Yeah, sweetiepie, I guess it does, at that." And we poked a couple in together.

So Dustin leaves the frog eggs on that little side cart thing by the kitchen table and one day about a week later Mom comes in from gardening and she's all thirsty and what does she do? She looks around, and sees a half-full water bottle and reaches for it and takes a swig.

And there I am sitting at the table, eating some microwave shrimp dinner or something, and I'm in a hurry because I have to go to a soccer game.

Mom turns to tell me probably to hurry up or we'll be late.

She realizes her mouth is full of water.

Then she realizes what's *in* that water.

Spew!

Week-old frog egg water all over the side of my face, in my hair, on my jersey sleeve, in the macaroni and shrimp. And there's even some of it on the fork that's just going into my mouth. Frog water—and into my mouth before I can stop it.

Disgusting!

I spit out the frog water shrimp and macaroni on the plate. Meanwhile, Mom runs over to the sink and gags, trying to throw up, but she can't get herself to.

And I, I remember, I went over there too, and I couldn't help it, and I shouldn't have done what I did next, because I was just as grossed out as she was, but I couldn't help it. I laughed.

And she turned and looked at me so hurt, that I would laugh at her at a time like that. She didn't say anything, but I'll never forget that look she gave me.

And I felt really bad and started to cry, "Sorry, Mommy. Sorry, sorry, sorry." Because I still called her that sometimes back then, "Mommy."

And then Mom smiled. Everything was all right.

Except that she went ahead and threw up right then and there into the sink, of course. After all, she'd drunk a huge swallow of frog egg water.

I was ten at the time. It was not long before that night with the glowing light, and the bad dream, and the next thing I know I woke up in the crèche, and then there was Aleria hunched over me, staring at me with those eye stalks of hers.

But back to the frog water: the smell of it hit us both. It was *on* me, and it was *rancid*. And we both started to gag and laugh, and Mom helped me clean up real quick, and she brushed her teeth and gargled with some old mouthwash she found under the bathroom cabinet, *Tangerine* or *Listerane* or something, I can't remember, and we made it to the soccer game just in time. But I had to keep the same jersey on since I only had the one, and I smelled that gag-me frog water smell the whole time and it made me so mad I scored a goal *and* took another girl out with a slide tackle when I was on defense and got yellow-carded and almost thrown out. Anyway, we won that time, and all the other girls jumped on me, and high-fived me for playing so good. And I forgot all about the frog water after that. Until now.

The slop wand goo had been in storage probably for years, and, like everything else on Aleria's ship, was kind of stale smelling or tasting.

I dried myself off with a towel that came out of another maker-bump from the ship wall. You have to dry yourself off in zero g. Any liquid that's water-based will stick to you like a layer of paste or cooking oil or something, and it won't just run off, because there's no "down" for it to run toward. I gave the wet towel to a disposal tube, which sucked it down.

"Space or recycle?" asked the ship.

"Recycle," I answered.

There wasn't any reason to throw the thing away, even though interstellar space was pretty empty and could use maybe a towel floating out there between stars to give it some character.

After Aleria had detached herself from my legs, she slid over to her resting globe. It was kind of like a chair for Aleria, and it floated in the exact middle of the bridge pod. It was held in place by magnets or some kind of forcefield thing like that, because if you tried to move the globe from the center, it would pop back into position. It had an opening on one side, so Aleria, who didn't have any skeleton or exoskeleton at all, could slide into there like a, say, one of those sea slugs from the Science Channel, and bunch up in a ball. This was relaxing to Aleria's type, the Meebs. I'd never met any others, but she'd had me watch plenty of videos.

"You'll be meeting them soon, after all," she said. "Your new brothers and sisters and aunts and uncles. By the time we arrive, you'll really be looking forward to it."

So there she sat in the middle of the bridge pod. This was what I called the room, anyway. It was oval shaped, like an egg. There wasn't really any floor or ceiling, just a wall, because this was zero g. The resting globe was clear and it looked like one of those terrariums I used to see in Pet Mart or whatever that place was called. I guess the globe ones were supposed to look cool. They sat on a stand and you put turtles or frogs or whatever air breathing stuff in them. Dustin and I only ever had gold fish.

Thinking about Dustin made me whimper a little. I guess it was pretty loud. I didn't cry anymore, but I couldn't help sometimes letting out something like that. I hated it when I did. I hated to let Aleria know anything about how I was really feeling. She was going to own my thoughts and feelings pretty soon, and I wanted to keep them for myself as long as I could before that happened.

"Honey, won't you tell me what's the matter?" said the voice from the ship's speakers. This was Aleria talking. The regular ship voice was just a voice, maybe a woman, maybe a man. Gray, like everything else here. But Aleria's voice was all honey-sweet. She kind of sounded like when Da would do the helium breath voice at my and Dustin's birthday parties, but full of "oohs," and "aahs," and "dears" and "darlings."

She didn't have a real voice, of course. She was a blob, not a human. She talked to the ship the way her kind did—through chemical packets that she kind of flicked at the walls, where they were absorbed. I thought of them as booger-filled snot. The ship then translated the packets and spoke in the made-up voice it had for her.

"The nodes are hurting me inside," I said. Which was true. The implants, which she'd put into me, were growing inside my muscles and would one day take over all of me, did hurt. This was an always and forever ache, and I didn't let it affect me anymore. But it was a good excuse.

"I'm sorry, Megan, but one day the pain will be gone, I promise."

"And I'll be like you."

"You'll be part of me," Aleria said. "I'll hug you really tight, and we'll be together forever."

You're not my mother, I thought. *My mother is ten thousand light-years behind me.*

I didn't really care about what the change was doing to my body that much. Oh, I did a little. But one day my *thoughts* were not going to be my own. That was what I really hated, hated, hated.

One day, all my memories of Mom, Da, Dustin and the rest would belong to Aleria. And I knew what she'd do with them, all right. She was jealous. She would keep the knowledge, but wipe the love away. She wanted me all for herself.

"Darling, you're so sweet, I need another sip of you," Aleria said through the ship speaker. "Bring the conditioner over and bathe me, there's a good girl."

The ship wall made a faucet. That was the only way I could think to describe it. You squeezed the outside of the faucet like maybe you would milk a cow—even though I never milked a cow in my life, we lived in the suburbs—and this kind of gloppy sausage filling stuff would come out. It was some kind of enzyme that softened up Aleria's membrane artificially so she could feed again without having to wait her normal period, which could be a couple of hours. I caught the glop in a balloon bag, then pinched the balloon closed, and slid the end from the faucet. There was another maker-cone thingie nearby, more or less permanent, for water. I put the lip of the balloon over this one and squeezed out some water to mix with the enzyme-glop inside the balloon.

When I took the balloon off the water maker-cone, a few drops of water escaped. Water drops didn't just float off into space like you might think. They were still touching my hand, and water has this weird surface tension. In zero g it will stick to you. I remember when we had toast for breakfast and I would get some strawberry jelly on my hands and you couldn't wipe it off with a napkin and even if you licked your fingers—gross!—that jelly-slimy feeling would still be there until you gave your hands a good washing.

Water does that in zero g. A thin coat will stick to you no matter how hard you shake your hand or whatever to get it off. The only way to get rid of it is to find something absorbent and let that soak it up. I wiped these water drops on the side of my pants. I wear these kind of gray pajama top and bottoms made out of some kind of thin material. I don't know what they're made of, but I'm pretty sure they aren't one hundred percent cotton. They fit me okay, but I've been growing a lot lately and my wrists and ankles are starting to stick way out.

Anyway, I kept the balloon pinched off and then sloshed around the water and enzyme goop solution inside, mixing it. After a while, it started to make a solution with no lumps. That was the way Aleria liked it. Absolutely no lumps. I kicked off from the wall and floated over to Aleria's globe. She was packed in there pretty good, but a couple of pseudopods were sticking out, drifting kind of lazily around. There was a holding strap attached to the globe especially for me, so I hooked in with a foot and kind of bent myself around the globe. I'd gotten really good at swimming in zero g. If there was zero g soccer, I was sure I'd be good enough to score goals.

I squeezed the conditioning solution into the top of the tank. It hung onto Aleria's outer membrane the same way water clung to my skin. I spread it around. A little stream of snot-talk shot out from her and right by my face. I heard it splat, soft-like, into the ship wall.

"Wonderful," said the wall speaker. "That's it. Rub it in. Get me soft, dear."

I remembered getting hugged by Mom. The hug I used the most was the big one she gave me when I was finally starting to get okay grades on my language art quizzes. I was kind of slow learning to read—I was still on second grade books when I was already in third grade—but then one day in fourth grade, it just seemed a lot easier. And Mom was this big reader—she always had a book around—and she wanted us to share that, liking books and all. We never really got a chance.

I used that hug a lot, though.

I spread on the rest of the conditioner. I reached into the tank and kind of kneaded her like a giant ball of Play-doh. She could squeeze up real tight, about the size of a basketball, when she wanted to.

"Careful, careful, child," said the wall. "Not too much on the underside. I'll turn blue."

Aleria was kind of a clear color, but not see-through. She looked like gloppy Elmer's glue if it had dark chunks floating around in it like Aleria's organs and nodules and stuff did.

"Why will you turn blue, Aleria?" I asked,

"I do wish you'd call me Mother, as we discussed."

"Why will you turn blue, Mother?"

"I'm not sure," she said. "I never was much of a chemist. My specialty is scouting, as you know. But you humans and we Meebs do need oxygen in about the same amounts. That's why I picked you out at the crèche, of course. You and I can share the same atmosphere."

The crèche, I thought with a shudder. It was a collection station, staffed by Meeb robots. I only found that out later.

One day I went to sleep in my room. Mine was the one over the garage. It was farther from Mom and Da's bedroom that Dustin's was, but it was a little bigger than his. Mom and I painted it up with peace signs and flowers and stuff.

I dreamed about a bright light.

And when I woke up, I wasn't in my room anymore. I was in a cage.

There were other people in there with me from all different parts of the world, like India and Australia and China and like that. Some were kids, some were adults. It was like this white room we couldn't see the walls of, but we couldn't get out of. I was the youngest.

What none of us knew what that we were in a Pet Mart. I mean, an alien Pet Mart.

I used to love going to Pet Mart. I really liked watching those cuddly looking chinchillas, and the cute little mice running around and around to nowhere in those wheels of theirs. I liked it when they grabbed the wheels and took a ride around and around for a few turns. It made you think that they weren't completely stupid, and kind of knew what they were doing.

Or no. The crèche was not like the pet store. It was lots worse. Because I knew now what it meant to be *picked out* at the crèche. To be the one who gets selected by that floating glob outside the cage window.

Kind of like a pet store crossed with a grocery store. That was maybe the closest way of looking at it. Kind of, but not really.

The ones Aleria didn't pick out of her trap got recycled, of course. Aleria was very big on a recycling.

I emptied the rest of the balloon then kicked over to the disposal. I stuck my hand into the blister orifice and let it suck away the used balloon skin. The reason the disposal blister didn't suck me away was because of the mechs in my skin. They got pinged and identified me, my body, as "keep." The disposal unit then asked the question it always asked.

"Space or recycle?"

"Recycle," I answered.

And that was all there was to it. The blister didn't care; it just needed the answer to follow its programming. The ship might be an artificial intelligence of some sort, but it sure wasn't any kind of genius.

I pushed off and went back to Aleria. She was conditioned now. All her pseudopods were retracted which I knew meant she was waiting expectantly. It was time.

I stuck my hands into the globe, into the main opening, and stuck them into *her,* pushing into her gooey flesh. The outside of her dimpled for a ways, like the plastic wrap on those cases of water bottles did, then it gave away completely, and my hands and arms were within the milky glop that floated inside Aleria, that *was* Aleria.

A stream of her speech-mucus twisted past me. It hit the walls and got absorbed and translated.

"Aaah," the wall speaker sighed. "That's it. Deeper, deeper."

I plunged in up to my shoulders. I felt the goo of her surround my arms. And then I felt the prickles where she broke the skin and where parts of her slid inside *me*.

She wasn't just feeding on me, she was changing me. Changing me into more of *her*. One day, when the nodules she left inside me reached maturity, I would be "ripe," and she would be able to absorb me completely. We would be one.

"My youth will be restored, darling, and your youth will last forever."

She never told me exactly how the process worked. "I'm not a biologist, dear. I'm a scout," was her only reply when I asked. But I knew a lot more about Meebs now that I'd been on the ship for a year and seen the videos. At least I thought it was a year I'd been here. I figured I was about the size of an eleven-year-old, even though there were no mirrors, and if there had been, I would have avoided them. I hadn't seen myself in a long time. I was kind of afraid to look, afraid to see what the mechs had done to my face. My skin was as gray as my pajamas. But at least, with the mechs in it, it was kind of shiny.

I pushed into Aleria as deep as I could, because I knew if I didn't, she would demand it of me anyway.

"Is that good, Mother?"

"You have no idea, dear. Replenishment is the greatest pleasure in life, and don't let anybody tell you different."

Finally, after what seemed like hours and hours, but I knew was maybe thirty minutes—two *Sponge Bob* episodes, Da used to say, when I asked how long that was—a deep sigh came from the wall speakers.

"Perfect. That will be all dear," Aleria said.

I pulled out my arms. They came out coated in her milky interior fluid. I had towels, the ship made them for me, but I knew not to rub my arms off just yet. My skin was blistered, and the skin mechs needed time to fix what they could of the damage before I went to dry myself. The mechs never really did a great job. I thought that, like a lot of the stuff on Aleria's ship, they were kind of stale or something like that. I knew my arms would be red and hurt for at least a light cycle.

When I first got on the ship, I used to call a light cycle a day, but pretty soon I figured out that they were exactly the same length every time. The light came from everywhere in the ship, and then didn't. Nearly ten Earth hours on. A little over four off. I asked once, and Aleria explained this was the Meeb active-rest cycle. And when the lights went off, it became so pitch black I couldn't see my hand in front of my face in the ship's bridge or the recreation room or the waste room, which was where both Aleria and I went to the bathroom. It got sort of sucked dry and cleaned after we left. This was done with mech crawlies that looked like baby spiders, maybe. They clumped together while you were going, then swarmed the place after you left and carried off whatever.

Anyway, there *was* one place where the faintest of light remained during lights-out. This was in the supply room. There were observation portals there. Each one was about as big as the windows used to be in my bedroom, but they were roundish, kind of egg-shaped. They were shaped to fit a Meeb optical stalk. There were four windows around the supply room, and I could always see the stars through them. We were traveling faster than light, but it was still slow enough so the stars didn't look like they were moving. I usually slept floating near one of those portals. I pretended that I knew the one that was facing Earth, and I would look out and pretend I could see the sun, even if it was only a pinprick in the dark. I knew this wasn't true, that I didn't know which one was the sun, but I could sort of fake my way to sleep that way.

So I let the mech work, and then I patted my arms and hands dry with an absorption towel, and was careful not to take off too much of my tenderized skin. Even though I was going easy with the towel, it still felt like I was rubbing sandpaper against myself. The towels were the same gray color as my pajamas, by the way, and not pretty the way

Mom's always were, with flowers on them and stuff. Everything in the ship was gray like that, and even I was now.

This time when I dried off the milk, something felt different. My skin wasn't just blistered; it was changing shape, too. It was kind of crunchy-lumpy. And it looked *thinner*. In fact, I touched it with a finger and it popped like a pear skin. Something oozed out, but it wasn't red like blood. It was white and looked like puss.

I felt the swollen nodes under my chin, the nodes in my neck. They were big and as tight as little nuts, like pecans or those hard, dark brown ones you could barely break with the nutcracker. I never knew what those kinds of nuts were called, and now I didn't have anyone to ask.

Aleria had said this would happen, that all my lymph nodes would swell up more and more. That would mean my body's defenses were getting taken over, and would start to tag the biological elements she implanted in me as "friend" instead of "enemy." That was what was happening, I supposed.

While I was drying off and feeling my nodes and all that, Aleria was babbling away, the way she often did after a replenishing. Talk, talk, talk. Snot flying everywhere. She got nostalgic, too—you know, talking about the old days and all that. She talked a lot about the Meeb home system. The Meebs didn't live on planet surfaces, but in a bunch of big space stations spread around their star's biological sweet spot. That's where we were headed at the moment, to one of those habitats, even though the trip was going to take another Earth year. We were one year into it. Which was another reason I figured I was eleven.

I could tell that Aleria was particularly relaxed today. She had fed well. And I guess she could feel that my resistance was really starting to break down.

"The clan will be so happy to meet you, my darling daughter," Aleria said. She was glowing white in the tank now, about to ooze her way out and back to her usual spot near the main ship interaction console. "And I think they'll be very pleased with the bounty I bring them from this journey. Also for the information. We'll get a fine reward."

Here was something I hadn't heard from her before.

"The information?" I asked. "I don't understand, Mother. What do you mean?"

"The knowledge of where the system is, of course, and what to expect when they get there."

"Get where?"

"The systems where the new children are to be found, dear," she replied. The wall speakers made it sound like she was sleepy, dreamy, the way I felt when I was drifting off to sleep all safe and sound and tucked in. It had been a long way since I felt that way.

"Why would the clan want to go there?"

"Why, to protect your kind, dear," she said. "To absorb and protect. That's what parents are *for*."

"They'll take children?"

"It's better that way," she said. "Believe me, I've had to absorb a full grown adult before, and it was an unpleasant process for both of us. Integrating those kinds of ingrained memories is difficult. So much resentment and anger to deal with in adults of a species."

"I guess so," I said.

"Children are so much easier to handle," she continued. "But not all species *have* children, you know. Juvenile and nymph forms, I mean. Only special ones. Like yours, my darling."

And then it hit me. What she *was*. Her job. She'd told me over and over, but I hadn't been listening, or it hadn't, you know, registered.

She was a scout.

"Now darling, I need to get dried off and ready for my rest period," Aleria said. "Come and wipe me down, there's a dear."

My jaw hurt. I had been grinding my teeth again.

"Yes, Mother dear," I replied.

So I guess I was thinking about Dustin when I did it. I was thinking about the way she would send back more Meebs. I knew how many existed in the space stations of Aleria's home system. I'd watched the videos. My troubles in third grade were behind me. I was a good student now. Anyway, it didn't take a genius to do the math.

There were enough Meebs for every child on Earth, and then some.

Aleria was a scout. Scouts find the way. Then they go back and lead others on the same path. To the same destination.

A year to go, and then two years for a return trip. Those habitats were capable of faster than light travel. Imagine that: a whole city of a billion Meebs headed for Earth.

Dustin would be eleven when they arrived.

This would happen to him.

I floated over to the water maker-cone and planted my feet against the ship wall. I pulled on the end of the bump. The ship wall dimpled out at my touch. I pulled harder. The cone grew in length, became more a tube than a cone. It reeled out like a hose, flowing from the material of the wall itself. I needed it to be long enough to reach Aleria.

So I pulled it out farther and farther. I wrapped it around my elbow and a thumb, the way I'd seen Da roll up the extension cord for the leaf blower. The extension cord was orange. The hose was a light shade of gray. I missed colors.

When I had enough length, I pushed off. I let the water hose trail out behind me as I sailed across the room.

Aleria had flowed out of the globe and pushed off a way, like a couple of yard sticks away. She was beginning her after-feed stretch. I needed to catch her before she spread out to her full size. At the moment, she was about the size of one of those big rubbery exercise balls like Mom used to have. A Pilamies ball, or something like that.

Aleria extended a sensing stalk in time to notice what I was doing.

"Darling daughter, I said to bring a towel, not more water, now please—"

"Stop calling me that," I said. My voice was sort of a growl and it surprised even me. I'd never made that mean a sound before. "I'm not your child, and you're not my mother."

I reached the end of my tether, the water tube. With a squeeze of my hands around the tube's end—the end looked kind of a like the tip of an elephant trunk—I opened the spigot and let the water flow. There was back pressure behind it, and out the water came.

Water doesn't flow in zero g the way it does in gravity. Even before Aleria took me, I knew about zero g. I had seen Youtube videos from space shuttles and the space station and stuff in science class at school. But the one thing I had never seen was what water does when it meets something floating in zero g.

It clings.

It jiggles like crazy, but it won't come off.

You can't shake it off. You can shake off a few droplets, but if there is enough of it, it isn't going anywhere no matter what you do. Without something to absorb it and overcome that surface tension, water sticks like glue.

It sticks like frog egg glop does to frog eggs, the gunk that holds the eggs together in a big clump. All for one. One for all.

In the creek, or in some little kid's water bottle.

Living or dead.

For a second, it seemed like Aleria thought I was trying to do something nice for her, something extra. She paused there, floating, out of the globe and maybe a yard or two away from it, but not completely expanded yet. She let me bathe her. And then I bathed the other side of her. I bathed her all over.

And I kept the spigot open. It's pretty simple. You squeeze the orifice and it relaxes some kind of stopper on the end.

And when she tried to move, to ooze outward, the water went with her.

I squeezed the spigot open, and then the bubble of water around her expanded. She was inside it, like a milky-white pit. It was jiggling around her, but it wouldn't come off.

I remembered those frog eggs.

Oh, she struggled. She twisted and turned. On her own, all the squirming would have gotten her to a wall, certainly. If she'd been by herself in the ship, she would have had a scare, but even her random motion would probably have saved her, allowed her to intersect with a hard surface, an extended piece of the bridge pod, anything. And then one of her pseudopods would have been able to find a footing, pull herself free from the coating of water.

But I was here now.

I was careful and alert, like the teachers always wanted us to be during carpool pickup. I circled Aleria with the water hose. I used pressure from the water tube hose for flying around fast, and the strap holds the ship had grown for me all around the wall for anchoring myself when I needed to. The moment Aleria looked like she was drifting close to a wall, I sent a stream of water toward her to push her away. I hadn't spent a year in zero g for nothing; I had a feel for how to do this now.

I kept her away from the pod walls, all of them. I held her away from saving herself.

Inside the ball of water, I saw the shooting snot, the little chemical speaking packets, dart out into the liquid. But they couldn't escape. The water tension held them in. Her words of command couldn't get to the ship wall and receive activation.

Frog glop, I thought. *Frog water.*

I had to smile.

She couldn't turn off the water.

She couldn't tell the ship to save her.

She couldn't even scream.

I watched her in that frog water. She turned from milky white to blue. And when she was blue, I saw something else she was doing. She was forming a picture on the surface of her membrane.

Not fair.

It was Mom. Her face. Frowning, the way she'd looked when I hurt her feelings. After she drank the frog water and was gagging over the kitchen sink and I was laughing at her.

Aleria had stolen enough of me to show me that.

But I'm eleven. I know real from fake.

I kept on laughing.

I mean, she was a blob in a quivery, jiggly coating of froggy, jumpy water. It was the water I was laughing at, the way it moved.

I kept on laughing while Aleria went from blue to green and from green to brown.

She stayed brown.

My laugh turned into a kind of a chuckle, then a wheezing kind of thing, and then it felt like it was going to turn into crying. I didn't want that, so I stopped as quickly as I'd started and held it all in. After that, I stared at Aleria for a long, long time.

She drowned—suspended in a quivering coating of water, only a few meters from safety. A dead blob in frog water.

When I finally spoke, it was a whisper. "Is Aleria dead, ship?"

"Affirmative. Captain Aleria is dead." The voice was neutral. No feeling. Gray. And it was a huge relief to hear after Aleria's honey-sweet Mother voice. I could go with gray for now.

Of course I didn't take the ship's word for it, not entirely. Like I said, the ship wasn't the brightest brain in the universe. No, I left Aleria floating there for another light cycle. When I woke up from a tired, restless sleep, she hadn't wiggled free. Hadn't somehow come back to life. There she hung.

Aleria was dead. I made double sure of it by expelling her remains via the disposal unit.

"Space or recycle?" asked the ship.

You can guess the answer I gave.

I ate. The stuff the ship fed me through a food maker-bump was gray and didn't taste like much, but it kept me alive.

It was time to have a serious talk with the ship.

I went to the bridge. There were still lots of gobs of water hanging around. I hadn't managed to suck the place dry yet. Floating around there felt a little like walking in that misty stuff when Da took us on the hike up to that overlook one time. I couldn't remember the name of the place. Mount Overlook or something like that, but I knew that couldn't be the right name. Who would call a mountain Mount Overlook? I wished, like I always wished, that I had been paying better attention.

That's okay. I was just a kid, I thought.

And then I realized I wasn't anymore. Not now.

So I was all ready to have an argument with ship, for it to be a struggle. The truth was I was expecting to have to figure out some way to sabotage the vessel if I had to. There was no way we were going to the Meeb system. I'd blow us up first.

"Ship," I said. "We need to talk."

And the ship answered in its neutral, gray tone with maybe the sweetest words I've ever heard.

"Yes, Captain Aleria, how may I serve you?"

"But ship, you *know* Aleria is dead. You said she was dead yourself."

"Speaker mech signal identifies as Captain Aleria," the ship replied. "Previous reading has been discarded."

I sighed, and felt the tightness and a little bit of the scared-ness and terrified-ness leak out of me.

And then, I think I started to cry. And I let myself. Just a little. My face was already wet, with all that mist in the air. When I first woke up in the crèche trap and then when Aleria took me on board her ship, I had cried a lot. But then I stopped, and I hadn't for a long, long time. Maybe this was because tears are hard to deal with in zero g. They kind of stick to your eyes when you don't wipe them and make little globs. They don't run down your face and they don't go away. In zero g, you have to do something about tears or they'll just, you know, *stay*.

"Do you have a fix on the system we recently visited, ship? The one with the crèche trap in orbit around the planet called Earth?"

"Yes, captain."

"If we turned around and started immediately, do we have enough fuel and supplies to make it back there?"

"Yes, captain."

Was this really what I wanted? I was more than half a Meeb, or the ship wouldn't have recognized me as captain. I was afraid to have the ship make a mirror. I was afraid to look myself in the face. My skin was gray and glinted a little from the mech. What would the rest of me look like?

But I was still me. Still Megan. I was just—*different*, now.

And I had to make sure that the next time a Meeb scout showed up to steal a human child, she got met by some very angry very dangerous moms and dads.

I wiped my tears. *Oh, whatever.* I was gray. Okay, maybe I was half-human, half-Meeb. This was the way things were. I had to deal with it. I wasn't a kid anymore. I was eleven. Practically a teenager.

"Take us to Earth, ship."

Take me home.

((((Peter Phillips))))

Say you're an intrepid space explorer and your ship happens to crash on an uncharted planet—but then you receive radio transmissions from someone outside who's actually speaking your language. Your obvious reaction would be to take heart and await help. And the ones sending those transmissions are very eager to help, but unfortunately both you and they have not understood the grim realities of the situation . . .

Peter Phillips (1920-2012) was born in London, England. He made a big splash with his story, "Dreams are Sacred" in the September 1948 issue of *Astounding Science-Fiction*. The story, in which the narrator's psyche is sent into the mind of a patient who has withdrawn from reality, is now recognized as a classic, and was soon followed by another remarkable story, *Manna*, in the February 1949 issue of the same magazine. The two stories were noted for striking originality of concept and cheerfulness of outlook. The first quality is certainly true of the story which follows, but "Lost Memory" has an outlook which is anything but cheerful.

((((**LOST MEMORY**))))

Peter Phillips

I collapsed joints and hung up to talk with Dak-whirr. He blinked his eyes in some discomfort.

"What do you want, Palil?" he asked complainingly.

"As if you didn't know."

"I can't give you permission to examine it. The thing is being saved for inspection by the board. What guarantee do I have that you won't spoil it for them?"

I thrust confidentially at one of his body-plates. "You owe me a favor," I said. "Remember?"

"That was a long time in the past."

"Only two thousand revolutions and a reassembly ago. If it wasn't for me, you'd be eroding in a pit. All I want is a quick look at its thinking part. I'll vrull the consciousness without laying a single pair of pliers on it."

He went into a feedback twitch, an indication of the conflict between his debt to me and his self-conceived duty.

Finally he said, "Very well, but keep tuned to me. If I warn that a board member is coming, remove yourself quickly. Anyway how do you know it has consciousness? It may be mere primal metal."

"In that form? Don't be foolish. It's obviously a manufacture. And I'm not conceited enough to believe that we are the only form of intelligent manufacture in the Universe."

"Tautologous phrasing, Palil," Dak-whirr said pedantically. "There could not conceivably be 'unintelligent manufacture.' There can be no consciousness without manufacture, and no manufacture without intelligence. Therefore there can be no consciousness without intelligence. Now if you should wish to dispute—"

I tuned off his frequency abruptly and hurried away. Dak-whirr is a fool and a bore. Everyone knows there's a fault in his logic circuit, but he refuses to have it traced down and repaired. Very unintelligent of him.

The thing had been taken into one of the museum sheds by the carriers. I gazed at it in admiration for some moments. It was beautiful, having suffered only slight exterior damage, and was obviously no mere conglomeration of sky metal.

In fact, I immediately thought of it as "he" and endowed it with the attributes of self-knowing, although, of course, his consciousness could not be functioning or he would have attempted communication with us.

I fervently hoped that the board, after his careful disassembly and study, could restore his awareness so that he could tell us himself which solar system he came from.

Imagine it! He had achieved our dream of many thousands of revolutions—space flight—only to be fused, or worse, in his moment of triumph.

I felt a surge of sympathy for the lonely traveller as he lay there, still, silent, non-emitting. Anyway, I mused, even if we couldn't restore him to self-knowing, an analysis of his construction might give us the secret of the power he had used to achieve the velocity to escape his planet's gravity.

In shape and size he was not unlike Swen—or Swen Two, as he called himself after his conversion—who failed so disastrously to reach our satellite, using chemical fuels. But where Swen Two had placed his tubes, the stranger had a curious helical construction studded at irregular intervals with small crystals.

He was thirty-five feet tall, a gracefully tapering cylinder. Standing at his head, I could find no sign of exterior vision cells, so I assumed he had some kind of vrulling sense. There seemed to be no exterior markings at all, except the long, shallow grooves dented in his skin by scraping to a stop along the hard surface of our planet.

I am a reporter with warm current in my wires, not a cold-thinking scientist, so I hesitated before using my own vrulling sense. Even though the stranger was non-aware—perhaps permanently—I felt it would be a presumption, an invasion of privacy. There was nothing else I could do, though, of course.

I started to vrull, gently at first, then harder, until I was positively glowing with effort. It was incredible; his skin seemed absolutely impermeable.

The sudden realisation that metal could be so alien nearly fused something inside me. I found myself backing away in horror, my self-preservation relay working overtime.

Imagine watching one of the beautiful cone-rod-and-cylinder assemblies performing the Dance of the Seven Spanners, as he's conditioned to do, and then suddenly refusing to do anything except stump around unattractively, or even becoming obstinately motionless, unresponsive. That might give you an idea of how I felt in that dreadful moment.

Then I remembered Dak-whirr's words—there could be no such thing as an "unintelligent manufacture." And a product so beautiful could surely not be evil. I overcame my repugnance and approached again.

I halted as an open transmission came from someone near at hand.

"Who gave that squeaking reporter permission to snoop around here?"

I had forgotten the museum board. Five of them were standing in the doorway of the shed, radiating anger. I recognised Chirik, the chairman, and addressed myself to him. I explained that I'd interfered with nothing and pleaded for permission on behalf of my subscribers to watch their investigation of the stranger. After some argument, they allowed me to stay.

I watched in silence and amusement as one by one they tried to vrull the silent being from space. Each showed the same reaction as myself when they failed to penetrate the skin.

Chirik, who is wheeled—and inordinately vain about his suspension system—flung himself back on his supports and pretended to be thinking.

"Fetch Fiff-fiff," he said at last. "The creature may still be aware, but unable to communicate on our standard frequencies."

Fiff-fiff can detect anything in any spectrum. Fortunately he was at work in the museum that day and soon arrived in answer to the call. He stood silently near the stranger for some moments, testing and adjusting himself, then slid up the electromagnetic band.

"He's emitting," he said.

"Why can't we get him?" asked Chirik.

"It's a curious signal on an unusual band."

"Well, what does he say?"

"Sounds like utter nonsense to me. Wait, I'll relay and convert it to standard."

I made a direct recording naturally, like any good reporter.

"—after planetfall," the stranger was saying. "Last dribble of power. If you don't pick this up, my name is Entropy. Other instruments knocked to hell, airlock jammed and I'm too weak to open it manually. Becoming delirious, too, I guess. Getting strong undirectional ultra-wave reception in Inglish, craziest stuff you ever heard, like goblins muttering, and I know we were the only ship in this sector. If you pick this up, but can't get a fix in time, give my love to the boys in the mess. Signing off for another couple of hours, but keeping this channel open and hoping . . ."

"The fall must have deranged him," said Chirik, gazing at the stranger. "Can't he see us or hear us?"

"He couldn't hear you properly before, but he can now, through me," Fiff-fiff," pointed out. "Say something to him, Chirik."

"Hello," said Chirik doubtfully. "Er—welcome to our planet. We are sorry you were hurt by your fall. We offer you the hospitality of our assembly shops. You will feel better when you are repaired and repowered. If you will indicate how we can assist you—"

"What the hell! What ship is that? Where are you?"

"We're here," said Chirik. "Can't you see us or vrull us? Your vision circuit is impaired, perhaps? Or do you depend entirely on vrulling? We can't find your eyes and assumed either that you protected them in some way during flight, or dispensed with vision cells altogether in your conversion."

Chirik hesitated, continued apologetically: "But we cannot understand how you vrull, either. While we thought that you were unaware, or even completely fused, we tried to vrull you. Your skin is quite impervious to us, however."

The stranger said: "I don't know if you're batty or I am. What distance are you from me?"

Chirik measured quickly. "One meter, two-point-five centimeters from my eyes to your nearest point. Within touching distance, in fact." Chirik tentatively put out his hand. "Can you not feel me, or has your contact sense also been affected?"

It became obvious that the stranger had been pitifully deranged. I reproduce his words phonetically from my record, although some of them make little sense. Emphasis, punctuative pauses and spelling of unknown terms are mere guesswork, of course.

He said : "For godsakemann stop talking nonsense, whoever you are. If you're outside, can't you see the airlock is jammed? Can't shift it myself. I'm badly hurt. Get me out of here, please."

"Get you out of where?" Chirik looked around, puzzled. "We brought you into an open shed near our museum for a preliminary examination. Now that we know you're intelligent, we shall immediately take you to our assembly shops for healing and recuperation. Rest assured that you'll have the best possible attention."

There was a lengthy pause before the stranger spoke again, and his words were slow and deliberate. His bewilderment is understandable, I believe, if we remember that he could not see, vrull or feel.

He asked: "What manner of creature are you? Describe yourself."

Chirik turned to us and made a significant gesture toward his thinking part, indicating gently that the injured stranger had to be humoured.

"Certainly," he replied. "I am an unspecialised bipedal manufacture of standard proportions, lately self-converted to wheeled traction, with a hydraulic suspension system of my own devising which I'm sure will interest you when we restore your sense circuits."

There was an even longer silence.

"You are robots," the stranger said at last. "Crise knows how you got here or why you speak Inglish, but you must try to understand me. I am mann. I am a friend of your master, your maker. You must fetch him to me at once."

"You are not well," said Chirik firmly. "Your speech is incoherent and without meaning. Your fall has obviously caused several serious feedbacks, of a very serious nature. Please lower your voltage. We are taking you to our shops immediately. Reserve your strength to assist our specialists as best you can in diagnosing your troubles."

"Wait. You must understand. You are—ogodno that's no good. Have you no memory of mann? The words you use—what meaning have they for you? Manufacture—made by hand hand hand damyou. Healing. Metal is not healed. Skin. Skin is not metal. Eyes. Eyes are not scanning cells. Eyes grow. Eyes are soft. My eyes are soft. Mine eyes have seen the glory—steady on, sun. Get a grip. Take it easy. You out there listen."

"Out where?" asked Prrr-chuk, deputy chairman of the museum board.

I shook my head sorrowfully. This was nonsense, but, like any good reporter, I kept my recorder running.

The mad words flowed on. "You call me he. Why? You have no seks. You are knewter. You are *it it it*! I am he, he who made you, sprung from shee, born of wumman. What is wumman, who is silv-ya what is shee that all her swains commend her ogod the bluds flowing again. Remember. Think back, you out there. These words were made by mann, for mann. Hurt, healing, hospitality, horror, deth by loss of blud. *Deth Blud*. Do you understand these words? Do you remember the soft things that made you? Soft little mann who konkurred the Galaxy and made sentient slaves of his machines and saw the wonders of a million worlds, only this miserable representative has to die in lonely desperation on a far planet, hearing goblin voices in the darkness."

Here my recorder reproduces a most curious sound, as though

the stranger were using an ancient type of vibratory molecular vocaliser in a gaseous medium to reproduce his words before transmission, and the insulation on his diaphragm had come adrift.

It was a jerky, high-pitched, strangely disturbing sound; but in a moment the fault was corrected and the stranger resumed transmission.

"Does blud mean anything to you?"

"No," Chirik replied simply.

"Or deth?"

"No."

"Or wor?"

"Quite meaningless."

"What is your origin? How did you come into being?"

"There are several theories," Chirik said. "The most popular one—which is no more than a grossly unscientific legend, in my opinion—is that our manufacturer fell from the skies, imbedded in a mass of primal metal on which He drew to erect the first assembly shop. How He came into being is left to conjecture. My own theory, however—"

"Does legend mention the shape of this primal metal?"

"In vague terms, yes. It was cylindrical, of vast dimensions."

"An interstellar vessel," said the stranger.

"That is my view also," said Chirik complacently.

"And—"

"What was the supposed appearance of your—manufacturer?"

"He is said to have been of magnificent proportions, based harmoniously on a cubical plan, static in Himself, but equipped with a vast array of senses."

"An automatic computer," said the stranger.

He made more curious noises, less jerky and at a lower pitch than the previous sounds.

He corrected the fault and went on: "God that's funny. A ship falls, menn are no more, and an automatic computer has pupps. Oh, yes, it fits in. A self-setting computer and navigator, operating on verbal orders. It learns to listen for itself and know itself for what it is, and to absorb knowledge. It comes to hate menn—or at least their bad qualities—so it deliberately crashes the ship and pulps their puny bodies with a calculated nicety of shock. Then it propagates and does a dam fine job of selective erasure on whatever it gave its pupps to use for a memory. It passes on only the good it found in menn, and purges the memory of him completely. Even purges all of his vocabulary except scientific terminology. Oil is thicker than blud. So may they live without the burden of knowing that they are—ogod they must know, they must understand. You outside, what happened to this manufacturer?"

Chirik, despite his professed disbelief in the supernormal aspects of the ancient story, automatically made a visual sign of sorrow.

"Legend has it," he said, "that after completing His task, He fused himself beyond possibility of healing."

Abrupt, low-pitched noises came again from the stranger.

"Yes. He would. Just in case any of His pupps should give themselves forbidden knowledge and an infeeryorrity komplecks by probing his mnemonic circuits. The perfect self-sacrificing muther. What sort of environment did He give you? Describe your planet."

Chirik looked around at us again in bewilderment, but he replied courteously, giving the stranger a description of our world.

"Of course," said the stranger. "Of course. Sterile rock and metal suitable only for you. But there must be some way . . ."

He was silent for a while.

"Do you know what growth means?" he asked finally. "Do you have anything that grows?"

"Certainly," Chirik said helpfully. "If we should suspend a crystal of some substance in a saturated solution of the same element or compound—"

"No, no," the stranger interrupted. "Have you nothing that grows of itself, that fruktiffies and gives increase without your intervention?"

"How could such a thing be?"

"Criseallmytee I should have guessed. If you had one blade of gras, just one tiny blade of growing gras, you could extrapolate from that to me. Green things, things that feed on the rich brest of erth, cells that divide and multiply, a cool grove of treez in a hot summer, with tiny warm-bludded burds preening their fethers among the leeves; a feeld of spring weet with newbawn mice timidly threading the dangerous jungul of storks; a stream of living water where silver fish dart and pry and feed and procreate; a farm yard where things grunt and cluck and greet the new day with the stirring pulse of life, with a surge of blud. Blud—"

For some inexplicable reason, although the strength of his carrier wave remained almost constant, the stranger's transmission seemed to be growing fainter.

"His circuits are failing," Chirik said. "Call the carriers. We must take him to an assembly shop immediately. I wish he would reserve his power."

My presence with the museum board was accepted without question now. I hurried along with them as the stranger was carried to the nearest shop.

I now noticed a circular marking in that part of his skin on which he had been resting, and guessed that it was some kind of orifice through which he would have extended his planetary traction mechanism if he had not been injured.

He was gently placed on a disassembly cradle. The doctor in charge that day was Chur-chur, an old friend of mine. He had been listening to the two-way transmissions and was already acquainted with the case.

Chur-chur walked thoughtfully around the stranger.

"We shall have to cut," he said. "It won't pain him, since his infra-molecular pressure and contact senses have failed. But since we can't vrull him, it'll be necessary for him to tell us where his main brain is housed or we might damage it."

Fiff-fiff was still relaying, but no amount of power boost would make the stranger's voice any clearer. It was quite faint now, and there are places on my recorder tape from which I cannot make even the roughest phonetic transliteration.

". . . strength going. Can't get into my zoot . . . done for if they bust through lock, done for if they don't . . . must tell them I need oxygen . . ."

"He's in bad shape, desirous of extinction," I remarked to

Chur-chur, who was adjusting his arc-cutter. "He wants to poison himself with oxidation now."

I shuddered at the thought of that vile, corrosive gas he had mentioned, which causes that almost unmentionable condition we all fear—rust.

Chirik spoke firmly through Fiff-fiff. "Where is your thinking part, stranger? Your central brain?"

"In my head," the stranger replied. "In my head ogod my head . . . eyes blurring everything going dim . . . luv to mairee . . . kids . . . a carry me home to the lone prayree . . . get this bluddy airlock open then they'll see me die . . . but they'll see me . . . some kind of atmosphere with this gravity . . . see me die . . . extrapolate from body what I was . . . what they are damthem damthem damthem . . . mann . . . master . . . I AM YOUR MAKER!"

For a few seconds the voice rose strong and clear, then faded away again and dwindled into a combination of those two curious noises I mentioned earlier. For some reason that I cannot explain, I found the combined sound very disturbing despite its faintness. It may be that it induced some kind of sympathetic oscillation.

Then came words, largely incoherent and punctuated by a kind of surge like the sonic vibrations produced by variations of pressure in a leaking gas-filled vessel.

". . . done it . . . crawling into chamber, closing inner . . . must be mad . . . they'd find me anyway . . . but finished . . . want to see them before I die . . . want see them see me . . . liv few seconds, watch them . . . get outer one open . . ."

Chur-chur had adjusted his arc to a broad, clean, blue-white glare. I trembled a little as he brought it near the edge of the circular marking in the stranger's skin. I could almost feel the disruption of the infra-molecular sense currents in my own skin.

"Don't be squeamish, Palil," Chur-chur said kindly. "He can't feel it now that his contact sense has gone. And you heard him say that his central brain is in his head." He brought the cutter firmly up to the skin. "I should have guessed that. He's the same shape as Swen Two, and Swen very logically concentrated his main thinking part as far away from his explosion chambers as possible."

Rivulets of metal ran down into a tray which a calm assistant had placed on the ground for that purpose. I averted my eyes quickly. I could never steel myself enough to be a surgical engineer or assembly technician.

But I had to look again, fascinated. The whole area circumscribed by the marking was beginning to glow.

Abruptly the stranger's voice returned, quite strongly, each word clipped, emphasised, high-pitched.

"Ar no no no . . . god my hands . . . they're burning through the lock and I can't get back I can't get away . . . stop it you feens stop it can't you hear . . . I'll be burned to deth I'm here in the airlock . . . the air's getting hot you're burning me alive . . ."

Although the words made little sense, I could guess what had happened and I was horrified.

"Stop, Chur-chur," I pleaded. "The heat has somehow brought back his skin currents. It's hurting him."

Chur-chur said reassuringly: "Sorry, Palil. It occasionally happens during an operation—probably a local thermoelectric effect. But even if his contact senses have started working again and he can't switch them off, he won't have to bear this very long."

Chirik shared my unease, however. He put out his hand and awkwardly patted the stranger's skin.

"Easy there," he said. "Cut out your senses if you can. If you can't, well, the operation is nearly finished. Then we'll repower you, and you'll soon be fit and happy again, healed and fitted and reassembled."

I decided that I liked Chirik very much just then. He exhibited almost as much self-induced empathy as any reporter; he might even come to like my favourite blue stars, despite his cold scientific exactitude in most respects.

My recorder tape shows, in its reproduction of certain sounds, how I was torn away from this strained reverie.

During the one-and-a-half seconds since I had recorded the distinct vocables "burning me alive," the stranger's words had become quite blurred, running together and rising even higher in pitch until they reached a sustained note—around E-flat in the standard sonic scale.

It was not like a voice at all.

This high, whining noise was suddenly modulated by apparent words without changing its pitch. Transcribing what seem to be words is almost impossible, as you can see for yourself—this is the closest I can come phonetically:

"Eeeeahahmbeeeeing baked aliiive in an uvennn ahdeeer-jeeesussunmuuutherrr! "

The note swooped higher and higher until it must have neared supersonic range, almost beyond either my direct or recorded hearing.

Then it stopped as quickly as a contact break.

And although the soft hiss of the stranger's carrier wave carried on without perceptible diminution, indicating that some degree of awareness existed, I experienced at that moment one of those quirks of intuition given only to reporters:

I felt that I would never greet the beautiful stranger from the sky in his full senses.

Chur-chur was muttering to himself about the extreme toughness and thickness of the stranger's skin. He had to make four complete cutting revolutions before the circular mass of nearly white-hot metal could be pulled away by a magnetic grapple.

A billow of smoke puffed out of the orifice. Despite my repugnance, I thought of my duty as a reporter and forced myself to look over Chur-chur's shoulder.

The fumes came from a soft, charred, curiously shaped mass of something which lay just inside the opening. "Undoubtedly a kind of insulating material," Chur-chur explained.

He drew out the crumpled blackish heap and placed it carefully on a tray. A small portion broke away, showing a red, viscid substance.

"It looks complex," Chur-chur said, "but I expect the stranger will be able to tell us how to reconstitute it or make a substitute."

His assistant gently cleaned the wound of the remainder of the material, which he placed with the rest; and Chur-chur resumed his inspection of the orifice.

You can, if you want, read the technical accounts of Chur-chur's discovery of the stranger's double skin at the point where the cut was made; of the incredible complexity of his driving mechanism, involving principles which are still not understood to this day; of the museum's failure to analyse the exact nature and function of the insulating material found in only that one portion of his body; and of the other scientific mysteries connected with him.

But this is my personal, non-scientific account. I shall never forget hearing about the greatest mystery of all, for which not even the most tentative explanation has been advanced, nor the utter bewilderment with which Chur-chur announced his initial findings that day.

He had hurriedly converted himself to a convenient size to permit actual entry into the stranger's body.

When he emerged, he stood in silence for several minutes. Then, very slowly, he said:

"I have examined the 'central brain' in the forepart of his body. It is no more than a simple auxiliary computer mechanism. It does not possess the slightest trace of consciousness. And there is no other conceivable centre of intelligence in the remainder of his body."

There is something I wish I could forget. I can't explain why it should upset me so much. But I always stop the tape before it reaches the point where the voice of the stranger rises in pitch, going higher and higher until it cuts out.

There's a quality about that noise that makes me tremble and think of rust.

(((((Sarah A. Hoyt)))))

Being afraid of the dark is common among children, and would probably be considered more common among adults, if they weren't embarrassed to admit it. Once, there actually were dangerous things out there, circling the fire (better not let it go out), looking in to the cave mouth with eyes reflecting that firelight, but now things are different. The night can be banished with a flip of an electric switch, and the deadliest predators are either extinct or kept in zoo cages. But suppose there were other, even deadlier creatures who moved away from the realm of machines and lights. Suppose they now lurk in the dark of space . . . waiting for an opportunity to show their power again.

Sarah A. Hoyt won the Prometheus Award for her novel *Darkship Thieves*, published by Baen, and has authored *Darkship Renegades* and *A Few Good Men*, two more novels set in the same universe, as was "Angel in Flight," a story in the first installment of *A Cosmic Christmas*. *Darkship* Renegades is presently a Prometheus Award nominee. She has written numerous short stories and novels in a number of genres, science fiction, fantasy, mystery, historical novels and historical mysteries, much under a number of pseudonyms, and has been published—among other places—in *Analog*, *Asimov's* and *Amazing*. For Baen, she has also written three books in her popular shape-shifter fantasy series, *Draw One in the Dark*, *Gentleman Takes a Chance*, and *Noah's Boy*. Her *According to Hoyt* is one of the most interesting blogs on the internet. Originally from Portugal, she lives in Colorado with her husband, two sons and the surfeit of cats necessary to a die-hard Heinlein fan.

(((((DRAGONS)))))

Sarah A. Hoyt

"What if they were really there," Jack said. He came out of the engine room, looking like something dredged up from a dark sea—all flying white hair, and wide blue eyes that looked like they should be blind. Spacer's eyes they call them. "What if they were really there?" he asked. "Those monsters, those dragons, those creatures ready to swallow ships, ready to render humans mad, ready to tear apart the faint shell of reason we use to paint over what we don't know?"

He'd been enlarging on this theme for the last three hours: the monsters who'd once threatened seafarers. He'd read to me from an account in the ship's database—not standard issue I was sure—of a dragon-like creature flying round and round a ship's sails and finally making them burn, and all the sailors lost, which made me wonder who'd written the account and known how many times the monster went around the mast and how his wings sounded like moth's wings in the wind, and how he obscured the sun.

He'd been talking about it, all the while he was in the engine room, working on the faltering engine of this fifty year old mining ship. And from outside, now and then, as I listened to the tinker and swish of tools, to the idiot beeping of the machine as it tried to establish normal function, I'd shouted, "Then they weren't. If they existed where did they go? Where did they hide?" Now I said it again, quietly, and I added, "Because we've crisscrossed the Earth with ships, and we've gridded her with communications satellites, and these monsters don't exist."

Jack gave me a slitty-eyed look, and a corner of his mouth twitched up. He was wiping his hands to a huge, oil-stained rag. It was as if the ship's engine had bled all over them.

A two-man ship, is all this was. A two-man asteroid miner ship, one step up from a robot one, in that we could avoid collisions most of the time, and we didn't get confused about what to mine.

My dad had done this for most of his life—had gone out and harvested minerals and rare earths from the asteroid belt. A month, two months, three months at a time, and come back home a little more tired, a little grayer, but with money to keep me in educational modules, and to keep Mom and me comfortable in our little house. He'd gone and come back, gone and come back, a fisherman in an endless sea, until the cold of space and the emptiness had bleached him away entirely. He'd died of one of those cancers long-time space miners get, and faded away into death like someone washed out to sea.

He'd left almost enough money to complete my training—almost—to become an interstellar navigator, to work in those ships that went out to the new colony worlds. Almost. I needed another six months, another module and then I could apply.

One trip out to the asteroids ought to do it, I'd thought, and I'd tried to find a ship that would take me—inexperienced and raw. There had been only Jack. Jack who'd taught Dad, Jack who'd been old when dad was an apprentice. Jack and the *Gone Done It*, his forever-breaking-down ship, cobbled together of salvage and will power.

And so here I was. A month trip. All I had to do was survive a month.

"Have you ever thought," Jack said. He crossed the common room that was all we had outside the engine room and the storage room for our found materials, and dove into the cupboard for a piece of cheese. Hard cheese. He bit into it, leaving the mark of his teeth in the white-yellowness of the cheese. "Have you ever thought," he said, "that the monsters were there; that they moved on? They were there when man first woke, when man first said *I am*, there in the darkness of the cave away from the camp fire, waiting, waiting. Any human who wandered away from the camp fire was slash, cut, gash." He made vicious motions with the hand holding the piece of cheese. "Nothing but the remains found in the morning, half-eaten."

"I imagine there were tigers and bears and stuff," I said. I'd almost said saber-tooth tigers, but then I wasn't sure if those had lived at the same time as humans. Natural history modules were extra and not needed for a space ship navigator. "Waiting to snack on a human," I said. "But not supernatural monsters."

Jack quirked an eyebrow at me. He had bushy eyebrows, very white, like the tentacles that grow over the eyes of certain dark-dwelling fish, and which give a sort of light to move by. "No?" he said. "But what if there were? And what is supernatural, exactly? Just a word people use to hide what they can't explain. There's always things people can't explain. Imagine that there were those things, there, in the dark, waiting for humans to stray beyond safety and then—"

"I won't suppose anything of the sort," I said. "Stop trying to scare me. Did you fix the engine?"

He shoved the rest of the cheese in his mouth, wiped his fingers to the coveralls, leaving crumbs of cheese behind amid the oil smears. He waggled his hand at me. "Almost," he said. "I can keep the artificial gravity on and the air purifying, but we're still not moving. We're marooned here. I'll go do battle with it again."

The engine room swallowed him. He left the door open, though, so he could talk. I wondered why he was talking to me about monsters, and figured it was part hazing since I didn't quite belong to his world and never would, and part to keep himself amused while he worked.

I knew how to repair engines, too, at least in theory. I'd taken the module just before coming on this trip. But I didn't know what had happened to the *Gone Done It* in the fifty years since she'd left the factory, and I doubted very much that her entrails resembled much of anything that the modules had shown me.

Jack had changed her, at least for the last thirty years, and he should know her way around her twisted, convoluted interior.

"Consider, young Pete, consider. Perhaps there were things out there. Why else would our ancestors write about them, our oldest songs and legends sing of them: of things of claw and tooth and scale, of night and infinite malice. Suppose they were made of something not-flesh, something our ancestors couldn't kill. Consider they were rivals with humans—rival intelligences, zealously defending their space against the curious monkey-minds. When humans left the campfire, the place all other human minds know, the place all other humans tell each human he is safe and lit and rational, then these things pounce. They pounce in defense of their lair, of their secret dark. They kill and rend in order to be allowed to go on living."

He banged something. It sounded like he was hitting metal hard with a hammer, and then there was a series of pings, that sounded like he'd managed to loosen a piece and was pulling it around, the other way, slowly. "They were there," his voice came above the other sounds. "In the dark of the cave. But then more and more humans ventured out into that dark, humans learned to make torches, take the fire with them, make the darkness less dark.

"And the monsters fled, before the light of the torches, before the certainty of the human minds that they were safe. They gathered in distant lands, in forests, in plains where they could ambush the human mind, feed on human fear. The few who ventured there and survived brought out stories. Fearful stories of those who lurked there. They came with claw and tentacle and with tearing fang, and humans ran back with stories and warnings. *Don't go into the forest*, they said. And *don't stray far from the shore*. And maps were drawn with vast areas marked *Here there be dragons*.

"But the humans came, over hill, around trees. They came in numbers, in family groups, in migratory bands. They cut down trees and built among them. What had been strange and wonderful became familiar, safe. The dangerous animals were killed and the suggestion of fangs, the shadow of claws retreated. The monsters retreated, to the cold, salty, trackless deep ocean, hovering over the unexplored waters. Till the humans went there too, and above the Earth, in the sky. And then the monsters fled, still further.

"These things were chased from Earth," Jack put his head in the opening of the door, and grinned at me, a pantomime devil, his forehead sooted with machine oil, his eyes slanted and amused, and I thought he was laughing at me. This was almost all hazing, and he was laughing at me, amused at my discomfiture, waiting for my reaction. "Do you ever wonder?" he asked me, and raised his tumultuous eyebrows at me. "Do you ever wonder where they went? Where they are?"

"I imagine they went back to hiding under beds and scaring children," I said, sardonically.

He went on, as if he hadn't heard me, "They went out to the dark of space, to the unknown land out there—claw and wing, tentacle and fang. They wait out here, they wait—"

There was a particularly loud and vicious clang. "There will never be enough of us out here, far enough out here, to carry our light, our certainty of safety. Even the asteroid miners . . . How many are there at any time? A hundred? Fewer? Most places still send up robots to do the mining. It's more loss of robots and time, more wasted trips, but fewer lives lost. There's few of us, and space is immense. Out here—" Another clang, which gave me the impression that he'd gestured wide with his hand and hit something nearby. "Out here, they can live, undisturbed, they can spread and mutate and grow. They've found a place where we can't overwhelm them, we can't despoil them. They found their realm of cold and dark. We're as nothing here. And when we venture here, they pounce—they come at us, to avenge their old wrong, their stolen paradise. We pushed them from the warm nights of Earth to here, and in the process we made them harder, sharper, more malicious. And they wait—for us."

I sighed, and let my sigh be really audible. "I'm not going to be scared, Jack, I really am not. Did you tell these stories to my father? Was he scared?"

There was something like a short bark of laughter, and then, "I didn't have to tell your father anything. He knew it already. There was this time, out in the belt—"

And then his voice died away, and a triumphant "aha!" came back, and there was a clang, and Jack came out, looking like he'd been crawling around in someone's chimney, soot on his hair, soot marking his white eyebrows. He threw a wrench on the floor of the main cabin, and retreated to the fresher in the corner, with its vibro-clean.

I picked up the wrench and set it in the tool cabinet. When I'd come into the *Gone Done It*, there had been tools everywhere, and bits and pieces of material used for repairs. I'd tagged, organized it, put it away, and kept it put away, with no help from Jack. No wonder, I thought, the man dreamed of monsters hiding in dark and cluttered places. He'd been living in a dark and cluttered place when I'd got here.

That night we ate some dried fish, and a bit of hard bread. Food for asteroid miners was about as good as food had been for mariners. At least we didn't have to drink grog, though given the *Gone Done It's* ancient purification arrangements, it didn't do to dwell too long on where the water we drank came from. And we didn't.

We ate, and then we went to bed. The beds let down from the wall, each with a thin mattress and an ancient blanket that smelled as much of oil and soot as the rags that Jack used in the engine room.

We were in bed, one on either side of the cabin, when Jack said, "There was this one time, out in the belt—"

He sounded thoughtful, reminiscent, not at all like he'd sounded when he'd oh so obviously been trying to scare me. "Your father was standing guard—"

I didn't say anything. It was one of those things. I knew Jack and Dad had taken some trips together. It was part of the reason that Jack had given me this chance at a trip, even though I was completely inexperienced. But the father I remembered was the man who came home with substantial funds for our account, the man who sat quietly, reading. The man who made Mother smile, and who never raised his voice to me.

I'd been torn, since I'd come on the ship with Jack, afraid of what he'd say. It sounds stupid and cowardly, but I wasn't sure I was prepared to hear the man who was so neat at home had left tools and wrenches all over in the *Gone Done It*. It would be like looking at a side of him that my father had kept quiet, like peeking into someone who had been part of my father, but not the part Mother and I knew.

So I stayed quiet, and Jack was quiet a long time, and it seemed to me that he'd fallen asleep, but then he went on as though he'd been talking all alone, as though he spoke out of a deeper silence, as though I were remembering or seeing the same things he was remembering and seeing, and all he needed to do was give me a few words to remind me. "If he hadn't been so fast on the uptake, Pete, the truth is, neither the *Gone Done It* nor I would be here. But it was all the work of a moment. By the time I came in, he'd chopped off the part of the thing that was inside the engine room, and he'd stopped the leak, and the only thing to say something odd had happened was that tentacle . . . It was the oddest thing, Pete . . . writhing and alive, but not flesh at all. It was as if it were made of darkness, built of shadow and gathered fear.

"When I turned the lights on, it vanished, but it left an icy feel in the air. An icy feel."

I didn't answer. I wasn't sure he wasn't asleep and talking out of a nightmare. Surely what he was talking about was a nightmare. My father—

If my father had seen something that fantastic, he would have spoken. When I talked of going to the stars, he would have warned me. Surely—

There was no time to dwell on it, and in the morning I woke to Jack shaking me. He'd fixed the sensors, and we'd located an asteroid that was all platinum and some rare isotopes, and he wanted my help with the robots, to do the mining.

Asteroid mining is not a physical occupation, not even when humans go out as miners. You don't put on your spacesuit and step out, and grunt and sweat with your pickax, to extract minerals from the wandering space junk. No, you use the sensors to detect the ore or the minerals or the rare Earths. And then you send out a probe that brings the stuff in to be analyzed and confirm your find. And finally you send little robots out, an army of ant-shaped homunculi who crawled all over the asteroid and cleaned it of anything that might be valuable on Earth.

I was better at controlling the harvesting robots than Jack was. Visual acuity and hand-eye coordination get worse with age. It fell to me to spend three days in front of the screen, manipulating the buttons and the pad, working to get those robots to harvest every last particle of saleable stuff, and to store it in our holds.

It was a small asteroid—maybe twenty feet across. But ours was a small ship. Once I was done, exhausted, my eyes burning from strain, my hands shaking from the days and days of close in work, the holds were full. And all I wanted was to sleep.

Jack had rested, and slept and played solitary while I harvested, and now he took over, as I crawled into my bed and fell into a sleep full of images of robots moving across the uncertain, flickering screen of the *Gone Done IT*, my hand still reflexively moving, in my sleep, trying to gather more wealth into the hold, trying—

Jack meanwhile woke, and got on the controls. The last thing he said to me was, "I'll take her home now, Pete. I'll take us home now, son."

I don't know how long I slept. I thought it might have been hours, but it could as well be days. I hadn't slept at all while harvesting, because we didn't have the tech to hold onto the asteroid, and we had to harvest while we could, while we could follow its orbit, and before a smaller asteroid—or larger—hit against our relatively fragile side. Asteroid hits were always a danger in the asteroid belt, and probably the reason why the profession was considered hazardous, the one reason beyond the radiation why so few miners made old bones.

You couldn't harden these small mining ships enough while keeping them light enough to carry ore and valuables back to Earth in quantity enough to justify the trip. Instead, every ship was provided with quick patches and fast-fix-it for the walls, and you hoped the meteor that hit you wouldn't be big enough to take the ship out, and that it wouldn't hit anyone on the way through the ship.

The *Gone Done It* had so many quick patches on her walls that there might be more of them than of the original walls. I knew no one had ever died in it. Which meant, I guess, it was better to be lucky than good.

I slept—I rocked in an ocean of deep and dark slumber, in a dream full of small asteroids zooming and dancing around the *Gone Done It*, slowly metamorphosing into dragons and ants and things with claws, dancing, safe, in the dark of space.

I don't know how long.

I know I woke. I woke startled and shocked, from deep, dark sleep to wide awake, sitting on my bed, heart hammering, eyes open, trying to see into darkness.

There had been a sound. A clang.

An asteroid strike. It had to be an asteroid strike. I called into the darkness, "Jack?" but there was no sound. No. I lie. There was a sound. The sound was a whoosh, as though every wind on Earth had gathered there, to blow into the ship. No. To blow out of the ship.

Before the pressure and air alarm sounded its first jangling peep, I was up, and halfway in the space suit.

Bolting the helmet on, turning on my oxygen, I lurched into the engine room where the steering apparatus was, the place where Jack would be when he was driving us out of the asteroid belt, carefully trying to avoid just this kind of—

Just this kind of disaster. There was a hole on the wall in the engine room. Jack was on the floor, unconscious. I thought he was bleeding but it was hard to tell. It could be true. Or it could be that he'd passed out through lack of oxygen. It was probably pretty low in here, while the air hissed outside the ship.

I groped for the hole. And that's when I felt it: the tentacle wrapped around my waist, pulling out. There was a claw clamped around my ankle. I saw, through my visor, fearful and intent, a large, slitty yellow eye, something like a malevolent cat, full of fury and vengeance.

The tentacle squeezed. The claw would pierce through the suit. There was a suggestion of teeth, a feeling of things, small, large, hungry, gnawing at the space suit.

I screamed. And then I reached for the emergency lights. As the tentacle dragged me inexorably, my hand fell on the button for the emergency light.

The light would have been turned off in here, of course, while we were underway, to allow Jack to concentrate on the screens that showed the view all around the ship. So he could avoid—

My hand, in its heavy glove, found the button and punched it.

For just a moment there was the feeling of tightening, of harder clawing. Then a shriek like a million damned forced out into the outer darkness.

The outer darkness—

Light coming on must have startled them. I had time to pull away from the tentacle, the claw, the myriad malevolent teeth without mouths that were trying to eat me into a maw of darkness.

And then by rote, without even glancing at Jack, without looking at the things of darkness and cold, insubstantial but real, which filled the engine room, I applied patch and fast-fix-it. I slammed the controls to bring the emergency oxygen into circulation.

I fixed, I cleaned, I made all safe.

I didn't go to Jack till it was all done, because I had a feeling what I would find. It was as I'd expected. The old miner was dead, on the floor, sprawled like a broken doll, his skin gone the pallor of a landed fish, his eyes wide open and staring at some unimaginable horror.

What I wasn't expecting, what I wasn't prepared for, was his wounds: A hundred piercings, a thousand cruel rents where claw and fang had gone in.

I gave him a burial in space, as best I could, and I cleaned the floor of the engine room, and I tried to forget the brief view I had when the lights came on, of tentacle and claw and fang.

I never spoke of it. Won't speak of it. What good would it do? At best people would think I was playing an hoax on them . . . At worst—

There was enough money, even when I'd split with Jack's widow, to get me the module to become a navigator.

The bigger ships, the interstellar ones that do commerce with the colonies are well-armored enough. There's no reason to fear the sort of asteroid strike that was carefully recorded in the log book of the *Gone Done It* as having caused Jack's death.

There is nothing to fear. I'm told that our interstellar ships are some of the safest forms of transportation. You stand a better chance of dying on Earth from having an asteroid fall on your head out of a clear blue sky than you stand of dying in one of these.

Deaths happen, of course. Nothing is ever completely safe. We lose a ship or three every few decades. But the causes, though often not explained, simply because the ships can't be recovered from the immensity of space, are usually obvious and mundane: engine failure, human error and, often presumed, simply landing in a place other than where the ship meant to go. Not hard to do with quantum ships that navigate the n-dimensional folds of an infinite space.

My cabin in the interstellar ship is large, well appointed, bigger than my parents' house, back on Earth.

It's impossible that, lying there, snug in my comfortable bed, I can actually hear anything through the thick walls of the ship.

And yet, often and often I wake in the night, my heart pounding and my mouth dry. If anyone heard of these night terrors, they'd invalid me out of the service as unstable, so I tell no one.

But in the deep dark of ship night, while everyone else sleeps, I hear the wings of something large, gross and unnamable circling round and round the ship, just touching. I hear tentacles scraping the outside, searching, trying to find me again, trying to pull me out there, into the dark, the cold.

I hear Jack's voice say, "They grew bigger out here, more vicious. They wait to take vengeance on those who expelled them from the warm and bountiful Earth."

My heart pounds, and my palms sweat. My throat closes with terror. How big have they grown? How vicious? Big enough to pierce the skin of an interstellar ship? To devour us all, crew and passengers, suddenly, half-roused from our slumbers and screaming from terror nothing can appease?

Screaming for help that will never come?

Here there be dragons.

((((**Robert Sheckley**))))

The planet obviously had been home to a civilization with a technology advanced far beyond that of Earth, but apparently not much more advanced in other ways, since their records revealed a history of wars. There were no more wars going on now, because all of the inhabitants had disappeared, and those records gave no clue as to what had happened to them. Not that the three humans let the mystery concern them. They were looking for a legendary cache of high-tech weapons more powerful than anything in Earth's arsenals which they could sell to the highest bidder, and weren't bothered by that enigmatic disappearance. But they should have been . . .

Robert Sheckley (1928-2005) seemed to explode into print in the early 1950s with stories in nearly every science fiction magazine on the newsstands. Actually, the explosion was bigger than most realized, since he was simultaneously writing even more stories under a number of pseudonyms. His forte was humor, wild and unpredictable, often absurdist, much like the work of Douglas Adams three decades later. His work has been compared to the Marx Brothers by Harlan Ellison®, to Voltaire by both Brian W. Aldiss and J.G. Ballard, and Neil Gaiman has called Sheckley "Probably the best short-story writer during the 50s to the mid-1960s working in any field." Of course, Robert Sheckley's ingenious and inventive humor often took very dark turns—as in the story which follows.

(((((THE LAST WEAPON)))))

Robert Sheckley

Edsel was in a murderous mood. He, Parke, and Faxon had spent three weeks in this part of the deadlands, breaking into every mound they came across, not finding anything, and moving on to the next. The swift Martian summer was passing, and each day became a little colder. Each day Edsel's nerves, uncertain at the best of times, had frayed a little more. Little Faxon was cheerful, dreaming of all the money they would make when they found the weapons, and Parke plodded silently along, apparently made of iron, not saying a word unless he was spoken to.

Bud Edsel had reached his limit. They had broken into another mound, and again there had been no sign of the lost Martian weapons. The watery sun seemed to be glaring at him, and the stars were visible in an impossibly blue sky. The afternoon cold seeped into Edsel's insulated suit, stiffening his joints, knotting his big muscles.

Quite suddenly, Edsel decided to kill Parke. He had disliked the silent man since they had formed the partnership on Earth. He disliked him even more than he despised Faxon.

Edsel stopped.

"Do you know where we're going?" he asked Parke, his voice ominously low.

Parke shrugged his slender shoulders, negligently. His pale, hollow face showed no trace of expression.

Robert Sheckley

"Do you?" Edsel asked.

Parke shrugged again.

A bullet in the head, Edsel decided, reaching for his gun.

"Wait!" Faxon pleaded, coming up between them. "Don't fly off, Edsel. Just think of all the money we can make when we find the weapons!" The little man's eyes glowed at the thought. "They're right around here somewhere, Edsel. The next mound, maybe."

Edsel hesitated, glaring at Parke. Right now he wanted to kill more than anything else in the world. If he had known it would be like this when they formed the company on Earth . . . It had seemed so easy then. He had the plaque, the one which told where a cache of the fabulous lost Martian weapons were. Parke was able to read the Martian script, and Faxon could finance the expedition. So, he had figured all they'd have to do would be to land on Mars and walk up to the mound where the stuff was hidden.

Edsel had never been off Earth before. He hadn't counted on the weeks of freezing, starving on concentrated rations, always dizzy from breathing thin, tired air circulating through a replenisher. He hadn't though about the sore, aching muscles you get, dragging your way through the thick Martian brush.

All he had thought about was the price a Government—any Government—would pay for those legendary weapons.

"I'm sorry," Edsel said, making up his mind suddenly. "This place gets me. Sorry I blew up, Parke. Lead on."

Parke nodded and started again. Faxon breathed a sigh of relief, and followed Parke.

After all, Edsel thought, I can kill them any time.

They found the correct mound in mid-afternoon, just as Edsel's patience was wearing thin again. It was a strange, massive affair, just as the script had said. Under a few inches of dirt was metal. The men scraped and found a door.

"Here, I'll blast it open," Edsel said, drawing his revolver.

Parke pushed him aside, turned the handle and opened the door.

Inside was a tremendous room. And there, row upon gleaming

row, were the legendary lost weapons of Mars, the missing artifacts of Martian civilization.

The three men stood for a moment, just looking. Here was the treasure that men had almost given up looking for. Since man had landed on Mars, the ruins of great cities had been explored. Scattered across the plains were ruined vehicles, art forms, tools, everything indicating the ghost of a titanic civilization, a thousand years beyond Earth's. Patiently deciphered scripts had told of the great wars ravaging the surface of Mars. The scripts stopped too soon, though, because nothing told what had happened to the Martians. There hadn't been an intelligent being on Mars for several thousand years. Somehow, all animal life on the planet had been obliterated.

And, apparently, the Martians had taken their weapons with them.

Those lost weapons, Edsel, knew, were worth their weight in radium. There just wasn't any thing like them.

The men went inside. Edsel picked up the first thing his hand reached. It looked like a .45, but bigger. He went to the door and pointed the weapon at a shrub on the plain.

"Don't fire it," Faxon said, as Edsel took aim. "It might backfire or something. Let the Government men fire them, after we sell."

Edsel squeezed the trigger. The shrub, seventy-five feet away, erupted in a bright red flash.

"Not bad," Edsel said, patting the gun. He put it down and reached for another.

"Please, Edsel," Faxon said, squinting nervously at him. "There's no need to try them out. You might set off an atomic bomb or something."

"Shut up," Edsel said, examining the weapon for a firing stud.

"Don't shoot any more," Faxon pleaded. He looked to Parke for support, but the silent man was watching Edsel. "You know, something in this place might have been responsible for the destruction of the Martian race. You wouldn't want to set it off again, would you?"

Edsel watched a spot on the plain glow with heat as he fired at it.

"Good stuff." He picked up another, rod-shaped instrument. The cold was forgotten. Edsel was perfectly happy now, playing with all the shiny things.

"Let's get started," Faxon said, moving towards the door.

"Started? Where?" Edsel demanded. He picked up another glittering weapon, curved to fit his wrist and hand.

"Back to the port," Faxon said. "Back to sell this stuff, like we planned. I figure we can ask just about any price, any price at all. A Government would give billions for weapons like these."

"I've changed my mind," Edsel said. Out of the corner of his eye he was watching Parke. The slender man was walking between the stacks of weapons, but so far he hadn't touched any.

"Now listen," Faxon said, glaring at Edsel. "I financed this expedition. We planned on selling the stuff. I have a right to—well, perhaps not."

The untried weapon was pointed squarely at his stomach.

"What are you going to do?" he asked, trying not to look at the gun.

"To hell with selling it," Edsel said, leaning against the cave wall where he could also watch Parke. "I figure I can use this stuff myself." He grinned broadly, still watching both men.

"I can outfit some of the boys back home. With the stuff that's here, we can knock over one of those little Governments in Central America easy. I figure we could hold it forever."

"Well," Faxon said, watching the gun, "I don't want to be a party to that sort of thing. Just count me out."

"All right," Edsel said.

"Don't worry about me talking," Faxon said quickly. "I won't. I just don't want to be in on any shooting or killing. So I think I'll go back."

"Sure," Edsel said. Parke was standing to one side, examining his fingernails.

"If you get that kingdom set up, I'll come down," Faxon said, grinning weakly. "Maybe you can make me a duke or something."

"I think I can arrange that."

"Swell. Good luck." Faxon waved his hand and started to walk away. Edsel let him get twenty feet, then aimed the new weapon and pressed the stud.

The gun didn't make any noise; there was no flash, but Faxon's arm was neatly severed. Quickly, Edsel pressed the stud again and swung the gun down on Faxon. The little man was chopped in half, and the ground on either side of him was slashed also.

Edsel turned, realized that he had left his back exposed to Parke. All the man had to do was pick up the nearest gun and blaze away. But Parke was just standing there, his arms folded over his chest.

"That beam will probably cut though anything," Parke said. "Very useful."

Edsel had a wonderful half-hour, running back and forth to the door with different weapons. Parke made no move to touch anything, but watched with interest. The ancient Martian arms were as good as new, apparently unaffected by their thousands of years of disuse. There were many blasting weapons, of various designs and capabilities. Then heat and radiation guns, marvelously compact things. There were weapons which would freeze and weapons which would burn; others which would crumble, cut, coagulate, paralyze, and do any of the other things to snuff out life.

"Let's try this one," Parke said. Edsel, who had been on the verge of testing an interesting-looking three-barrelled rifle, stopped.

"I'm busy," he said.

"Stop playing with those toys. Let's have a look at some real stuff."

Parke was standing near a squat black machine on wheels. Together they tugged it outside. Parke watched while Edsel moved the controls. A faint hum started deep in the machine. Then a blue haze formed around it. The haze spread as Edsel manipulated the controls until it surrounded the two men.

"Try a blaster on it," Parke said. Edsel picked up one of the explosive pistols and fired. The charge was absorbed by the haze. Quickly he tested three others. They couldn't pierce the blue glow.

"I believe," Parke said softly, "this will stop an atomic bomb. This is a force field."

Edsel turned it off and they went back inside. It was growing dark in the cave as the sun neared the horizon.

"You know," Edsel said, "you're a pretty good guy, Parke. You're OK."

"Thanks," Parke said, looking over the mass of weapons.

"You don't mind my cutting down Faxon, do you? He was going straight to the Government."

"On the contrary, I approve."

"Swell. I figure you must be OK. You could have killed me when I was killing Faxon." Edsel didn't add that it was what he would have done.

Parke shrugged his shoulders.

"How would you like to work on this kingdom deal with me?" Edsel asked, grinning. "I think we could swing it. Get ourselves a nice place, plenty of girls, lots of laughs. What do you think?"

"Sure," Parke said. "Count me in." Edsel slapped him on the shoulder, and they went through the ranks of weapons.

"All those are pretty obvious," Parke said as they reached the end of the room. "Variations on the others."

At the end of the room was a door. There were letters in Martian script engraved on it.

"What's that stuff say?" Edsel asked.

"Something about 'final weapons,'" Parke told him, squinting at the delicate tracery. "A warning to stay out." He opened the door. Both men started to step inside, then recoiled suddenly.

Inside was a chamber fully three times the size of the room they had just left. And filling the great room, as far as they could see, were soldiers. Gorgeously dressed, fully armed, the soldiers were motionless, statue-like.

They were not alive.

There was a table by the door, and on it were three things. First, there was a sphere about the size of a man's fist, with a calibrated dial set in it. Beside that was a shining helmet. And next was a small, black box with Martian script on it.

"Is it a burial place?" Edsel whispered, looking with awe at the strong unearthly faces of the martian soldiery. Parke, behind him, didn't answer.

Edsel walked to the table and picked up the sphere. Carefully he turned the dial a single notch.

"What do you think it's supposed to do?" he asked Parke. "Do you think—" Both men gasped and moved back.

The lines of fighting men had moved. Men in ranks swayed, then came to attention. But they no longer held the rigid posture of death. The ancient fighting men were alive.

One of them, in an amazing uniform of purple and silver, came forward and bowed to Edsel.

"Sir, your troops are ready." Edsel was too amazed to speak.

"How can you live after thousands of years?" Parke answered. "Are you Martians?"

"We are the servants of the Martians." The soldier said. Parke noticed that the soldier's lips hadn't moved. The man was telepathic. "Sir, we are Synthetics."

"Whom do you obey?" Parke asked.

"The Activator, sir." The Synthetic was speaking directly to Edsel, looking at the sphere in his hand. "We require no food or sleep, sir. Our only desire is to serve you and to fight." The soldiers in the ranks nodded approvingly.

"Lead us into battle, sir!"

"I sure will!" Edsel said, finally regaining his senses. "I'll show you boys some fighting, you can bank on that!"

The soldiers cheered him, solemnly, three times. Edsel grinned, looking at Parke.

"What do the rest of these numbers do?" Edsel asked. But the soldier was silent. The question was evidently beyond his built-in knowledge.

"It might activate other Synthetics," Parke said. "There are probably more chambers underground."

"Brother!" Edsel shouted. "*Will* I lead you into battle!" Again the soldiers cheered, three solemn cheers.

"Put them to sleep and let's make some plans," Parke said. Dazed, Edsel turned the switch back. The soldiers froze again into immobility.

"Come on outside."

"Right."

"And bring that stuff with you." Edsel picked up the shining helmet and the black box and followed Parke outside. The sun had almost disappeared now, and there were black shadows over the red land. It was bitterly cold, but neither man noticed.

"Did you hear what they said, Parke? Did you hear it? They said I was their leader! With men like those—" He laughed at the sky. With those soldiers, those weapons, nothing could stop him. He'd really stock his land—prettiest girls in the world, and would he have a time!

"I'm a general!" Edsel shouted, and slipped the helmet over his head. "How do I look, Parke? Don't I look like a—" He stopped. He was hearing a voice in his ears, whispering, muttering. What was it saying?

"*. . . damned idiot, with his little dream of a kingdom. Power like this is for a man of genius, a man who can remake history. Myself!*"

"Who's talking? That's you, isn't it Parke?" Edsel realized suddenly that the helmet allowed him to listen in on thoughts. He didn't have time to consider what a weapon this would be for a ruler.

Parke shot him neatly through the back with a gun he had been holding all the time.

"What an idiot," Parke told himself, slipping the helmet on his head. "A kingdom! All the power in the world and he dreamed of a little kingdom!" He glanced back at the cave.

"With those troops—the force field—and the weapons—I can take over the world." He said it coldly, knowing it was a fact. He turned to go back to the cave to activate the Synthetics, but stopped first to pick up the little black box Edsel had carried.

Engraved on it, in flowing Martian script, was, "The Last Weapon."

I wonder what it could be, Parke asked himself. He had let Edsel live long enough to try out all the others; no use chancing a misfire himself. It was too bad he hadn't lived long enough to try out this one, too.

Of course, I really don't need it, he told himself. He had plenty. But this might make the job a lot easier, a lot safer. Whatever it was, it was bound to be good.

Well, he told himself, let's see what the Martians considered their last weapon. He opened the box.

A vapor drifted out, and Parke threw the box from him, thinking about poison gas.

The vapor mounted, drifted haphazardly for a while, then began to coalesce. It spread, grew and took shape.

In a few seconds, it was complete, hovering over the box. It glimmered white in the dying light, and Parke saw that it was just a tremendous mouth, topped by a pair of unblinking eyes.

"Ho ho," the mouth said. "Protoplasm!" It drifted to the body of Edsel. Parke lifted a blaster and took careful aim.

"Quiet protoplasm," the thing said, nuzzling Edsel's body. "I like quiet protoplasm." It took down the body in a single gulp.

Parke fired, blasting a ten-foot hole in the ground. The giant mouth drifted out of it, chuckling.

"It's been so long," it said.

Parke was clenching his nerves in a forged grip. He refused to let himself become panicked. Calmly he activated the force field, forming a blue sphere around himself.

Still chuckling, the thing drifted through the blue haze.

Parke picked up the weapon Edsel had used on Faxon, feeling the well-balanced piece swing up in his hand. He backed to one side of the force field as the thing approached, and turned on the beam.

The thing kept coming.

"Die, die!" Parke screamed, his nerves breaking.

But the thing came on, grinning broadly.

"I like *quiet* protoplasm," the thing said as its gigantic mouth converged on Parke.

"But I also like *lively* protoplasm."

It gulped once, then drifted out of the other side of the field, looking anxiously around for the millions of units of protoplasm, as there had been in the old days.

(((((Elizabeth Bear and Sarah Monette)))))

Pest control is a necessity everywhere, even on a space station, and this station was overdue for a heavy dose of it. Particularly since the pests were breaking through from another dimension, and leaving holes through which even bigger alien creatures could emerge into our space, creatures which were much too dangerous to be called mere "pests" . . .

"Moongoose" is set in the same universe as the authors' "Boojum," a story I heartily recommend, and last year's podcasted novelette, "The Wreck of the *Charles Dexter Ward*." And this story will provide extra fun for H.P. Lovecraft fans, spotting all the places where his story titles, place names, and so on have been pressed into unusual service. That is not dead which can eternally be referenced and in strange footnotes, even death may die.

Elizabeth Bear was born on the same day as Frodo and Bilbo Baggins, but in a different year. When coupled with a tendency to read the dictionary for fun as a child, this led her inevitably to penury, intransigence, and the writing of speculative fiction. She is the Hugo, Sturgeon, and Campbell Award winning author of 25 novels and almost a hundred short stories. Her most recent series is the Eternal Sky trilogy from Tor, beginning with Range of Ghosts. She and Sarah Monette have written two novels and a number of short stories together.

Her dog lives in Massachusetts; her partner, writer Scott Lynch, lives in Wisconsin. She spends a lot of time on planes.

Sarah Monette was born and raised in Oak Ridge, Tennessee; she began writing at the age of 12, and hasn't stopped yet. Appropriately, her PhD in English Literature was earned with a dissertation on ghosts in English Renaissance revenge tragedy. Her novels include

Melusine, *The Virtu,* *The Mirador,* and *Corambis.* Her next novel, *The Goblin Emperor,* will come out from Tor under the pen-name Katherine Addison. She won the Spectrum award in 2003 for her short story "Three Letters from the Queen of Elfland," and many of her short stories have been cited on Best of the Year lists, and included in anthologies of the year's best sf and/or fantasy. She currently lives in a 107-year-old house in the Upper Midwest with a great many books, two cats, and a husband. (There's also a horse. He does not live in the house.) Her website is www.sarahmonette.com.

((((MONGOOSE))))

Elizabeth Bear and Sarah Monette

Izrael Irizarry stepped through a bright-scarred airlock onto Kadath Station, lurching a little as he adjusted to station gravity. On his shoulder, Mongoose extended her neck, her barbels flaring, flicked her tongue out to taste the air, and colored a question. Another few steps, and he smelled what Mongoose smelled, the sharp stink of toves, ammoniac and bitter.

He touched the tentacle coiled around his throat with the quick double tap that meant *soon*. Mongoose colored displeasure, and Irizarry stroked the slick velvet wedge of her head in consolation and restraint. Her four compound and twelve simple eyes glittered and her color softened, but did not change, as she leaned into the caress. She was eager to hunt and he didn't blame her. The boojum *Manfred von Richthofen* took care of its own vermin. Mongoose had had to make do with a share of Irizarry's rations, and she hated eating dead things.

If Irizarry could smell toves, it was more than the "minor infestation" the message from the station master had led him to expect. Of course, that message had reached Irizarry third or fourth or fifteenth hand, and he had no idea how long it had taken. Perhaps when the stationmaster had sent for him, it *had* been minor.

But he knew the ways of bureaucrats, and he wondered.

People did double-takes as he passed, even the heavily-modded

Christian cultists with their telescoping limbs and biolin eyes. You found them on every station and steelships too, though mostly they wouldn't work the boojums. Nobody liked Christians much, but they could work in situations that would kill an unmodded human or a even a gilly, so captains and station masters tolerated them.

There were a lot of gillies in Kadath's hallways, and they all stopped to blink at Mongoose. One, an indenturee, stopped and made an elaborate hand-flapping bow. Irizarry felt one of Mongoose's tendrils work itself through two of his earrings. Although she didn't understand staring exactly—her compound eyes made the idea alien to her—she felt the attention and was made shy by it.

Unlike the boojum-ships they serviced, the stations—Providence, Kadath, Leng, Dunwich, and the others—were man-made. Their radial symmetry was predictable, and to find the station master, Irizarry only had to work his way inward from the *Manfred von Richthofen*'s dock to the hub. There he found one of the inevitable safety maps (you are here; in case of decompression, proceed in an orderly manner to the life vaults located here, here, or here) and leaned close to squint at the tiny lettering. Mongoose copied him, tilting her head first one way, then another, though flat representations meant nothing to her. He made out STATION MASTER'S OFFICE finally, on a oval bubble, the door of which was actually in sight.

"Here we go, girl," he said to Mongoose (who, stone-deaf though she was, pressed against him in response to the vibration of his voice). He hated this part of the job, hated dealing with apparatchiks and functionaries, and of course the Station Master's office was full of them, a receptionist, and then a secretary, and then someone who was maybe the *other* kind of secretary, and then finally—Mongoose by now halfway down the back of his shirt and entirely hidden by his hair and Irizarry himself half stifled by memories of someone he didn't want to remember being—he was ushered into an inner room where Station Master Lee, her arms crossed and her round face set in a scowl, was waiting.

"Mr. Irizarry," she said, unfolding her arms long enough to stick one hand out in a facsimile of a congenial greeting.

He held up a hand in response, relieved to see no sign of

recognition in her face. It was Irizarry's experience that dead lives were best left lie where they fell. "Sorry, Station Master," he said. "I can't."

He thought of asking her about the reek of toves on the air, if she understood just how bad the situation had become. People could convince themselves of a lot of bullshit, given half a chance.

Instead, he decided to talk about his partner. "Mongoose hates it when I touch other people. She gets jealous, like a parrot."

"The cheshire's here?" She let her hand drop to her side, the expression on her face a mixture of respect and alarm. "Is it out of phase?"

Well, at least Station Master Lee knew a little more about cheshire-cats than most people. "No," Irizarry said. "She's down my shirt."

Half a standard hour later, wading through the damp bowels of a ventilation pore, Irizarry tapped his rebreather to try to clear some of the tove-stench from his nostrils and mouth. It didn't help much; he was getting close.

Here, Mongoose wasn't shy at all. She slithered up on top of his head, barbels and graspers extended to full length, pulsing slowly in predatory greens and reds. Her tendrils slithered through his hair and coiled about his throat, fading in and out of phase. He placed his fingertips on her slick-resilient hide to restrain her. The last thing he needed was for Mongoose to go spectral and charge off down the corridor after the tove colony.

It wasn't that she wouldn't come back, because she would—but that was only if she didn't get herself into more trouble than she could get out of without his help. "Steady," he said, though of course she couldn't hear him. A creature adapted to vacuum had no ears. But she could feel his voice vibrate in his throat, and a tendril brushed his lips, feeling the puff of air and the shape of the word. He tapped her tendril twice again—*soon*—and felt it contract. She flashed hungry orange in his peripheral vision. She was experimenting with jaguar rosettes—they had had long discussions of jaguars and tigers after their nightly reading of Pooh on the *Manfred von Richthofen*, as Mongoose had wanted to know what jagulars and tiggers were. Irizarry had already taught her about mongooses, and he'd read *Alice in Wonderland* so she would know what a Cheshire Cat was. Two days later—he still remembered it vividly—she had disappeared quite slowly, starting with the tips of the long coils of her tail and tendrils and ending with the needle-sharp crystalline array of her teeth. And then she'd phased back in, all excited aquamarine and pink, almost bouncing, and he'd praised her and stroked her and reminded himself not to think of her as a cat. Or a mongoose.

She had readily grasped the distinction between jaguars and jagulars, and had almost as quickly decided that she was a jagular; Irizarry had almost started to argue, but then thought better of it. She was, after all, a Very Good Dropper. And nobody ever saw her coming unless she wanted them to.

When the faint glow of the toves came into view at the bottom of the pore, he felt her shiver all over, luxuriantly, before she shimmered dark and folded herself tight against his scalp. Irizarry doused his own lights as well, flipping the passive infrared goggles down over his eyes. Toves were as blind as Mongoose was deaf, but an infestation this bad could mean the cracks were growing large enough for bigger things to wiggle through, and if there were raths, no sense in letting the monsters know he was coming.

He tapped the tendril curled around his throat three times, and whispered, "Go." She didn't need him to tell her twice; really, he thought wryly, she didn't need him to tell her at all. He barely felt her featherweight disengage before she was gone down the corridor as silently as a hunting owl. She was invisible to his goggles, her body at ambient temperature, but he knew from experience that her barbels and vanes would be spread wide, and he'd hear the shrieks when she came in among the toves.

The toves covered the corridor ceiling, arm-long carapaces adhered by a foul-smelling secretion that oozed from between the sections of their exoskeletons. The upper third of each tove's body bent down like a dangling bough, bringing the glowing, sticky lure and flesh-ripping pincers into play. Irizarry had no idea what they fed on in their own phase, or dimension, or whatever.

Here, though, he knew what they ate. Anything they could get.

He kept his shock probe ready, splashing after, to assist her if it turned out necessary. That was sure a lot of toves, and even a cheshire-cat could get in trouble if she was outnumbered. Ahead of him, a tove warbled and went suddenly dark; Mongoose had made her first kill.

Within moments, the tove colony was in full warble, the harmonics making Irizarry's head ache. He moved forward carefully, alert now for signs of raths. The largest tove colony he'd ever seen was on the derelict steelship *Jenny Lind*, which he and Mongoose had explored when they were working salvage on the boojum *Harriet Tubman*. The hulk had been covered inside and out with toves; the colony was so vast that, having eaten everything else, it had started cannibalizing itself, toves eating their neighbors and being eaten in turn. Mongoose had glutted herself before the *Harriet Tubman* ate the wreckage, and in the refuse she left behind, Irizarry had found the strange starlike bones of an adult rath, consumed by its own prey. The bandersnatch that had killed the humans on the *Jenny Lind* had died with her reactor core and her captain. A handful of passengers and crew had escaped to tell the tale.

He refocused. This colony wasn't as large as those heaving masses on the *Jenny Lind*, but it was the largest he'd ever encountered not in a quarantine situation, and if there weren't raths somewhere on Kadath Station, he'd eat his infrared goggles.

A dead tove landed at his feet, its eyeless head neatly separated from its segmented body, and a heartbeat later Mongoose phased in on his shoulder and made her deep clicking noise that meant, *Irizarry! Pay attention!*

He held his hand out, raised to shoulder level, and Mongoose flowed between the two, keeping her bulk on his shoulder, with tendrils resting against his lips and larynx, but her tentacles wrapping around his hand to communicate. He pushed his goggles up with his free hand and switched on his belt light so he could read her colors.

She was anxious, strobing yellow and green. *Many*, she shaped against his palm, and then emphatically, *R.*

"R" was bad—it meant rath—but it was better than "B." If a

bandersnatch had come through, all of them were walking dead, and Kadath Station was already as doomed as the *Jenny Lind*. "Do you smell it?" he asked under the warbling of the toves.

Taste, said Mongoose, and because Irizarry had been her partner for almost five Solar, he understood: the toves tasted of rath, meaning that they had recently been feeding on rath guano, and given the swiftness of toves' digestive systems, that meant a rath was patrolling territory on the station.

Mongoose's grip tightened on his shoulder. *R*, she said again. *R. R. R.*

Irizarry's heart lurched and sank. More than one rath. The cracks were widening.

A bandersnatch was only a matter of time.

Station Master Lee didn't want to hear it. It was all there in the way she stood, the way she pretended distraction to avoid eye-contact. He knew the rules of this game, probably better than she did. He stepped into her personal space. Mongoose shivered against the nape of his neck, her tendrils threading his hair. Even without being able to see her, he knew she was a deep, anxious emerald.

"A rath?" said Station Master Lee, with a toss of her head that might have looked flirtatious on a younger or less hostile woman, and moved away again. "Don't be ridiculous. There hasn't been a rath on Kadath Station since my grandfather's time."

"Doesn't mean there isn't an infestation now," Irizarry said quietly. If she was going to be dramatic, that was his cue to stay still and calm. "And I said raths. Plural."

"That's even more ridiculous. Mr. Irizarry, if this is some ill-conceived attempt to drive up your price—"

"It isn't." He was careful to say it flatly, not indignantly. "Station Master, I understand that this isn't what you want to hear, but you have to quarantine Kadath."

"Can't be done," she said, her tone brisk and flat, as if he'd asked her to pilot Kadath through the rings of Saturn.

"Of course it can!" Irizarry said, and she finally turned to look at him, outraged that he dared to contradict her. Against his neck,

Mongoose flexed one set of claws. She didn't like it when he was angry.

Mostly, that wasn't a problem. Mostly, Irizarry knew anger was a waste of time and energy. It didn't solve anything. It didn't fix anything. It couldn't bring back anything that was lost. People, lives. The sorts of things that got washed away in the tides of time. Or were purged, whether you wanted them gone or not.

But this was . . . "You do know what a colony of adult raths can do, don't you? With a contained population of prey? Tell me, Station Master, have you started noticing fewer indigents in the shelters?"

She turned away again, dismissing his existence from her cosmology. "The matter is not open for discussion, Mr. Irizarry. I hired you to deal with an alleged infestation. I expect you to do so. If you feel you can't, you are of course welcome to leave the station with whatever ship takes your fancy. I believe the *Arthur Gordon Pym* is headed in-system, or perhaps you'd prefer the Jupiter run?"

He didn't have to win this fight, he reminded himself. He could walk away, try to warn somebody else, get himself and Mongoose the hell off Kadath Station. "All right, Station Master. But remember that I warned you, when your secretaries start disappearing."

He was at the door when she cried, "Irizarry!"

He stopped, but didn't turn.

"I can't," she said, low and rushed, as if she was afraid of being overheard. "I can't quarantine the station. Our numbers are already in the red this quarter, and the new political officer . . . it's my head on the block, don't you understand?"

He didn't understand. Didn't want to. It was one of the reasons he was a wayfarer, because he never wanted to let himself be like her again.

"If Sanderson finds out about the quarantine, she finds out about you. Will your papers stand up to a close inspection, Mr. Irizarry?"

He wheeled, mouth open to tell her what he thought of her and her clumsy attempts at blackmail, and she said, "I'll double your fee."

At the same time, Mongoose tugged on several strands of his hair, and he realized he could feel her heart beating, hard and rapid, against his spine. It was her distress he answered, not the Station Master's bribe. "All right," he said. "I'll do the best I can."

Toves and raths colonized like an epidemic, outward from a single originating point, Patient Zero in this case being the tear in spacetime that the first tove had wriggled through. More tears would develop as the toves multiplied, but it was that first one that would become large enough for a rath. While toves were simply lazy— energy efficient, the Arkhamers said primly—and never crawled farther than was necessary to find a useable anchoring point, raths were cautious. Their marauding was centered on the original tear because they kept their escape route open. And tore it wider and wider.

Toves weren't the problem, although they were a nuisance, with their tendency to use up valuable oxygen, clog ductwork, eat pets, drip goo from ceilings, and crunch wetly when you stepped on them. Raths were worse; raths were vicious predators. Their natural prey might be toves, but they didn't draw the line at disappearing weakened humans or small gillies, either.

But even they weren't the danger that had made it hard for Irizarry to sleep the past two rest shifts. What toves tore and raths widened was an access for the apex predator of this alien food chain.

The bandersnatch: *Pseudocanis tindalosi.* The old records and the indigent Arkhamers called them hounds, but of course they weren't, any more than Mongoose was a cat. Irizarry had seen archive video from derelict stations and ships, the bandersnatch's flickering angular limbs appearing like spiked mantis arms from the corners of sealed rooms, the carnage that ensued. He'd never heard of anyone left alive on a station where a bandersnatch manifested, unless they made it to a panic pod damned fast. More importantly, even the Arkhamers in their archive-ships, breeders of Mongoose and all her kind, admitted they had no records of anyone *surviving* a bandersnatch rather than *escaping* it.

And what he had to do, loosely put, was find the core of the infestation before the bandersnatches did, so that he could eradicate the toves and raths and the stress they were putting on this little corner of the universe. Find the core—somewhere in the miles upon miles of Kadath's infrastructure. Which was why he was in this little-used service corridor, letting Mongoose commune with every ventilation duct they found.

Anywhere near the access shafts infested by the colony, Kadath Station's passages reeked of tove—ammoniac, sulfurous. The stench infiltrated the edges of Irizarry's mask as he lifted his face to a ventilation duct. Wincing in anticipation, he broke the seal on the rebreather and pulled it away from his face on the stiff elastic straps, careful not to lose his grip. A broken nose would not improve his day.

A cultist engineer skittered past on sucker-tipped limbs, her four snake-arms coiled tight beside her for the narrow corridor. She had a pretty smile, for a Christian.

Mongoose was too intent on her prey to be shy. The size of the tove colony might make her nervous, but Mongoose loved the smell—like a good dinner heating, Irizarry imagined. She unfolded herself around his head like a tendriled hood, tentacles outreached, body flaring as she stretched towards the ventilation fan. He felt her lean, her barbels shivering, and turned to face the way her wedge-shaped head twisted.

He almost tipped backwards when he found himself face to face with someone he hadn't even known was there. A woman, average height, average weight, brown hair drawn back in a smooth club; her skin was space-pale and faintly reddened across the cheeks, as if the IR filters on a suit hadn't quite protected her. She wore a sleek space-black uniform with dull silver epaulets and four pewter-colored bands at each wrist. An insignia with a stylized sun and Earth-Moon dyad clung over her heart.

The political officer, who was obviously unconcerned by Mongoose's ostentatious display of sensory equipment.

Mongoose absorbed her tendrils in like a startled anemone, pressing the warm underside of her head to Irizarry's scalp where the hair was thinning. He was surprised she didn't vanish down his shirt, because he felt her trembling against his neck.

The political officer didn't extend her hand. "Mr. Irizarry? You're a hard man to find. I'm Intelligence Colonel Sadhi Sanderson. I'd like to ask you a few quick questions, please."

"I'm, uh, a little busy right now," Irizarry said, and added uneasily, "Ma'am." The *last* thing he wanted was to offend her.

Sanderson looked up at Mongoose. "Yes, you would appear to be hunting," she said, her voice dry as scouring powder. "That's one of the things I want to talk about."

Oh *shit*. He had kept out of the political officer's way for a day and a half, and really that was a pretty good run, given the obvious tensions between Lee and Sanderson, and the things he'd heard in the Transient Barracks: the gillies were all terrified of Sanderson, and nobody seemed to have a good word for Lee. Even the Christians, mouths thinned primly, could say of Lee only that she didn't actively persecute them. Irizarry had been stuck on a steelship with a Christian congregation for nearly half a year once, and he knew their eagerness to speak well of everyone; he didn't know whether that was actually part of their faith, or just a survival tactic, but when Elder Dawson said, "She does not trouble us," he understood quite precisely what that meant.

Of Sanderson, they said even less, but Irizarry understood that, too. There was no love lost between the extremist cults and the government. But he'd heard plenty from the ice miners and dock workers and particularly from the crew of an impounded steelship who were profanely eloquent on the subject. Upshot: Colonel Sanderson was new in town, cleaning house, and profoundly not a woman you wanted to fuck with.

"I'd be happy to come to your office in an hour, maybe two?" he said. "It's just that—"

Mongoose's grip on his scalp tightened, sudden and sharp enough that he yelped; he realized that her head had moved back toward the duct while he fenced weakly with Colonel Sanderson, and now it was nearly *in* the duct, at the end of a foot and a half of iridescent neck.

"Mr. Irizarry?"

He held a hand up, because really this wasn't a good time, and yelped again when Mongoose reached down and grabbed it. He knew better than to forget how fluid her body was, that it was really no more than a compromise with the dimension he could sense her in, but sometimes it surprised him anyway.

And then Mongoose said, *Nagina,* and if Colonel Sanderson hadn't been standing right there, her eyebrows indicating that he was already at the very end of the slack she was willing to cut, he would have cursed aloud. Short of a bandersnatch—and that could still be along any time now, don't forget, Irizarry—a breeding rath was the worst news they could have.

"Your cheshire seems unsettled," Sanderson said, not sounding in the least alarmed. "Is there a problem?"

"She's eager to eat. And, er. She doesn't like strangers." It was as true as anything you could say about Mongoose, and the violent colors cycling down her tendrils gave him an idea what her chromatophores were doing behind his head.

"I can see that," Sanderson said. "Cobalt and yellow, in that stippled pattern—and flickering in and out of phase—she's acting aggressive, but that's fear, isn't it?"

Whatever Irizarry had been about to say, her observation stopped him short. He blinked at her—*like a gilly,* he thought uncharitably—and only realized he'd taken yet another step back when the warmth of the bulkhead pressed his coveralls to his spine.

"You know," Sanderson said mock-confidentially, "this entire corridor *reeks* of toves. So let me guess: it's not just toves anymore."

Irizarry was still stuck at her being able to read Mongoose's colors. "What do you know about cheshires?" he said.

She smiled at him as if at a slow student. "Rather a lot. I was on the *Jenny Lind* as an ensign—there was a cheshire on board, and I saw . . . It's not the sort of thing you forget, Mr. Irizarry, having been there once." Something complicated crossed her face—there for a flash and then gone.

"The cheshire that died on the *Jenny Lind* was called Demon," Irizarry said, carefully. "Her partner was Long Mike Spider. You knew them?"

"Spider John," Sanderson said, looking down at the backs of her hands. She picked a cuticle with the opposite thumbnail. "He went by Spider John. You have the cheshire's name right, though."

When she looked back up, the arch of her carefully shaped brow told him he hadn't been fooling anyone.

"Right," Irizarry said. "Spider John."

"They were friends of mine." She shook her head. "I was just a pup. First billet, and I was assigned as Demon's liaison. Spider John liked to say he and I had the same job. But I couldn't make the captain believe him when he tried to tell her how bad it was."

"How'd you make it off after the bandersnatch got through?" Irizarry asked. He wasn't foolish enough to think that her confidences were anything other than a means of demonstrating to him why he could trust her, but the frustration and tired sadness sounded sincere.

"It went for Spider John first—it must have known he was a threat. And Demon—she threw herself at it, never mind it was five times her size. She bought us time to get to the panic pod and Captain Golovnina time to get to the core overrides." She paused. "I saw it, you know. Just a glimpse. Wriggling through this . . . this *rip* in the air, like a big gaunt hound ripping through a hole in a blanket with knotty paws. I spent years wondering if it got my scent. Once they scent prey, you know, they never stop . . ."

She trailed off, raising her gaze to meet his. He couldn't decide if the furrow between her eyes was embarrassment at having revealed so much, or the calculated cataloguing of his response.

"So you recognize the smell, is what you're saying."

She had a way of answering questions with other questions. "Am I right about the raths?"

He nodded. "A breeder."

She winced.

He took a deep breath and stepped away from the bulkhead. "Colonel Sanderson—I have to get it *now* if I'm going to get it at all."

She touched the microwave pulse pistol at her hip. "Want some company?"

He didn't. Really, truly didn't. And if he had, he wouldn't have chosen Kadath Station's political officer. But he couldn't afford to offend her . . . and he wasn't licensed to carry a weapon.

"All right," he said and hoped he didn't sound as grudging as he felt. "But don't get in Mongoose's way."

Colonel Sanderson offered him a tight, feral smile. "Wouldn't dream of it."

The only thing that stank more than a pile of live toves was a bunch of half-eaten ones.

"Going to have to vacuum-scrub the whole sector," Sanderson said, her breath hissing through her filters.

If we live long enough to need to, Irizarry, thought, but had the sense to keep his mouth shut. You didn't talk defeat around a politico. And if you were unfortunate enough to come to the attention of one, you certainly didn't let her see you thinking it.

Mongoose forged on ahead, but Irizarry noticed she was careful to stay within the range of his lights, and at least one of her tendrils stayed focused back on him and Sanderson at all times. If this were a normal infestation, Mongoose would be scampering along the corridor ceilings, leaving scattered bits of half-consumed tove and streaks of bioluminescent ichor in her wake. But this time, she edged along, testing each surface before her with quivering barbels so that Irizarry was reminded of a tentative spider or an exploratory octopus.

He edged along behind her, watching her colors go dim and cautious. She paused at each intersection, testing the air in every direction, and waited for her escort to catch up.

The service tubes of Kadath Station were mostly large enough for Irizarry and Sanderson to walk through single-file, though sometimes they were obliged to crouch, and once or twice Irizarry found himself slithering on his stomach through tacky half-dried tove slime. He imagined—he hoped it was imagining—that he could sense the thinning and stretch of reality all around them, see it in the warp of the tunnels and the bend of deck plates. He imagined that he glimpsed faint shapes from the corners of his eyes, caught a whisper of sound, a hint of scent, as of something almost there.

Hypochondria, he told himself firmly, aware that that was the wrong word and not really caring. But as he dropped down onto his belly again, to squeeze through a tiny access point—this one clogged with the fresh corpses of newly-slaughtered toves—he needed all the comfort he could invent.

He almost ran into Mongoose when he'd cleared the hole. She scuttled back to him and huddled under his chest, tendrils writhing, so close to out of phase that she was barely a warm shadow. When he saw what was on the other side, he wished he'd invented a little more.

This must be one of Kadath Station's recycling and reclamation centers, a bowl ten meters across sweeping down to a pile of rubbish in the middle. These were the sorts of places you always found minor tove infestations. Ships and stations might be supposed to be kept clear of vermin, but in practice, the dimensional stresses of sharing the spacelanes with boojums meant that just wasn't possible. And in Kadath, somebody hadn't been doing their job.

Sanderson touched his ankle, and Irizarry hastily drew himself aside so she could come through after. He was suddenly grateful for her company.

He really didn't want to be here alone.

Irizarry had never seen a tove infestation like this, not even on the *Jenny Lind*. The entire roof of the chamber was thick with their sluglike bodies, long lure-tongues dangling as much as half a meter down. Small flitting things—young raths, near-transparent in their phase shift—filled the space before him. As Irizarry watched, one blundered into the lure of a tove, and the tove contracted with sudden convulsive force. The rath never stood a chance.

Nagina, Mongoose said. *Nagina, Nagina, Nagina.*

Indeed, down among the junk in the pit, something big was stirring. But that wasn't all. That pressure Irizarry had sensed earlier, the feeling that many eyes were watching him, gaunt bodies stretching against whatever frail fabric held them back—here, it was redoubled, until he almost felt the brush of not-quite-in-phase whiskers along the nape of his neck.

Sanderson crawled up beside him, her pistol in one hand. Mongoose didn't seem to mind her there.

"What's down there?" she asked, her voice hissing on constrained breaths.

"The breeding pit," Irizarry said. "You feel that? Kind of funny, stretchy feeling in the universe?"

Sanderson nodded behind her mask. "It's not going to make you any happier, is it, if I tell you I've felt it before?"

Irizarry was wearily, grimly unsurprised. But then Sanderson said, "What do we do?"

He was taken aback and it must have shown, even behind the rebreather, because she said sharply, "*You*'re the expert. Which I assume is why you're on Kadath Station to begin with and why Station Master Lee has been so anxious that I not know it. Though with an infestation of this size, I don't know how she thought she was going to hide it much longer anyway."

"Call it sabotage," Irizarry said absently. "Blame the Christians. Or the gillies. Or disgruntled spacers, like the crew off the *Caruso*. It happens a lot, Colonel. Somebody like me and Mongoose comes in and cleans up the toves, the station authorities get to crack down on whoever's being the worst pain in the ass, and life keeps on turning over. But she waited too long."

Down in the pit, the breeder heaved again. Breeding raths were slow—much slower than the juveniles, or the sexually dormant adult rovers—but that was because they were armored like titanium armadillos. When threatened, one of two things happened. Babies flocked to mama, mama rolled herself in a ball, and it would take a tactical nuke to kill them. Or mama went on the warpath. Irizarry had seen a pissed off breeder take out a bulkhead on a steelship once; it was pure dumb luck that it hadn't breached the hull.

And, of course, once they started spawning, as this one had, they could produce between ten and twenty babies a day for anywhere from a week to a month, depending on the food supply. And the more babies they produced, the weaker the walls of the world got, and the closer the bandersnatches would come.

"The first thing we have to do," he said to Colonel Sanderson, "as in, *right now,* is kill the breeder. Then you quarantine the station and get parties of volunteers to hunt down the rovers, before they can bring another breeder through, or turn into breeders, or however the fuck it works, which frankly I don't know. It'll take fire to clear this nest of toves, but Mongoose and I can probably get the rest. And *fire,* Colonel Sanderson. Toves don't give a shit about vacuum."

She could have reproved him for his language; she didn't. She just nodded and said, "How do we kill the breeder?"

"Yeah," Irizarry said. "That's the question."

Mongoose clicked sharply, her *Irizarry!* noise.

"No," Irizarry said. "Mongoose, don't—"

But she wasn't paying attention. She had only a limited amount of patience for his weird interactions with other members of his species and his insistence on *waiting*, and he'd clearly used it all up. She was Rikki Tikki Tavi, and the breeder was Nagina, and Mongoose knew what had to happen. She launched off Irizarry's shoulders, shifting phase as she went, and without contact between them, there was nothing he could do to call her back. In less than a second, he didn't even know where she was.

"You any good with that thing?" he said to Colonel Sanderson, pointing at her pistol.

"Yes," she said, but her eyebrows were going up again. "But, forgive me, isn't this what cheshires are for?"

"Against rovers, sure. But—Colonel, have you ever seen a breeder?"

Across the bowl, a tove warbled, the chorus immediately taken up by its neighbors. Mongoose had started.

"No," Sanderson said, looking down at where the breeder humped and wallowed and finally stood up, shaking off ethereal babies and half-eaten toves. "Oh. *Gods*."

You couldn't describe a rath. You couldn't even look at one for more than a few seconds before you started getting a migraine aura. Rovers were just blots of shadow. The breeder was massive, armored, and had no recognizable features, save for its hideous, drooling, ragged edged maw. Irizarry didn't know if it had eyes, or even needed them.

"She can kill it," he said, "but only if she can get at its underside. Otherwise, all it has to do is wait until it has a clear swing, and she's . . ." He shuddered. "I'll be lucky to find enough of her for a funeral. So what *we* have to do now, Colonel, is piss it off enough to give her a chance. Or"—he had to be fair; this was not Colonel Sanderson's job—"if you'll lend me your pistol, you don't have to stay."

She looked at him, her dark eyes very bright, and then she turned to look at the breeder, which was swinging its shapeless head in slow arcs, trying, no doubt, to track Mongoose. "Fuck that, Mr. Irizarry," she said crisply. "Tell me where to aim."

"You won't hurt it," he'd warned her, and she'd nodded, but he was pretty sure she hadn't really understood until she fired her first shot and the breeder didn't even *notice*. But Sanderson hadn't given up; her mouth had thinned, and she'd settled into her stance, and she'd fired again, at the breeder's feet as Irizarry had told her. A breeding rath's feet weren't vulnerable as such, but they were sensitive, much more sensitive than the human-logical target of its head. Even so, it was concentrating hard on Mongoose, who was making toves scream at various random points around the circumference of the breeding pit, and it took another three shots aimed at that same near front foot before the breeder's head swung in their direction.

It made a noise, a sort of "wooaaurgh" sound, and Irizarry and Sanderson were promptly swarmed by juvenile raths.

"Ah, fuck," said Irizarry. "Try not to kill them."

"I'm sorry, try *not* to kill them?"

"If we kill too many of them, it'll decide we're a threat rather than an annoyance. And then it rolls up in a ball, and we have no chance of killing it until it unrolls again. And by then, there will be a lot more raths here."

"And quite possibly a bandersnatch," Sanderson finished. "But—" She batted away a half-corporeal rath that was trying to wrap itself around the warmth of her pistol.

"If we stood perfectly still for long enough," Irizarry said, "they could probably leech out enough of our body heat to send us into hypothermia. But they can't bite when they're this young. I knew a cheshire-man once who swore they ate by crawling down into the breeder's stomach to lap up what it'd digested. I'm still hoping that's not true. Just keep aiming at that foot."

"You got it."

Irizarry had to admit, Sanderson was steady as a rock. He shooed juvenile raths away from both of them, Mongoose continued her depredations out there in the dark, and Sanderson, having found her target, fired at it in a nice steady rhythm. She didn't miss; she didn't try to get fancy. Only, after a while, she said out of the corner of her mouth, "You know, my battery won't last forever."

"I know," Irizarry said. "But this is good. It's working."

"How can you tell?"

"It's getting mad."

"How can you *tell*?"

"The vocalizing." The rath had gone from its "wooaaurgh" sound to a series of guttural huffing noises, interspersed with high-pitched yips. "It's warning us off. Keep firing."

"All right," Sanderson said. Irizarry cleared another couple of juveniles off her head. He was trying not to think about what it meant that no adult raths had come to the pit—just how much of Kadath Station had they claimed?

"*Have* there been any disappearances lately?" he asked Sanderson.

She didn't look at him, but there was a long silence before she said, "None that *seemed* like disappearances. Our population is by necessity transient, and none too fond of authority. And, frankly, I've had so much trouble with the stationmaster's office that I'm not sure my information is reliable."

It had to hurt for a political officer to admit that. Irizarry said, "We're very likely to find human bones down there. And in their caches."

Sanderson started to answer him, but the breeder decided it had had enough. It wheeled toward them, its maw gaping wider, and started through the mounds of garbage and corpses in their direction.

"What now?" said Sanderson.

"Keep firing," said Irizarry. *Mongoose, wherever you are, please be ready.*

He'd been about seventy-five percent sure that the rath would stand up on its hind legs when it reached them. Raths weren't sapient, not like cheshires, but they were smart. They knew that the quickest way to kill a human was to take its head off, and the second quickest was to disembowel it, neither of which they could do on all fours.

And humans weren't any threat to a breeder's vulnerable abdomen; Sanderson's pistol might give the breeder a hot foot, but there was no way it could penetrate the breeder's skin.

It was a terrible plan—there was that whole twenty-five percent where he and Sanderson died screaming while the breeder ate them from the feet up—but it worked. The breeder heaved itself upright, massive, indistinct paw going back for a blow that would shear Sanderson's head off her neck and probably bounce it off the nearest bulkhead, and with no warning of any kind, not for the humans, not for the rath, Mongoose phased viciously in, claws and teeth and sharp edged tentacles all less than two inches from the rath's belly and moving fast.

The rath screamed and curled in on itself, but it was too late. Mongoose had already caught the lips of its—oh gods and fishes, Irizarry didn't know the word. Vagina? Cloaca? Ovipositor? The place where little baby raths came into the world. The only vulnerability a breeder had. Into which Mongoose shoved the narrow wedge of her head, and her clawed front feet, and began to rip.

Before the rath could even reach for her, her malleable body was already entirely inside it, and it—screaming, scrabbling—was doomed.

Irizarry caught Sanderson's elbow and said, "Now would be a good time, *very slowly*, to back away. Let the lady do her job."

Irizarry almost made it off of Kadath clean.

He'd had no difficulty in getting a berth for himself and Mongoose—after a party or two of volunteers had seen her in action, after the stories started spreading about the breeder, he'd nearly come to the point of beating off the steelship captains with a stick. And in the end, he'd chosen the offer of the captain of the *Erich Zann*, a boojum; Captain Alvarez had a long-term salvage contract in the Kuiper belt—"cleaning up after the ice miners," she'd said with a wry smile—and Irizarry felt like salvage was maybe where he wanted to be for a while. There'd be plenty for Mongoose to hunt, and nobody's life in danger. Even a bandersnatch wasn't much more than a case of indigestion for a boojum.

He'd got his money out of the stationmaster's office—hadn't even had to talk to Station Master Lee, who maybe, from the things he was hearing, wasn't going to be stationmaster much longer. You could either be ineffectual *or* you could piss off your political officer. Not both at once. And her secretary so very obviously didn't want to bother her that it was easy to say, "We had a contract," and to plant his feet and smile. It wasn't the doubled fee she'd promised him, but he didn't even want that. Just the money he was owed.

So his business was taken care of. He'd brought Mongoose out to the *Erich Zann*, and insofar as he and Captain Alvarez could tell, the boojum and the cheshire liked each other. He'd bought himself new underwear and let Mongoose pick out a new pair of earrings for him. And he'd gone ahead and splurged, since he was, after all, *on* Kadath Station and might as well make the most of it, and bought a selection of books for his reader, including *The Wind in the Willows*. He was looking forward, in an odd, quiet way, to the long nights out beyond Neptune: reading to Mongoose, finding out what she thought about Rat and Mole and Toad and Badger.

Peace—or as close to it as Izrael Irizarry was ever likely to get.

He'd cleaned out his cubby in the Transient Barracks, slung his bag over one shoulder with Mongoose riding on the other, and was actually in sight of the *Erich Zann*'s dock when a voice behind him called his name.

Colonel Sanderson.

He froze in the middle of a stride, torn between turning around to greet her and bolting like a rabbit, and then she'd caught up to him. "Mr. Irizarry," she said. "I hoped I could buy you a drink before you go."

He couldn't help the deeply suspicious look he gave her. She spread her hands, showing them empty. "Truly. No threats, no tricks. Just a drink. To say thank you." Her smile was lopsided; she knew how unlikely those words sounded in the mouth of a political officer.

And any other political officer, Irizarry wouldn't have believed them. But he'd seen her stand her ground in front of a breeder rath, and he'd seen her turn and puke her guts out when she got a good look at what Mongoose did to it. If she wanted to thank him, he owed it to her to sit still for it.

"All right," he said, and added awkwardly, "Thank you."

They went to one of Kadath's tourist bars: bright and quaint and cheerful and completely unlike the spacer bars Irizarry was used to. On the other hand, he could see why Sanderson picked this one. No one here, except maybe the bartender, had the least idea who she was, and the bartender's wide-eyed double take meant that they got excellent service: prompt and very quiet.

Irizarry ordered a pink lady—he liked them, and Mongoose, in delight, turned the same color pink, with rosettes matched to the maraschino "cherry." Sanderson ordered whisky, neat, which had very little resemblance to the whisky Irizarry remembered from planetside. She took a long swallow of it, then set the glass down and said, "I never got a chance to ask Spider John this: how did you get your cheshire?"

It was clever of her to invoke Spider John and Demon like that, but Irizarry still wasn't sure she'd earned the story. After the silence had gone on a little too long, Sanderson picked her glass up, took another swallow, and said, "I know who you are."

"I'm *nobody*," Irizarry said. He didn't let himself tense up, because Mongoose wouldn't miss that cue, and she was touchy enough, what with all the steelship captains, that he wasn't sure what she might think the proper response was. And he wasn't sure, if she decided the proper response was to rip Sanderson's face off, that he would be able to make himself disagree with her in time.

"I promised," Sanderson said. "No threats. I'm not trying to trace you, I'm not asking any questions about the lady you used to work for. And, truly, I'm only *asking* how you met *this* lady. You don't have to tell me."

"No," Irizarry said mildly. "I don't." But Mongoose, still pink, was coiling down his arm to investigate the glass—not its contents, since the interest of the egg-whites would be more than outweighed by the sharp sting to her nose of the alcohol, but the upside-down cone on a stem of a martini glass. She liked geometry. And this wasn't a story that could hurt anyone.

He said, "I was working my way across Jupiter's moons, oh, five years ago now. Ironically enough, I got trapped in a quarantine. Not for vermin, but for the black rot. It was a long time, and things got . . . ugly."

He glanced at her and saw he didn't need to elaborate.

"There were Arkhamers trapped there, too, in their huge old scow of a ship. And when the water rationing got tight, there were people that said the Arkhamers shouldn't have any—said that if it was the other way 'round, they wouldn't give us any. And so when the Arkhamers sent one of their daughters for their share . . ." He still remembered her scream, a grown woman's terror in a child's voice, and so he shrugged and said, "I did the only thing I could. After that, it was safer for me on their ship than it was on the station, so I spent some time with them. Their professors let me stay.

"They're not bad people," he added, suddenly urgent. "I don't say I understand what they believe, or why, but they were good to me, and they did share their water with the crew of the ship in the next berth. And of course, they had cheshires. Cheshires all over the place, cleanest steelship you've ever seen. There was a litter born right about the time the quarantine finally lifted. Jemima—the little girl I helped—she insisted they give me pick of the litter, and that was Mongoose."

Mongoose, knowing the shape of her own name on Irizarry's lips, began to purr, and rubbed her head gently against his fingers. He petted her, feeling his tension ease, and said, "And I wanted to be a biologist before things got complicated."

"Huh," said Sanderson. "Do you know what they are?"

"Sorry?" He was still mostly thinking about the Arkhamers, and braced himself for the usual round of superstitious nonsense: demons or necromancers or what-not.

But Sanderson said, "Cheshires. Do you know what they are?"

"What do you mean, 'what they are'? They're cheshires."

"After Demon and Spider John . . . I did some reading and I found a professor or two—Arkhamers, yes—to ask." She smiled, very thinly. "I've found, in this job, that people are often remarkably willing to answer my questions. And I found out. They're bandersnatches."

"Colonel Sanderson, not to be disrespectful—"

"Sub-adult bandersnatches," Sanderson said. "Trained and bred and intentionally stunted so that they never mature fully."

Mongoose, he realized, had been watching, because she caught his hand and said emphatically, *Not.*

"Mongoose disagrees with you," he said and found himself smiling. "And really, I think she would know."

Sanderson's eyebrows went up. "And what does Mongoose think she is?"

He asked, and Mongoose answered promptly, pink dissolving into champagne and gold: *Jagular.* But there was a thrill of uncertainty behind it, as if she wasn't quite sure of what she stated so emphatically. And then, with a sharp toss of her head at Colonel Sanderson, like any teenage girl: *Mongoose.*

Sanderson was still watching him sharply. "Well?"

"She says she's Mongoose."

And Sanderson really wasn't trying to threaten him, or playing some elaborate political game, because her face softened in a real smile, and she said, "Of course she is."

Irizarry swished a sweet mouthful between his teeth. He thought of what Sanderson had said, of the bandersnatch on the *Jenny Lind* wriggling through stretched rips in reality like a spiny, deathly puppy tearing a blanket. "How would you domesticate a bandersnatch?"

She shrugged. "If I knew that, I'd be an Arkhamer, wouldn't I?" Gently, she extended the back of her hand for Mongoose to sniff. Mongoose, surprising Irizarry, extended one tentative tendril and let it hover just over the back of Sanderson's wrist.

Sanderson tipped her head, smiling affectionately, and didn't move her hand. "But if I had to guess, I'd say you do it by making friends."

««« Theodore Sturgeon »»»

The ship was crewed with men who had been deliberately, painstakingly driven insane, except for one man. They had told him that he wasn't insane—but then, they might have been lying to him. Then they sent them to a place in space from which ships did not return. The mission was insane in *every* meaning of the word . . .

Theodore Sturgeon (1918-1985) was one of the great writers of science fiction's "golden age" in the 1940s, and by the 1950s was renowned for his three-dimensional characters and his highly individual style. His early works, of which "Medusa" is an example, were elegantly constructed, fast-paced stories told by a wisecracking narrator, but he soon developed a fluent prose poetry of style that accomplished wonders. Another notable prose poet, Ray Bradbury, admitted the strong influence Sturgeon's writing had on his own work in the introduction he wrote for *Without Sorcery*, Sturgeon's first story collection. His now-classic novel, *More Than Human*, won the International Fantasy Award, the first of a number of awards (though there should have been many more). The distinguished editor and reviewer Groff Conklin once wrote, "You don't read [Sturgeon's] stories. They happen to you." (Nailed it, Mr. Conklin!) Two *Star Trek* episodes were scripted by him, and one of them, "The Amok Time," was a high point of that program. He wrote over 200 short stories, all of which have now been collected in thirteen volumes published by North Atlantic Books. (Many thanks to the late Paul Williams and Noël Sturgeon for bringing this miracle to pass.) He was also the author of unforgettable horror stories, such as "It!," "The Professor's Teddy Bear," "Farewell to Eden," and, of course, "Bianca's Hands." Not to mention the story which follows . . .

(((((MEDUSA)))))

Theodore Sturgeon

I wasn't sore at them. I don't know what they'd done to me, exactly—
I knew that some of it wasn't so nice, and that I'd probably never be
the same again. But I was a volunteer, wasn't I? I'd asked for it. I'd
signed a paper authorizing the department of commerce of the league
to use me as they saw fit. When they pulled me out of the fleet for
routine examination, and when they started examinations that were
definitely not routine, I didn't kick. When they asked for volunteers
for a project they didn't bother to mention by name, I accepted it sight
unseen. And now—

"How do you feel, Rip?" old Doc Renn wanted to know. He spoke
to me easylike, with his chin on the backs of his hands and his elbows
on the table. The greatest name in psychoscience, and he talks to me
as if he were my old man. Right up there in front of the whole psycho
board, too.

"Fine, sir," I said. I looked around. I knew all the doctors and one
or two of the visitors. All the medicos had done one job or another on
me in the last three years. Boy, did they put me through the mill. I
understood only a fraction of it all—the first color tests, for instance,
and the electro-coordination routines. But that torture machine of
Grenfell's and that copper helmet that Winton made me wear for two
months—talk about your nightmares! What they were doing to or for
me was something I could only guess at. Maybe they were testing me

111

for something. Maybe I was just a guinea pig. Maybe I was in training for something. It was no use asking, either. I volunteered, didn't I?

"Well, Rip," Doc Renn was saying, "It's all over now—the preliminaries, I mean. We're going ahead with the big job."

"Preliminaries?" I goggled. "You mean to tell me that what I've been through for the last three years was all preliminaries?"

Renn nodded, watching me carefully. "You're going on a little trip. It may not be fun, but it'll be interesting."

"Trip? Where to?" This was good news; the repeated drills on spaceship techniques, the refresher courses on astrogation, had given me a good-sized itch to get out into the black again.

"Sealed orders," said Renn, rather sharply. "You'll find out. The important thing for you to remember is that you have a very important role to play." He paused. I could see him grimly ironing the snappiness out of his tone. Why in Canaan did he have to be so careful with *me*? "You will be put aboard a Forfield Super—the latest and best equipped that the league can furnish. Your job is to tend the control machinery, and to act as assistant astrogator no matter what happens. Without doubt, you will find your position difficult at times. You are to obey your orders as given, without question, and without the use of force where possible."

This sounded screwy to me. "That's all written up, just about word for word, in the 'Naval Manual,'" I reminded him gently, "under 'Duties of Crew.' I've had to do all you said every time I took a ship out. Is there anything special about this one, that it calls for all this underlining?"

He was annoyed, and the board shuffled twenty-two pairs of feet. But his tone was still friendly, half-persuasive when he spoke. "There is definitely something special about this ship, and—its crew. Rip, you've come through everything we could hand you, with flying colors. Frankly, you were subjected to psychic forces that were enough to drive a normal man quite mad. The rest of the crew—it is only fair to tell you—are insane. The nature of this expedition necessitates our manning the ship that way. Your place on the ship is a key position. Your responsibility is a great one."

"Now—hold on, sir," I said. "I'm not questioning your orders, sir, and I consider myself under your disposition. May I ask a few questions?"

He nodded.

"You say the crew is insane. Isn't that a broad way of putting it—" I couldn't help needling him; he was trying so hard to keep calm— "for a psychologist?"

He actually grinned. "It is. To be more specific, they're schizoids— dual personalitites. Their primary egos are paranoiac. They're perfectly rational except on the subject of their particular phobia—or mania as the case may be. The recessive personality is a manic depressive."

Now, as I remembered it, most paranoiacs have delusions of grandeur coupled with a persecution mania. And a manic depressive is the "Yes master" type. They just didn't mix. I took the liberty of saying as much to one of Earth's foremost psychoscientists.

"Of course they don't mix," snapped Renn. "I didn't say they did. There's no interflowing egos in these cases. They are schizoids. The cleavage is perfect."

I have a mole under my arm that I scratch when I'm thinking hard. I scratched it. "I didn't know anything like that existed," I said. Renn seemed bent on keeping this informal, and I was playing it to the limit. I sensed that this was the last chance I'd have to get any information about the expedition.

"There never were any cases like that until recently," said Renn patiently. "Those men came out of our laboratories."

"Oh. Sort of made-to-order insanity?"

He nodded.

"What on earth for, sir?"

"Sealed orders," he said immediately. His manner became abrupt again. "You take off tomorrow. You'll be put aboard tonight. Your commanding officer is Captain William Parks." I grinned delightedly at this. Parks—the horny old fireater! They used to say of him that he could create sunspots by spitting straight up. But he was a real spaceman—through and through. "And don't forget, Rip," Renn finished. "There is only one sane man aboard that ship. That is all."

I saluted and left.

A Forfield Super is as sweet a ship as anything ever launched. There's none of your great noisy bulk pushed through the ether by a cityful of men, nor is it your completely automatic "Eyehope"—so called because after you slipped your master control tape into the automatic pilot you always said, "you're on your way, you little hunk of tinfoil—I hope!"

With an eight-man crew, a Forfield can outrun and outride anything else in space. No rockets—no celestial helices—no other such clumsy nonsense drives it. It doesn't go places by going—it gets there by standing still. By which I mean that the ship achieves what laymen call "Universal stasis."

The Galaxy is traveling in an orbit about the mythical Dead Center at an almost incredible velocity. A Forfield, with momentum nullified, just stops dead while the Galaxy streams by. When the objective approaches, momentum is resumed, and the ship appears in normal space with only a couple of thousand miles to go. That is possible because the lack of motion builds up a potential in motion; motion, being a relative thing, produces a set of relative values.

Instead of using the terms "action" and "reaction" in speaking of the Forfield drive, we speak of "stasis" and "re-stasis." I'd explain further but I left my spherical slide rule home. Let me add only that a Forfield can achieve stasis in regard to planetary, solar, galactic, or universal orbits. Mix 'em in the right proportions, and you get resultants that will take you anywhere, fast.

I was so busy from the instant I hit the deck that I didn't have time to think of all the angles of this more-than-peculiar trip. I had to check and double-check every control and instrument from the milliammeter to the huge compound integrators, and with a twenty-four-hour deadline that was no small task. I also had to take a little instruction from a league master mechanic who had installed a couple of gadgets which had been designed and tested at the last minute expressly for this trip. I paid little attention to what went on round me. I didn't even know the skipper was aboard until I rose from my knew before the integrators, swiveled around on my way to the control board, and all but knocked the old war horse off his feet.

"Rip! I'll be damned!" he howled. "Don't tell me—you're not signed on here?"

"Yup," I said. "Let go my hand, skipper—I got to be able to hold a pair of needle noses for another hour or so. Yeah, I heard you were going to captain this barrel. How do you like it?"

"Smooth," he said, looking around, then bringing his grin back to me. He only grinned twice a year because it hurt his face; but when he did, he did it all over. "What do you know about the trip?"

"Nothing except that we have sealed orders."

"Well, I'll bet there's some kind of a honkatonk at the end of the road," said Parks. "You and I've been on . . . how many is it? Six? Eight . . . anyway, we've been on plenty of ships together, and we managed to throw a whingding ashore every trip. I hope we can get out Aldebaran way. I hear Susie's place is under new management again. Heh! Remember the time we—"

I laughed. "Let's save it, skipper. I've got to finish this check-up, and fast. But, man, it's good to see you again." We stood looking at each other, and then something popped into my head and I felt my smile washing off. What was it that Dr. Renn had said—"Remember there's only one sane man aboard!" Oh, no—they hadn't put Captain Parks through that! Why—

I said, "How do you—feel, cap'n?"

"Swell," he said. He frowned. "Why? You feel all right?"

Not right then, I didn't. Captain Parks batty? That was just a little bit lousy. If Renn was right—and he was always right—then his board had given Parks the works, as well as the rest of the crew. All but me, that is. I *knew* I wasn't crazy. I didn't feel crazy. "I feel fine," I said.

"Well, go ahead then," said Parks, and turned his back.

I went over to the control board, disconnected the power leads from the radioscope, and checked the dials. For maybe five minutes I felt the old boy's eyes drilling into the nape of my neck, but I was too upset to say anything more. It got very quiet in there. Small noises drifted into the control room from other parts of the ship. Finally I heard his shoulder brush the doorpost as he walked out.

How much did the captain know about this trip? Did he know that he had a bunch of graduates from the laughing academy to man his ship? I tried to picture Renn informing Parks that he was a paranoiac and a manic depressive, and I failed miserably. Parks would probably take a swing at the doctor. Aw, it just didn't make sense. It occurred to me that "making sense" was a criterion that we put too much faith in. What do you do when you run across something that isn't even supposed to make sense?

I slapped the casing back on the radioscope, connected the leads, and called it quits. The speaker over the forward post rasped out, "All hands report to control chamber!" I started, stuck my tools into their clips under the chart table, and headed for the door. Then I remembered I was already in the control room, and subsided against the bulkhead.

They straggled in. All hands were in the pink, well fed and eager. I nodded to three of them, shook hands with another. The skipper came in without looking at me—I rather thought he avoided my eyes. He went straight forward, faced about and put his hands low enough on the canted control board so he could sit on them. Seabiscuit, the quartermaster, and an old shipmate of mine, came and stood beside me. There was an embarrassed murmur of voices while we all awaited the last two stragglers.

Seabiscuit whispered to me, "I once said I'd sail clear to Hell if Bill Parks was cap'n of the ship."

I said, out of the side of my face, "So?"

"So it looks like I'm goin' to," said the Biscuit.

The captain called the roll. That crew was microscopically hand picked. I had heard every single one of the names he called in connection with some famous escapade or other. Harry Voight was our chemist. He is the man who kept two hundred passengers alive for a month with little more than a week's supply of air and water to work with, after the liner crossed bows with a meteorite on the Pleione run. Bort Brecht was the engineer, a man who could do three men's work with his artificial hand alone. He lost it in the *Pretoria* disaster. The gunner was Hoch McCoy, the guy who "invented" the bow and arrow and saved his life when he was marooned on an asteroid in the middle of a pack of poison-toothed "Jackrabbits." The mechanics were Phil and Jo Hartley, twins, whose resemblance enabled them to change places time and again during the Insurrection, thus running bales of vital information to the league high command.

"Report," he said to me.

"All's well in the control chamber, sir," I said formally.

"Brecht?"

"All's well back aft, sir."

"Quartermaster?"

"Stores all stored and stashed away, sir," said the Biscuit.

Parke turned to the control board and threw a lever. The air locks slid shut, the thirty-second departure signal began to sound from the oscillator on the hull and from signals here and in the engineer's chamber. Parks raised his voice to be heard over their clamor.

"I don't know where we're goin'," he said, with an odd smile, "but—" the signals stopped, and that was deafening—"we're on our way!"

The master control he had thrown had accomplished all the details of taking off—artificial gravity, "solar" and "planetary" stases, air pumps, humidifiers—everything. Except for the fact that there was suddenly no light streaming in through the portholes any more, there was no slightest change in sensation. Parks reached out and tore the seals off the tape slot on the integrators and from the door of the orders file. He opened the cubbyhold and drew out a thick envelope. There was something in my throat I couldn't swallow.

He tore it open and pulled out eight envelopes and a few folded sheets of paper. He glanced at the envelopes and, with raised eyebrows, handed them to me. I took them. There was one addressed to each member of the crew. At a nod from the skipper, I distributed them. Parks unfolded his orders and looked at them.

"Orders," he said. "By authority of the Solar League, pertaining to destination and operations of Xantippean Expedition No. 1."

Startled glances were batted back and forth. Xantippe! No one had ever been to Xantippe. The weird, cometary planet of Betelgeuse was, and had always been, taboo—and for good reason.

Park's voice was tight. "Orders to be read to crew by the captain immediately upon taking off." The skipper went to the pilot chair, swiveled it, and sat down. The crew edged closer.

"The League congratulates itself on its choice of a crew for this most important mission. Out of twenty-seven hundred volunteers, these eight men survived the series of tests and conditioning exercises provided by the league.

"General orders are to proceed to Xantippe. Captain and crew have been adequately protected against the field. Object of the expedition is to find the cause of the Xantippe Field and to remove it.

"Specific orders for each member of the crew are enclosed under separate sealed covers. The crew is ordered to read these instructions, to memorize them, and to destroy the orders and envelopes. The league desires that these orders be read in strictest secrecy by each member of the crew, and that the individual contents of the envelopes be held as confidential until contrary orders are issued by the league." Parks drew a deep breath and looked around at his crew.

They were a steady lot. There was evidence of excitement, of surprise, and in at least one case, of shock. But there was no fear. Predominantly, there was a kind of exultance in the spaceburned, hard-bitten faces. They bore a common glory, a common hatred. "That isn't sensible," I told myself. "It isn't natural, or normal, or sane, for eight men to face madness, years of it, with that joyous light in their eyes. But then—they're mad already, aren't they? *Aren't they?*"

It was catching, too. I began to hate Xantippe. Which was, I suppose, silly. Xantippe was a planet, of a sort. Xantippe never killed anybody. It drove them mad, that was all. More than mad—it fused their synapses, reduced them to quivering, mindless hulks, drooling, their useless minds turned supercargo in a useless body. Xantippe had snared ship upon ship in the old days; ships bound for the other planets of the great star. The mad planet used to blanket them in its mantle of vibrations, and they were never heard from again. It was years before the league discovered where the ships had gone, and then they sent patrols to investigate. They lost eighteen ships and thirty thousand men that way.

And then came the Forfield Drive. In the kind of static hyperspace which these ships inhabited, surely they would pass the field unharmed. There were colonists out there on the other planets, depending on supplies from Sol. There were rich sources of radon, uranium, tantalum, copper. Surely a Forfield ship could—

But they couldn't. They were the first ships to penetrate the field, to come out on the other side. The ships were intact, but their crews could use their brains for absolutely nothing. Sure, I hated Xantippe. Crazy planet with its cometary orbit and its unpredictable complex ecliptic. Xantippe had an enomous plot afoot. It was stalking us—even now it was ready to pounce on us, take us all and drain our minds—

I shook myself and snapped out of it. I was dreaming myself into a case of the purple willies. If I couldn't keep my head on my shoulders about this spacegoing padded cell, then who would? Who else could?

The crew filed out, muttering. Parks sat on the pilot's chair, watching them, his bright gaze flitting from face to face. When they had gone, he began to watch me. Not look at me. Watch me. It made me sore.

"Well?" he said after a time.

"Well *what*?" I barked, insubordinately.

"Aren't you going to read your bedtime story? I am."

"Bed—oh." I slit the envelope, unfolded my orders. The captain did likewise at the extreme opposite side of the chamber. I read:

"Orders by authority of the Solar League pertaining to course of action to be taken by Harl Ripley, astromechanic on Xantippean Expedition No. 1.

"Said Harl Ripley shall follow the rules and regulations as set forth in the naval regulations, up until such time as the ship engages the Xantippean Field. He is then to follow the orders of the master, except in case of the master's removal from active duty from some unexpected cause. Should such an emergency arise, the command does not necessarily revert to said Harl Ripley, but to the crew member who with the greatest practicability outlines a plan for the following objective: The expedition is to land on Xantippe; if uninhabited, the planet is to be searched until the source of the field is found and destroyed. If inhabited, the procedure of the pro-tem commander must be dictated by events. He is to bear in mind, however, that the primary and only purpose of the expedition is to destroy the Xantippean Field."

That ended the orders; but scrawled across the foot of the page was an almost illegible addendum: "Remember your last board meeting, Rip. And good luck!" The penciled initials were C. Renn, M. Ps. S. That would be Doc Renn.

I was so puzzled that my ears began to buzz. The government had apparently spent a huge pile of money in training us and outfitting the expedition. And yet our orders were as hazy as they could possibly be. And what was the idea of giving separate orders to each crew member? And such orders! "The procedure of the pro-tem commander must be dictated by events." That's what you'd call putting us on our own! It wasn't like the crisp, detailed commands any navy man is used to. It was crazy.

Well, of course it was crazy, come to think of it. What else could you expect with this crew? I began to wish sincerely that the board had driven me nuts along with the rest of them.

I was at the chart table, coding up the hundred-hour log entry preparatory to slipping it into the printer, when I sensed someone behind me. The skipper, of course. He stayed there a long time, and I knew he was watching me.

I sat there until I couldn't stand it any longer. "Come on in." I said without moving. Nothing happened. I listened carefully until I could hear his careful breathing. It was short, swift. He was trying to breathe in a whisper. I began to be really edgy. I had a nasty suspicion that if I whirled I would be just in time to catch a bolt from a by-by gun.

Clenching my jaw till my teeth hurt, I rose slowly, and without looking around, went to the power-output telltales and looked at them. I didn't know what was the matter with me. I'd never been this way before—always expecting attack from somewhere. I used to be a pretty nice guy. As a matter of fact, I used to be the nicest guy I knew. I didn't feel that way any more.

Moving to the telltales took me another six or eight feet from the man at the door. Safer for both of us. And this way I had to turn around to get back to the table. I did. It wasn't the skipper. It was the chemist, Harry Voight. We were old shipmates, and I knew him well.

"Hello, Harry. Why the dark companion act?"

He was tense. He was wearing a little mustache of perspiration on his upper lip. His peculiar eyes—the irises were as black as the pupils—were set so far back in his head that I couldn't see them, for the alleyway light was directly over his head. His bald, bulging forehead threw two deep purple shadows, and out of them he watched me.

"Hi, Rip. Busy?"

"Not too busy. Put it in a chair."

He came in and sat down. He turned as he passed me, backed into the pilot's seat. I perched on the chart table. It looked casual, and kept my weight on one foot. If I had to move in any direction, including up, I was ready to.

After a time, he said, "What do you think of this, Rip?" His gesture took in the ship, Xantippe, the league, the board.

"I only work here." I quoted. That was the motto of the navy. Our insignia is the league symbol superimposed on a flaming sun, under which is an ultraradio screen showing the words, "I only work here." The famous phrase expresses the utmost in unquestioning, devoted duty.

Harry smiled a very sickly smile. If ever I saw a man with something eating him, it was Harry Voight. "S'matter?" I asked quietly. "Did somebody do you something?"

He looked furtively about him, edged closer. "Rip, I want to tell you something. Will you close the door?"

I started to refuse, and then reflected that regulations could stand a little relaxing in a coffin like this one. I went and pressed the panel, and it slid closed. "Make it snappy," I said. "If the skipper comes up here and finds that door closed he'll slap some wrists around here."

As soon as the door closed, Harry visibly slumped. "this is the first time in two days I've felt—comfortable," he said. He looked at me with sudden suspicion. "Rip—when we roomed together in Venus City, what color was that jacket I used to keep my 'Naval Manual' in?"

I frowned. I'd only seen the thing a couple of times— "Blue," I said.

"That's right." He wiped his forehead. "You're O.K." He made a couple of false starts and then said, "Rip, will you keep everything I say strictly to yourself? Nobody can be trusted here—nobody!" I nodded. "Well," he went on in a strained voice. "I know that this is a screwy trip. I know that the crew is—has been made—sort of—well, not normal—"

He said, with conviction, "The league has its own reason for sending us, and I don't question them. But something has gone wrong. You think Xantippe is going to get us? Ha! Xantippe is getting us *now*!" He sat back triumphantly.

"You don't say."

"But I do! I know she's countless thousands of light years away. But I don't have to tell you of the power of Xantippe. For a gigantic power like that, a little project like what they're doing to us is nothing. Any force that can throw out a field three quarters of a billion miles in diameter can play hell with us at a far greater distance."

"Could be," I said. "Just what are they doing?"

"They're studying us," he hissed. "They're watching each of us, our every action, our every mental reflex. And one by one they are—taking us away! They're got the Hartley twins, and Bort Brecht, and soon they'll have me. I don't know about the others, but their turns will come. They are taking away our personalities, and substituting their own. I tell you, those three men—and soon now, I with them—those men are not humans, but Xantippeans!"

"Now wait," I said patiently. "Aren't you going on guesswork. Nobody knows if Xantippe's inhabited. And I doubt that this substitution you speak of can be done."

"You don't think so? For pity's sake, Rip—for your own good, try to believe me! The Xantippean Field is a thought force, isn't it? And listen—I know it if you don't—this crew was picked for its hatred of Xantippe. Don't you see why? The board expects that hatred to act as a mental 'fender'—to partly ward off the field. They think there might be enough left of our minds when we're inside the field to accomplish our objective. They're wrong, Rip—*wrong!* The very existence of our communal hatred is the thing that has given us away. They have been ready for us for days now—and they are already doing their work aboard."

He subsided, and I prodded him with gentle questions.

"How do you know the Xantippeans have taken away those three men?"

"Because I happened to overhear the Hartley twins talking in the messroom two days ago. They were talking about their orders. I know I should not have listened, but I was already suspicious."

"They were talking about their orders? I understood that the orders were confidential."

"They were. But you can't expect the Hartleys to pay much attention to that. Anyway, Jo confided that a footnote on his orders had intimated that there was only one sane man aboard. Phil laughed that off. He said he knew he was sane, and he knew that Jo was sane. Now, I reason this way. Only a crazy man would question the league; a crazy man or an enemy. Now the Hartleys may be unbalanced, but they are still rational. They are still navy men. Therefore, they must be enemies, because navy men never question the league."

I listened to that vague logic spoken in that intense, convincing voice, and I didn't know what to think. "What about Bort Brecht—and yourself?"

"Bort! Ahh!" His lips curled. "I can sense an alien ego when I speak to him. It's overwhelming. I hate Xantippe," he said wildly, "but I hate Bort Brecht more! The only thing I could possibly hate more than Xantippe would be a Xantippean. That proves my point!" He spread his hands. "As for me—Rip, I'm going mad. I feel it. I see things—and when I do, I will be another of them. And then we will all be lost. For there is only one sane man aboard this ship, and that is me, and when I'm turned into a Xantippean, we will be doomed, and I want you to kill me!" He was half hysterical. I let him simmer down.

"And do I look crazy?" I asked. "If you are the only sane man—"

"Not crazy," he said quickly. "A schizoid—but you're perfectly rational. You must be, or you wouldn't have remembered what color my book jacket was."

I got up, reached out a hand to help him to his feet. He drew back. "Don't touch me!" he screamed, and when I recoiled, he tried to smile. "I'm sorry, Rip, but I can't be sure about anything. You may be a

Xantippean by now, and touching me might . . . I'll be going now . . .
I—" He went out, his black, burning eyes half closed.

I stood at the door watching him weave down the alleyway. I
could guess what was the matter. Paranoia—but bad! There was the
characteristic persecution mania, the intensity of expression, the
peculiar single-track logic—even delusions of grandeur. Hah! He
thought he was the one mentally balanced man aboard!

I walked back to the chart table, thinking hard. Harry always had
been pretty tight-lipped. He probably wouldn't spread any panic
aboard. But I'd better tip the captain off. I was wondering why the
Hartley twins and Harry Voight had all been told that all hands but
me were batty, when the skipper walked in.

"Rip," he said without preamble. "Did you ever have a fight with
Hoch McCory?"

"Good gosh, no!" I said. "I never saw him in my life until the day
we sailed. I've heard of him, of course. Why?"

Parks looked at me oddly. "He just left my quarters. He had the
most long-winded and detailed song and dance about how you were
well known as an intersolar master saboteur. Gave names and dates.
The names I know well. But the dates—well, I can alibi you for half of
'em. I didn't tell him that. But—Lord! He almost had me convinced!"

"Another one!" I breathed. And then I told him about Harry
Voight.

"I don't imagine Doc Renn thought they would begin to break so
soon," said Parks when I had finished. "These boys were under
laboratory conditions for three solid years, you know."

"I didn't know," I said. "I don't know a damn thing that's going
on around here and I'd better learn something before I go off my
kilter, too."

"Why, Ripley," he said mockingly. "You're overwrought!" Well, I
was. Parks said, "I don't know much more than you do, but that goofy
story of Harry Voight's has a couple of pretty shrewd guesses in it. For
instance, I think he was right in assuming that the board had done
something to the minds of . . . ah . . . some of the crew as armor against
the field. Few men have approached it consciously—those who have

were usually scared half to death. It's well known that fear forms the easiest possible entrance for the thing feared—ask any good hypnotist. Hate is something different again. Hate is a psychological block against fear and the thing to be feared. And the kind of hate that these guys have for Xantippe and the field is something extra special. They're mad, but they're not afraid—and that's no accident. When we do hit the field, it's bound to have less effect on us than it had on the crews of poor devils who tried to attack it."

"That sounds reasonable. Er . . . skipper, about this 'one sane man' business. What do you think of that?"

"More armor," said Parks. "But armor against the man himself. Harry, for instance, was made a paranoiac, which is a very sensible kind of nut; but at the same time he was convinced that he alone was sane. If he thought his mind had been actually tampered with instead of just—tested, he'd get all upset about it and, like as not, undo half the Psy Board's work."

Some of that struck some frightening chords in my memory. "Cap'n—do you believe that there is one sane, normal man aboard?"

"I do. One." He smiled slowly. "I know what you're thinking. You'd give anything to compare your orders with mine, wouldn't you?"

"I would. But I won't do it. Confidential. I couldn't let myself do it even if you agreed, because—" I paused.

"Well?"

"Because you're an officer and I'm a gentleman."

In my bunk at last, I gave over wishing that we'd get to the field and have it over with, and tried to do some constructive thinking. I tried to remember exactly what Doc Renn had said, and when I did, I was sorry I'd made the effort. "You are sane," and "You have been subjected to psychic forces that are sufficient to drive a normal man quite mad" might easily be totally different things. I'd been cocky enough to assume that they meant the same thing. Well, face it. Was I crazy? I didn't feel crazy. Neither did Harry Voight. He thought he was going crazy, but he was sure he hadn't got there yet. And what was "crazy," anyway? It was normal, on this ship, to hate Xantippe so much that you felt sick and sweated cold when you thought of it. Paranoia—persecution. Did I feel persecuted? Only by the thought of our duty toward Xantippe, and the persecution was Xantippe, not the duty. Did I have delusions of grandeur? Of course not; and yet— hadn't I blandly assumed that Voight had such delusions because he thought *he* was the one sane man aboard?

What was the idea of that, anyway? Why had the board put one sane man aboard—if it had? Perhaps to be sure that one man reacted differently to the others at the field, so that he could command. Perhaps merely to make each man feel that he was sane, even though he wasn't. My poor, tired brain gave it up and I slept.

We had two casualties before we reached the field. Harry Voight cut his throat in the washroom, and my gentle old buddy, Seabiscuit, crushed in the back of Hoch McCoy's head. "He was an Insurrectionist spy," he insisted mildly, time and again, while we were locking him up.

After that, we kept away from each other. I don't think I spoke ten words to anyone outside of official business, from that day until we snapped into galactic stasis near Betelgeuse. I was sorry about Hoch, because he was a fine lad. But my sorrow was tempered by the memory of his visit to the captain. There had been a pretty fine chance of his doing that to me.

In normal space once more, we maneuvered our agile little craft into an orbit about the huge sun and threw out our detectors. These wouldn't tell us much when the time came, for their range wasn't much more than the radium of the field.

The mad planet swam up onto the plates and I stared at it as I buzzed for the skipper. Xantippe was a strangely dull planet, even this close to her star. She shone dead silver, like a moonlit corpse's flesh. She was wrinkled and patched, and—perhaps it was an etheric disturbance—she seemed to pulsate slowly from pole to pole. She wasn't quite round: more nearly an ovoid, with the smaller end toward Betelgeuse! She was between two and three times the size of Luna. Gazing at her, I thought of the thousands of men of my own service who had fallen prey to her, and of the fine ships of war that had plunged into the field and disappeared. Had they crashed? Had they been tucked into some weird warp of space? Were they captives of some strange and horrible race?

Xantippe had defied every type of attack so far. She swallowed up atomic mines and torpedoes with no appreciable effect. She was apparently impervious to any rayed vibration known to man; but she was matter, and should be easy meat for an infragun—if you could get an infragun close enough. The gun's twin streams of highly charged particles, positrons on one side, mesatrons on the other, would destroy anything that happened to be where they converged. But an infragun has an effective range of less than five hundred miles. Heretofore, any ship which carried the weapon that close to Xantippe carried also a dead or mindless crew.

Captain Parks called the crew into the control room as soon as he arrived. No one spoke much: they didn't need any more information after they had glanced at the viewplate which formed the forward wall of the chamber. Bort Brecht, the swarthy engineer, wanted to know how soon we'd engage the field.

"In about two hours," said the captain glibly. I got a two-handed grip on myself to keep from yapping. He was a cold-blooded liar—we'd hit it in half an hour or less, the way I figured it. I guessed that he had his own reasons. Perhaps he thought it would be easier on the crew that way.

Parks leaned casually against the integrators and faced the crew. "Well, gentlemen," he said as if he were banqueting on Earth, "we'll soon find out what this is all about. I have instructions from the league to place certain information at your disposal.

"All hands are cautioned to obey the obvious commander once we're inside the field. That commander may or may not be myself. That has been arranged for. Each man must keep in mind the objective—the destruction of the Xantippean Field. One of us will lead the others toward that objective. Should no one seem to be in command a pro-tem captain is to be elected."

Brecht spoke up. "Cap'n, how do we know that this 'commander' that has been arranged for isn't Harry Voight or Hoch McCoy?"

"We don't know," said Parks gravely. "But we will. We will."

Twenty-three minutes after Xantippe showed up on the plates, we engaged her field.

All hands were still in the control room when we plunged in. I remember the sudden weakness of my limbs, and the way all five of the others slipped and slid down to the deck. I remember the Biscuit's quaver, "I tell you it's all a dirty Insurrectionist plot." And then I was down on the deck, too.

Something was hurting me, but I knew exactly where I was. I was under Dr. Grenfell's torture machine; it was tearing into my mind, chilling my brain. I could feel my brains, every last convolution of them. They were getting colder and colder, and bigger and bigger, and pretty soon now they would burst my skull and the laboratory and the building and chill the Earth. Inside my chest I was hot, and of course I knew why. I was Betelgeuse, mightiest of suns, and with my own warmth. I warmed half a galaxy. Soon I would destroy it, too, and that would be nice.

All the darkness in Great Space came to me.

Leave me alone. I don't care what you want done. I just want to lie here and— But nobody wanted me to do anything. What's all the hollering about, then? Oh. *I* wanted something done. There's something that has to be done, so get up, get up, get—

"He *is* dead. Death is but a sleep and a forgetting, and he's asleep, and he's forgotten everything, so he must be dead!" It was Phil Hartley. He was down on his hunkers beside me, shrieking at the top of his voice, mouthing and pointing like an ape completely caught up in the violence of his argument. Which was odd, because he wasn't arguing with anybody. The skipper was sitting silently in the pilot's chair, tears streaming down his cheeks. Jo Hartley was dead or passed out on the deck. The Biscuit and Bort Brecht were sitting on the deck holding hands like children, starring entranced into the viewplate. It showed a quadrant of Xantippe, filing the screen. The planet's surface did indeed pulsate, and it was a beautiful sight. I wanted to watch it drawing closer and closer, but there was something that had to be done first.

I sat up achingly. "Get me some water," I muttered to Phil Hartley. He looked at me, shrieked, and went and hid under the chart table.

The vision of Xantippe caught and held me again, but I shook it off. It was the most desirable thing I'd ever seen and it promised me all I could ever want, but there was something I had to do first. Maybe someone could tell me. I shook the skipper's shoulder.

"Go away," he said. I shook him again. He made no response. Fury snapped into my brain. I cuffed him with my open hand, front and back, front and back. He leaped to his feet, screamed, "Leave me alone!" and slumped back into the chair. At the sound Bort Brecht lurched to his feet and came over to us. When he let go Seabiscuit's hand, the Biscuit began to cry quietly.

"I'm giving the orders around here," Bort said.

I was delighted. There had been something, a long time ago, about somebody giving orders. "I have to do something," I said. "Do you know what it is?"

"Come with me." He led the way, swaggering, to the screen. "Look," he commanded, and then sat down beside Seabiscuit and lost himself in contemplation. Seabiscuit kept on crying.

"That's not it," I said doubtfully. "I think you gave me the wrong orders."

"Wrong?" he bellowed. "Wrong? I am never wrong!" He got up, and before I knew what was coming, he hauled off and cracked three knuckles with my jawbone. I hit the deck with a crash and slid up against Jo Hartley. Jo didn't move. He was alive, but he just didn't seem to give a damn. I lay there for a long time before I could get up again. I wanted to kill Bort Brecht, but there was something I had to do first.

I went back to the captain and butted him out of the chair. He snarled at me and went and crouched by the bulkhead, tears still streaming down his cheeks. I slumped into the seat, my fingers wandering idly about the controls without touching them, my eyes desperately trying to avoid the glory of Xantippe.

It seemed to me that I was very near to the thing I was to do. My right hand touched the infragun activator switch, came away, went back to it, came away. I boldly threw the other switch; a network of crosshairs and a bright central circle appeared on the screen. This was it, I thought. Bort Brecht yelped like a kicked dog when the crosshairs appeared, but did not move. I activated the gun, and grasped the range lever in one hand and the elevation control in the other. A black-centered ball of flame hovered near the surface of the planet.

This was it! I laughed exultantly and pushed the range lever forward. The ball plunged into the dull-silver mystery, leaving a great blank crater. I pulled and pushed at the elevation control, knowing that my lovely little ball was burning and tearing its inexorable way about in the planet's vitals. I drew it out to the surface, lashed it up and down and right and left, cut and slashed and tore.

Bort Brecht was crouched like an anthropoid, knees bent, knuckles on the deck, fury knotting his features, eyes fixed on the scene of destruction. Behind me, Phil Hartley was teetering on tiptoe, little cries of pain struggling out of his lips every time the fireball appeared. Bort spun and was beside me in one great leap. "What's happening? Who's doing that?"

"He is," I said immediately, pointing at Jo Hartley. I knew that this was going to be tough on Jo, but I was doing the thing I had to do, and I knew Bort would try to stop me. Bort leaped on the prone figure, using teeth and nails and fists and feet; and Phil Hartley hesitated only a minute, torn between the vision of Xantippe and something that called to him from what seemed a long, long while ago. Then Jo cried out in agony, and Phil, a human prototype of my fireball, struck Bort amidships. Back and forth, fore and aft, the bloody battle raged, while Seabiscuit whimpered and the skipper, still sunk in his introspective trance, wept silent. And I cut and stabbed and ripped at Xantippe.

I took care now, and cut a long slash almost from pole to pole; and the edges opened away from the wound as if the planet had been wrapped in a paper sheath. Underneath it was an olive-drab color, shot with scarlet. I cut at this incision again and again, sinking my fireball in deeper at each slash. The weakened ovoid tended to press the edges together, but the irresistible ball sheared them away as it passed; and when it had cut nearly all the through, the whole structure fell in on itself horribly. I had a sudden feeling of lightness, and then unbearable agony. I remember stretching back and back over the chair in the throes of some tremendous attack from inside my body, and then I struck the deck with my head and shoulders, and I was all by myself again in the beautiful black.

There was a succession of lights that hurt, and soothing smells, and the sound of arcs and the sound of falling water. Some of them were weeks apart, some seconds. Sometimes I was conscious and could see people tiptoeing about. Once I thought I heard music.

But at last I awoke quietly, very weak to a hand on my shoulder. I looked up. It was Dr. Renn. He looked older.

"How do you feel, Rip?"

"Hungry."

He laughed. "That's splendid. Know where you are?"

I shook my head, marveling that it didn't hurt me.

"Earth," he said. "Psy hospital. You've been through the mill, son."

"What happened?"

"Plenty. We got the whole story from the picrecording tapes inside and outside of your ship. You cut Xantippe all to pieces. You incidentally got Bort Brecht started on the Hartley family, which later literally cut *him* to pieces. It cost three lives, but Xantippe is through."

"Then—I destroyed the projector, or whatever it was—"

"You destroyed Xantippe. You—killed Xantippe. The planet was a . . . a thing that I hardly dare think about. You ever see a hydromedusa here on Earth?"

"You mean one of those jellyfish that floats on the surface of the sea and dangles paralyzing tentacles down to catch fish?"

"That's it. Like a Portugese man-of-war. Well, that was Xantippe, with that strange mind field about her for her tentacles. A space dweller; she swept up anything that came her way, killed what was killable, digested what was digestible to her. Examination of the pictures, incidentally, shows that she was all set to hurl out a great cloud of spores. One more revolution about Betelgeuse and she'd have done it."

"How come I went under like that?" I was beginning to remember.

"You weren't as well protected as the others. You see, when we trained that crew we carefully split the personalities; paranoiac hatred to carry them through the field and an instant reversion to manic depressive under the influence of the field. But yours was the only personality we couldn't split. So you were the leader—you were delegated to do the job. All we could do to you was to implant a desire to destroy Xantippe. You did the rest. But when the psychic weight of the field was lifted from you, your mind collapsed. We had a sweet job rebuilding it, too, let me tell you!"

"Why all that business about the 'one sane man'?"

Renn grinned. "That was to keep the rest of the crew fairly sure of themselves, and to keep you from the temptation of taking over before you reached the field, knowing that the rest, including the captain, were not responsible for their actions."

"What about the others, after the field disappeared?"

"They reverted to something like normal. Not quite, though. The quartermaster tied up the rest of the crew just before they reached Earth and handed them over to us as Insurrectionist spies!

"But as for you, there's a command waiting for you if you want it."

"I want it," I said. He clapped me on the shoulder and left. Then they brought me a man-sized dinner.

««« James H. Schmitz »»»

Here's another ominous region of space from which few ships have returned. The two undercover agents were aware of that (one of them painfully so), but their job at hand was getting the goods on a smuggling operation that was stealing valuable items from a scientific repository. Then a ship full of well-armed smugglers showed up. And so did a *thing* from that deadly region of lost starships, looking for something that had been stolen from its domain . . .

James H. Schmitz (1911-1981) was a master of action-adventure science fiction, notably his stories of the Hub, a loosely-bound confederation of star systems. His most popular characters were Telzey Amberdon, the spunky teenage telepath, and Trigger Argee, a crack shot with a gun and reflexes that made lighting look lethargic. His most popular novel, *The Witches of Karres*, though not part of the Hub universe, is a classic space opera. Many of his sf adventure tales have scary moments, and this one has them in spades.

((((THE SEARCHER))))

James H. Schmitz

It was night in that part of the world of Mezmiali—deep night, for much of the sky was obscured by the dense cosmic cloud called the Pit, little more than two light-years away. Overhead, only a scattering of nearby stars twinkled against the sullen gloom of the cloud. Far to the east, its curving edges were limned in brilliance, for beyond it, still just below the horizon, blazed the central sun clusters of the Hub.

The landscaped private spaceport was well lit but almost deserted. A number of small ships stood about in their individual stations, and two watchmen on a pair of float scooters were making a tour of the grounds, moving along unhurriedly twenty feet up in the air. They weren't too concerned about intruders—the ships were locked and there was little else of value around to steal. But their duties included inspecting the area every two hours, and they were doing it.

One of them checked his scooter suddenly, said through his mike, "Take a look at Twenty-two, will you!"

His companion turned his head in the indicated direction. The ship at Station Twenty-two was the largest one here at present, an interstellar yacht which had berthed late in the afternoon, following an extensive pleasure cruise. He stared in surprise, asked, "Nobody on board, is there?"

The first watchman was checking his list. "Not supposed to be until tomorrow. She's getting a standard overhaul then. What do you suppose that stuff is?"

The stuff he referred to looked like a stream of pale, purple fire welling silently out of the solid hull of the yacht, about halfway up its side. It flowed down along the side of the ship, vanishing as it touched the ground—appeared actually to be pouring on unchecked through the base of Station Twenty-two into the earth. Both men had glanced automatically at the radiation indicators on the scooters and found them reassuringly inactive. But it was a puzzling, eerie sight.

"It's new to me!" the other man said uneasily. "Better report it right away! There might be somebody on board, maybe messing around with the engines. Wait a moment. It's stopping!"

They looked on in silence as the last of the fiery flow slid down the yacht, disappeared soundlessly into the station's foundation.

The first watchman shook his head.

"I'll call the super," he said. "He'll—"

A sharp whistling rose simultaneously from the two radiation indicators. Pale fire surged out of the ground beneath the scooters, curved over them, enclosing the men and their vehicles. For a moment, the figures of the watchmen moved convulsively in a shifting purple glow; then they appeared to melt, and vanished. The fire sank back to the ground, flowed down into it. The piercing clamor of the radiation indicators faded quickly to a whisper and ended.

The scooters hung in the air, motionless, apparently undamaged. But the watchmen were gone.

Eighty yards underground, the goyal lay quiet while the section it had detached to assimilate the two humans who had observed it as it left the ship returned and again became a part of it. It was a composite of billions of units, an entity now energy, now matter, vastly extensible and mobile in space, comparatively limited in the heavy mediums of a planet. At the moment, it was close to its densest material form, a sheet of unseen luminescence in the ground, sensor groups probing the spaceport area to make sure there had been no other witnesses to its arrival on Mezmiali.

There appeared to have been none. The goyal began to drift

underground toward a point on the surface of the planet about a thousand miles away from the spaceport. . . .

And, about a thousand miles away, in the direction the goyal was heading, Danestar Gems raked dark-green fingernails through her matching dark-green hair, and swore nervously at the little spy-screen she'd been manipulating.

Danestar was alone at the moment, in a small room of the University League's Unclassified Specimens Depot on Mezmiali. The Depot was composed of a group of large, heavily structured, rather ugly buildings, covering about the area of an average village, which stood in the countryside far from any major residential sections. The buildings were over three centuries old and enclosed as a unit by a permanent energy barrier, presenting to the world outside the appearance of a somewhat flattened black dome which completely concealed the structures.

Originally, there had been a fortress on this site, constructed during a period when Mezmiali was subject to periodic attacks by space raiders, human and alien. The ponderous armament of the fortress, designed to deal with such enemies, had long since been dismantled; but the basic buildings remained, and the old energy barrier was the one still in use—a thing of monstrous power, retained only because it had been simpler and less expensive to leave it in place than to remove it.

Nowadays, the complex was essentially a warehouse area with automatic maintenance facilities, an untidy giant museum of current and extinct galactic life and its artifacts. It stored mineral, soil, and atmosphere samples, almost anything, in fact, that scientific expeditions, government exploration groups, prospectors, colonial workers, or adventuring private parties were likely to pick up in space or on strange worlds and hand over to the University League as being perhaps of sufficient interest to warrant detailed analysis of its nature and properties. For over a century, the League had struggled—and never quite managed—to keep up with the material provided it for study in this manner. Meanwhile, the specimens continued to come in and were routed into special depots for preliminary cataloging and storage. Most of them would turn out to be without interest, or of interest only to the followers of some esoteric branch of science. A relatively very small number of items, however, eventually might become very valuable, indeed, either because of the new scientific information they would provide or because they could be commercially exploited, or both. Such items had a correspondingly high immediate sales value as soon as their potential qualities were recognized.

Hence the Unclassified Specimens Depots were, in one way or another, well protected areas; none of them more impressively so than the Mezmiali Depot. The lowering black barrier enclosing it also served to reassure the citizenry of the planet when rumors arose, as they did periodically, that the Depot's Life Bank vaults contained dormant alien monstrosities such as human eyes rarely looked upon.

But mainly the barrier was there because the University League did not want some perhaps priceless specimens to be stolen.

That was also why Danestar Gems was there.

Danestar was a long-waisted, lithe, beautiful girl, dressed severely in a fitted black coverall suit and loose short white jacket, the latter containing numerous concealed pockets for the tools and snooping devices with which she worked. The wide ornamental belt enclosing the suit under the jacket similarly carried almost indetectable batteries of tiny control switches. Her apparently frivolous penchant for monocolor make-up—dark-green at the moment: green hair and lashes, green eyes, lips, nails, all precisely the same shade—was part of the same professional pattern. The hair was a wig, like a large flowing helmet, designed for Danestar personally, with exquisite artistry, by a stylist of interstellar fame; but beneath its waves was a mass of miniature gadgetry, installed with no less artistry by Danestar herself. On another day, or another job, depending on the purpose she was pursuing, the wig and other items might be sea-blue, scarlet, or a somewhat appalling pale-pink. Her own hair was dark brown, cut short. In most respects, Danestar actually was a rather conservative girl.

For the past ten minutes, she had been trying unsuccessfully to contact her colleague, Corvin Wergard. Wergard's last report, terminated abruptly, had reached her from another section of the Depot. He'd warned her that a number of armed men were trying to close in on him there and that it would be necessary for him to take prompt evasive action.

Danestar Gems and Corvin Wergard were employees of the Kyth Interstellar Detective Agency, working in the Depot on a secret assignment for University League authorities. Officially, they had been sent here two weeks before as communications technicians who were to modernize the Depot's antiquated systems. Danestar was, as a matter of fact, a communications expert, holding an advanced degree in the subject. Corvin Wergard had a fair working knowledge of communication systems; but they were not his specialty. He was a picklock in the widest sense. Keeping him out of a place he wanted to get into or look into was a remarkably difficult thing to do.

Their working methods differed considerably. Danestar was an instrument girl. The instruments she favored were cobwebby miniatures; disassembled, all fitted comfortably into a single flat valise which went wherever Danestar did. Most of them she had built herself, painstakingly and with loving care like a fly fisherman creating the gossamer tools of his hobby. Next to them, their finest commercial equivalents looked crude and heavy—not too surprisingly, since Danestar's instruments were designed to be handled only by her own slender, extremely deft fingers. On an operation, she went about, putting out ten, twenty, fifty or a hundred eyes and ears, along with such other sensors, telltales, and recorders of utterly inhuman type as were required by the circumstances, cutting in on established communication lines and setting up her own, masked by anti-antispying devices. In many cases, of course, her touch had to be imperceptible; and it almost always was. She was a confirmed snoop, liked her work, and was very good at it.

Wergard's use of tools, on the other hand, was restricted to half a dozen general-utility items, not particularly superior to what might be expected of the equipment of any enterprising and experienced burglar. He simply knew locks and the methods used to protect them against tampering or to turn them into deadly traps inside and out;

and, by what might have been in part an intuitive process of which he was unaware, he knew what to do about them, whether they were of a type with which he was familiar or not, almost in the instant he encountered them. To observers, he sometimes appeared to pass through the ordinary run of locked doors without pausing. Concealed alarms and the like might delay him a minute or two; but he rarely ran into any contrivance of the sort that could stop him completely.

The two had been on a number of previous assignments together and made a good team. Between them, the Unclassified Specimens Depot became equipped with a satisfactorily comprehensive network of Danestar's espionage devices within twenty-four hours after their arrival.

At that point, a number of complications made themselves evident.

Their principal target here was the director of the Depot, Dr. Hishkan. The University League had reason to believe—though it lacked proof—that several items which should have been in the Depot at present were no longer there. It was possible that the fault lay with the automatic storage, recording, and shipping equipment; in other words, that the apparently missing items were simply not in their proper place and would eventually be found. The probability, however, was that they had been clandestinely removed from the Depot and disposed of for profit.

In spite of the Depot's size, only twenty-eight permanent employees worked there, all of whom were housed in the Depot itself. If any stealing was going on, a number of these people must be involved in it. Among them, Dr. Hishkan alone appeared capable of selecting out of the vast hodgepodge of specimens those which would have a genuine value to interested persons outside the University League. The finger of suspicion was definitely pointed at him.

That made it a difficult and delicate situation. Dr. Hishkan had a considerable reputation as a man of science and friends in high positions within the League. Unquestionable proof of his guilt must be provided before accusations could be made. . . .

Danestar and Corvin Wergard went at the matter unhurriedly, feeling their way. They would have outside assistance available if needed but had limited means of getting information out of the Depot. Their private transmitter could not drive a message through the energy barrier, hence could be used at most for a short period several times a day when airtrucks or space shuttles passed through the entrance lock. The Depot's communicators were set up to work through the barrier, but they were in the main control station near the entrance lock and under observation around the clock.

Two things became clear almost immediately. The nature of their assignment here was suspected, if not definitely known; and every U-League employee in the Depot, from Dr. Hishkan on down, was involved in the thefts. It was not random pilfering but a well-organized operation with established outside contacts and with connections in the League to tip them off against investigators.

Except for Wergard's uncanny ability to move unnoticed about an area with which he had familiarized himself almost as he chose, and Danestar's detection-proof instrument system, their usefulness in the Depot would have been over before they got started. But within a few days, they were picking up significant scraps of information. Dr. Hishkan did not intend to let their presence interfere with his activities; he had something going on too big to postpone until the supposed communications technicians gave up here and left. In fact, the investigation was forcing him to rush his plans through, since he might now be relieved of his position as head of the Depot at any time, on general suspicions alone.

They continued with the modernization of the communications systems, and made respectable progress there. It was a three months' job, so there was no danger they would get done too quickly with it. During and between work periods, Danestar watched, listened, recorded; and Wergard prowled. The conspirators remained on guard. Dr. Hishkan left the Depot for several hours three times in two weeks. He was not trailed outside, to avoid the chance of a slip which might sharpen his suspicions. The plan was to let him make his arrangements, then catch him in the act of transferring University League property out of the Depot and into the hands of his contacts. In other respects, he was carrying out his duties as scientific director in an irreproachable manner.

They presently identified the specimen which Dr. Hishkan appeared to be intending to sell this time. It seemed an unpromising choice, by its looks a lump of asteroid material which might weigh around half a ton. But Dr. Hishkan evidently saw something in it, for it had been taken out of storage and was being kept in a special vault near his office in the main Depot building. The vault was left unguarded—presumably so as not to lead to speculations about its contents—but had an impressive series of locks, which Wergard studied reflectively one night for several minutes before opening them in turn in a little less than forty seconds. He planted a number of Danestar's observation devices in the vault, locked it up again and went away.

The devices, in their various ways, presently took note of the fact that Dr. Hishkan, following his third trip outside the Depot, came into the vault and remained occupied for over an hour with the specimen. His activities revealed that the thing was an artifact, that the thick shell of the apparent asteroid chunk could be opened in layers within which nestled a variety of instruments. Hishkan did something with the instruments which created a brief but monstrous blast of static in Danestar's listening recorders.

As the next supplies truck left the Depot, Danestar beamed a shortcode message through the open barrier locks to their confederates outside, alerting them for possibly impending action and describing the object which would be smuggled out. Next day, she received an acknowledgment by the same route, including a summary of two recent news reports. The static blast she had described apparently had been picked up at the same instant by widely scattered instruments as much as a third of the way through the nearest Hub cluster. There was some speculation about its source, particularly—this was the subject of the earlier report—because a similar disturbance had been noted approximately three weeks before, showing the same mysteriously widespread pattern of simultaneous occurrence.

Wergard, meanwhile, had dug out and copied the Depot record of the item's history. It had been picked up in the fringes of the cosmic dust cloud of the Pit several years earlier by the only surviving ship of a three-vessel U-League expedition, brought back because it was emitting a very faint, irregular trickle of radiation, and stored in the Unclassified Specimens Depot pending further investigation. The possibility that the radiation might be coming from instruments had not occurred to anybody until Dr. Hishkan took a closer look at the asteroid from the Pit.

"Floating in space," Danestar said thoughtfully. "So it's a signaling device. An alien signaling device. Probably belonging to whatever's been knocking off Hub ships in the Pit."

"Apparently," Wergard said. He added, "Our business here, of course, is to nail Hishkan and stop the thieving. . . . "

"Of course," Danestar said. "But we can't take a chance on this thing's getting lost. The Federation has to have it. It will tell them more about who built it, what they're like, than they've ever found out since they began to suspect there's something actively hostile in the Pit."

Wergard looked at her consideringly. Over two hundred ships, most of them Federation naval vessels, had disappeared during the past eighty years in attempts to explore the dense cosmic dust cloud near Mezmiali. Navigational conditions in the Pit were among the worst known. Its subspace was a seething turmoil of energies into which no ship could venture. Progress in normal space was a matter of creeping blindly through a murky medium stretching out for twelve light-years ahead where contact with other ships and with stations beyond the cloud was almost instantly lost. A number of expeditions had worked without mishap in the outer fringes of the Pit, but ships attempting penetration in depth simply did not return. A few fragmentary reports indicated the Pit concealed inimical intelligent forces along with natural hazards.

Wergard said, "I remember now . . . you had a brother on one of the last Navy ships lost there, didn't you?"

"I did," Danestar said. "Eight years ago. I was wild about him—I thought I'd never get over it. The ship sent out a report that its personnel was being wiped out by what might be a radiation weapon. That's the most definite word they've ever had about what happens there. And that's the last they heard of the ship."

"All right," Wergard said. "That makes it a personal matter.

I understand that. And it makes sense to have the thing wind up in the hands of the military scientists. But I don't want to louse up our operation."

"It needn't be loused up," Danestar said. "You've got to get me into the vault, Wergard. Tonight, if possible. I'll need around two hours to study the thing."

"Two hours?" Wergard looked doubtful.

"Yes. I want a look at what it's using for power to cut through standard static shielding, not to mention the Depot's force barrier. And I probably should make duplos of at least part of the system."

"The section patrol goes past there every hour," Wergard said. "You'll be running a chance of getting caught."

"Well, you see to it that I don't," Danestar told him.

Wergard grunted. "All right," he said. "Can do."

She spent her two hours in Dr. Hishkan's special vault that night, told Wergard afterwards, "It's a temporal distorter, of course. A long-range communicator in the most simple form—downright primitive. At a guess, a route marker for ships. A signaling device. . . . It picks up impulses, can respond with any one of fourteen signal patterns. Hishkan apparently tripped the lot of them in those blasts. I don't think he really knew what he was doing."

"That should be really big stuff commercially, then," Wergard remarked.

"Decidedly! On the power side, it's forty percent more efficient than the best transmitters I've heard about. Nothing primitive there! Whoever got his hands on the thing should be able to give the ComWeb system the first real competition it's had. . . . "

She added, "But this is the most interesting part. Wergard, that thing is *old!* It's an antique. At a guess, it hasn't been used or serviced within the past five centuries. Obviously, it's still operational—the central sections are so well shielded they haven't been affected much. Other parts have begun to fall apart or have vanished. That's a little bit sinister, wouldn't you say?"

Wergard looked startled. "Yes, I would. If they had stuff five hundred years ago better in some respects than the most sophisticated systems we have today . . . "

"In some rather important respects, too," Danestar said. "I didn't get any clues to it, but there's obviously a principle embodied designed to punch an impulse through all the disturbances of the Pit. If our ships had that . . . "

"All right," Wergard said. "I see it. But let's set it up to play Dr. Hishkan into our hands besides. How about this—you put out a shortcode description at the first opportunity of what you've found and what it seems to indicate. Tell the boys to get the information to Federation agents at once."

Danestar nodded. "Adding that we'll go ahead with our plans as they are, but they're to stand by outside to make sure the gadget doesn't get away if there's a slip-up?"

"That's what I had in mind," Wergard agreed. "The Feds should cooperate—we're handing them the thing on a platter."

He left, and Danestar settled down to prepare the message for transmission. It was fifteen minutes later, just before she'd finished with it, that Wergard's voice informed her over their private intercom that the entry lock in the energy barrier had been opened briefly to let in a space shuttle and closed again.

"I wouldn't bet," he said, "that this one's bringing in specimens or supplies. . . . " He paused, added suddenly, "Look out for yourself! There're boys with guns sneaking into this section from several sides. I'll have to move. Looks like the word's been given to pick us up!"

Danestar heard his instrument snap off. She swore softly, turned on a screen showing the area of the lock. The shuttle stood there, a sizable one. Men were coming out of it. It clearly hadn't been bringing in supplies or specimens.

Danestar stared at it, biting her lip. In another few hours, they would have been completely prepared for this! The airtruck which brought supplies from the city every two days would have come and left during that time; and as the lock opened for it, her signal to set up the trap for the specimen smugglers would have been received by the Kyth Agency men waiting within observation range of the Depot. Thirty minutes later, any vehicle leaving the Depot without being given a simultaneous shortcode clearance by her would be promptly intercepted and searched.

But now, suddenly, they had a problem. Not only were the smugglers here, they had come prepared to take care of the two supposed technicians the U-League had planted in the Depot to spy on Dr. Hishkan. She and Corvin Wergard could make themselves very difficult to find; but if they couldn't be located, the instrument from the Pit would be loaded on the shuttle and the thieves would be gone again with it, probably taking Dr. Hishkan and one or two of his principal U-League confederates along. Danestar's warning message would go out as they left, but that was cutting it much too fine! A space shuttle of that type was fast and maneuverable, and this one probably carried effective armament. There was a chance the Kyth operators outside would be able to capture it before it rejoined its mother ship and vanished from the Mezmiali System—but the chance was not at all a good one.

No, she decided, Dr. Hishkan's visitors had to be persuaded to stay around a while, or the entire operation would go down the drain. Switching on half a dozen other screens, she set recorders to cover them, went quickly about the room making various preparations to meet the emergency, came back to her worktable, completed the message to their confederates and fed it into a small shortcode transmitter. The transmitter vanished into a deep wall recess it shared with a few other essential devices. Danestar settled down to study the screens, in which various matters of interest could now be observed, while she waited with increasing impatience for Wergard to call in again.

More minutes passed before he did, and she'd started checking over areas in the Depot where he might have gone with the spy-screen. Then his face suddenly appeared in the instrument.

"Clear of them now," he said. "They got rather close for a while. Nobody's tried to bother you yet?"

"No," said Danestar. "But our Depot manager and three men from the shuttle came skulking along the hall a minute or two ago. They're waiting outside the *door.*"

"Waiting for what?"

"For you to show up."

"They know you're in the room?" Wergard asked.

"Yes. One of them has a life detector."

"The group that's looking around for me has another of the gadgets," Wergard said. "That's why it took so long to shake them. I'm in a sneaksuit now. You intend to let them take you?"

"That's the indicated move," Danestar said. "Everything's set up for it. Let me brief you. . . . "

The eight men who had come off the shuttle belonged to a smuggling ring which would act as middleman in the purchase of the signaling device from the Pit. They'd gone directly to Dr. Hishkan's office in the Depot's main building, and Danestar had a view of the office in one of her wall screens when they arrived. The specimen already had been brought out of the vault, and she'd been following their conversation about it.

Volcheme, the chief of the smugglers, and his assistant, Galester, who appeared to have had scientific training, showed the manner of crack professionals. They were efficient businessmen who operated outside the law as a calculated risk because it paid off. This made dealing with them a less uncertain matter than if they had been men of Dr. Hishkan's caliber—intelligent, amoral, but relatively inexperienced amateurs in crime. Amateurs with a big-money glint in their eyes and guns in their hands were unpredictable, took very careful handling. Volcheme and Galester, on the other hand, while not easy to bluff, could be counted on to think and act logically under pressure.

Danestar was planning to put on considerable pressure.

"They aren't sure about us," she said. "Hishkan thinks we're U-League spies but that we haven't found out anything. Volcheme wants to be certain. That's why he sent in word to have us picked up before he got here. Hishkan is nervous about getting involved in outright murder but will go along with it."

Wergard nodded. "He hasn't much choice at this stage. Well, play it straight then—or nearly straight. I'll listen but won't show unless there's a reason. While I'm at large, you have life insurance. I suppose you're quizproofed. . . . "

"Right." Danestar checked her watch. "Doped to the eyebrows. I took it twenty minutes ago, so the stuff should be in full effect now. I'll make the contact at once."

Wergard's face vanished from the spy-screen. Danestar turned the sound volume on the wall screen showing the group in Dr. Hishkan's office back up. Two sets of recorders were taking down what went on in there and already had stored away enough evidence to convict Dr. Hishkan on a number of counts. One of the sets was a decoy; it was concealed in the wall, cleverly enough but not so cleverly that the smugglers wouldn't find it when they searched the room. The duplicate set was extremely well concealed. Danestar had made similar arrangements concerning the handful of other instruments she couldn't allow them to discover. When they took stock of the vast array of miniature espionage devices they'd dig up here, it should seem inconceivable to them that anything else might still be hidden.

She sent a final glance around the room. Everything was as ready as she could make it. She licked her lips lightly, twisted a tiny knob on her control belt, shifted her fingers a quarter-inch, turned down a switch. Her eyes went back to the view in Dr. Hishkan's office.

Dr. Hishkan, Volcheme, and Galester were alone in it at the moment. Three of Volcheme's men waited with Tornull, the Depot manager, in the hall outside of Danestar's room; the remaining three had been sent to join the search for Wergard. The craggy lump of the asteroid which wasn't an asteroid stood in one corner. Several of its sections had been opened, and Galester was making a careful examination of a number of instruments he'd removed from them.

Dr. Hishkan, showing signs of nervousness, evidently had protested that this was an unnecessary delay because Galester was now saying to Volcheme, "Perhaps he doesn't understand that when our clients pay for this specimen, they're buying the exclusive privilege of studying it and making use of what they learn."

"Naturally I understand that!" Dr. Hishkan snapped.

"Then," Galester went on, "I think we should have an explanation for the fact that copies have been made of several of these subassemblies."

"Copies?" Dr. Hishkan's eyes went wide with amazed suspicion. "Ridiculous! I—"

"You're certain?" Volcheme interrupted.

"Absolutely," Galester told him. "There's measurable duplo

radiation coming from four of the devices I've checked so far. There's no point in denying that, Doctor. We simply want to know why you made the duplicates and what you've done with them."

"Excuse me!" Danestar said crisply as Dr. Hishkan began to splutter an indignant denial. "I can explain the matter. The duplos are here."

In the office, a brief silence followed her announcement. Eyes switched right and left, then, as if obeying a common impulse, swung suddenly around to the wall screen in which Danestar's image had appeared.

Dr. Hishkan gasped, "Why—why that's—"

"Miss Gems, the communications technician, no doubt," Volcheme said dryly.

"Of course, it is," Danestar said. "Volcheme, I've listened to this discussion. You put yourself in a jam by coming here. But, under the circumstances, we can make a deal."

The smuggler studied her. He was a lean, blond man, no longer young, with a hard, wise face. He smiled briefly, said, "A deal I'll like?"

"If you like an out. That's what you're being offered."

Dr. Hishkan's eyes had swiveled with growing incredulity between the screen and Volcheme's face. He said angrily, "What nonsense is this? Have her picked up and brought here at once! We must find out what—"

"I suggest," Volcheme interrupted gently, "you let me handle the matter. Miss Gems, I assume your primary purpose here is to obtain evidence against Dr. Hishkan?"

"Yes," said Danestar.

"You and your associate—Mr. Wergard—are U-League detectives?"

She shook her head.

"No such luck, Volcheme! We're private agency, full-privilege, Federation charter."

"I suspected it." Volcheme's lips pulled back from his teeth in a grimace of hostility. "You show the attributes of the breed. Do I know the agency?"

"Kyth Interstellar."

He was silent a moment, said, "I see. . . . Is Mr. Wergard available for negotiations?"

"No. You'll talk to me."

"That will be satisfactory. You realize, of course, that I don't propose to buy your deal blind. . . . "

"You aren't expected to," Danestar said.

"Then let's get the preliminaries out of the way." The smuggler's face was bleak and watchful. "I have men guarding your room. Unlock the door for them."

"Of course." Danestar turned toward the door's lock control in the wall on her left. Volcheme pulled a speaker from his pocket.

They understood each other perfectly. One of the last things a man of Volcheme's sort cared to do was get a major private detective agency on his neck. It was a mistake, frequently a fatal one. As a matter of principle and good business, the agencies didn't get off again.

But if he saw a chance to go free with the loot, leaving no witnesses to point a finger at him, he'd take it. Danestar would remain personally safe so long as Volcheme's men didn't catch up with Wergard. After that, she'd be safe only if she kept the smuggler convinced he was in a trap from which there was no escape. Within a few hours he would be in such a trap, but he wasn't in it at present. Her arrangements were designed to keep him from discovering that.

The door clicked open and four men came quickly and cautiously into the room. Three of them were smugglers; the fourth was Tornull, the U-League depot manager. The one who'd entered first stayed at the door, pointing a gun at Danestar. Volcheme's other two men separated, moved toward her watchfully from right and left. They were competent professionals who had just heard that Danestar was also one. The gun aimed at her from the door wasn't there for display.

"As a start, Decrain," Volcheme's voice said from the screen, "have Miss Gems give you the control belt she's wearing."

Danestar unsnapped the belt, making no unnecessary motions, and handed it to the big man named Decrain. They were pulling her teeth, or thought they were, which was sensible from their point of view and made no immediate difference from hers; the belt could be of no use at present. Decrain drew out a chair, told her to sit down and keep her hands in sight. She complied, and the man with the gun came up and stood eight feet to her left. Decrain and his companion began a quick, expert search of her living quarters with detectors. Tornull, Dr. Hishkan's accomplice in amateur crime, watched them, now and then giving Danestar and her guard a puzzled look which indicated the girl didn't appear very dangerous to him and that he couldn't understand why they were taking such elaborate precautions with her.

Within six minutes, Decrain discovered as much as Danestar had wanted them to find of her equipment and records. Whenever the detector beams approached the rest of it, other beams reached out gently and blended with them until they'd slid without a quiver past the shielded areas. The collection of gadgetry Decrain laid out on Danestar's worktable was impressive and exotic enough to still suspicions, as she had expected. When he announced yet another discovery, Galester observed thoughtfully from the screen, "That's a dangerously powerful anti-interrogation drug you use, Miss Gems!"

"It is," Danestar acknowledged. "But it's dependable. I'm conditioned to it."

"How much have you taken?"

"My limit. A ten-hour dose . . . sixty-five units."

She was telling the truth—her developed ability to absorb massive dosages of quizproof without permanent ill effects had pulled her out of more than one difficult situation. But a third of the amount she'd mentioned was considered potentially lethal. Decrain studied her dubiously a moment as if pondering the degree of her humanity. Decrain appeared to be a stolid type, but the uncovering of successive batteries of spidery instruments unlike anything he had encountered in his professional career had caused him mental discomfort; and when he brought Danestar's set of gimmicked wigs—to which the green one she'd been wearing was now added—out of a shrinkcase and watched them unfold on the table, he'd seemed shaken.

"You'll be brought over here now, Miss Gems," Volcheme said, his face sour. "We want a relaxed atmosphere for our discussion, so

Decrain will search you thoroughly first. As far as possible, he'll be a gentleman about it, of course,"

"I'm sure he will be," Danestar said agreeably. "Because if he isn't, his hide becomes part of the deal."

The muscles along Decrain's jaw tightened, but he continued packaging the sections of Danestar's instruments Galester wanted to examine without comment. Tornull began to laugh, caught sight of the big man's expression, and sobered abruptly, looking startled.

The semi-material composite body of the goyal flowed below the solid surface of the world of Mezmiali toward the Unclassified Specimens Depot, swerving from its course occasionally to avoid the confusing turbulences of radiation about the larger cities. Its myriad units hummed with coordinating communal impulses of direction and purpose.

Before this, in all its thousand years of existence, the goyal had known only the planets of the Pit, murkily lit by stars which swam like patches of glowing fog in the dark. Once those worlds had supported the civilization of an inventive race which called itself the Builders.

The Builders developed spaceships capable of sliding unharmed through the cosmic dust at a speed above that of light, and a location system to guide them infallibly through the formless gloom where ordinary communication methods were useless. Eventually they reached the edges of the Pit . . . and shrank back. They had assumed the dust cloud stretched on to the end of the universe, were appalled when they realized it was limited, seemed suspended in some awesome, gleaming, impossibly *open* void.

To venture into that terrible alien emptiness themselves was unthinkable. But the urge to explore it by other means grew strong. The means they presently selected was a lowly form of energy life, at home both in the space and on the planets of the Pit. The ingenuity of the Builders produced in it the impulse to combine with its kind into increasingly large, more coherent and more purposeful groups; and the final result of their manipulations was the goyal, a superbeing which thought and acted as an individual, while its essential structure was still that of a gigantic swarm of the minor uncomplicated prototypes of energy life with which the Builders had begun. The goyal was intended to be their galactic explorer, an intelligent, superbly adaptable servant, capable of existing and sustaining itself as readily in space as on the worlds it encountered.

In its way, the goyal was an ultimate achievement of the Builders' skills. But it was to become also the monument to an irredeemable act of stupidity. They had endowed it with great and varied powers and with keen, specialized intelligence, but not with gratitude. When it discovered it was stronger than its creators and swifter than their ships, it turned on the Builders and made war on them, exterminating them on planet after planet until, within not much more than a century, it became sole master of the Pit.

For a long time, it remained unchallenged there. It shifted about the great dust cloud at will, guided by the Builders' locator system, feeding on the life of the dim worlds. During that period, it had no concept of intelligence other than its own and that of the Builders. Then a signal which had not come into use since the last of the Builders vanished alerted the locator system. A ship again had appeared within its range.

The goyal flashed through the cloud on the locator impulses like a great spider darting along the strands of its web. At the point of disturbance, it found an alien ship groping slowly and blindly through the gloom. Without hesitation, it flowed aboard and swept through the ship, destroying all life inside.

It had been given an understanding of instruments, and it studied the ship in detail, then studied the dead beings. They were not Builders though they showed some resemblance to them. Their ship was not designed to respond to the locator system; it had come probing into the Pit from the surrounding void.

Other ships presently followed it, singly and in groups. They came cautiously, scanning the smothering haze for peril, minds and instruments alert behind a variety of protective devices which seemed adequate until the moment the goyal struck. The enveloping protective screens simply were too light to hamper it seriously; and once it was through the screens, the alien crew was at its mercy. But the persistence these beings showed in intruding on its domain was disturbing to it. It let some of them live for a time on the ships it captured while it watched and studied them, manipulated them, experimented with them. Gradually, it formed a picture of an enemy race in the void which must be destroyed as it had destroyed the Builders if its supremacy was to be maintained.

It did not intend to venture into the void alone. It had planted sections of its body on a number of the worlds of the Pit. The sections were as yet immature. They could not move about in space as the parent body did, possessed barely enough communal mind to know how to nourish themselves from the planetary life about them. But they were growing and developing. In time the goyal would have others of its kind to support it. Until then, it planned to hold the Pit against the blind intruders from the void without letting the enemy race become aware of its existence.

Then the unforeseeable happened. An entire section of the locator system suddenly went dead, leaving the remainder functioning erratically. For the first time in its long existence, the goyal was made aware of the extent of its dependence on the work of the Builders. After a long difficult search, it discovered the source of the trouble. A key locator near the edge of the dust cloud had disappeared. Its loss threatened to make the entire system unusable.

There was no way of replacing it. The goyal's mind was not that of a Builder. It had learned readily to use instruments, but it could not construct them. Now it realized its mistake in exterminating the only civilized race in the Pit. It should have kept the Builders in subservience to itself so that their skills would always be at its disposal. It could no longer be certain even of detecting the intruding aliens when they came again and preventing them from discovering the secrets of the cloud. Suddenly, the end of its reign seemed near.

Unable to develop a solution to the problem, the goyal settled into a kind of apathy, drifted with dimming energies aimlessly about the Pit . . . until, unmistakably, the lost locator called it! Alert at once, the goyal sped to other units of the system, found they had recorded and pinpointed the distant blast. It had come from beyond the cloud, out of the void! Raging, the goyal set off in the indicated direction. It had no doubt of what had happened—one of the alien ships had discovered the locator and carried it away. But now it could be and would be recovered.

Extended into a needle of attenuated energy over a million miles in length, the goyal flashed out into the starlit void, its sensor units straining. There was a sun dead ahead; the stolen instrument must be within that system. The goyal discovered a spaceship of the aliens moving in the same direction, closed with it and drew itself on board. For a time, its presence unsuspected, it remained there, forming its plans. It could use the ship's energies to build up its reserves, but while the ship continued toward Mezmiali, it made no move.

Presently it noted a course shift which would take the ship past the Mezmiali system but close enough to it to make the transfer to any of the sun's four planets an almost effortless step. The goyal remained quiet. Not long afterwards, its sensors recorded a second blast from the lost locator. Now it knew not only to which planet it should go but, within a few hundred miles, at what point of that planet the instrument was to be found.

Purple fire lashed out from the ship's bulkheads to engulf every human being on board simultaneously. Within moments, the crew was absorbed. The goyal drank energy from the drive generators to the point of surfeit, left the ship and vanished in the direction of Mezmiali. Within the system, it again closed in on a ship and rode down with it to the planet.

It had reached its destination undetected and at the peak of power, its reserves intact. But this was unknown enemy territory, and it remained cautious. For hours, its sensors had known precisely where the locator was to be found. The goyal waited until the humans had disembarked from the ship, until the engines were quiet and it could detect no significant activity in the area immediately about it. Then it flowed out of the ship and into the ground. The two humans who saw it emerge were absorbed before they could make a report.

There was no reason to hesitate longer. Moving through the dense solid matter of the planet was a tedious process by the goyal's standards; but, in fact, only a short time passed before it reached the University League's isolated Depot.

There it was brought to a very abrupt stop.

It had flowed up to the energy barrier surrounding the old fortress site and partly into it. Hostile forces crashed through it instantly with hideous, destructive power. A quarter of its units died in that moment. The remaining units whipped back out of the boiling fury of the field, reassembled painfully underground near the Depot. The body was reduced and its energy depleted, but it had suffered no lasting damage.

The communal mind remained badly shocked for minutes; then it, too, began to function again. There was not the slightest possibility of breaking through that terrible barrier! In all its experience, the goyal had never encountered anything similar to it. The defensive ship screens it had driven through in its secretive murders in the Pit had been fragile webs by comparison, and the Builders' stoutest planetary energy shields had been hardly more effective. It began searching cautiously along the perimeter of the barrier. Presently it discovered the entrance lock.

It was closed, but the goyal knew about locks and their uses. The missing locator was so close that the sensors' reports on it were blurred, but it was somewhere within this monstrously guarded structure. The goyal decided it needed only to wait. In time, the lock would open and it would enter. It would destroy the humans inside, and be back on its way to the Pit with the locator before the alien world realized that anything was amiss. . . .

Approximately an hour later, a slow bulky vehicle came gliding down from the sky toward the Depot. Messages were exchanged between it and a small building on the outside of the barrier in the language employed on the ships which had come into the Pit. A section of the communal mind interpreted the exchange without difficulty, reported:

The vehicle was bringing supplies, was expected, and would be passed through the barrier lock.

At the lock, just below the surface of the ground, the goyal waited, its form compressed to near-solidity, to accompany the vehicle inside.

In Dr. Hishkan's office in the central building of the Depot, the arrival of the supplies truck was being awaited with a similar degree of interest by the group assembled there. Their feelings about it varied. Danestar's feeling—in part—was vast relief. Volcheme was a very tough character, and there was a streak of gambler's recklessness in him which might have ruined her plan.

"Any time anything big enough to have that apparatus on board leaves the Depot now, we clear it by shortcode before the lock closes," she'd said. "You don't know what message to send. You can't get it from me, and you can't get it from Wergard. The next truck or shuttle that leaves won't get cleared. And it will get stopped almost as soon as it's outside."

That was it—the basic lie! If they'd been willing to take the chance, they could have established in five minutes that it was a lie.

"You're bluffing," Volcheme had said, icily hating her. "The bluff won't stop us from leaving when we're ready to go. We won't have to run any risks. We'll simply go out with the shuttle to check your story before we load the thing on."

"Then why don't you do it? Why wait?" She'd laughed, a little high, a little feverish, with the drugs cooking in her—her own and the stuff Galester had given her in an attempt to counteract the quizproof effect. She'd told them it wasn't going to work; and now, almost two hours later, they knew it wasn't going to work.

They couldn't make her feel physical pain, they couldn't intimidate her, they couldn't touch her mind. They'd tried all that in the first fifteen minutes when she came into the office, escorted by Decrain and Tornull, and told Volcheme bluntly what the situation was, what he had to do. They could, of course, as they suggested, kill her, maim her, disfigure her. Danestar shrugged it off. They could, but she didn't have to mention the price tag it would saddle them with. Volcheme was all too aware of it.

The threats soon stopped. Volcheme either was in a trap, or he wasn't. If the Kyth Agency had him boxed in here, he would have to accept Danestar's offer, leave with his group and without the specimen. He could see her point—they had an airtight case against Dr. Hishkan and his accomplices now. The specimen, whatever its nature, was a very valuable one; if it had to be recaptured in a running fight with the shuttle, it might be damaged or destroyed. That was the extent of the agency's responsibility to the U-League. They had no interest in Volcheme.

The smuggler was being given an out, as Danestar had indicated. But he'd had the biggest, most profitable transaction of his career set up, and he was being told he couldn't go through with it. He didn't know whether Danestar was lying or not, and he was savage with indecision. If the Depot was being watched—Volcheme didn't much doubt that part of the story—sending the shuttle out to check around and come back could arouse the suspicions of the observers enough to make them halt it when it emerged the second time. That, in fact, might be precisely what Danestar wanted him to do.

He was forced to conclude he couldn't take the chance. To wait for the scheduled arrival of the supplies truck was the smaller risk. Volcheme didn't like waiting, either. Wergard hadn't been found; and he didn't know what other tricks the Kyth agents could have prepared. But, at any rate, the truck was the answer to part of his problem. It would be let in, unloaded routinely, allowed to depart, its men unaware that anything out of the ordinary was going on in the Depot. They would watch then to see if the truck was stopped outside and searched. If that happened, Volcheme would be obliged to agree to Danestar's proposal.

If it didn't happen, he would know she'd been lying on one point; but that would not be the end of his difficulties. Until Wergard was captured or killed, he still couldn't leave with the specimen. The Kyth agents knew enough about him to make the success of the enterprise depend on whether he could silence both of them permanently. If it was possible, he would do it. With stakes as high as they were, Volcheme was not inclined to be squeamish. But that would put an interstellar organization of experienced man-hunters on an unrelenting search for the murderers of two of its members. . . .

Whatever the outcome, Volcheme wasn't going to be happy. What had looked like the haul of a lifetime, sweetly clean and simple, would wind up either in failure or as a dangerously messy partial success. Galester and Decrain, seeing the same prospects, shared their chief's feelings. And while nobody mentioned that the situation looked even less promising for Dr. Hishkan and Tornull, those two had at least begun to suspect that if the smugglers succeeded in escaping with the specimen, they would not want to leave informed witnesses behind.

When the voice of an attendant in the control building near the lock entry finally announced from the wall screen communicator that the supplies truck had arrived and was about to be let into the Depot, Danestar therefore was the most composed of the group. Even Decrain, who had been detailed to keep his attention on her at all times, stood staring with the others at the screen where Dr. Hishkan was switching on a view of the interior lock area.

Danestar made a mental note of Decrain's momentary lapse of alertness, though it could make no difference to her at present. The only thing she needed to do, or could do, now was wait. Her gaze shifted to the table where assorted instruments Galester had taken out of the alien signaling device still stood. At the other side of the table was the gadgetry Decrain had brought here from her room, a toy-sized shortcode transmitter among it. Volcheme had wanted to be sure nobody would send out messages while the lock was open.

And neither she nor Wergard would be sending any messages. But automatically, as the lock switches were thrown, the duplicate transmitter concealed in the wall of her room would start flicking its coded alert out of the Depot, repeating it over and over until the lock closed.

And twenty or thirty minutes later, when the supplies truck slid back out through the lock and lifted into the air, it would be challenged and stopped.

Then Volcheme would give up, buy his pass to liberty on her terms. There was nothing else he could do.

It wasn't the kind of stunt she'd care to repeat too often—her nerves were still quivering with unresolved tensions. But she'd carried it off without letting matters get to a point where Wergard might have had to help her out with some of his fast-action gunplay. Danestar told herself to relax, that nothing at all was likely to go wrong now.

Her gaze slipped over to Volcheme and the others, silently

watching the wall screen, which was filled with the dead, light-drinking black of the energy barrier, except at the far left where the edge of the control building blocked the barrier from view. A great glowing circle, marking the opened lock in the barrier, was centered on the screen. As Danestar looked at it, it was turning a brilliant white.

Some seconds passed. Then a big airtruck glided out of the whiteness and settled to the ground. The lock faded behind it, became reabsorbed by the dull black of the barrier. Several men climbed unhurriedly out of the truck, began walking over to the control building.

Danestar started upright in her chair, went rigid.

A wave of ghostly purple fire had lifted suddenly out of the ground about the truck, about the walking men, enclosing them.

There was a general gasp from the watching group in Hishkan's office. Then, before anyone moved or spoke, a voice roared from the communicator:

"Control office, attention! Radiation attack! Close internal barrier fields at once! *Close all internal Depot barrier fields at once!*"

Volcheme, whatever else might be said of him, was a man of action. Perhaps, after two hours of growing frustration, he was ready to welcome action. Apparently, a radiation weapon of unidentified type had been used inside the Depot. Why it had been turned on the men who had got off the supplies truck was unexplained. But it had consumed them completely in an instant, though the truck itself appeared undamaged.

Coming on top of the tensions already seething in the office, the shock of such an attack might have brought on complete confusion. But Volcheme immediately was snapping out very practical orders. The four smugglers detailed to help find Corvin Wergard were working through the Depot's underground passage system within a few hundred yards of the main building. They joined the group in the office minutes later. The last of Volcheme's men was stationed in the control section. He confirmed that the defensive force fields enclosing the individual sections of the Depot inside the main barrier had been activated. Something occurred to Volcheme then. "Who gave that order?"

"Wergard did," said Danestar.

They stared at her. "That *was* Wergard," Tornull agreed. "I didn't realize it, but that was his voice."

Volcheme asked Danestar. "Do you know where he is?"

She shook her head. She didn't know, as a matter of fact. Wergard might have been watching the lock from any one of half a hundred screens in the Depot. He could have been in one of the structures adjacent to the control building . . . too close to that weird fiery phenomenon for comfort. Radiation attack? What had he really made of it? Probably, Danestar thought, the same fantastic thing she'd made of it. His reaction, the general warning shouted into the communications system, implied that; very likely had been intended to imply it to her. She was badly frightened, very much aware of it, trying to decide how to handle the incredibly bad turn the situation might have taken.

Volcheme, having hurried Tornull off to make sure the space shuttle, which had been left beside the building's landing dock, was within the section's barrier field, was asking Galester and Dr. Hishkan, "Have you decided what happened out there?"

Galester shrugged. "It appears to be a selective antipersonnel weapon. The truck presumably was enclosed by the charge because there was somebody still on it. But it shows no sign of damage, while the clothing the men outside were wearing disappeared with them. It's possible the weapon is stationed outside the Depot and fired the charge through the open lock. But my opinion is that it's being operated from some concealed point within the Depot."

Volcheme looked at Hishkan. "Well? Could it have been something that was among your specimens here? Something Miss Gems and Wergard discovered and that Wergard put to use just now?"

The scientist gave Danestar a startled glance.

Danestar said evenly, "Forget that notion, Volcheme. It doesn't make sense."

"Doesn't it? What else makes sense?" the smuggler demanded. "You've been here two weeks. You're clever people, as you've demonstrated. Clever enough to recognize a really big deal when Hishkan shoved it under your noses. Clever enough to try to frighten competitors away. You know what I think, Miss Gems? I think that when I showed up here today, it loused up the private plans you and Wergard had for Hishkan's specimen."

"We do have plans for it," said Danestar. "It goes to the Federation. And now you'd better help us see it gets there."

Volcheme almost laughed. "I should?"

Danestar said, "You asked what else makes sense. There's one thing that does. You might have thought of it. That U-League specimen didn't just happen to be drifting around in the Pit where it was found. *Somebody made it and put it there!*"

She had the full attention of everyone in the office now, went on quickly. It was a space-signaling device which could tell human scientists a nearly complete story of how its unknown designers were able to move about freely in the dust cloud and how they communicated within it. And recently Dr. Hishkan had twice broadcast the information that human beings had the space instrument. The static bursts he'd produced had been recorded a great deal farther away from Mezmiali than the Pit.

Volcheme interrupted with angry incredulity. "So you're suggesting aliens from the Pit have come here for it!"

"I'm suggesting just that," Danestar said. "And Dr. Hishkan, at least, must be aware that a ship which vanished in the Pit a few years ago reported it was being attacked with what appeared to be radiation weapons."

"That's true! That's true!" Dr. Hishkan's face was white.

"I think," Danestar told them, "that when that airtruck came into the Depot, something came in with it the truckers didn't know was there. Something that had a radiation weapon of a kind we don't know about. Volcheme, if you people have a single functioning brain cell left between you, you'll tell the control building right now to put out a call for help! We're going to need it. We want the heaviest Navy ships near Mezmiali to get down here to handle this, and—"

"Volcheme!" a voice cut in urgently from the screen communicator.

The smuggler's head turned. "Go ahead, Yee!" His voice was harsh with impatience.

"The U-League group that's been hunting for this Wergard fellow doesn't answer!" Yee announced. He was the man Volcheme had stationed in the control building. "Seven men—two wearing communicators. We've been trying to contact them for eight minutes. Looks like they might have got wiped out somewhere in the Depot the same way as the truck crew!"

There was an uneasy stir among the men in the office. Volcheme said sharply, "Don't jump to conclusions! Have the operators keep calling them. They may have some reason for staying quiet at the moment. The others have checked in?"

"Yes," said Yee. "Everyone else who isn't in the control building is sitting tight behind defense screens somewhere."

"They've been told to stay where they are and report anything they observe?"

"Yes. But nobody's reported anything yet."

"Let me know as soon as someone does. And, Yee, make very sure everyone in the control building is aware that until this matter is settled, the control building takes orders only from me."

"They're *real* aware of that, Volcheme," said Yee.

The smuggler turned back to the group in the office. "Of course, we're not going to be stupid enough to take Miss Gems's advice!" he said. If he felt any uncertainty, it didn't show in his voice or face. "Somebody has pulled a surprise trick with some radiation device and killed a number of people. But we're on guard now, and we're very far from helpless! Decrain will stay here to make sure Miss Gems does not attempt to interfere in any way. The rest of us will act as a group."

He indicated the men who had been searching for Wergard. "There are four high-powered energy rifles on the shuttle. You four will handle them. Galester, Dr. Hishkan, Tornull, and I will have handguns. Dr. Hishkan tells me that the radiation suits used for dangerous inspection work in the Depot are stored on the ground level of this building.

"Remember, this device is an antipersonnel weapon. We'll be in the suits, which will block its effect on us at least temporarily; we'll be armed, and we'll be in the shuttle. There's a barrier exit at the building loading dock, through which we can get the shuttle out into the Depot. Scanscreens are being used in the control building to locate the device or its operator. When they're found—"

The communicator clicked. Wergard's voice said, "Volcheme, this is Wergard. Better listen!"

Volcheme's head swung around. "What do you want?" It was almost a snarl.

"If you'd like a look at that antipersonnel weapon," Wergard's voice told him drily, "switch your screen to Section Thirty-six. You may change your mind about chasing it around in the shuttle."

A few seconds later, the wall screen flickered and cleared. For an instant, they all stared in silence.

Like a sheet of living purple fire, the thing flowed with eerie swiftness along the surface of one of the Depot's side streets toward a looming warehouse. Its size, Danestar thought, was the immediately startling factor—it spread across the full width of the street and was a hundred and fifty, perhaps two hundred, yards long. As it reached the warehouse, the big building's defense field flared into activity. Instantly, the fiery apparition veered sideways, whipped around the corner of the street and was gone from sight.

Shifting views of the Depot flicked through the screen as Dr. Hishkan hurriedly manipulated the controls. He glanced around, eyes wide and excited. "I've lost it! It appears to be nowhere in the area."

"I wouldn't worry," Volcheme said grimly. "It will show up again." He asked Galester, "What did you make of that? What *is* it?"

Galester said, "It's identical, of course, with what we saw engulfing the truck and the men at the lock. We saw only one section of it there. It emerged partly above the surface of the Depot and withdrew into it again. As to what it is . . . " He shrugged. "I know of nothing to compare it to precisely!" He hesitated again, went on. "My impression was that it was moving purposefully—directing itself. Conceivably an energy weapon could control a mobile charge in such a manner that it would present that appearance."

Dr. Hishkan added, "Whatever this is, Volcheme, I believe it would be very unwise to attempt to oppose it with standard weapons!"

The smuggler gave him a tight grin. "Since there's no immediate need to make the attempt, we'll postpone it, at any rate, Doctor. To me, the significant part of what we just saw was that the thing avoided contact with the defense field of that building . . . or was turned away from it, if it's the mobile guided charge Galester was talking about. In either case, our enemy can't reach us until we decide what we're dealing with and how we should deal with it."

Danestar said sharply, "Volcheme, don't be a fool—don't count on that! The ships that disappeared in the Pit carried defense fields, too."

Volcheme gave her a venomous glance but didn't answer. Dr. Hishkan said thoughtfully, "What Miss Gems says is technically true. But even if we are being subjected to a similar attack, this is a very different situation! This complex was once a fort designed to defend a quarter of the continent against the heaviest of spaceborne weapons. And while the interior fields do not compare with the external barrier in strength, they are still far denser than anything that would or could be carried by even the largest exploration ships. I believe we can depend on the field about this building to protect us while we consider means to extricate ourselves from the situation." He added, "I feel far more optimistic now! When we have determined the nature of the attacking entity, we should find a method of combating it available to us in the Depot. There is no need to appeal to the authorities for help, as Miss Gems suggested, and thereby have our personal plans exposed to them—which was, of course, what she intended!"

Wergard's voice said from the communicator, "If you want to continue your studies, Dr. Hishkan, you'll get the chance immediately! The thing is now approaching the main building from the north, and it's coming fast."

Dr. Hishkan turned quickly back to the screen controls.

There was a wide square enclosed by large buildings directly north of the main one. The current of fire was half across the square as it came to view in the screen. As Wergard had said, it was approaching very swiftly and there was a suggestion of purposeful malevolence in that rushing motion which sent a chill down Danestar's spine. In an instant, it seemed, it reached the main building and the energy field shielding it; and now, instead of veering off to the side as it had done before, the tip of the fiery body curved upwards. It flowed vertically up along the wall of the building, inches away from the flickering defense field. For seconds, the wall screen showed nothing but pale purple flame streaming across it. Then the flame was gone; and the empty square again filled the screen.

From the communicator, Wergard's voice said quickly, "It crossed the top of the building, went down the other side and disappeared below the ground level surface—"

The voice broke off. Almost immediately, it resumed. "I've had more luck keeping it in view than you. It's been half around the Depot by now, and my impression is it's been looking things over before it makes its next move—whatever that's going to be.

"But one thing I've noticed makes me feel much less secure behind a section energy field than some of you people think you are. The thing has kept carefully away from the outer Depot barrier—a hundred yards or so at all times—and it cuts its speed down sharply when it gets anywhere near that limit. On the other hand, as you saw just now, it shows very little respect for the sectional building fields. I haven't seen it attempt to penetrate one of them, but it's actually contacted them a number of times without apparent harm to itself, as it did again in passing over the main building a moment ago."

Volcheme snapped, "What's that supposed to tell us?"

"I think," Wergard said, "that, among other things, our visitor has been testing the strength of those barriers. I wouldn't care to bet my life on what it's concluded, as you seem willing to do. Another point—it may be developing a particular interest in the building you're in. I suggest you take a close look at the square on the north again."

At first glance, the square still seemed empty. Then one noticed that its flat surface was alive with tiny sparks, with flickers and ripplings of pale light. The thing was there, almost completely submerged beneath the Depot's ground level, apparently unmoving.

Tornull said, staring fascinatedly, "Perhaps it knows we have that specimen in here!"

Nobody answered. But in the square, as if aware its presence had been discovered, the fire shape rose slowly to the surface of the ground until it lay in full view, flat and monstrous, sideways to the main building. The silence in the office was broken suddenly by a chattering sound. It had not been a loud noise, but everyone started nervously and looked over at the table where the pile of instruments had been assembled.

"What was that?" Volcheme demanded.

"My shortcode transmitter," Danestar told him.

"It's recorded a message?"

"Obviously."

"From whom?"

"I'm not sure," said Danestar evenly. "But let's guess. It's not from outside the Depot because shortcode won't go through the barrier. It's not from Wergard, and it's not from one of your people. What's left?"

The smuggler stared at her. "That's an insane suggestion!"

"Perhaps," Danestar said. "Why don't we listen to the translation?"

"We will!" Volcheme jerked his head at Decrain. "Go over to the table with her. She isn't to touch anything but the transmitter!"

He watched, mouth twisted unpleasantly, as Decrain followed Danestar to the table. She picked up the miniature transmitter, slid a fingernail quickly along a groove to the phonetic translator switch. As she set the instrument back on the table, the words began.

"Who . . . has . . . it . . . where . . . is . . . it . . . I . . . want . . . it . . . who . . . has . . . it . . . where . . . "

It went on for perhaps a minute and a half, three sentences repeated monotonously over and over, then stopped with a click. Danestar wasn't immediately aware of the effect on the others. She'd listened in a mixture of fear, grief, hatred, and sick revulsion. Shortcode was speech, transmitted in an economical flash, restored to phonetic speech in the translator at the reception point. Each of the words which made up the three sentences had been pronounced at one time by a human being, were so faithfully reproduced one could tell the sentences had, in fact, been patched together with words taken individually from the speech of three or four different human beings. Human beings captured by the enemy in the Pit, Danestar thought, long dead now, but allowed to live while the enemy learned human speech from them, recorded their voices for future use. . . .

She looked around. The others seemed as shaken as she was. Volcheme's face showed he no longer doubted that the owner of the alien instrument had come to claim it.

Dr. Hishkan remarked carefully, "If it should turn out that we are unable to destroy or control this creature, it is possible we can get rid of it simply by reassembling the device it's looking for and placing it outside the defense screen. If it picks it up, we can open the barrier lock as an indication of our willingness to let it depart in peace with its property."

Volcheme looked at him. "Doctor," he said, "don't panic just because you've heard the thing talk to you! What this does seem to prove is that the specimen you're selling through us is at least as valuable as it appeared to be—and I for one don't intend to be cheated out of my profit."

"Nor I," Dr. Hishkan said hastily. "But the creature's ability to utilize shortcode to address us indicates a dangerous level of intelligence. Do you have any thoughts on how it might be handled now?"

Galester interrupted, indicating the screen. "I believe it's beginning to move. . . . "

There was silence again as they watched the fire body in the square. Its purple luminescence deepened and paled in slowly pulsing waves; then the tip swung about, swift as a flicking tongue, first toward the building, then away from it; and the thing flowed in a darting curve across the square and into a side street.

"Going to nose around for its treasure somewhere else!" Volcheme said after it had vanished. "So, while it may suspect it's here, it isn't sure. I'm less impressed by its apparent intelligence than you are, Doctor. A stupid man can learn to use a complicated instrument, if somebody shows him how to do it. This may be a stupid alien . . . a soldier type sent here from the Pit to carry out a specific, limited mission."

Galester nodded. "Possibly a robot."

"Possibly a robot," Volcheme agreed. "And, to answer your question of a moment ago, Doctor—yes, I have thought of a way to get it off our necks."

"What's that?" Dr. Hishkan inquired eagerly.

"No need to discuss it here!" Volcheme gave Danestar a glance of mingled malevolence and triumph. She understood its meaning well enough. If Wergard could be located, Volcheme could now rid himself of the Kyth operators with impunity. There were plenty of witnesses to testify that the monstrous creature which had invaded the Depot had destroyed over a dozen men. She and Wergard would be put down as two more of its victims.

"We won't use the shuttle at present," Volcheme went on. "But we want the portable guns, and we'll get ourselves into antiradiation suits immediately. Decrain, watch the lady until we get back—use any methods necessary to make sure she stays where she is and behaves herself. We'll bring a suit back up for you. The rest of you come along. Hurry!"

Decrain started to say something, then stood silent and scowling as the others filed quickly out of the office and started down the hall to the right. The big man looked uneasy. With a gigantic fiery alien around, he might not appreciate being left alone to guard the prisoner while his companions climbed into the security of antiradiation suits. As the last of the group disappeared, he sighed heavily, shifted his attention back to Danestar.

His eyes went huge with shocked surprise. The chair in which she had been sitting was empty. Decrain's hand flashed to his gun holster, stopped as it touched it. He stood perfectly still.

Something hard was pushing against the center of his back below his shoulder blades.

"Yes, I've got it," Danestar whispered behind him. "Not a sound, Decrain! If you even breathe louder than I like, I'll split your spine!"

They waited in silence. Decrain breathed cautiously while the voices and footsteps in the hall grew fainter, became inaudible. Then the gun muzzle stopped pressing against his back.

"All right," Danestar said softly—she'd moved off but was still close behind him—"just stand there now!"

Decrain moistened his lips.

"Miss Gems," he said, speaking with some difficulty, "I was, you remember, a gentleman!"

"So you were, buster," her voice agreed. "And a very fortunate thing that is for you at the moment. But—"

Decrain dropped forward, turning in the air, lashing out savagely with both feet in the direction of the voice. It was a trick that worked about half the time. A blurred glimpse of Danestar flashing a white smile above him and of her arm swinging down told him it hadn't worked here. The butt of the gun caught the side of his head a solid wallop, and Decrain closed his eyes and drifted far, far away.

She bent over him an instant, half-minded to give him a second rap for insurance, decided it wasn't necessary, shoved the gun into a pocket of her coveralls and went quickly to the big table in the center of the office. Her control belt was there among the jumble of things they'd brought over from her room. Danestar fastened it about her waist, slipped on the white jacket lying beside it, rummaged hurriedly among the rest, storing the shortcode transmitter and half a dozen other items into various pockets before she picked up her emptied instrument valise and moved to the opposite end of the table where Galester had arranged the mechanisms he'd removed for examination from the false asteroid.

She'd had her eye on one of those devices since she'd been brought to the office. It was enclosed in some brassy pseudometal, about the size of a goose egg and shaped like one. Galester hadn't known what to make of it in his brief investigation, and Dr. Hishkan had offered only vague conjectures; but she had studied it and its relationship to a number of other instruments very carefully on the night she'd been in Dr. Hishkan's vault, and knew exactly what to make of it. She placed it inside her valise, went back to the collection of her own instruments, turned on the spy-screen and fingered a switch on the control belt. The spy-screen made a staccato chirping noise.

"I'm alone here," she told it quickly. "Decrain's out cold. Now, how do I get out of this building and to some rendezvous point—fastest? Volcheme's gone berserk, as you heard. I don't want to be anywhere near them when they start playing games with that animated slice of sheet lightning!"

"Turn left when you leave the office," Wergard's voice said from the blank screen. "Take the first elevator two levels down and get out."

"And then?"

"I'll be waiting for you there."

"How long have you been in the building?" she asked, startled.

"About five minutes. Came over to pick up a couple of those antiradiation suits for us, which I have. The way things were going then, I thought I'd better hang around and wait for a chance to get you away from our friends."

"I was about to start upstairs when Volcheme and the others left. Then I heard a little commotion in the office and decided you were doing something about Decrain. So I waited."

"Bless you, boy!" Danestar said gratefully. "Be with you in a minute!"

She switched off the spy-screen, went out of the office, skirting Decrain's harshly snoring form on the carpet, and turned left down the quiet hall.

The hideaway from which Corvin Wergard had been keeping an observer's eye on events in the Depot was one of a number he'd set up for emergency use shortly after their arrival. He'd selected it for operations today because it was only a few steps from an exit door in the building, and less than a hundred and twenty yards from both the control section and the outer barrier lock—potential critical points in whatever action would develop. Guiding Danestar back to it took minutes longer than either of them liked, but the route Wergard had worked out led almost entirely through structures shielded from the alien visitor by section defense screens.

She sat across the tiny room from him, enclosed in one of the bulky antiradiation suits, the shortcode transmitter on a wall shelf before her, fingers delicately, minutely, adjusting another of the instruments she had brought back from Hishkan's office. Her eyes were fixed on the projection field above the instrument. Occasional squigglings and ripples of light flashed through it—meaningless static. But she'd had glimpses of light patterns which seemed far from meaningless here, was tracking them now through the commband detector to establish the settings which would fix them in the visual projection field for study. That was a nearly automatic process—her hands knew what to do and were doing it. Her thoughts kept turning in nightmare fascination about other aspects of the gigantic raider.

What did they know about it? And what did it know about them?

That living, deadly energy body, or its kind, had not built the signaling device. If it was not acting for itself, if it had hidden masters in the Pit, the masters had not built the device, either. Regardless of its origin, the instrument, though centuries old, still had been in use; and in the dust cloud its value in establishing location, in permitting free purposeful action, must be immense. But whoever was using it evidently had lacked even the ability to keep it in repair. Much less would they have been able to replace it after it disappeared—and they must be in mortal fear that mankind would discover the secrets of the instrument and return to meet them on even terms in the cloud. . . .

So this creature had traversed deep space to reach Mezmiali and recover it.

Volcheme, conditioned to success in dealing with human opponents, still believed his resourcefulness was sufficient to permit him to handle the emissary from the Pit. To Danestar it seemed approximately like attempting to handle an animated warship. The thing was complex, not simply an elemental force directed by a limited robotic mind. It had demonstrated it could use its energies to duplicate the human shortcode system, and the glimpse she'd had in the detector's field of one of its patterns implied it was capable of much more than had been shown so far. And it might not have come here alone. There could be others of its kind undetected beyond the Depot's barrier with whom it was in communication.

In the face of such possibilities, Volcheme's determination

amounted to lunacy. They might have convinced the others of the need to call for outside help; but the intercom system had been shut off, evidently on the smuggler's orders, when Danestar's escape was discovered. Through various spy devices they knew he was coordinating the activities of his men with personal communicators, and that a sectional force barrier was being set up across the center of the main building, connected to the external ones. Completed, the barrier system would transform half the building into a box trap, open at the end. The men and the specimen from the Pit would be in the other half. When the monster flowed into the trap to get at them, observers in the control building would snap a barrier shut across the open end. The thing would be safely inside . . . assuming that barriers of sectional strength were impassable to it.

Volcheme's calculations were based entirely on that assumption. So far, nothing had happened to prove him wrong. The alien creature was still moving about the Depot. Wergard, before the multiple-view screen through which he had followed the earlier events of the day, reported glimpses of it every minute or two. And there were increasing indications of purpose in its motions. It had passed along this building once, paused briefly. But it had shown itself three times about the control section, three times at the main building. Its interest appeared to be centering on those points.

Until it ended its swift and unpredictable prowling, they could only wait here. Wergard was ready to slip over to a personnel lock in the barrier about the control building when an opportunity came. A gas charge would knock out the men inside, and the main barrier would open long enough then to let out their prepared shortcode warning. Their main concern after that would be to stay alive until help arrived.

Their heads turned sharply as the shortcode transmitter on the shelf before Danestar gave its chattering pickup signal. She stood up, snapped the headpiece of her radiation suit into position, collapsed the other instruments on the shelf, slid them into the suit's pockets, and picked up the valise she'd brought back from Dr. Hishkan's office.

". . . where . . . is . . . it . . . I . . . want . . . it . . ." whispered the transmitter.

"Pickup range still set at thirty yards?" Wergard asked.

"Yes," she said.

"There's nothing in sight around here."

Danestar glanced over at him. He'd encased himself in the other radiation suit. A small high-power energy carbine lay across a chair beside him. His eyes were on the viewscreen which now showed only the area immediately around the building. She didn't answer. The transmitter continued to whisper.

It wasn't in sight, but it was nearby. Very near. Within thirty yards of the transmitter, of their hideout, of them. And pausing now much longer than it had the first time it passed the building.

". . . who . . . has . . . it . . . where . . . is . . . it . . ."

Her skin crawled, icy and uncontrollable. If it had any way of sensing what she held concealed inside the valise, it would want it. She didn't think it could. No spying device she knew of could pierce the covering of the valise. But the egg-shaped alien instrument within—no bigger than her two fists placed together—was the heart and core of the specimen from the Pit, its black box, the part which must hold all significant clues to the range and penetrating power of its signals. Without it, the rest of the contents of that great boulder-shaped thing would be of no use now—to Volcheme or to the alien.

They waited, eyes on the viewscreen, ready to move. If the building was attacked and the creature showed it could force its way through the enclosing energy barrier, there was an unlocked door behind them. An elevator lay seconds beyond the door; and two levels down, they would be in the underground tunnel system where a transport shell waited. If they were followed, they could continue along the escape route Wergard had marked out, moving from barrier to barrier to slow the pursuer. Unless it overtook them, they would eventually reach the eastern section of the Depot, known as the Keep, where ancient defense screens formed so dense a honeycomb that they should be safe for hours from even the most persistent attacks.

But retreat would cost them their chance to make use of the control section. . . .

The transmitter's whisper faded suddenly. For some seconds, neither stirred. Then Wergard said, relief sharp in his voice: "It may have moved off!"

He shifted the screen mechanisms. A pattern of half a dozen simultaneous views appeared. "There it is!"

On the far side of the control building, flowing purple fire lifted into view along fifty yards of one of the Depot's streets like the back of a great surfacing sea beast, sank from sight again. Danestar hesitated, took the commband detector quickly out of her suit pocket, placed it on the wall shelf. She pressed a button on the little instrument and the projection field sprang into semi-visibility above it.

Wergard, eyes shifting about the viewscreen, said, "It's still only seconds away from us. Don't get too absorbed in whatever you're trying to do."

"I won't."

Danestar released the bulky radiation headpiece, turned it back out of her way. Her fingertips slipped along the side of the detector, touched a tiny adjustment knob, began a fractional turn, froze.

The visual projection she'd been hunting had appeared in the field before her.

A flickering, shifting, glowing galaxy of tiny momentary sparks and lines of light . . . the combined communication systems of a megacity might have presented approximately such a picture if the projector had presented them simultaneously. She licked her lips, breath still, as her fingers shifted cautiously, locking the settings into place.

When she drew her hand away, Wergard's voice asked quietly, "What's that?"

"The thing's intercom system. It's . . . let me think—Wergard! What's it doing now?"

"It's beside the control building." Wergard paused. He hadn't asked what her manipulations with the detector were about; she seemed to be on the trail of something, and he hadn't wanted to distract her.

But now he added, "Its behavior indicates . . . yes! Apparently it is going to try to pass through the section barrier there!"

The viewscreen showed the ghostly, reddish glittering of an activated defense barrier along most of the solid front wall of the control building. Two deep-rose glowing patches, perhaps a yard across, marked points where the alien had come into direct contact with the barrier's energies.

It hadn't, Danestar thought, liked the experience, though in each case it had maintained the contact for seconds, evidently in a deliberate test of the barrier's strength. Her eyes shifted in a brief glance to the viewscreen, returned to the patterns of swarming lights in the projector field.

The reaction of the creature could be observed better there. As it touched the barrier, dark stains had appeared in the patterns, spread, then faded quickly after it withdrew. There was a shock effect of sorts. But not a lasting one. Danestar's breathing seemed constricted. She was badly frightened now. The section barriers did hurt this thing, but they wouldn't stop it if it was determined to force its way through their energies. Perhaps the men in the control building weren't yet aware of the fact. She didn't want to think of that—

She heard a brief exclamation from Wergard, glanced over again at the screen.

And here it comes, she thought.

The thing was rising unhurriedly out of the street surface before the control building, yards from the wall. When it tested the barrier, it had extruded a fiery pointed tentacle and touched it to the building. Now it surged into view as a rounded luminous column twenty feet across, widening as it lifted higher. The top of the column began to lean slowly forward like a ponderous cresting wave, reached the wall, passed shuddering into it. The force field blazed in red brilliance about it and its own purple radiance flared, but the great mass continued to flow steadily through the barrier.

And throughout the galaxy of dancing, scintillating, tiny lights in the projector field, Danestar watched long shock shadows sweep, darken, and spread . . . then gradually lighten and commence to fade.

When she looked again at the viewscreen, the defense barrier still blazed wildly. But the street was empty. The alien had vanished into the control building.

"It isn't one being," Danestar said. "It's probably several billion. Like a city at work, an army on the march. An organization. A system. The force field did hurt it—but at most it lost one half of one percent of the entities that make it up in going through the barrier."

Wergard glanced at the projection field, then at her.

"Nobody in the control building had access to a radiation suit," he said. "So they must have been dead in an instant when the thing reached them. If it can move through a section barrier with no more damage than you feel it took, why hasn't it come out again? It's been in there for over five minutes now."

Danestar, eyes on the pattern in the projection field, said, "It may have been damaged in another way. I don't know. . . . "

"What do you mean?"

She nodded at the pattern. "It's difficult to describe. But there's a change there! And it's becoming more distinct. I'm not sure what it means."

Wergard looked at the field a moment, shrugged. "I'll take your word for it. It's a jumble to me. I don't see any changes in it."

Danestar hesitated. She had almost intuitive sensitivity for the significance of her instruments' indications; and that something was being altered now, moment by moment, in the millionfold interplay of signals in the pattern seemed certain.

She said suddenly, "There's a directing center to the thing, of course, or it couldn't function as it does. Before it went through the force field, every part of it was oriented to that center. There was a kind of rhythm to the whole which showed that. Now, there's a section that's going out of phase with the general rhythm."

"What does that add up to?"

Danestar shook her head. "I can't tell that yet. But if the shock it got from the barrier disrupted part of its internal communication system, it might be, in our terms, at least partly paralyzed now. A percentage of the individual entities—say about one-tenth—are no longer coordinating with the whole, are disconnected from it. . . . Of course, we can't count on it, but it would explain why it hasn't reappeared."

Both were silent a moment. Then Wergard said, "If it is immobilized, it killed everyone in the control building before the shock got through to it. Otherwise we would have had indications of action by Volcheme by now."

She nodded. The intercom switch on the viewscreen was open, but the system remained dead. And whatever the smuggler and the group in the main building were engaged in, they were not at present in an area covered by her spy devices. But the space shuttle had not left the building, so they were still there. If the creature from the Pit was no longer a menace and Volcheme knew it, every survivor of the gang would be combing the Depot for traces of Wergard and herself. Since they weren't, Volcheme had received no such report from the control building. Whatever else had happened, the men stationed there had died as the alien poured in through the barrier.

Her breath caught suddenly. She said, "Wergard, I think . . . it's trying to come out again!"

"The barrier's flickering," he acknowledged from the viewscreen. An instant later: "Full on now! Afraid you're right! Watch for signs of damage. If it isn't crippled, and if it suspects someone is here, it may hit this building next, immediately! It isn't in sight . . . must be moving out below ground level."

Danestar snapped the radiation headpiece back in position without taking her eyes from the projection field. Shock darkness crisscrossed the pattern of massed twinkling pinpoints of brightness again, deepened. She could judge the thing's rate of progress through the barrier by that now. There were no indications of paralysis; if anything, its passage seemed swifter. Within seconds, the darkness stopped spreading, began to fade. "It's outside," she said. "It doesn't seem seriously injured."

"And it's still not in sight," said Wergard. "Stay ready to move!"

They were both on their feet. The shortcode transmitter on the shelf was silent, but this time the creature might not be announcing its approach. Danestar's eyes kept returning to the projection field. Again the barrier had achieved minor destruction, but she could make out no further significant changes. The cold probability was now that there was no practical limit to the number of such passages the creature could risk if it chose. But something about the pattern kept nagging at her mind. What was it?

A minute passed in a humming silence that stretched her nerves, another . . . and now, Danestar told herself, it was no longer likely that the monster's attention would turn next to this building, to them. The barrier had remained quiet, and there had been no other sign of it. Perhaps it wasn't certain humans were hiding here; at any rate, it must have shifted by now to some other section of the Depot.

Almost with the thought, she saw Wergard's hand move on the viewscreen controls, and in the screen the area about them was replaced by a multiple-view pattern.

Nothing stirred in the various panels; no defense field was ablaze about any of the buildings shown. The entire great Depot seemed empty and quiet.

"At a guess," Wergard remarked thoughtfully, "it's hanging around the main building again now." He moved back a step from the screen, still watching it, began to unfasten his antiradiation suit.

"What are you doing?" she asked.

He glanced over at her. "Getting out of it. One thing these suits weren't made for is fast running. I expect to be doing some of the fastest running in my career in perhaps another minute or two."

"Running? You're not—"

"Our alien," Wergard said, "should take action concerning Volcheme's boys next. But whatever it does, the instant we see it involved somewhere else, I'll sprint for the control building. It may be the last chance we get to yell for help from outside. And I don't want to be slowed down by twenty pounds of suit while I'm about it."

Danestar swallowed hard. He was right. But there was something, a feeling. . . .

"No! Don't go there!" she said sharply, surprising herself.

He looked around in bewilderment. "Don't go there? What are you—watch that!"

His eyes had shifted back to the screen. For an instant, she couldn't tell what he had seen. Then, just as the view began to blur into another, she found it.

Volcheme's space shuttle had darted out of the cover of the main building, swung right, was flashing up a wide street toward the eastern section of the Depot.

"Making a run for the Keep!" Wergard said harshly. He fingered the controls, following the shuttle from view section to view section. "They might just—no, there it is!"

The great fire body—flattened, elongated—whipped past between two warehouse complexes, a rushing brightness fifty feet above the ground, vanished beyond the buildings.

"Too fast for them!" Wergard shook his head. "It knows what they're doing and is cutting them off. Perhaps their guns can check it! You watch what happens—I'm going now."

"No! I . . ."

Then at last the realization surged up. Danestar stared at him, completely dismayed.

"It's a trap," she said evenly. "Of course!"

"What is? What are you talking about?"

"The control building! Don't you see?" She jerked her head at the projection field. "I *said* a section of the thing was splitting off from the main body! When it came out through the barrier again, *that* section wasn't showing any shock effects. I saw it but didn't understand what it meant. Of course! It didn't come through the barrier at all. It's still *in there*, Wergard! In the control building. Waiting for any of us to show up. There're two of them now. . . ."

She watched stunned comprehension grow in his face as she spoke.

The smugglers' shuttle was caught not much more than a minute later. It had discovered the enemy between it and the Keep section, turned back. When the space thing followed, tiny bursts of dazzling white light showed the shuttle's energy guns were in action. The fire body jerked aside and paused . . . and now the shuttle turned again, flashed straight at its pursuer, guns blazing full out.

For a moment, it seemed a successful maneuver. The great creature swept up out of the path of the machine, slipped over the top of a building, disappeared. The shuttle rushed on toward the Keep—and at the next corner a loop of purple radiance snared it, drove it smashing into a building front. The fire giant flowed down, sent the shuttle hurtling against the building again, closed over it. For seconds, the radiance pulsed about the engulfed vehicle, then lifted into the air, moved off. There was no sign of the shuttle until, some hundreds of yards away, the fire body opened to let the shattered machine slide out, drop to the surface of the Depot. Its lock door was half-twisted away; and Volcheme and his companions clearly were no longer within it.

To Danestar, watching in sick fascination, it had seemed as if a great beast of prey had picked up some shelled, stinging creature, disarmed it, cracked it to draw out the living contents, and flung aside the empty shell.

The alien swung west, toward the central section of the Depot, seemed to be returning to the main building complex, but then flowed down to the surface, sank into it and vanished.

Minutes passed and it did not reappear. Again the Depot's sections stood quiet and lifeless in the viewscreen.

"It may be waiting for somebody else to break from cover," Wergard said suddenly. "But you'd think the first thing it would do now is push into the main building and get its gadget! Volcheme must have left it there—the thing wouldn't have slammed the shuttle around like that if it hadn't been sure the contraption wasn't inside."

Danestar didn't reply. Their nerves were on edge, and Wergard was simply thinking aloud. They had no immediate explanation for the thing's behavior. But it had been acting purposefully throughout, and there must be purpose in its disappearance.

All they could do at present was wait, alert for signs of an approach on any level. She had discarded her antiradiation suit, as Wergard had done previously. The men in the shuttle might have gained a second or two of life because of the protection the suits gave them; but against so overwhelmingly powerful a creature they obviously had made no real difference. And they were cumbersome enough to be a serious disadvantage in other respects. If there were indications that the second energy body, the smaller one in the control building, had left it, Wergard would still attempt a dash over there.

There were no such indications. There were, in fact, no indications of any kind of activity whatever until, approximately ten minutes after it vanished, the big space creature showed itself again.

It was rising slowly from the ground into the square before the deserted main building when Wergard detected it in the screen. Then, while they watched, it flowed deliberately up to the building and into it.

And no defending force fields flared into action.

As it disappeared, they exchanged startled looks. Wergard said quickly, "Volcheme must have had the barriers shut off just before they left by the lock—so the thing could pick up its device. . . . "

"And let them get away?" Danestar hesitated. There'd been talk of that before she escaped from Volcheme's group. But she was not at all certain that the smuggler, even under such intense immediate pressures, would abandon his prize completely. The flight might even have been designed in part to draw the raider away from it.

"Otherwise—" Wergard scowled, chewed his lip. "Has there been anything in the projection pattern to show it's split again?"

She shook her head. "No. But if you're thinking it could detach a section small enough to get in through a personnel lock and turn off the building's barrier—"

"That's what I'm thinking."

Danestar shrugged, said, "I wouldn't be able to tell that, Wergard. I've been watching the projection. But it would be too minor a difference to be noticeable. It may have done it."

He was silent a moment. "Well," he said then, "it has the gadget it came for now. We'll see what it does next." He added, without change of tone, "Incidentally, it doesn't have all of it, does it?"

Danestar gave him a startled glance.

"How did you guess?" she asked.

A half-grin flicked over Wergard's tense face. "It's the sort of thing you'd do. You've been hanging on to that valise as if there were something very precious inside."

"There is," Danestar agreed. "It's not very big, but the specimen won't work without it. And when those things in the Pit realize it's gone, they won't be able to replace it."

"Very dirty trick!" Wergard said approvingly. He glanced at the valise. "Supposing we manage to get out of this alive—how useful could the item become?"

"Extremely useful, if it gets to really capable people. As far as I could make out, it must embody all the essentials of that system."

Wergard nodded. "We'll hang on to it, then. As long as we can, anyway. We may have to destroy it, of course. Think the thing could spot there's a part missing?"

"It could if it has a way of testing it," said Danestar. "But if the specimen's been reassembled and resealed, nothing will show. . . . There the creature comes now!"

They watched its emergence from the main building. It poured out of the landing lock area, swung west across the central square, moving swiftly. It might be carrying the specimen with it, as it had carried the shuttle.

"Coming back here!" Wergard remarked some seconds later. "And if it can open sectional barriers, it can open the main Depot lock in the control building. . . . "

Danestar knew what he meant. The Pit creature might believe it had achieved its objective in regaining the lost signaling instrument and simply leave now. She began to feel almost feverish with hope, warned herself it was much more probable it did not intend to let any human being in the Depot remain alive to tell about it.

Her gaze shifted again to the patterns in the projection field. No further changes had been apparent, but a sense of dissatisfaction, of missing some hidden significance, still stirred in her each time she studied them. I'm not seeing everything they should tell me, she thought. She shook her head tiredly. Too much had happened these hours! Now her thinking seemed dulled.

She heard Wergard say, "It's stopped for something!"

It had come to an intersection, paused. Then suddenly it veered to the right, moved swiftly past three buildings, checked again before a fourth. A probing fire tentacle reached toward the building, and defense barriers promptly blazed into activity.

The creature withdrew the tentacle, remained where it was, half-submerged in the street. Activated by its proximity, the defense field continued to flare while one or two minutes passed. Then the field subsided, vanished. The creature moved forward until some two-thirds of it appeared to be within the building. Barely seconds later, it drew back again, swung away. . . .

"It caught somebody inside there!" Wergard said. "It couldn't have been looking for anything else. How did it know some poor devils had holed up in that particular section?"

The intercom signal on the viewscreen burred sharply with his last words, then stopped. They stared at it, glanced at each other. Neither attempted to move toward the switch.

The intercom began ringing again. It rang, insistently, jarringly, with brief pauses, for a full minute now before it went silent.

"So that's how!" Wergard said heavily. He shrugged. "Well, if it—or a section of it—can manipulate a barrier lock and reproduce shortcode impulses, it can grasp and manipulate an intercom system. Not a bad way to locate survivors. If we don't answer—"

"We can't stay here, anyway," Danestar told him, frowning at the projection field. She had spoken in an oddly flat, detached manner.

"No. It's mopping up before it heads home—and now it can apparently cut off every sectional barrier that isn't locally maintained directly from the control building. It won't be long before it discovers that—if it hasn't already done it." Wergard picked up the energy gun. "Grab what you need and let's move! I've thought of something better than trying to make it to the Keep and playing hide-and-seek with it there. With the tricks it's developed, we wouldn't last—" He looked over, said quickly, sharply, "Danestar!"

Danestar glanced around at him, bemused, lips parted. "Yes? I . . ."

"Wake up!" Wergard's voice was edged with nervous impatience. "I think I can work us over to the section the thing just cleared out. If we leave the barrier off, there's a good chance it won't check that building again. Let's not hang around here!"

"No." She shook her head, turned to the instruments on the shelf. "You've got to get me to our quarters, Wergard—immediately!"

"From here? Impossible! There're several stretches—over three hundred yards in all—where we'd be in the open without the slightest cover. It's suicide! We—" Wergard checked himself, staring at her. "You've thought up something? Is it going to work?"

"It might, if we can get there."

He swore, blinked in scowling reflection.

"All right!" he said suddenly. "Can do—I hope! Tell me on the way or when we're there what you're after. We'll make a short detour. There's something I could do to keep our friend occupied for a while. It may buy us an additional twenty, thirty minutes. . . . "

Hurrying up a narrow dim passage behind Wergard, Danestar felt clusters of eerie fears hurry along with her. Wergard swung on at a fast walking pace. Now and then she broke into a run to keep up with him; and when she did, he slowed instantly to let her walk again. It was sensible—they might have running enough to do shortly. But staying sensible wasn't easy. Her legs *wanted* to run.

They were blind here, she thought. Her awareness of it was what had built up the feeling of frightened helplessness during the past minutes to the point where it seemed hardly bearable. She couldn't use her instruments, and the sectional barriers in this area were turned off; they were also deprived of that partial protection. As Wergard had suspected, the alien had discovered the force fields could be operated from the central control office. The Depot was open to it now except in sections where human beings had taken refuge and cut in defense barriers under local control. Such points, of course, were the ones it would investigate.

And they might encounter it at any moment, with no warning at all. Whether they got through to their quarters had become a matter of luck—good luck or bad—and Danestar, who always prepared, always planned, found herself unable to accept that condition.

Wergard halted ahead of her; and she stopped, watched him cautiously edge a door open, glance out. He looked back, slid the energy carbine from his shoulder, held it in one hand, made a beckoning motion with the other. Danestar followed him through the door and he eased it back into its lock. They had come out into one of the Depot's side streets. It stretched away on either side between unbroken building fronts, a strip of the dull black dome of the main barrier arching high above.

They darted across the street, ran fifty feet along the building on the far side before Wergard stopped at another door. This one opened on a pitch-dark passage; and, a moment later, the darkness closed in about them.

Wergard produced a light, said quietly, "Watch your step here! The section was sealed off officially fifty years ago and apparently hasn't been inspected since."

He moved ahead, rapidly but carefully, holding the light down for her. They were some five minutes from their starting point. Beyond that, Danestar did not know what part of the Depot they'd come to, but Wergard had told her about this building. It had been part of the old fortress system, cheaper to seal off than remove, an emergency unit station which operated the barrier defenses of the complexes surrounding it. If the equipment was still in working order, Wergard would turn on those barriers. Approximately a tenth of Depot would again be shielded then, beyond manipulation by the control office. That should draw the creature's attention to the area, while they moved on. Their living quarters were in a building a considerable distance away.

Eyes shifting about, Danestar followed the pool of light dancing ahead of her feet. The flooring was decayed here and there; little piles of undefinable litter lay about, and the air was stale and musty. Wergard, in his prowling, might in fact have been the first to enter the building in fifty years. They turned a corner of the passage, came to a dark doorspace. There he stopped.

"You'd better wait here," he told her. "There's a mess of machinery inside, and some of it's broken. I'll have to climb around and over it. If the barrier system is operating, I'll have it going within three or four minutes."

He vanished through the door. Danestar watched the receding light as it moved jerkily deeper into a forest of ancient machines, lost it when it went suddenly around a corner. There was complete darkness about her then. She fingered a lighter in her pocket but left it there. No need to nourish the swirling tide of apprehensions within her by peering about at shadows. Darkness wasn't the enemy. After a minute or two, she heard a succession of metallic sounds in the distance. Presently they ended, and a little later Wergard returned. He was breathing hard and his face was covered with dirt-streaked sweat.

"As far as I can make out, the barriers are on," he said briefly. "Now we'd better get out of the neighborhood fast!"

But they made slower overall progress than before, because now they had to use the personnel locks in the force fields as they moved from one complex section to the next. In between, they ran where they could. They crossed two more side streets. After the second one, Wergard said, "At the end of this building we'll be out of the screened area."

"How far beyond that?" Danestar asked.

"Three blocks. Two big sprints in the open!" He grimaced. "We *could* use the underground systems along part of the stretch. But they won't get us across the main streets unless we follow them all the way to the Keep and back down."

She shook her head. "Let's stick to your route." A transport shell of the underground system could have taken them to the Keep and into the far side of the Depot in minutes. But its use would register on betraying instruments in the control building, and might too easily draw the alien to the moving shell.

The personnel lock at the other end of the building let them into a narrow alley. Across it was the flank of one of the Depot's giant warehouses. As they started along the alley, there was a crackling, spitting, explosive sound—the snarl of a defense field flashing into action.

Wergard reached out, snatched the valise from Danestar's hand. "*Run!*"

They raced up the alley. The furious crackle of the force field came from behind them, from some other building. It was not far away, and it was continuing. A hundred yards on, Wergard halted abruptly, caught Danestar as she plowed into him, thrust the valise at her.

"Here—!" he gasped. She saw they'd reached a door to the warehouse; now Wergard was turning to open it. Clutching the valise, thoughts a roiling confusion of terror, she looked back, half-expecting to see a wave of purple fire sweeping up the alley toward them.

But the alley was empty, though the building front along which the barrier blazed was only a few hundred yards away. Then, as Wergard caught her arm, hauled her in through the door, a closer section—the building from which they had emerged a moment before—erupted in glittering fury. The door slammed in back of her, and they were running again, through a great hall, along aisles between high-stacked rows of packing cases. And—*where was the valise?* Then she realized Wergard had taken it.

She followed him into a cross-aisle. Another turn to the right, and the end of the hall was ahead, a wide passage leading off it. She had a glimpse of Wergard's strained face looking back for her; then, suddenly, he swerved aside against the line of cases, crouched, his free arm making a violent gesture, motioning her to the floor.

Danestar dropped instantly. A moment later, he was next to her.

"Keep . . . down!" he warned. "*Way* . . . down!"

Sobbing for breath, flattened against the cases, she twisted her head around, saw what he was staring at over the stacked rows behind them. A pale purple reflection went gliding silently along the ceiling at the far end of the hall, seemed to strengthen for an instant, abruptly faded out.

They scrambled to their feet, ran on into the passage.

Even after they'd slowed to a walk again, had reached a structure beyond the warehouse, they didn't talk about it much. Both were badly winded and shaken. It had been difficult to believe that the thing could have failed to detect them. Its attention must have been wholly on the force fields it was skirting, even as a section of it flowed through the warehouse within a few hundred feet of them.

If they'd been a few seconds later reaching the alley. . . .

Danestar reached into her white jacket, turning up its cooling unit. Wergard glanced at her. His face was dripping sweat. He wiped at it with his sleeve.

She asked, "You're still wearing the sneaksuit?"

Wergard lifted a strand of transparent webbing from under his collar, let it snap back. "Think it might have helped?"

"I don't know." But the creature might have the equivalent of a life detector unit as part of its sensory equipment, and a sneaksuit, distorting and blurring the energy patterns of a living body, would perhaps afford some protection. She said, "I'll get into one as soon as we reach our quarters. It may have known somebody was around but didn't want to waste time picking up another human until it found out why the defense barriers were turned on again in that area."

Wergard remarked dubiously, "It seems to me it's got picking up humans at the top of its priority list!" After a moment, he added, "The long sprint comes next. Feel up to it?"

Danestar looked at him. "I'd better feel up to it! If we see that thing again—I'm one inch this side of pure panic right now!"

He grunted. "Quit bragging!" He slid the carbine from his shoulder. "It's that door ahead. Let me have a look out first."

As he began to unlock the door, Danestar found herself glancing back automatically once more at the long, lit, empty corridor through which they had come, their hurried steps echoing in the silence of the building. Then she saw Wergard had paused, half-crouched and motionless, at the barely opened door.

"What is it?" she asked quickly.

"I don't know!" The face he turned to her was puzzled and apprehensive. "Come up and take a look!"

She moved to where she could look out past him. After a moment, she said, "There are adjustment instruments for the Depot lighting somewhere in the control section."

"Uh-huh," said Wergard. "Another item that's been sealed away for a hundred years or so. But our Number Two Thing in the control building seems to have got to them. I'd like to know what it means."

He opened the door wider. Both moved forward carefully, glancing along the street outside.

This was one of the main streets of the Depot. Across from them, a hundred and fifty yards away, was the massive white front of the structure which housed the central generators. Approximately two hundred yards to the left, it was pierced by a small entrance door which was the next step on Wergard's route to their quarters. To west and east, the street stretched away for half a mile before rows of buildings crossed it.

But all this was in semi-darkness now; too dim to let them make out the door in the wall of the generator building from where they stood. A hazy brightness above the line of buildings across the street indicated the rest of the Depot was still flooded by the projection lighting system which was that of the old fortress—wear-proof and ageless. If not deliberately tampered with, it would go on filling the Depot with eternal day-brightness for millennia.

But something had tampered with it and was still tampering with it. As they looked, the gloom along the street deepened perceptibly, then, slowly, lightened to its previous level.

"There can't be much light in the Pit, of course," Wergard said, staring up the street to the west. The control section, Danestar realized suddenly, lay in that direction. "It may be trying to improve visibility in the Depot for its perceptions."

"Or," said Danestar, "ruin visibility for ours."

Wergard looked at her. "We don't have the time left to try another route," he said. "Whatever it's doing, we may make a mistake in crossing the street while it's experimenting. But waiting here makes no sense."

She shook her head. "The intention might be to keep us waiting here."

"Yes, I thought of that. So let's go. Right now. Top speed across. I'll stay behind you."

For an instant, Danestar hesitated. Her feeling that the uncertain darkness of the wide street was under the scrutiny of alien senses, that they would be observed and tracked, like small scuttling animals, as soon as they left the shelter of the doorway, became almost a conviction in that moment. The fact remained that they could not stay where they were. She tightened her grip on the handle of the valise, drew a deep breath, darted out.

They were half-across when the darkness thickened so completely that they might have moved in mid-stride into a black universe. Blind, she thought. It was an abrupt mental shock. She faltered, almost stumbled, felt she had swerved from the line she was following, tried to turn back to it . . . suddenly didn't know at all in which direction to move. Now panic closed in.

"*Wergard!*"

"That way!" His voice, hoarse and strained, was on her right, rather than behind her. As she turned toward it, his light flicked on, narrowed to a pale thread, marking a small circle on the wall of the generator building ahead of Danestar. She was hurrying toward the wall again as the thread of light cut out . . . and seconds later, the wall and the street began to reappear, dim and vague as before, but tangibly present. They reached the wall together, turned left along it. Again the street darkened, became lost in absolute blackness.

Wergard's hand caught her arm. "Just walk." He added something, muttered and indistinct, which might have been a curse. They went on, breathing raggedly. Wergard's hand remained on Danestar's arm. The darkness lightened a trifle, grew dense again. "Hold on a moment!" Wergard said, very softly.

She stopped instantly, stood unmoving, let her breath out slowly. Wergard's hand left her arm. She had an impression of cautious motion from him, decided he'd raised the carbine to fire-ready position. Then he, too, was still.

He'd speak when he thought he could. Danestar's eyes shifted quickly, scanning the unrelieved dark about them. The only sound was a dim faint hum of machinery from within the structure on their right.

Then she realized something had appeared in her field of vision.

It was ahead and to the left. A small pale patch of purple luminescence, moving swiftly but in an oddly jerky manner, its outline shifting and wavering, as it approached their path at what might be a right angle. How far away? If it was touching the ground, Danestar thought, or just above it, it must be at least two hundred yards farther up the street. That would make it a considerably larger thing than her first impression had suggested.

As these calculations flicked through her mind, their object passed by ahead, moved on to the right, abruptly vanished.

"You saw it?" Wergard whispered.

"Yes."

"Went in between a couple of buildings. Not so good—but it was some distance off. We don't seem to have been noticed. Let's go on."

Wergard had glimpsed another of the minor fire shapes just before they stopped. That one had been smaller—or farther away—and had been in sight for only an instant, on the left side of the street.

"They shouldn't be too large to get through a personnel lock and switch off a barrier for Thing Number One," he said as they hurried along a catwalk in the generator building. "But that doesn't necessarily mean Number One is in this area."

"Scouts?" Danestar suggested.

That had been Wergard's thought. The Pit creature could have split off several dozen autonomous sections of itself of the size they had observed without noticeably reducing its main bulk, and scattered them about the Depot to speed up the search for any humans still hiding out. The carbine couldn't have done significant damage to the alien giant but should have the power to disrupt essential force patterns in these lesser replicas. "They don't make things easier for us," Wergard said, "but we'll have to show ourselves only once more. After that, we'll have cover. And we can change our tactics a little. . . . "

At the end of the generator building was the central street of the Depot, slightly wider than the last one they had crossed. It was almost startling to find it normally lit. Directly opposite was the entrance recess to another building. This was the final open stretch on the way to their quarters. Wergard mopped his forehead, asked, "Ready to try it?"

Danestar nodded. She felt lightly tensed, not at all tired. Dread had its uses—her body had recognized an ultimate emergency and responded. She thought it would go on running now when she called on it until it fell dead.

Wergard was wearing a sneaksuit; she wasn't. It was possible they were being followed, that the light-shapes they'd seen were casting about in the area for the source of the life energy they'd detected here, of which she was the focus. In that case, getting across the central street might be the point of greatest danger. They'd decided she should go first while Wergard covered her with the carbine. He would follow as soon as she was within the other building.

She slipped out the door ahead of him, drew a deep breath, ran straight across the too-silent, bright-lit street toward the entrance recess.

And nothing happened. The carbine stayed quiet. The paving flowed by, and it seemed only an instant then before the building front swayed close before her. Danestar flung herself into the recess, came up gasping against the wall.

A door on the left, Wergard had said. Where?—she discovered it next to her, pulled it open.

For a moment, her mind seemed about to spin into insanity. Then she was backing away from the door, screaming with all her strength, while two shapes of pale fire glided out through it toward her. Somewhere, she heard the distant sharp snarl of the carbine. A blizzard of darting, writhing lines of purple light enveloped her suddenly, boiled in wild turmoil about the recess. The closer of the shapes had vanished, and the carbine was snarling again.

Abruptly, her awareness was wiped out.

"Got your third setting now, I think!" Wergard announced.

Danestar glanced at him. He sat at a table a few feet to her left, hunched forward, elbows planted on the table, face twisted in concentration as he peered at the tiny paper-flat instrument in his left hand.

"Uh-huh, that's it!" He sighed heavily. "Four to go."

His right forefinger and thumb closed cautiously down on the device, shifted minutely, shifted back again. It was an attachment taken from Danestar's commband detector. She had designed it, used it on occasion to intrude on covert communications in which she had a professional interest, sometimes blanking a band out gently at a critical moment, sometimes injecting misinformation.

But it was an instrument designed for her fingers, magical instruments themselves in their sensitized skill, deftness, and experience. It had not been designed for Wergard's fingers, or anyone else's; and the only help she could give him with it was to tell him what must be done. Both hands were needed to operate the settings, and at present she couldn't use her left hand. What had knocked her out in the building entrance, an instant before Wergard's gun disrupted the second of the two Pit things that surprised her there, seemed to have been the approximate equivalent of a near miss from a bolt of lightning. Wergard had carried her two Depot blocks to their quarters, was working a sneaksuit over her, before she regained consciousness. Then she woke up suddenly, muscles knotted, trying to scream, voice thick and slurred when she started to answer Wergard's questions. They discovered her left side was almost completely paralyzed, her tongue partly affected. As soon as he could make out what she wanted, what her plan had been, Wergard hauled her down to the ground-level barrier room of the building, along with an assortment of hastily selected gadgetry, settled her in a chair next to the barrier control panel, arranged the various instruments on a table before her where she could reach them with her right hand. Then he went to work on the attachment's miniature dials to adjust them to the seven settings she'd told him were needed.

He swore suddenly, in a gust of savage impatience, asked without looking up, "How long have I been playing around with this midget monster of yours?"

"Sixteen minutes," Danestar told him. The paralysis had begun to lift; she could enunciate well enough, though the left side of her face remained numb. But she still couldn't force meaningful motion into her left hand. If she had been able to use it, she wouldn't have needed half a minute to flick in the dial readings, slap the attachment back into the detector. It was a job no more involved than threading a series of miniature needles. The problem was simply that Wergard's hands weren't made for work on that scale, weren't trained to it.

"Sixteen minutes!" He groaned. His face was beaded with the sweat of effort. "Well, I seem to be getting the hang of it. Our luck may hold up."

It might, she thought. It was still a matter of luck. They'd had good luck and bad luck both during the past half-hour. Until now, the main alien body had been engaged in the cluster of activated defense barriers on the north side of the Depot. The viewscreen on the table showed her the intermittent flickering of force fields there; now and then, a section blazed brightly. And sometimes she'd seen the great purple glow passing among the buildings. While it remained in that area, they had time left. But the barriers were being shut off, one by one. Detached work segments of the thing would be able to enter by a personnel lock and cut the controls. And—perhaps when the locks could not be immediately found—the main body was again driving directly through the force fields and absorbing what damage it must to get into a protected building.

During the past four minutes alone, it appeared to have passed through three such sectional barriers. Changes in the detector's visual pattern revealed the damage. The accumulated effect was not inconsiderable.

Danestar's gaze went to the locked instrument valise, lying on the table between the detector and the shortcode transmitter, in immediate reach of her right hand. Within it was still the alien instrument she'd taken from Dr. Hishkan's office, the small, all-essential coordinating device without which the artificial asteroid from the cosmic cloud was a nonoperative, useless, meaningless lump of deteriorating machinery.

Had the alien mind discovered it wouldn't function, that the humans here had removed a section of it?

She thought it had. The repeated acceptance, during these last minutes, of the destruction of whole layers of its units in the raging force fields, to allow it to reach the barrier controls more quickly, suggested a new urgency in its search for human survivors. It would have been logical for it to assume that whoever had the missing instrument had sought refuge in the one area still shielded by multiple barriers.

But when the last of those defense fields was shut off and the last of the northern buildings hunted through, the creature would turn here. In that, their luck had been bad—very bad! To avoid attracting attention to the building, they'd planned to leave its barrier off as long as possible. They were in sneaksuits, perhaps untraceable. They might have remained undetected indefinitely.

But they had been in the barrier room only a few minutes before one of the prowling segments found them. Danestar had the streets along two sides of the building under observation, and nothing had been in sight there. Evidently, the thing had approached through an adjacent building. Without warning, it erupted from an upper corner of the room, swept down toward them. Danestar barely glimpsed it before Wergard scooped up the carbine placed across the table beside him and triggered it one-handed.

The segment vanished, as its counterparts in the building entry had done, in an exploding swirl of darting, purple-gleaming lines of light. The individual energy entities which had survived the gun's shock-charge seemed as mindless and purposeless as an insect swarm whirled away on a sudden gust of wind. Danestar had slapped on the building's defense fields almost as Wergard fired; and in seconds, the indicators showed the fields flickering momentarily at thousands of points as the glittering purple threads flashed against them and were absorbed. Within a minute, the building was clear again.

But almost immediately afterwards, the barrier was impacted in a far more solid manner; and now the viewscreen showed a sudden shifting and weaving of fire shapes in one of the streets beside the building. Four or five segments had appeared together; one had attempted to slip into the building and encountered the force field. Lacking the protective bulk of the main body, it was instantly destroyed. The others obviously had become aware of the danger.

"If they can find the personnel lock here, they should try that!" Wergard remarked.

He laid Danestar's instrument carefully to one side, stood waiting with the gun. The entry surface of the lock was in the wall across from them, ringed in warning light to show the field was active. Danestar kept her eyes on the control panel. After a moment, she said sharply, "They have found the lock!" A yellow light had begun to flash beside the field indicators, signaling that the lock was in use. As it began to open on the room, the carbine flicked a charge into it, and the purple glow within exploded in glittering frenzies.

The attempt to use the lock wasn't repeated. The scouting segments were not in themselves an immediate danger here. But in the open, away from the building, where they could bring their destructive powers into play, a few of them should be more than a match for the carbine. To retreat again to some other point of the Depot had become impossible. The things remained in the vicinity and were on guard, and other segments began to join them.

That made it simply a question of how many minutes it still would be before the main body appeared to deal with the humans pinned down in this building. Neither Wergard nor Danestar mentioned it. They'd had good luck and bad, lasted longer than there had been any real reason to expect; now they'd run out of alternative moves. Nothing was left to discuss. Wergard had laid the carbine down, resumed his carefully deliberate groping with the spidery dials of Danestar's device. Danestar watched the instruments; and the instruments, in their various ways, watched the enemy. A tic began working in the corner of Wergard's jaw; sweat ran down his face. But his hands remained steady. After a time, he announced he had locked in the first setting. Then the second, and the third. . . .

There were developments in the instruments Danestar didn't tell him about. That the main body of the alien was absorbing savage punishment in its onslaught on the force fields became increasingly evident. The detector's projection field pattern almost might have been that of a city undergoing an intermittent brutal barrage. Blacked-out sections remained lifeless now, and there were indications of an erratically spreading breakdown in general organization.

But it should know, she thought, how much of that it could tolerate. Meanwhile it was achieving its purpose with frightening quickness. Barrier after barrier blazed in sudden bright fury along the line of search through the northern complex, subsided again. The viewscreen panels kept shifting as Danestar followed the thing's progress. Then she cut in one more panel, and knew it was the last. The alien had very little farther to go.

She switched the screen back momentarily to the local area, the streets immediately around their building. There was evidence here, she thought, in the steadily increasing number of ghostly darting light shapes beyond the barrier, that alien control of the Depot was almost complete. The segments had been sent through it like minor detachments of an invading army to make sure no humans were left in hiding anywhere. They were massing about this building now because the composite mind knew that within the building were the only survivors outside of the northern complex.

The thing was intelligent by any standards, had used its resources methodically and calculatingly. The major section which had been detached from it after it captured the control building apparently had remained there throughout, taking no part in other action. That eliminated the possibility that humans might escape from the Depot or obtain outside help. Only during the past few minutes, after the alien mind was assured that the last survivors were pinned down, had there been a change in that part of the pattern in the projector field. The thing seemed to be on the move now, filling some other role in the overall plan. Perhaps, Danestar thought, it would rejoin the main body as a reserve force, to make up for the losses suffered in the barriers. Or it might be on its way here.

Wergard said absently, as if it had occurred to him to mention in passing something that was of no great interest to either of them, "Got that fourth setting now. . . ."

Less than a minute later, in the same flat, perfunctory tone, he announced the fifth setting was locked in; and hope flared in Danestar so suddenly it was like a shock of hot fright.

She glanced quickly at him. Staring down at the instrument he fingered with infinite two-handed deliberation, Wergard looked drugged, in a white-faced trance. She didn't dare address him, do anything that might break into that complete absorption.

But mentally she found herself screaming at him to hurry. There was so little time left. The last barrier in the northern complex had flared, gone dead, minutes before. The giant main body of the alien seemed quiescent then. There were indications of deep continuing disturbances in the scintillating signal swarms in the projector, and briefly Danestar had thought that the last tearing shock of force field energies could have left the great mass finally disorganized, crippled and stunned.

But then evidence grew that the component which had remained in the control station was, in fact, rejoining the main body. And its role became clear. As the two merged, the erratic disturbances in the major section dimmed, smoothed out. A suggestion of swift, multitudinous rhythms coordinating the whole gradually returned.

The Pit thing was the equivalent of an army of billions of individuals. And that entity had a directing intelligence—centered in the section which had held itself out of action until the energy defenses of the Depot were neutralized. Now it had reappeared, unaffected by the damage the main body had suffered, to resume control, restore order. Quantitatively, the composite monster was reduced, shrunken. But its efficiency remained unimpaired; and as far as she and Wergard were concerned, the loss in sheer mass made no difference at all.

And where was it now? She'd kept the panels of the viewscreen shifting about along the line of approach it should take between the northern complex and this building. She did not catch sight of it. But, of course, if it was in motion again, it could as easily be flowing toward them below ground level where the screen wouldn't show it. . . .

Danestar paused, right hand on the screen mechanism.

Had there been the lightest, most momentary, betraying quiver in a section of the defense barrier indicator: just then? The screen was turned to the area about the building; and only the swift gliding ghost shapes of the segments were visible in the streets outside.

But that meant nothing. She kept her eyes on the barrier panel. Seconds passed; then a brief quivering ran through the indicators and subsided.

The thing was here, beneath the building, barely beyond range of its force field.

Danestar drew the instrument valise quietly toward her, opened its dial lock and took out the ovoid alien device and a small gun lying in the valise beside it. She laid the device on the table, placed the gun's muzzle against it. A slight pull of her trigger finger would drive a shattering charge into the instrument. . . .

Her eyes went back to the viewscreen. The swirling mass of light shapes out there abruptly had stopped moving.

She and Wergard had discussed this. The alien had traced the U-League's asteroid specimen from the Pit to Mezmiali, and to the Depot. While the instrument now missing from the specimen had been enclosed by the spyproof screens of Danestar's valise, the alien's senses evidently had not detected it. But it should register on them as soon as it was removed again from the valise.

One question had been then whether the alien would be aware of the device's importance to it. Danestar thought now that it was. The other question was whether it had learned enough from its contacts with humans to realize that, cornered and facing death, they might destroy such an instrument to keep it from an enemy.

If the alien knew that, it might, in the final situation, gain them a little more time.

She would not have been surprised if the barrier indicators had blazed red the instant after she opened the valise. And she would, in that moment, which certainly must be the last of her life and Wergard's, have pulled the gun trigger.

But nothing happened immediately, except that the segments in the streets outside the building went motionless. That, of course, should have some significance. Danestar waited now as motionlessly. Perhaps half a minute passed. Then the rattling pickup signal of the shortcode transmitter on the table suddenly jarred the stillness of the room.

Some seconds later, three spaced words, stolen from living human voices, patched together by the alien's cunning, came from the transmitter:

"I . . . want . . . it. . . ."

There was a pause. On Danestar's left, Wergard made a harsh laughing sound. She watched the barrier panel. The indicators there remained quiet.

"I . . . want . . . it. . . ." repeated the transmitter suddenly. It paused again.

"Six, Danestar!" Wergard's voice told her. He added something in a mutter, went silent.

"I . . . want—"

The transmitter cut off abruptly. The force field indicators flickered very slightly and then were still. But in the viewscreen there was renewed motion.

The segments in the street to the left of the building lifted like burning leaves caught by the breath of an approaching storm, swirled up together, streamed into and across the building beyond. In an instant, the street was empty of them. In the street on the right, ghostly fire shapes also were moving off, more slowly, gliding away to the east, while the others began pouring out of building fronts and down through the air again to join the withdrawal. Some four hundred yards away, the swarm came to a stop, massing together. Seconds later, the paving about them showed the familiar purple glitter and the gleaming mass of the Pit creature lifted slowly into view from below, its minor emissaries merging into it and vanishing as it arose. It lay there quietly then, filling the width of the street.

The situation had been presented in a manner which could not be misunderstood. The alien mind wanted the instrument. It knew the humans in this building had it. It had communicated the fact to them, then drawn back from the building, drawn its segments with it.

The humans, it implied, were free to go now, leaving the instrument behind. . . .

But, of course, that was not the real situation. There was no possible compromise. The insignificant-looking device against which Danestar's gun was held was the key to the Pit. To abandon it to the alien at this final moment was out of the question. And the act, in any case, would not have extended their lives by more than a few minutes.

So the muzzle of the gun remained where it was, and Danestar made no other move. Revealing they had here what the creature wanted had gained them a trifling addition in time. Until she heard Wergard tell her he had locked in the seventh and final setting on the diabolically tiny instrument with which he had been struggling for almost twenty minutes, she could do nothing else.

But Wergard stayed silent while the seconds slipped away. When some two minutes had passed, Danestar realized the giant fire shape was settling back beneath the surface of the street. Within seconds then it disappeared.

A leaden hopelessness settled on her at last. When they saw the thing again, it would be coming in for the final attack. And if it rose against the force fields from below the building, they would not see it then. She must remember to pull the trigger the instant the barrier indicators flashed their warning. Then it would be over.

She looked around at Wergard, saw he had placed the instrument on the table before him and was scowling down at it, lost in the black abstraction that somehow had enabled his fingers to do what normally must have been impossible to them. Only a few more minutes, Danestar thought, and he might have completed it. She parted her lips to warn him of what was about to happen, then shook her head silently. Why disturb him now? There was nothing more Wergard could do, either.

As she looked back at the viewscreen, the Pit creature began to rise through the street level a hundred yards away. It lifted smoothly, monstrously, a flowing mountain of purple brilliance, poured toward them.

Seconds left . . . Her finger went taut on the trigger.

A bemused, slow voice seemed to say heavily, "My eyes keep blurring now. Want to check this, Danestar? I think I have the setting, but—"

"*No time!*" She screamed it out, as the gun dropped to the table. She twisted awkwardly around on the chair, right hand reaching. "Let me have it!"

Then Wergard, shocked free of whatever trance had closed on him, was there, slapping the device into her hand, steadying her as she twisted back toward the detector and fitted it in. He swung away from her. Danestar locked the attachment down, glanced over her shoulder, saw him standing again at the other table, eyes fixed on her, hand lifted above the plunger of the power pack beside the carbine.

"Now!" she whispered.

Wergard couldn't possibly have beard it. But his palm came down in a hard slap on the plunger as the indicators of the entire eastern section of the barrier flared red.

Danestar was a girl who preferred subtle methods in her work when possible. She had designed the detector's interference attachment primarily to permit careful, unnoticeable manipulations of messages passing over supposedly untappable communication lines; and it worked very well for that purpose.

On this occasion, however, with the peak thrust of the power pack surging into it, there was nothing subtle about its action. A storm of static howled through the Depot along the Pit creature's internal communication band. In reaction to it, the composite body quite literally shattered. The viewscreen filled with boiling geysers of purple light. Under the dull black dome of the main barrier, the rising mass expanded into a writhing, glowing cloud. Ripped by continuing torrents of static, it faded further, dissipated into billions of flashing lines of light, mindlessly seeking escape. In their billions, they poured upon the defense globe of the ancient fortress.

For three or four minutes, the great barrier drank them in greedily.

Then the U-League Depot stood quiet again.

((((Neal Asher))))

The military team had pulled off their mission and now their problem was to get off the planet again while staying alive. They were only worried about human enemies who might be on their trail. That was a big mistake . . .

Neal Asher is one of the brightest of British science fiction writers (though many of his stories are more dark than bright), and has been very prolific since his first story was published in 1989, publishing fifteen novels and three short story collections (one of which was later reprinted in an expanded version), and numerous novellas and short stories. Most of his works (including "The Rhine's World Incident") are set in a future history called the Polity Universe. His stories have no shortage of action and violence and have been described as space opera with a cyberpunk sensibility (I would have described them as hard-boiled space opera, but then I'm not a critic). His stories, "Suckers" and "Mason's Rats III," were finalists for the British Science Fiction Award. Among the earlier novels in his Polity series are *Gridlinked*, *The Line of Polity*, *The Skinner*, *Brass Man*, and *Polity Agent*. For more information about the series, and his non-Polity works, see his website, http://freespace.virgin.net/n.asher/. Many of his short stories and novelettes fit nicely into the horror in space category, so picking one for this anthology was not easy. I finally decided that this one made me more uneasy than the others.

THE RHINE'S WORLD
((((INCIDENT))))

Neal Asher

The remote control rested dead in Reynold's hand, but any moment now Kirin might make the connection, and the little lozenge of black metal would become a source of godlike power. Reynold closed his hand over it, sudden doubts assailing him, and as always felt a tight stab of fear. That power depended on Kirin's success, which wasn't guaranteed, and on the hope that the device the remote connected to had not been discovered and neutralized.

He turned towards her. "Any luck?"

She sat on the damp ground with her laptop open on a mouldering log before her, with optics running from it to the framework supporting the sat dish, spherical laser com unit and microwave transmitter rods. She was also auged into the laptop; an optic lead running from the bean-shaped augmentation behind her ear to plug into it. Beside the laptop rested a big flat memstore packed with state-of-the-art worms and viruses.

"It is not a matter of luck," she stated succinctly.

Reynold returned his attention to the city down on the plain. Athelford was the centre of commerce and Polity power here on Rhine's World, most of both concentrated at its heart where skyscrapers reared about the domes and containment spheres of the runcible port. However, the unit first sent here had not been able to position the device right next to the port itself and its damned controlling AI—Reynold felt an involuntary shudder at the thought of the kind of icy artificial intelligences they were up against. The unit had been forced to act fast when the plutonium processing plant, no doubt meticulously tracked down by some forensic AI, got hit by Earth Central Security. They'd also not been able to detonate. Something had taken them out before they could even send the signal.

"The yokels are calling in," said Plate. He was boosted and otherwise physically enhanced, and wore com gear about his head plugged into the weird scaley Dracocorp aug affixed behind his ear. "Our contact wants our coordinates."

"Tell him to head to the rendezvous as planned." Reynold glanced back at where their gravcar lay underneath its chameleoncloth tarpaulin. "First chance we get we'll need to ask our contact why he's not sticking to that plan."

Plate grinned.

"Are we still secure?" Reynold asked.

"Still secure," Plate replied, his grin disappearing. "But encoded Polity com activity is ramping up as is city and sat-scan output."

"They know we're here," said Kirin, still concentrating on her laptop.

"Get me the device, Kirin," said Reynold. "Get it to me now."

One of her eyes had gone metallic and her fingers were blurring over her keyboard. "If it was easy to find the signal and lock in the transmission key, we wouldn't have to be this damned close and, anyway, ECS would have found it by now."

"But we know the main frequencies and have the key," Reynold observed.

Kirin snorted dismissively.

Reynold tapped the com button on the collar of his fatigues. "Spiro," he addressed the commander of the four-unit of Separatist ground troops positioned in the surrounding area. "ECS are on to us but don't have our location. If they get it they'll be down on us like a falling tree. Be prepared to hold out for as long as possible—for the Cause I expect no less of you."

"They get our location and it'll be a sat-strike," Plate observed. "We'll be incinerated before we get a chance to blink."

"Shut up, Plate."

"I think I may—" began Kirin, and Reynold spun towards her. "Yes, I've got it." She looked up victoriously and dramatically stabbed a finger down on one key. "Your remote is now armed."

Reynold raised his hand and opened it, studying with tight cold fear in his guts the blinking red light in the corner of the touch console. Stepping a little way from his comrades to the edge of the trees, he once again gazed down upon the city. His mouth was dry. He knew precisely what this would set in motion: terrifying unhuman intelligences would focus here the moment he sent the signal.

"Just a grain at a time, my old Separatist recruiter told me," he said. "We'll win this like the sea wins as it laps against a sandstone cliff."

"Very poetic," said Kirin, now standing at his shoulder.

"This is gonna hurt them," said Plate.

Reynold tapped his com button. "Goggles everyone." He pulled his own flash goggles down over his eyes. "Kirin, get back to your worms." He glanced round and watched her return to her station and plug the memstore cable into her laptop. The worms and viruses the thing contained were certainly the best available, but they wouldn't have stood a chance of penetrating Polity firewalls *before* he initiated the device. After that they would penetrate local systems to knock out satellite scanning for, according to Kirin, ten minutes—time for them to fly the gravcar far from here, undetected.

"Five, four, three, two . . . one." Reynold thumbed the touch console on the remote.

Somewhere in the heart of the city a giant flashbulb came on for a second, then went out. Reynold pushed up his goggles to watch a skyscraper going over and a disk of devastation spreading from a growing and rising fireball. Now, shortly after the EM flash of the blast, Kirin would be sending her software toys. The fireball continued to rise, a sprouting mushroom, but despite the surface devastation many buildings remained disappointingly intact. Still, they would be irradiated and tens of thousands of Polity citizens now just ash. The sound reached them now, and it seemed the world was tearing apart.

"Okay, the car!" Reynold instructed. "Kirin?"

She nodded, already closing up her laptop and grabbing up as much of her gear as she could carry. The broadcast framework would have to stay though, as would some of the larger armaments Spiro had positioned in the surrounding area. Reynold stooped by a grey cylinder at the base of a tree, punched twenty minutes into the timer and set it running. The thermite bomb would incinerate this entire area and leave little evidence for the forensic AIs of ECS to gather. "Let's go!"

Spiro and his men, now armed with nothing but a few hand weapons, had already pulled the tarpaulin from the car and were piling into the back row of seats. Plate took the controls and Kirin and Reynold climbed in behind him. Plate took it up hard through the foliage, shrivelled seed husks and swordlike leaves falling onto them, turned it and hit the boosters. Glancing back Reynold could only see the top of the nuclear cloud, and he nodded to himself with grim satisfaction.

"This will be remembered for years to come," he stated.

"Yup, certainly will," replied Spiro, scratching at a spot on his cheek.

No one else seemed to have anything to say, but Reynold knew why they were so subdued. This was the come-down, only later would they realise just what a victory this had been for the Separatist cause. He tried to convince himself of that . . .

In five minutes they were beyond the forest and over rectangular fields of mega-wheat, hill slopes stitched with neat vineyards of protein gourds, irrigation canals and plascrete roads for the agricultural machinery used here. The ground transport—a balloon-tyred tractor towing a train of grain wagons—awaited where arranged.

"Irrigation canal," Reynold instructed.

Plate decelerated fast and settled the car towards a canal running parallel to the road on which the transport awaited, bringing it to a hover just above the water then slewing it sideways until it nudged the bank. Spiro and the soldiers were out first, then Kirin.

"You can plus-grav it?" Reynold asked.

Plate nodded, pulled out a chip revealed behind a torn-out panel, then inserted a chipcard into reader slot. "Ten seconds." He and Reynold disembarked, then bracing themselves against the bank, pushed the car so it drifted out over the water. After a moment smoke drifted up from the vehicle's console. Abruptly it was as if the car had been transformed into a block of lead. It dropped hard, creating a huge splash, then was gone in an instant. Plate and Reynold clambered up the bank after the others onto the road. Ahead, awaiting about the tractor stood four of the locals, or 'yokels' as Plate called them—four Rhine's World Separatists.

"Stay alert," Reynold warned.

As he approached the four he studied them intently. They all wore the kind of disposable overalls farmers clad themselves in on primitve worlds like this and all seemed ill-at-ease. For a moment Reynold focused on one of their number: a very fat man with a baby face and shaven head. With all the cosmetic and medical options available it was not often you saw people so obese unless they chose to look that way. Perhaps this Separatist distrusted what Polity technology had to offer, which wasn't that unusual. The one who stepped forwards, however, obviously did trust that technology, being big, handsome, and obviously having provided himself with emerald green eyes.

"Jepson?" Reynold asked.

"I am," said the man, holding out his hand.

Reynold gripped it briefly. "We need to get under cover quickly—sat eyes will be functioning again soon."

"The first trailer is empty." Jepson stabbed a finger back behind the tractor.

Reynold nodded towards Spiro and he and his men headed back towards the trailer. "You too," he said to Kirin and, as she departed, glanced at Plate. "You're with me in the tractor cab."

"There's only room for four up there," Jepson protested.

"Then two of your men best ride in the trailer." Reynold nodded towards the fat man. "Make him one of them—that should give us plenty of room."

The fat man dipped his head as if ashamed and trailed after Kirin, then at a nod from Jepson one of the others went too.

"Come on fat boy!" Spiro called as the fat man hauled himself up inside the trailer.

"I sometimes wonder what the recruiters are thinking," said Jepson as he mounted the ladder up the side of the big tractor.

"Meaning?" Reynold inquired as he followed.

"Me and Dowel," Jepson flipped a thumb towards the other local climbing up after Reynold, "have been working together for a year now, and we're good." He entered the cab. "Mark seems pretty able too, but I'm damned If I know what use we can find for Brockle."

"Brockle would be fat boy," said Plate, following Dowel into the cab.

"You guessed it." Jepson took the driver's seat.

Along one wall were three fold-down seats, the rest of the cab being crammed with tractor controls and a pile of disconnected hydraulic cylinders, universal joints and PTO shafts. Reynold studied these for a second, noted blood on one short heavy cylinder and a sticky pool of the same nearby. That was from the original driver of this machine . . . maybe. He reached down and drew his pulse-gun, turned and stuck it up under Dowel's chin. Plate meanwhile stepped up behind Jepson and looped a garrot about his neck.

"What the—" Jepson began, then desisted as Plate tightened the wire. Dowel simply kept very still, his expression fearful as he held his hands out from his body.

"We've got a problem," said Reynold.

"I don't understand," said Jepson.

"I don't either, but perhaps you can help." Reynold nodded to one of the seats and walked Dowel back towards it. The man cautiously pushed it down and sat. Gun still held at his neck, Reynold searched him, removing a nasty-looking snubnose, then stepped back knowing he could blow the top off the man's head before he got a chance to rise. "What I don't understand is why you contacted us and asked us for our coordinates."

Plate hit some foot lever on Jepson's seat and spun it round so the man faced Reynold, who studied his expression intently.

"You weren't supposed to get in contact, because the signal might have been traced," Reynold continued, "and there were to be no alterations to the plan unless I initiated them."

"I don't know what you mean," Jepson whispered. "We stuck to the plan—no one contacted you."

"Right frequency, right code—just before we blew the device."

"No, honestly—you can check our com record."

Either Jepson was telling the truth or he was a very good liar. Reynold nodded to Plate, who cinched the garrot into a loop around the man's neck and now, with one hand free, began to search him, quickly removing first a gas-system pulse-gun from inside his overalls then a comunit from the top pocket. Plate keyed it on, input a code, then tilted his head as if listening to something as the comunit's record loaded to his aug.

"Four comunits," said Plate. "One of them sent the message but the record has been tampered with so we don't know which one."

Jepson looked horrified. Reynold tapped his com button. "Spiro, disarm and secure those two in there with you." Then to Jepson, "Take us to the hideout."

Plate unlooped the garrot and spun Jepson's seat forwards again.

"It has to be one of the other two," said Jepson, looking back at Reynold. "Me and Dowel been working for the Cause for years."

"Drive the tractor," Reynold instructed.

The farm, floodlit now as twilight fell, was a great sprawl of barns, machinery garages and silos, whilst the farmhouse was a composite dome with rooms enough for twenty or more people. However, only three had lived there. One of them, according to Jepson, lay at the bottom of an irrigation canal with a big hydraulic pump in his overalls to hold him down. He had been the son. The parents were still here on the floor of the kitchen adjoining this living room, since Jepson and Dowel had not found time to clear up the mess before going to pick up their two comrades. Reynold eyed the two corpses for a moment, then returned his attention to Jepson and his men.

"Strip," he instructed.

"Look I don't know—" Jepson began, then shut up as Reynold shot a hole in the carpet moss just in front of the man's work boots.

The four began removing their clothes, all with quick economy but for Brockle, who seemed to be struggling with the fastenings. Soon they all stood naked.

"Jesu," said Spiro, "you could do with a makeover fat boy."

"Em alright," said Brockle, staring down at the floor, his hands, with oddly long and delicate fingers trying to cover the great white rolls of fat.

"Em alright is em?" said Spiro.

"Scan them," Reynold instructed.

Plate stepped forwards with a hand scanner and began running it from head to foot over each man, first up and down their fronts, then over them from behind. When Plate reached Brockle, Spiro called out, "Got a big enough scanner there, Plate?" which was greeted by hilarity from his four troops. When Plate came to one who had been in the grain carriage with Brockle, he reacted fast, driving a fist into the base of the man's skull then following him down to the floor. Plate pulled his solid-state laser from his belt, rested it beside the scanner then ran it down the man's leg, found something and fired. A horrible sputtering and sizzling ensued, black oily smoke and licks of flame rising from where the beam cut into the man's leg. After a moment, Plate inspected the readout from his scanner, nodded and stepped back.

"What have we got?" Reynold asked.

"Locater."

Reynold felt cold claws skittering down his backbone. "Transmitting?"

"No, but it could have been," Plate replied.

Reynold saw it with utter simplicity. If a signal had been sent, then ECS would be down on them very shortly, and shortly after that they would all be either dead or in an interrogation cell. He preferred dead. He did not want ECS taking his mind apart to find out what he knew.

"Spiro, put a watchman on the roof," he instructed.

Spiro selected one of his soldiers and sent him on their way.

Having already ascertained the layout of this place Reynold

pointed to a nearby door. "Now Spiro, I want you to take him in there," he instructed. "Tie him to a chair, revive him and start asking him questions. You know how to do that." He paused for a moment. They were all tired after forty-eight hours without sleep. "Work him for two hours then let one of your men take over. Rotate the watch on the roof too and make sure you all get some rest."

Spiro grinned, waved over one of his men and the two dragged their victim off into the room, leaving a trail of plasma and charred skin. Like all Separatist soldiers they were well versed in interrogation techniques.

"Oh, and gag him when he's not answering questions," Reynold added. "We all need to get some sleep."

Reynold turned back to the remaining three. "Get in there." He pointed towards another door. It was an internal store room without windows so would have to do.

"I didn't know," said Jepson. "You have to believe that."

"Move," Reynold instructed.

Jepson stooped to gather up his clothing, but Plate stepped over and planted his boot on the pile. Jepson hesitated for a moment then traipsed into the indicated room. One of the troops pulled up an armchair beside the door and plumped himself down in it, pulse-gun held ready in his right hand. Reynold nodded approval then sank down on a sofa beside where Kirin had tiredly seated herself, her laptop open before and connected to her aug. Plate moved over and dropped into an armchair opposite.

"That's everything?" Kirin asked Plate.

"Everything I've got," he replied.

"Could do with my sat-dish, but I'm into the farm system now—gives me a bit more range," said Kirin.

"You're running our security now?" Reynold asked.

"Well, Plate is better with the physical stuff so I might as well take it on now."

"Anything?"

"Lot of activity around the city, of course," she replied, "but nothing out this way. I don't think our friend sent his locator signal and I don't think ECS knows where we are. However, from what I've picked up it seems they do know they're looking for a seven-person specialist unit. Something is leaking out there."

"I didn't expect any less," said Reynold. "All we have to do now is keep our heads down for three days, separate to take up new identities then transship out of here."

"Simple hey," said Kirin, her expression grim.

"We need to get some rest," said Reynold. "I'm going to use one of the beds here and I suggest you do the same."

He heaved himself to his feet and went to find a bedroom. As his head hit the pillow he slid into a fugue state somewhere between sleep and waking. It seemed only moments had passed, when he heard the agonized scream, but checking his watch as he rolled from the bed he discovered two hours had passed. He crashed open the door to his room and strode out, angry. Kirin lay fast asleep on the sofa and a trooper in the armchair was gazing round with that bewildered air of someone only half-awake.

Reynold headed over to the room in which the interrogation was being conducted and banged open the door. "I thought I told you to keep him quiet?"

Their traitor had been strapped in a chair, a gag in his mouth. He was writhing in agony, skin stripped off his arm from elbow to wrist and one eye burnt out. The trooper in there with him had been rigging up something from the room's powerpoint, but now held his weapon and had been heading for the door.

"That wasn't him, sir," he said.

Reynold whirled, drawing his pulse-gun, then tapping his com button. "Report in." One reply from Spiro on the roof, one from the other trooper as he stumbled sleepily into the living room, nothing from Kirin, but then she was asleep, and nothing from Plate. "Plate?" Still nothing.

"Where did Plate go?" Reynold asked the seated guard.

The man pointed to a nearby hall containing bunk rooms. Signalling the two troopers to follow, Reynold headed over, opening the first door. The interior light came on immediately to show Plate, sprawled on a bed, his back arched and hands twisted in claws above him, fingers bloody. Reynold surveilled the room, but there was little to see. It possessed no window so the only access was the door, held just the one bed, some wall cupboards and a sanitary cubicle. Then he spotted the vent cover lying on the floor with a couple of screws beside it, and looked up. Something metallic and segmented slid out of sight into the air-conditioning vent.

"What the fuck was that?" asked one of the troops behind him.

"Any dangerous life forms on this world?" Reynold asked carefully, trying to keep his voice level.

"Dunno," came the illuminating reply. "We came in with you."

Reynold walked over to Plate and studied him. Blood covered his head and the pillow was deep red, soaked with it. Leaning closer Reynold saw holes in Plate's face and skull, each a few millimetres wide. Some were even cut through his aug.

"Get Jepson—bring him here."

Jepson seemed just as bewildered as Reynold. "I don't know. I just don't know."

"Are you a local or what?" asked Spiro, who had now joined them.

"Been in the city most of my life," said Jepson, then shifted back as Spiro stepped towards him. "Brockle . . . he might know. Brockle's a farm boy."

"Let's get fat boy," said Spiro, snagging the shoulder of one of his men and departing.

Brockle came stumbling into the room wiping tiredly at his eyes. He almost looked thinner to Reynold, maybe worn down by fear. His gaze wandered about the room for a moment in bewilderment, finally focusing on the corpse on the bed.

"Why you kill 'em?" he asked.

"We did not kill him," said Reynold, "but something did." He pointed to the open air-conditioning duct.

Brockle stared at that in bewilderment too, then returned his gaze to Reynold almost hopefully.

"What is there here on Rhine's World that could do this?"

"Rats?" Brockle suggested.

Spiro hit him hard, in the guts, and Brockle staggered back making an odd whining sound. Spiro, obviously surprised he hadn't gone down stepped in to hit him again but Reynold caught his shoulder. "Just lock them back up." But even as Spiro turned to obey, doubled shrieks of agony reverberated, followed by the sound of something heavy crashing against a wall.

Spiro led the way out and soon they were back in the living room. He kicked open the door to the room in which Jepson's comrades were incarcerated and entered, gun in hand, then on automatic he opened fire at something. By the time Reynold entered Spiro was backing up, staring at the smoking line of his shots traversing up the wall to the open air duct.

"What did you see?" Reynold asked, gazing at the two corpses on the floor. Both men were frozen in agonized rictus, their heads bloody pepper-pots. One of them had been opened up below the sternum and his guts bulged out across the floor.

"Some sort of snake," Spiro managed.

Calm, got to stay calm. "Kirin," said Reynold. "I'll need you to do a search for me." No reply. "Kirin?"

Whatever it was it had got her in her sleep, but the sofa being a dark terracotta colour had not shown the blood. Reynold spun her laptop round and flipped it open, turned it on. The screen just showed blank fuzz. After a moment he noticed the holes cut through the keyboard, and that seemed to make no sense at all. He turned to the others and eyed Jepson and Brockle.

"Put them back in there." He gestured to that bloody room.

"You can't do that," said Jepson.

"I can do what I fucking please." Reynold drew his weapon and pointed it, but Brockle moved in front of Jepson waving those long-fingered hands.

"We done nuthin! We done nuthin!"

Spiro and his men grabbed the two and shoved them back into the room, slamming the door shut behind them.

"What the fuck is this?" said Spiro, finally turning to face Reynold.

The laptop, with its holes . . .

Reynold stepped over to the room in which Spiro and his men had been torturing their other prisoner, and kicked the door open. The chair lay down on its side, the torture victim's head resting in a pool of blood. A sticking trail had been wormed across the floor, and up the wall to an open air vent. It seemed he only had a moment to process the sight before someone else shrieked in agony. The sound just seemed to go on and on, then something crashed against the inside of the door Jepson and Brockle had just been forced through, and the shrieking stopped. Brockle or Jepson, it didn't matter now.

"We get out of here," said Reynold. "They fucking found us."

"What the fuck do you mean?" asked Spiro.

Reynold pointed at the laptop then at Kirin, at the holes in her head. "Something is here . . ."

The lights went out and a door exploded into splinters.

Pulse-fire cut the pitch darkness and a silvery object whickered through the air. Reynold backed up and felt something slide over his foot. He fired down at the floor and briefly caught a glimpse of a long flat segmented thing, metallic, with a nightmare head decked with pincers, manipulators and tubular probes. He fired again. Someone was screaming, pulse-fire revealed Spiro staggering to one side. It wasn't him making that noise because one of the worm-things was pushing its way into him through his mouth. A window shattered and there came further screaming from outside.

Silence.

Then a voice, calm and modulated.

"Absolutely correct of course," it said.

"Who are you?" Reynold asked, backing up through the darkness. A hard hook caught his heel and he went over, then a cold tongue slammed between his palm and his pulse-gun and just flipped the weapon away into the darkness.

"I am your case worker," the voice replied.

"You tried to stop us," he said.

"Yes, I tried to obtain your location. Had you given it the satellite strike would have taken you out a moment later. This was also why I planted that locator in the leg of one of Jepson's men—just to focus attention away from me for a while."

"You're the one that killed our last unit here—the one that planted the device."

"Unfortunately not—they were taken out by satellite strike, hence the reason we did not obtain the location of the tactical nuclear device. Had it been me, everything would have been known."

Reynold thought about the holes through his comrades' heads, through their augs and the holes even through Kirin's laptop. Something had been eating the information out of them even as it killed them. Mind-reaming was the reason Separatists never wanted to be caught alive, but as far as Reynold knew that would happen in a white-tiled cell deep in the bowels of some ECS facility, not like this.

"What the hell are you?"

The lights came on.

"Courts do not sit in judgement," said the fat boy, standing naked before Reynold. "When you detonated that device it only confirmed your death sentence, all that remained was execution of that sentence. However, everyone here possessed vital knowledge of others in the Separatist organisation and of other atrocities committed by it— mental evidence requiring deep forensic analysis."

Fat boy's skin looked greyish, corpselike, but only after a moment did Reynold realise it was turning metallic. The fat boy leaned forwards a little. "I am the Brockle. I am the forensic AI sent to gather and analyse that evidence, and incidentally kill you."

Now fat boy's skin had taken on a transparency, and underneath it could be seen he was just made of knots of flat segmented worms some of which were already dropping to the floor, others in the process of unravelling. Reynold scrabbled across the carpet towards his gun as a cold metallic wave washed over him. Delicate tubular drills began boring into his head, into his mind. In agony he hoped for another wave called death to swamp him and, though it came physically, his consciousness did not fade. It remained, somewhere, in some no space, while a cold meticulous intelligence took it apart piece by piece.

((((Paul Ernst))))

Here's a story from the grand old days of the sf pulp magazines. The story's protagonist was the only one manning an emergency station on the Moon, and was bored out of his skull, wishing something would happen to ease the ennui. Be careful what you wish for . . .

(Incidentally, Ernst was obviously trying to get his facts right about the Moon—John W. Campbell was now the editor of *Astounding Science-Fiction*, after all—at least the facts which were known in 1939, but he made a few scientific mistakes. I'll leave spotting them as an exercise for the reader.)

Paul Ernst (1899-1985, though there is some doubt about these dates) was a prolific writer for the pulp magazines, and is best remembered for writing most of the 24 novels detailing the exploits of the pulp hero, The Avenger, in the magazine with the same name. These were written under the Street & Smith house name of Kenneth Robeson (the name also used on *Doc Savage* magazine, though most of Doc's adventures were written by Lester Dent). He also wrote the Doctor Satan series for *Weird Tales* in the 1930s. When the pulp magazines died in the 1950s, he began selling stories to the higher-paying (and supposedly more respectable) slick magazines, but in the heyday of the pulps he turned out stories in many categories: westerns, mysteries, science fiction, and horror. This one's a twofer of those last two types.

"NOTHING HAPPENS (((ON THE MOON")))

Paul Ernst

The shining ball of the full Earth floated like a smooth pearl between two vast, angular mountains. The full Earth. Another month had ticked by.

Clow Hartigan turned from the porthole beside the small airlock to the Bliss radio transmitter.

"RC3, RC3, RC3," he droned out.

There was no answer. Stacey, up in New York, always took his time about answering the RC3 signal, confound it! But then, why shouldn't he? There was never anything of importance to listen to from station RC3. Nothing of any significance ever happened on the Moon.

Hartigan stared unseeingly at the pink cover of a six-month-old *Tadio Gazette*, pasted to the wall over the control board. A pulchritudinous brunette stared archly back at him over a plump shoulder that was only one of many large nude areas.

"RC3, RC3—"

Ah, there Stacey was, the pompous little busybody.

"Hartigan talking. Monthly report."

"Go ahead, Hartigan."

A hurried, fussy voice. Calls of real import waited for Stacey, calls from Venus and Jupiter and Mars. Hurry up, Moon, and report that nothing has happened, as usual.

Hartigan proceeded to do so. "Lunar conditions the same. No ships have put in, or have reported themselves as being in distress. The hangar is in good shape, with no leaks. Nothing out of the way has occurred."

"Right," said Stacey pompously. "Supplies?"

"You might send up a blonde," said Hartigan.

"Be serious. Need anything?"

"No." Hartigan's eyes brooded. "How's everything in Little Old New York?"

"Sorry. Can't gossip. Things are pretty busy around here. If you need anything, let me know."

The burr of power went dead. Hartigan cursed with monotony, and got up.

Clow Hartigan was a big young man with sand-red hair and slightly bitter blue eyes. He was representative of the type Spaceways sent to such isolated emergency landing stations as the Moon.

There were half a dozen such emergency landing domes, visited only by supply ships, exporting nothing, but ready in case some passenger liner was crippled by a meteor or by mechanical trouble. The two worst on the Spaceways list were the insulated hell on Mercury, and this great lonely hangar on the Moon. To them Spaceways sent the pick of their probation executives. Big men. Powerful men. Young men. (Also men who were unlucky enough not to have an old family friend or an uncle on the board of directors who could swing a soft berth for them.) Spaceways did not keep them there long. Men killed themselves, or went mad and began inconsiderately smashing expensive equipment, after too long a dose of such loneliness as that of the Moon.

Hartigan went back to the porthole beside the small airlock. As he went, he talked to himself, as men do when they have been too long away from their own kind.

"I wish I'd brought a dog up here, or a cat. I wish there's be an attempted raid. Anything at all. If only something would *happen*."

Resentfully he stared out at the photographic, black-and-white lunar landscape, lighted coldly by the full Earth. From that his eye went to the deep black of the heavens. Then his heart gave a jump. There was a faint light up there where no light was supposed to be.

He hurried to the telescope and studied it. A space liner, and a big one! Out of its course, no matter where it was bound, or it couldn't have been seen from the Moon with the naked eye. Was it limping in here to the emergency landing for repairs?

"I don't wish them any bad luck," muttered Hartigan, "but I hope they've burned out a rocket tube."

Soon his heart sank, however. The liner soared over the landing dome a hundred miles up, and went serenely on its way. In a short time its light faded in distance. Probably it was one of the luxurious around-the-solar-system ships, passing close to the Moon to give the sightseers an intimate glimpse of it, but not stopping because there was absolutely nothing of interest there.

"Nothing *ever* happens in this Godforsaken hole," Hartigan gritted.

Impatiently he took his space suit down from the rack. Impatiently he stepped into the bulky, flexible metal thing and clamped down the headpiece. Nothing else to do. He'd take a walk. The red beam of the radio control board would summon him back to the hangar if for any reason anyone tried to raise RC3.

He let himself out through the double wall of the small airlock and set out with easy, fifteen-foot strides toward a nearby cliff on the brink of which it was sometimes his habit to sit and think nasty thoughts of the men who ran Spaceways and maintained places like RC3.

Between the hangar and the cliff was a wide expanse of gray lava ash, a sort of small lake of the stuff, feathery fine. Hartigan did not know how deep it might be. He did know that a man could probably sink down in it so far that he would never be able to burrow out again.

He turned to skirt the lava ash, but paused a moment before proceeding.

Behind him loomed the enormous half-globe of the hangar, like a phosphorescent mushroom in the blackness. One section of the halfglobe was flattened; and here were the gigantic inner and outer portals where a liner's rocket-propelled life shells could enter the dome. The great doors of this, the main airlock, reared halfway to the top of the hangar, and weighed several hundred tons apiece.

Before him was the face of the Moon: sharp angles of rock; jagged, tremendous mountains; sheer, deep craters; all picked out in black and white from the reflected light of Earth.

A desolate prospect. . . . Hartigan started on.

The ash beside him suddenly seemed to explode, soundlessly but with great violence. It spouted up like a geyser to a distance of a hundred feet, hung for an instant over him in a spreading cloud, then quickly began to settle.

A meteor! Must have been a fair-sized one to have made such a splash in the volcanic dust.

"Close call," muttered Hartigan, voice sepulchral in his helmet. "A little nearer and they'd be sending a new man to the lunar emergency dome."

But he only grimaced and went on. Meteors were like the lightning back on Earth. Either they hit you or they missed. There was no warning till after they struck; then it was too late to do anything about it.

Hartigan stumbled over something in the cloud of ash that was sifting down around him. Looking down, he saw a smooth, round object, black-hot, about as big as his head.

"The meteor," he observed. "Must have hit a slanting surface at the bottom of the ash heap and ricocheted up and out here. I wonder—"

He stooped clumsily toward it. His right "hand," which was a heavy pincer arrangement terminating the right sleeve of his suit, went out, then his left, and with some difficulty he picked the thing up. Now and then a meteor held splashes of previous metals. Sometimes one was picked up that yielded several hundred dollars' worth of platinum or iridium. A little occasional gravy with which the emergency-landing exiles could buy amusement when they got back home.

Through the annoying shower of ash he could see dimly the light of the hangar. He started back, to get out of his suit and analyze the meteor for possible value.

It was the oddest-looking thing he had ever seen come out of the heavens. In the first place, its shape was remarkable. It was perfectly round, instead of being irregular as were most meteors.

"Like an old-fashioned cannon ball," Hartigan mused, bending over it on a workbench. "Or an egg—"

Eyebrows raised whimsically, he played with the idea.

"Jupiter! What an egg it would be! A hundred and twenty pounds if it's an ounce and it smacked the Moon like a bullet without even cracking! I wouldn't want it poached for breakfast."

The next thing to catch his attention was the projectile's odd color, or, rather, the odd way in which the color seemed to be changing. It had been dull, black-hot, when Hartigan brought it in. It was now a dark green, and was getting lighter swiftly as it cooled!

The big clock struck a mellow note. Tiime for the dome keeper to make his daily inspection of the main doors.

Reluctantly Hartigan left the odd meteor, which was now as green as grass and actually seemed to be growing transparent, and walked toward the big airlock.

He switched on the radio power unit. There was no power plant of any kind in the hangar; all power was broadcast by the Spaceways central station. He reached for the contact switch which poured the invisible Niagara of power into the motor that moved the ponderous doors.

Cr-r-rack!

Like a cannon shot the sound split the air in the huge metal dome, echoing from wall to wall, to die at last in a muffled rumbling.

White-faced, Hartigan was running long before the echoes died away. He ran toward the workbench he had recently quitted. The sound seemed to have come from near there. His thought was that the hangar had been crashed by a meteor larger than its cunningly braced beams, tough metal sheath, and artful angles of deflection would stand.

That would mean death, for the air supply in the dome would race out through a fissure almost before he could don his space suit.

However, his anxious eyes, scanning the vaulting roof, could find no crumpled bracing or ominous download bulges. And he could hear no thin whine of air surging in the hangar to the almost nonexistent pressure outside.

Then he glanced at the workbench and uttered an exclamation. The meteor he had left there was gone.

"It must have rolled off the bench," he told himself. "But if it's on the floor, why can't I see it?"

He froze into movelessness. Had that been a sound behind him? A sound here, where no sound could possibly be made save by himself?

He whirled—and saw nothing. Nothing whatever, save the familiar expanse of smooth rock floor lighted with the cold white illumination broadcast on the power band.

He turned back to the workbench where the meteor had been, and began feeling over it with his hands, disbelieving the evidence of his eyes.

Another exclamation burst from his lips as his fingers touched something hard and smooth and round. The meteor. Broken into two halves, but still here. Only, *now it was invisible!*

"This," said Hartigan, beginning to sweat a little, "is the craziest thing I ever heard of!"

He picked up one of the two invisible halves and held it close before his eyes. He could not see it at all, though it was solid to the touch. Moreover, he seemed able to see through it, for nothing on the other side was blotted out.

Fear increased within him as his fingers told him that the two halves were empty, hollow. Heavy as the ball had been, it consisted of nothing but a shell about two inches thick. Unless—

"Unless something did crawl out of it when it split apart."

But that, of course, was ridiculous.

"It's just an ordinary metallic chunk," he told himself, "that split open with a loud bang when it cooled, due to contraction. The only thing unusual about it is its invisibility. That is strange."

He groped on the workbench for the other half of the thick round shell. With a half in each hand, he started toward the stock room, meaning to lock up this odd substance very carefully. He suspected he had something beyond price here. If he could go back to Earth with a substance that could produce invisibility, he could become one of the richest men in the universe.

He presented a curious picture as he walked over the brilliantly lighted floor. His shoulders sloped down with the weight of the two pieces of meteor. His bare arms rippled and knotted with muscular effort. Yet his hands seemed empty. So far as the eye could tell, he was carrying nothing whatever.

"What—"

He dropped the halves of the shell with a ringing clang, and began leaping toward the big doors. That time he *knew* he had heard a sound, a sound like scurrying steps! It had come from near the big doors.

When he got there, however, he could hear nothing. For a time the normal stillness, the ghastly phenomenal stillness, was preserved. Then from near the spot he had just vacated, he heard another noise. This time it was a gulping, voracious noise, accompanied by a sound that was like that of a rock crusher or a concrete mixer in action.

On the run, he returned, seeing nothing all this while, nothing, but smooth rock floor and plain, metal-ribbed walls, and occasional racks of instruments.

He got to the spot where he had dropped the parts of the meteor. The parts were no longer there. This time it was more than a question of invisibility. They had disappeared actually as well as visually.

To make sure, Hartigan got down on hands and knees and searched every inch of a large circle. There was no trace of the thick shell.

"Either something brand new to the known solar system is going on here," Hartigan declared, "or I'm getting as crazy as they insisted poor Stuyvesant was."

Increased perspiration glinted on his forehead. The fear of madness in the lonelier emergency fields was a very real fear. United Spaceways had been petitioned more than once to send two men instead of one to manage each outlying field; but Spaceways was an efficient corporation with no desire to pay two men where one could handle the job.

Again, Hartigan could hear nothing at all. And in swift though unadmitted fear that perhaps the whole business had transpired only in his own brain, he sought refuge in routine. He returned to his task of testing the big doors, which was important even though dreary in its daily repetition.

The radio power unit was on, as he had left it. He closed the circuit.

Smoothly the enormous inner doors swung open on their broad tracks to reveal the equally enormous outer portals. Hartigan stepped into the big airlock and closed the inner doors. He shivered a little. It was near freezing out here in spite of the heating units.

There was a small control room in the lock, to save an operator the trouble of always getting into a space suit when the doors were opened. Hartigan entered this and pushed home the switch that moved the outer portals.

Smoothly, perfectly, their tremendous bulk opened outward. They always worked smoothly, perfectly. No doubt they always would. Nevertheless, rules said test them regularly. And it was best to live up to the rules. With characteristic trustfulness, Spaceways had recording dials in the home station that showed by power marking whether or not their planetary employees were doing what they were supposed to do.

Hartigan reversed the switch. The doors began to close. They got to the halfway mark; to the three-quarters—

Hartigan felt rather than heard the sharp, grinding jar. He felt rather than heard the high, shrill scream, a rasping shriek, almost above the limit of audibility, that was something to make a man's blood run cold.

Still, without faltering, the doors moved inward and their serrated edges met. Whatever one of them had ground across had not been large enough to shake it.

"Jupiter!" Hartigan breathed, once more inside the huge dome with both doors closed.

He sat down to try to think the thing out.

"A smooth, round meteor falls. It looks like an egg, though it seems to be of metallic rock. As it cools, it gets lighter in color, till finally it disappears. With a loud bang, it bursts apart, and afterward

I hear a sound like scurrying feet. I drop the pieces of the shell to go toward the sound, and then I hear another sound, as if something were macerating and gulping down the pieces of shell, eating them. I come back and can't find the pieces. I go on with my test of opening and closing the main doors. As the outer door closes, I hear a crunching noise as if a rock were being pulverized, and a high scream like that of an animal in pain. All this would indicate that the meteor *was* a shell, and that some living thing *did* come out of it.

"But that is impossible.

"No form of life could live throuh the crash with which that thing struck the Moon, even though the lava ash did cushion the fall to some extent. No form of life could stand the heat of the meteor's fall and impact. No form of life could eat the rocky, metallic shell. It's utterly impossible!

"Or—is it impossible?"

He gnawed at his knuckles and thought of Stuyvesant.

Stuyvesant had been assigned to the emergency dome on Mercury. There was a place for you! An inferno! By miracles of insulation and supercooling systems the hangar there had been made livable. But the finest of space suits could not keep a man from frying to death outside. Nothing to do except stay cooped up inside the hangar, and pray for the six-month relief to come.

Stuyvesant had done that. And from Stuyvesant had begun to come queer reports. He thought he had seen something moving on Mercury near his landing field. Something like a rock!

Moving rocks! With the third report of that kind, the corporation had brought him home and turned him over to the board of science for examination. Poor Stuyvesant had barely escaped the lunatic asylum. He had been let out of Spaceways, of course. The corporation scrapped men suspected of being defective as quickly as they scrapped suspect material.

"When a man begins to see rocks moving, it's time to fire him," was the unofficial verdict.

The board of science had coldly said the same thing, though in more dignified language.

"No form of life as we know it could possibly exist in the high temperature and desert condition of Mercury. Therefore, in our judgment, Benjamin Stuyvesant suffered from hallucination when he reported some rocklike entity moving near Emergency Hangar RC10."

Hartigan glanced uneasily toward the workbench on which the odd meteor had rested.

"No form of life *as we know it*."

There was the catch. After all, this interplanetary travel was less than seventy years old. Might there not be many things still unknown to Earth wisdom?

"Not to hear the board of science tell it," muttered Hartigan, thinking of Stuyvesant's blasted career.

He thought of the Forbidden Asteroids. There were over two dozen on the chart on which, even in direst emergency, no ship was supposed to land. That was because ships had landed there, and had vanished without trace. Again and again. With no man able to dream of their fate. Till they simply marked the little globes "Forbidden," and henceforth ignored them.

"No form of life as we know it!"

Suppose something savage, huge, invisible, lived on those grim asteroids? Something that developed from egg form? Something that spread its young through the universe by propelling eggs from one celestial body to another? Something that started growth by devouring its own metallic shell, and continued it on a mineral instead of vegetable diet? Something that could live in any atmosphere or temperature?

"I *am* going crazy," Hartigan breathed.

In something like panic he tried to forget the affair in a great stack of books and magazines brought by the last supply ship.

The slow hours of another month ticked by. The full Earth waned, died, grew again. Drearily Hartigan went through the monotony of his routine. Day after day, the term "day" being a strictly figurative one on this drear lunar lump.

He rose at six, New York time, and sponged off carefully in a bit of precious water. He ate breakfast. He read. He stretched his muscles in a stroll. He read. He inspected his equipment. He read. He exercised on a set of homemade flying rings. He read.

"No human being should be called on to live like this," he said once, voice too loud and brittle.

But human beings did have to live like this, if they aspired to one of the big posts on a main planet.

He had almost forgotten the strange meteor that had fallen into lava ash at his feet a month ago. It was to be recalled with terrible abruptness.

He went for a walk in a direction he did not usually take, and came upon a shallow pit half a mile from the dome.

Pits, of course, are myriad on the Moon. The whole surface is made up of craters within craters. But this pit was not typical in conformation. Most are smooth-walled and flat-bottomed. This pit was ragged, as if it had been dug out. Besides, Hartigan had thought he knew every hole for a mile around, and he did not remember ever seeing this one.

He stood on its edge looking down. There was loose rock in its uncraterlike bottom, and the loose rock had the appearance of being freshly dislodged. Even this was not unusual in a place where the vibration of a footstep could sometimes cause tons to crack and fall.

Nevertheless, Hartigan could feel the hair rise a bit on the back of his neck as some deep, instinctive fear crawled within him at sight of the small, shallow pit. And then he caught his lips between his teeth and stared with wide, unbelieving eyes.

On the bottom of the pit a rock was moving. It was moving, not as if it had volition of its own, but as if it were being handled by some unseen thing.

A fragment about as big as his body, it rolled over twice, then slid along in impatient jerks as though a big head or hoof nudged at it. finally, it raised up from the ground and hung poised about seven feet in the air!

Restlessly, Hartigan watched, while all his former, almost superstitious fear flooded through him.

The rock fragment moved up and down in mid-space.

"Jupiter!" Clow Hartigan breathed hoarsely.

A large part of one end suddenly disappeared. A pointed

projection from the main mass of rock, it broke off and vanished from sight.

Another large chunk followed, breaking off and disappearing as though by magic.

"Jupiter!"

There was no longer doubt in Hartigan's mind. A live thing had emerged from the egglike meteor twenty-seven days ago. A live thing that now roamed loose over the face of the Moon.

But that section of rock, which was apparently being devoured, was held seven feet off the ground. What manner of creature could come from an egg no larger than his head and grow in one short month into a thing over seven feet tall? He thought of the Forbidden Asteroids, where no ships landed, though no man knew precisely what threat lurked there.

"It must be as big as a mastodon," Hartigan whispered. "What in the universe—"

The rock fragment was suddenly dropped, as if whatever invisible thing had held it had suddenly seen Hartigan at the rim of the pit. Then the rock was dashed to one side as if by a charging body. The next instant loose fragments of shale scattered right and left up one side of the pit as though a big body were climbing up and out.

The commotion in the shale was on the side of the pit nearest Hartigan. With a cry he ran toward the hangar.

With fantastic speed, sixty and seventy feet to a jump, he covered the ragged surface. But fast as he moved, he felt that the thing behind him moved faster. And that there *was* something behnd him he did not doubt for an instant, though he could neither see nor hear it.

It was weird, this pygmy human form in its bulky space suit flying soundlessly over the lunar surface under the glowing ball of Earth, racing like mad for apparently no reason at all, running insanely when so far as the eye could tell, nothing pursued.

But abysmal instinct told Hartigan that he was pursued, all right. And instinct told him that he could never reach the hangar in the lead. With desperate calmness he searched the ground still lying between him and the hangar.

A little ahead was a crack about a hundred feet wide and, as far as he knew, bottomless. With his oversized Earth muscles he could clear that in a gigantic leap. Could the ponderous, invisible thing behind him leap that far?

He was in mid-flight long enough to turn his head and look back, as he hurtled the chasm in a prodigious jump. He saw a flurry among the rocks at the edge he had just left as something jumped after him. Then he came down on the far side, lighting in full stride like a hurdler.

He risked slowing his speed by looking back again. A second time he saw a flurry of loose rock, this time on the near side of the deep crack. The thing had not quite cleared the edge, it seemed.

He raced on and came to the small air-lock door. He flung himself inside. He had hardly got the fastener in its groove when something banged against the outside of the door.

The thing pursuing him had hung on the chasm's edge long enough to let him reach safety, but had not fallen into the black depths as he had hoped it might.

"But that's all right," he said, drawing a great sigh of relief as he entered the hangar through the inner door. "I don't care what it does, now that I'm inside and it's out."

He got out of the space suit, planning as he moved.

The thing outside was over seven feet tall and made of some unfleshlike substance that must be practically indestructible. At its present rate of growth it would be as big as a small space liner in six months, if it weren't destroyed. But it would have to be destroyed. Either that, or Emergency Station RC3 would have to be abandoned, and his job with it, which concerned him more than the station.

"I'll call Stacey to send a destroyer," he said crisply.

He moved toward the Bliss transmitter, eyes glinting. Things were happening on the Moon, now, all right! And the thing that was happening was going to prove Stuyvesant as sane as any man, much saner than the gray-bearded goats on the board of science.

He would be confined to the hangar till Stacey could send a destroyer. No more strolls. He shuddered a little as he thought of how many times he must have missed death by an inch in his walks during the past month.

Hartigan got halfway to the Bliss transmitter, skirting along the wall near the small airlock.

A dull, hollow, booming sound filled the great hangar, ascending to the vaulted roof and seeming to shower down again like black water.

Hartigan stopped and stared at the wall beside him. It was bulging inward a little. Startled out of all movement, he stared at the ominous, slight bulge. And as he stared, the booming noise was repeated, and the bulge grew a bit larger.

"In the name of Heaven!"

The thing outside had managed to track him along the wall from the airlock, perhaps guided by the slight vibration of his steps. Now it was bindly charging the huge bulk of the hangar like a living, ferocious ram.

A third time the dull, terrible booming sound reverberated in the lofty hangar. The bulge in the tough metal wall spread again; and the two nearest supporting beams gave ever so little at the points of strain.

Hartigan moved back toward the airlock. While he moved, there was silence. The moment he stopped, there was another dull, booming crash and a second bulge appeared in the wall. The thing had followed him precisely, and was trying to get at him. The color drained from Hartigan's face. This changed the entire scheme of things.

It was useless to radio for help now. Long before a destroyer could get here, the savage, insensate monster outside would have opened a rent in the wall. That would mean Hartigan's death from escaping air in the hangar.

Crash!

Who would have dreamed that there lived anywhere in the universe, on no matter how far or wild a globe, a creature actually able to damage the massive walls of a Spaceways hangar? He could see himself trying to tell about this.

"An animal big enough to crack a hangar wall? And invisible? Well!"

Crash!

The very light globes, so far overhead, seemed to quiver a bit with the impact of this thing of unguessable nature against the vast semisphere of the hangar. The second bulge was deep enough so that the white enamel which coated it began chipping off in little flakes at the bulge's apex.

"What the devil am I going to do?"

The only thing he could think of for the moment was to move along the wall. That unleashed giant outside must not concentrate too long on any one spot.

He walked a dozen steps. As before, the ramming stopped while he was in motion, to start again as he halted. As before, it started at the point nearest to him.

Once more a bulge appeared in the wall, this time bigger than either of the first two. The metal sheets sheathing the hangar varied a little in strength. The invisible terror outside had struck a soft spot.

Hartigan moved hastily to another place.

"The whole base of the hangar will be scalloped like a pie crust at this rate," he gritted. "What can I—"

Crash!

He had inadvertently stopped near a rack filled with spare power bulbs. With its ensuing attack the blind fury had knocked the rack down onto the floor.

Hartigan's jaw set hard. Whatever he did must be done quickly. And it must be done by himself alone. He could not stay at the Bliss transmitter long enough to get New York and tell what was wrong, without giving the gigantic thing outside a fatal number of minutes in which to concentrate on one section of wall.

He moved slowly around the hangar, striving to keep the invisible fury too occupied in following him to get in more than an occasional charge. As he walked, his eyes went from one heap of supplies to another in search of a possible means of defense.

There were ordinary weapons in plenty, in racks along the wall. But none of these, he knew, could do material harm to the attacking fury.

He got to the great inner doors of the main airlock in his slow march around the hangar. And here he stopped, eyes glowing thoughtfully.

The huge doors had threatened in the early days to be the weak points in the Spaceways hangars. So the designers, like good engineers, had made the doors so massive that in the end they were stronger than the walls around them.

Bang!

A bulge near the massive hinges told Hartigan that the thing outside was as relentless as ever in its efforts to break through the wall and get at him. But he paid no attention to the new bulge. He was occupied with the doors.

If the invisible giant could be trapped in the main airlock between the outer and inner portals—

"Then what?" Hartigan wondered.

He could not answer his own question. But, anyway, it seemed like a step in the right direction to have the attacking fury penned between the doors rather than to have it loose and able to charge the more vulnerable walls.

"If I can coop it in the airlock, I might be able to think of some way to attack it," he went on.

He pushed home the control switch which set the broadcast power to opening the outer doors. And that gave him an idea that sent a wild thrill surging through him.

A heavy rumble told him that the motors were swinging open the outer doors.

"Will the thing come in?" he asked himself tensely. "Or has it sense enough to scent a trap?"

Bang!

The inner doors trembled a little on their broad tracks. The invisible monster had entered the trap.

"Trap?" Hartigan smiled mirthlessly. "Not much of a trap! Left to itself, it could probably break out in half an hour. But it won't be left to itself."

He reversed the switch to close the outer portals. Then, with the doors closed and the monster penned between, he got to work on the idea that had been born when he pushed the control switch.

Power, oceans of it, flooded from the power unit at the touch of a finger. A docile servant when properly channeled, it could be the deadliest thing on the Moon.

He ran back down the hangar to the stock room, and got out a drum of spare power cable. As quickly as was humanly possible, he rolled the drum back to the doors, unwinding the cable as he went.

It was with grim solemnity that he made his next move. He had to open the inner doors a few inches to go on with his frail plan of defense. And he had to complete that plan before the thing in the airlock could claw them open still more and charge through. For all their weight the doors rolled in perfect balance, and if the unseen terror could make dents in the solid wall, it certainly was strong enough to move the partly opened doors.

Speed! That was the thing that would make or break him. Speed, and hope that the power unit could stand a terrific overload without blowing a tube.

With a hand that inclined to tremble a bit, Hartigan moved the control switch operating the inner doors, and instantly cut the circuit again.

The big doors opened six inches or so, and stopped.

Hartigan cut off the power unit entirely, and dragged the end of the spare power cable to it. With flying fingers he disconnected the cable leading from the control switch to the motors that moved the portals, and connected the spare cable in its space.

He glanced anxiously at the doors, and saw the opening between them had widened to more than a foot. The left door moved a little even as he watched.

"I'll never make it."

But he went ahead.

Grabbing up the loose end of the cable, he threw it in a tangled coil as far as he could through the opening and into the airlock. Then he leaped for the power unit—and watched.

The cable lay unmoving on the airlock floor. But the left door moved! It jerked, and rolled open another six inches.

Hartigan clenched his hands as he stared at the inert cable. He had counted on the blind ferocity of the invisible terror, had counted on its attacking, or at least touching, the cable immediately. Had it enough intelligence to realize dimly that it would be best to avoid the cable? Was it going to keep working at those doors till—

The power cable straightened with a jerk. Straightened, and hung still, with the loose end suspended in midair about six feet off the airlock floor.

Hartigan's hand slammed down. The broadcast power was turned on to the last notch.

With his heart hammering in his throat, Hartigan gazed through the two-foot opening between the doors. Gazed at the cable through which was coursing oceans, Niagaras of power. And out there in the air-lock a thing began to build up from think air into a spectacle that made him cry out in wild horror.

He got a glimpse of a massive block of a head, eyeless and featureless, that joined with no neck whatever to a barrel of a body. He got a glimpse of five legs, like stone pillars, and of a sixth that was only a stump. ("That's what got caught in the doors a month ago—its leg," he heard himself babbling with insane calmness.) Over ten feet high and twenty feet long, the thing was a living battering ram, painted in the air in sputtering, shimmering blue sparks that streamed from its massive bulk in all directions.

Just a glimpse, he got, and then the monster began to scream as it had that first day when the door maimed it. Only now it was with a volume that tore at Hartigan's eardrums till he scremed himself in agony.

As he watched, he saw the huge carcass melt a little, like wax in flame, with the power cable also melting slowly and fusing into the cavernous, rocky jaws that had seized it. Then with a rush the whole bulk disintegrated into a heap of loose mineral matter.

Hartigan turned off the power unit and collapsed, with his face in his hands.

The shining ball of the full Earth floated like a smooth diamond between two vast, angular mountains. The full Earth.

Hartigan turned from the porthole beside the small airlock and strode to the Bliss radio transmitter.

"RC3, RC3, RC3," he droned out.

There was no answer. As usual, Stacey was taking his time about ansering the Moon's signal.

"RC3, RC3—"

There he was.

"Hartigan talking. Monthly report."

"All right, Hartigan."

A hurried fretful voice. Come on, Moon; report that, as always, nothing has happened.

"Lunar conditions the same," said Hartigan. "No ships have put in, or have reported themselves as being in distress. The hangar is in good shape, with no leaks."

"Right," said Stacey, in the voice of a busy man. "Supplies?"

"You might send up a blonde."

"Be serious, please. Supplies?"

"I need some new power bulbs."

"I'll send them on the next ship. Nothing irregular to report?"

Hartigan hesitated.

On the floor of the main airlock was a mound of burned, bluish mineral substance giving no indication whatever that it had once possessed outlandish, incredible life. In the walls of the hangar, at the base were half a dozen new dents, but ricocheting meteors might have made those. The meteoric shell from which this bizarre animal had come had been devoured, so even that was not left for investigation.

He remembered the report of the board of science on Stuyvesant.

"Therefore, in our judgment, Benjamin Stuyvesant suffered from hallucination—"

He would have liked to help Stuyvesant. But on the other hand Stuyvesant had a job with a second-hand space-suit store now, and was getting along pretty well in spite of Spaceways' dismissal.

"Nothing irregular to report?" repeated Stacey.

Hartigan stared, with one eyebrow sardonically raised, at the plump brunette on the pin *Radio Gazette* cover pasted to the wall. She stared coyly back over a bare shoulder.

"Nothing irregular to report," Hartigan said steadily.

(((((**Hank Davis**)))))

When an editor includes a story of his own in a book (a possibly disreputable but nonetheless common practice), a certain diffidence accompanied by a bit of foot-shuffling is in order, as when one is seen in public doing something legal but not quite respectable. So, I'll just mention that this turned out as a combination of Keith Laumer and H.P. Lovecraft, two writers who loom huge in my mental landscape. Of course, Laumer would have done it better, at least before his stroke, and while Lovecraft appreciated what he called "the interplanetary story" (as when he heaped praise on C.L. Moore's "Shambleau"), he never showed any interest in writing such yarns himself. Maybe if his beloved Providence had established a colony on another planet . . .

Hank Davis is an editor emeritus at Baen Books. While a naïve youth in the early 1950s (yes, he's *old*!), he was led astray by sf comic books, and then by A. E. van Vogt's *Slan*, which he read in the Summer 1952 issue of *Fantastic Story Quarterly* while in the second grade, sealing his fate. He has had stories published mumble-mumble years ago in *Analog*, *If*, *F&SF*, and Damon Knight's *Orbit* anthology series. (There was also a story sold to *The Last Dangerous Visions*, but let's not go there.) A native of Kentucky, he currently lives in North Carolina to avoid a long commute to the Baen office.

(((((VISITING SHADOW)))))

Hank Davis

"Yog-Sothoth knows the gate . . . He knows where the Old Ones broke through of old, and where They shall break through again . . . and why no one can behold Them as They tread. . . . Their hand is at your throats, yet ye see Them not; and Their habitation is even one with your guarded threshold."

—from *The Necronomicon*,
quoted in "The Dunwich Horror" by H.P. Lovecraft

If the planet hadn't reminded me so much of Earth, they might not have gotten me. But it did. And they did. I was being stupid, of course.

The Shadow wasn't there at the time, or I don't know what might have happened. Maybe nothing different. But it hadn't been at the edge of my vision for a couple of days, so I took a chance, docked the *Dutchman* at the Tucker Station at the L5 point, and stepped through the airlock.

I don't know where the thing goes when it's away, I don't know what it is, and I don't know why it . . . *takes* . . . other people, but not me. So far.

I wasn't going down to the planet, of course. Even if it hadn't been blue with white clouds, like Earth, and the clouds hid the shapes of the continents enough so that, if I didn't look too close, it might be Earth. I didn't know what the Shadow might do if it were on a planet. Maybe

I shouldn't have been on the space station. But it was between shifts and all the refreshments and amenities were closed. I saw that nobody else was in the observation dome for tourists and business types passing through, and went on in. It had a striking view of the Earthlike planet the station orbited.

It wasn't Earth, of course. I never go within a hundred lights of Earth.

It turned out that I shouldn't have gone within a hundred lights of this station, either. The back of my neck was itching, and I had a feeling somebody was watching me. Of course, I often have that feeling, but this didn't feel like the Shadow.

I turned around quickly. They had moved very quietly, which meant they were professionals. There were five of them, two women and three men, and they had surrounded me before I got the idea anybody was there. "Nice view," I said.

"You need to come with us," the beefiest of the bunch said. "Someone wants to have a talk with you."

They were wearing ordinary clothes, but I had the feeling they were also used to wearing uniforms. Maybe Terran Fleet uniforms. I had thought that after half a century, the Fleet would have stopped looking for me, but maybe I had underestimated their singlemindedness.

Or they might be cops, investigating a string of mysterious disappearances scattered across this arm of the Galaxy. I hadn't caused any of the disappearances—directly—but I was always there when they happened.

"Let's see some I.D.," I said. "And a warrant, if you're cops. I'll enjoy the view some more while you're looking for them," I said, and turned back to the planet that wasn't Earth, hanging in the blackness. And I kept turning, fast, but not fast enough. I got beefy boy, whom I took for the leader, in his midsection, but my hand barely clipped the one to his right on his ear, not what I was aiming for. I must have been out of practice.

Suddenly there was something barely noticeable, barely visible out of the corner of my eye, and then one of the women wasn't there anymore. Not entirely, anyway. As usual, there were pieces of her, falling to the floor in the low gravity of the station, along with her gun, but most of her had disappeared.

I thought that might distract them long enough for me to get the falling gun. I was wrong. The other three of them shot me, simultaneously as far as I could tell, three stunbeams converging on me while I was diving for the gun. I don't know how close I came to it, because I didn't know anything anymore, and that situation lasted for a long time. I was out before I even had time to regret they weren't shooting anything lethal. But maybe that wouldn't have worked. I've tried suicide and it doesn't work.

They may have shot me more than once, from the way I felt when I finally came out of it. I can't really blame them. They didn't know what had suddenly, terribly happened to one of them, and they were scared. Of course, I knew what had happened, and I was scared, too. Particularly since I didn't know *why* it happened, either this time or the many other times . . .

I knew Colonel Oberst didn't like me, but I didn't think he disliked me enough to get me killed. That might have been a mistake. He had called me into his office inside the officer's dome and offered me a smoke and a drink. That should have made me worry; but I wasn't worrying because I was a shorttimer. One more week, and I'd be heading back to Earth and my discharge from the Fleet. Marrying Angie, with a job as a civilian pilot lined up. Buzzing around the Solar System like an electron in a nanocircuit: nice, safe, routine. What could happen now?

"Kelly, I need a volunteer, and I think you're the best bet."

I had turned down the smoke, and now I wished I had turned down the drink. Uh-oh.

"Not the gate, I assume, sir?"

"Actually, it is the gate. The rats came back all right, and so did the monkey yesterday. We need a man to go."

We? This wasn't even the Fleet's job. We were on the outermost moon of a gas giant that didn't even have a name, just a number, to provide security for the scientists who were investigating the gate. The science guys were working for the Terran government, or else we wouldn't have been there, but the gate was their problem. Unless somebody ordered us to blow it up—but nobody was sure that was possible. Attempts to get samples from the gate's material for analysis hadn't worked. I'd heard one of the scientists saying it was like trying to get a sliver off of a endurosteel wall with only a modeling clay chisel to work with.

"Thank you for your confidence in me, sir, but I respectfully decline. I'm leaving in a week and—"

"I know, going back to Earth and getting married. It'd be a shame if you couldn't leave because of a problem with paperwork. After all, this has been determined to be a Priority One mission—one of the few signs of a technology of nonhuman origin that's more advanced than we or any of our e.t. allies have. In a P-1 mission, the commanding officer has considerable leeway in determining when critical personnel can be released. You might be in for the duration."

"Sir, I still decline, and I'll make a formal protest—"

"That's your right. Of course formal protests can take a long time to work through the legal plumbing. And in the meantime, your new job might not be there anymore. In fact, there might not be any other job openings for some time."

He wasn't being subtle. His brother was very high up in the Terran government, though nobody in the media or the government seemed to have any idea just exactly what Patrick Oberst's job was. He was probably the reason that Colonel Oberst was here in a nice safe assignment, no obvious dangers, nobody shooting at him, and if the mystery of the gate was solved on Oberst's watch it might mean at least one star on his shoulder. It'd look good on his resume when he retired and ran for office, keeping the running of the Terran government in the family. If either of the brothers Oberst wanted to get me blackballed from everywhere I might look for a piloting job . . .

"Let's hear it, sir." I wasn't saying "yes," yet. "What do I do that a monkey can't?"

His face had gotten hard, but now it eased up. Except for his eyes. They never eased up. "You know the story here, of course."

I knew the story. An expedition had found something that looked artificial: an arch about thirty feet high and twenty-five wide made of some white material which they couldn't identify, with what they thought was a jet black surface on one side, and a flat surface made of the same unidentifiable white material on the other. The black side turned out not to be solid. It was pure ebony blackness, not reflecting anything, and instruments poked into it went through like it was a vacuum, and came back apparently unaffected. Except that no information came back from them while they were on the other side of the black surface. Telemetry didn't transmit. Cameras and other gizmos on rods were poked through with wires leading back outside, but they didn't produce any info. Nothing came back on the wires. But the cameras, radars, thermometers, barometers, geigers, and so on, worked fine once they were back on our side of the black surface. And of course, the rods were long enough that they should have been stopped by the solid other side of the gate, but nothing stopped them. They apparently went—somewhere else.

So, they started calling it a "gate," and more equipment and more scientists were sent to the moon, along with Fleet personnel, including me, fully armed, in case somebody or something unfriendly came *out* of the gate. The few members of the original expedition had been housed in their ship when they weren't investigating. Now, the gate had several domes, including separate ones for the officers and the NCOs and enlisted men. So far, the military personnel had nothing much to do.

I wish it had stayed that way.

"You remember that they tried all sorts of recording devices, putting them through the gate, and they came out fine, except that nothing had been recorded. They even tried still photographs. With chemical film. God! I didn't know such things still existed. Then they tried putting a cage of lab rats through, and they came back perfectly healthy."

I was beginning to see where this was going . . .

". . . and the monkey came back fine. So now they have a chair big enough for a human, and they need somebody to sit in it while it's pushed through the gate. How about it, Lieutenant? It'll look good on your record. Volunteering for a dangerous mission. Maybe even a medal."

Nobody ever needs volunteers for a *safe* mission, I thought. Maybe I'd come through it all right, and be on my way in a week. Looked like I didn't have much choice.

"Okay, sir. Got any more bourbon?"

No more bourbon, as it happened. The scientists weren't happy about my having had even one shot. They didn't know what effect it might have on the other side of the gate. So I put on my pressure suit, and they strapped me into a plastic chair they'd taken out of the day room, removed the legs, added straps, and bolted it to a girder that was welded to the front of a deuce and a half vactrac. I could feel the vibrations of the tractor conducted through the girder behind me, and the gate got closer and closer, and I tried not to think of it as a mouth. A wide open mouth. The unreflecting black surface got closer, and I went through it with no resistance . . .

. . . and the next thing I remember was *walking* back out through the gate. I was wondering where the chair and the vactrac had gone, then I wondered why troops in pressure suits were running toward me, with their guns aimed in my direction. But I wasn't the complete center of attention. Several of the scientists were staring past me. So I turned around and saw that the black surface was gone. This side of the gate now looked like the opposite side. Solid. Then, Oberst came bouncing over in the low gravity. My radio was still on and I heard him yelling, "Where the hell were you? What did you do while you were gone?"

"What do you mean?" I said. "I haven't been gone more than a couple of seconds."

"How's your oxygen?" one of the scientists said.

I checked the digital readouts inside the helmet, and said, "It's fine. Nearly full tanks."

"You've been gone nearly two days," he said.

All this time, I had been noticing something odd. I once had an eye infection and my right eye had to be bandaged over for a couple of weeks. During that time, I kept looking to my right, because it was like a shadow was on my right side, and I kept reflexively turning to see what was making the shadow.

There was nothing covering either eye right now, but I kept seeing—almost seeing—something like a shadow, at first on my right, then on my left. I kept turning, but couldn't see anything casting a shadow. Then the part about how long I had been gone sank in: nearly two days. And I only had an eighteen-hour oxygen supply.

I should have been dead. But if the readouts were right, I hadn't consumed a noticeable amount of oxygen at all.

"Let's get to my office," Oberst said, and headed toward the officer's dome.

I followed, feeling very confused. Again, I thought I saw a shadow on my left side, but when I turned my head in the helmet, there was nothing close enough to me to cast a shadow.

Out of the suit, I needed a drink but decided not to ask Oberst for bourbon.

"That's ridiculous! You were gone for forty-six hours and thirteen minutes. You must have gotten your tanks refilled somewhere."

"Sir, I don't remember being in there for any time at all," I said. "The chair went through the black whatever-it-is . . ."

"Whatever-it-*was*. It's gone now. What did you do to turn it off?"

I was getting very annoyed. A drink probably wouldn't have helped. At least I was two days' closer to being a Proud Friggin' Civilian again. "Once again, sir, the chair put me through it, and the next thing I remember was walking out through it, on my own feet. What happened to the chair?"

"As per the plan, after one minute the tractor pulled you out again. Or pulled the chair out again. You weren't in it and the straps hadn't been unbuckled. What are you hiding, Kelly?"

Then his face got a look that told me he had just had an idea. I was was sure I wouldn't like it. I was right.

"If you *are* Kelly? Maybe I should put you in the brig until they can give you a full physical." He stood up, and I stood up, and I don't know if that's what caused it. I was very upset, and I still don't know if *that* caused it. But suddenly he was staring at my right and his eyes were very wide. And the shadow that was visible out of the corner of my eye was where he was staring as he pulled his gun from its holster. Then he was gone. Most of him.

There were pieces of his uniform scattered around his office, and little pieces of the colonel, and puddles of what looked like blood in unlikely places. But most of the colonel was gone.

They hadn't let me take a gun on the mission through the gate, so I didn't have mine, but Oberst's gun was on the floor. I moved as fast as I could in the low gravity and grabbed it up. Then I turned around. Several times. But I was apparently alone in the office. I didn't even see the shadow.

I thought about calling for help. Then I wondered which would be worse, being examined, maybe dissected, to see if I was really human—Oberst wouldn't be the only one to get that idea—or put on trial for Oberst's murder. There was enough of Oberst left to be identified, and I was the only one with him in his office when it happened. Whatever had happened.

On second thought, I probably wouldn't get a trial. One of the crown princes of the Oberst family was dead and I was the only fall guy around. I'd probably just disappear, unless I disappeared on my own.

Then I thought I saw the shadow again. Or Shadow—I wasn't thinking of it as capitalized yet, but I soon would. I turned quickly and aimed the gun, but there was nothing there.

Something had come through the gate with me. It was dangerous. Maybe it would attack me next, but if I went back to Earth—if they *let* me go back to Earth—it might attack someone else. Angie . . .

I left the office, saw there was nobody in sight, and went to get my pressure suit. On the way, Dr. Haber, one of the scientists, saw me and said, "Lieutenant Kelly, is it true you remember nothing of the time you were on the other side of the gate? We need to talk—"

"Right, Doctor. But I need to get something to eat first," I brushed him off.

"Hmmm, I don't know if you should eat anything until we've made an examina—"

"Later, please. I also need to use the latrine."

"Maybe we should have samples—"

I managed to get away from him without either stunning or cold-cocking him. Once I was back in my pressure suit, I headed for the launch pads, and opened the hatch to the ship I had piloted there from Earth. There shouldn't be anybody aboard, and there wasn't. Nobody would have any reason to steal a ship.

Except me.

I strapped in and again thought about heading for Earth. If I had left the thing behind—then I saw the Shadow again out of the corner of my eye, in the control room.

Eventually, I would quit turning my head, trying to see it clearly. There was never anything there. And there was nothing causing a shadow this time, either. But it was on the ship with me. Suppose I went back to Earth with the thing on board, and once it got there it reproduced? Maybe it could divide like an amoeba. Lots of little shadow-things swarming across the Earth.

I couldn't go back to Earth yet—maybe not ever.

I took off and ignored the anxious voices coming from the audio. Once I was far enough away, I'd set a course. My plans were vague, but I had to go somewhere to get supplies. The ship's atomic generator could run the reactionless drive and the hyperwarp engines for years, but I wasn't that well-supplied. I didn't guess then that I would keep needing supplies for a very long time.

Besides, I had to get rid of the Fleet ship. I knew about some independent and not particularly ethical colonies where I could turn it into currency, enough to get a smaller and less conspicuous ship and plenty of supplies. When I needed more currency, I could make some hauling small cargoes. But no passengers. Never any passengers.

Maybe I could get rid of my Shadow somehow. Or maybe it would get rid of me. But I was going to keep it away from Earth. And Angie. Oh, Angie . . .

Selling the Fleet ship turned out to be harder than I had expected. I wasn't going to land on the planet, and they wouldn't let me near the space station, but I couldn't blame them since I was piloting a fully-armed Fleet ship, nuke torpedoes and all. I asked the two in the ship that rendezvoused with me to stay in their ship. "Sure," one of them said from the vision screen, "we'll stay here and you'll come over and join us."

Somehow the old joke, "Why, are you coming apart?" didn't seem very funny. We argued for a while, but I finally went across the connecting tube. The two had guns trained on me, of course.

"So, you've deserted the Fleet and you want to sell that ship. Selling stolen goods, eh?" said the fat one. "You think we're pirates, maybe?"

I'd heard they didn't like to be called pirates. "No," I said, "just businessmen, trying to make a profit. Like I'm trying to make a deal."

The tall, bald one said, "Oh, I think you think we're pirates. You also think pirates are stupid, to believe a story like yours. I think right after we buy the ship, more Fleet ships'll show up, accuse us of stealing Terran government property and illegal weapons, and use that as an excuse for taking over the colony. Nobody'll care. After all, we're just pirates."

I was wondering if they were going to shoot me. I was a little surprised to find that I didn't much care. But only a little. I think they saw that and it made them nervous.

"Okay, Fleet boy," fat said, "let's take you to the station and find out what you're really up to." Then he noticed that the bald one wasn't there anymore. Most of him wasn't there.

"What the hell—" was what he said before I slugged him. Maybe I did care if he shot me. But not much.

Back in my stolen ship, I headed for another rogue colony and wondered how big the Shadow was. I had gone from one ship to another through a connecting tube barely big enough for me to stand up in. Maybe it hadn't needed the tube.

Much the same thing happened at my next stop. Maybe the dialogue was a little different. I had hoped I might have left the Shadow behind in the other ship, but hadn't hoped very hard.

I eventually found a buyer, then bought a smaller ship, stocked it with supplies, and headed outsystem, not caring where. Before that, the woman I bought the ship from asked me if I wanted a new name on the hull. I was about to say, "No," but I thought of something.

"Name it *Dutchman*," I said. As in *Flying Dutchman*, I thought. I was going to keep flying for a long time, I thought. But I didn't suspect then how long that would be. And how many other people would disappear at other stops.

After a while, I started feeling sorry for the occasional, ah, *businessmen* who stopped me and tried to take over *Dutchman*. There were a lot of them. Maybe they kept the Shadow entertained, if briefly.

There was darkness, and it lasted forever, then it began to fade as I noticed that someone had a major headache. Then I realized it was me. I was in a chair, and almost expected to see that black gate coming toward me, then remembered that was a long time ago, in a different chair. I wasn't strapped in as before, but I couldn't move. I was in a flexible but firm cocoon of some kind of foamy-looking material, and I wasn't wearing any clothes under it. I was looking at another man in a similar cocoon, then I woke up a little more and decided the other man was me. I looked like hell.

I wasn't looking in a mirror, though. I could see a couple of men with guns watching me through the semi-transparent reflection. I was on the other side of a transparent barrier.

One of them spoke into a wrist buzzer, and the pair quickly had company. I recognized four of them. My pals from the Tucker Station. The survivors from the station.

They stood there pointing guns in my general direction, then a screen I hadn't noticed until just then lit up, and an old man looked at me. If he was happy to see me, he hid it well. Then his eyes got even harder, and I thought it must be Colonel Oberst's father from the family resemblance. Another part of my aching brain woke up and I remembered that was over fifty years ago, and the Colonel's father was elderly even then, judging from newsflash pics of him which I'd seen.

"Pat Oberst?" I was thinking, then realized I'd said it out loud. The Colonel had always referred to his brother as Pat, and I had repeated his example, without thinking. I was coming out of the stunner-induced fog, but not fast enough.

There was a pause, indicating that he was a couple of light

seconds away, then, "My father and mother called me Pat," the man on the screen said, "and they're dead. My brother also called me Pat, but you murdered him somehow. To everyone still living, I'm Mr. Patrick Oberst, or just Mr. Oberst. But you're an exception, Mr. Kelly. How many languages do you speak?"

It was a crazy question, but my brain was still trying to come out of the fog, so I answered in detail, "One fluently, two others good enough for conversation, and a little of several more." Then I thought maybe I should be careful about answering questions.

"You probably know several words for death, then. And several for pain. I'll answer to all of them. And you'll have a choice of languages to scream in, Mr. Kelly." He took another look at me and seemed to find yet another reason to dislike me. "Votara, are you sure this is the right man. He looks like his photograph—too much like his photograph. He looks decades younger than he should be."

Maybe it was because of the Shadow, but I didn't seem to be aging much as the years passed. Maybe I wasn't aging at all, but there was no way I would go to a medtech to find out. I didn't seem to ever get sick, either. Maybe I'd live forever, just me and my pet monster, oh joy! Or maybe I was the pet.

"Positive, sir," said one of the women. "Fingerprints, retinas, DNA, brainechoes all match. If he isn't the right James Kelly, he's a perfect clone."

"You become more interesting, Mr. Kelly. I owe you for murdering my brother, but I was going to offer you an easier death than I would otherwise demand if you turned over the alien weapon you brought back through the gate and used to kill him. But if you also have a way of suspending or significantly slowing the aging process, and will share the secret, I might let you depart the world of the living with hardly any screaming at all. An hour or two at most."

"I wish I could hand them both over to you, but you wouldn't like the side effects." Then I woke up enough to realize what the slight time lag meant. "Where *are* you?" I yelled.

After a pause of two or three seconds, he said, "No need to shout, Mr. Kelly. Save your lungs for what you'll need them for very soon.

Why do you want to know where I am? I'm certainly out of your reach."

I looked more closely at the screen. He was sitting behind a huge polished desk. "You're in an office," I said. "Where is it?"

"A lot of people would give a lot to know that, Mr. Kelly. Just as I want to know where that alien weapon you've been using is hidden."

"Are you on *Earth*?"

He was not amused. "I suppose it's safe to tell you that I'm on Earth. Now it's your turn to answer questions . . ."

I was on the edge of panic. "This ship is in orbit around the Earth, isn't it? You've got to move it! Get it far from Earth immediately!"

The pause before he answered gave the thugs watching me time to look uneasy and grip their weapons more tightly. This time most of the weapons were lethal. I wondered if they could shoot through the transparent barrier.

Oberst spoke again, "Mr. Kelly, why do you want to get away from Earth? I doubt that even your unknown weapon can make the whole planet explode."

Forget about being on the edge of panic. I was neck-deep in it and trying to stay afloat. If they landed the ship, the Shadow would be loose on Earth. Maybe that was what it had been waiting for.

Then I realized that one of the thugs had left my sight while I was yelling, and was now returning with someone else. A woman. And then I saw her face—

She had a strip of tape over her mouth, but even so she looked like Angie. But it couldn't be Angie, because she looked like Angie had looked fifty years ago. For a wild second I wondered if the Shadow had somehow kept Angie from aging too. I didn't know what the thing was capable of doing . . .

Then my memory did a rewind and playback. I realized that Oberst had said, "Please bring in Ms. Maxwell now, Votara."

I was back in realtime, whatever "real" meant anymore, and Oberst said, "May I introduce Ms. Callie Maxwell? Ms. Maxwell, this is James Kelly, and he is reacting much the way I expected upon noticing your close resemblance to his former fiancée. And, no, Mr.

Kelly, I'm not planning on torturing her in hopes that the resemblance would make you disclose your secrets. Instead, I'm betting that if you somehow have the weapon concealed on your person, her resemblance to Angela Graham Hanson will keep you from using it on her. And perhaps the fact that she isn't here voluntarily will also make you hesitate."

Hanson! So she had married someone else. After that sank in, I wondered why Callie Maxwell was here . . .

"I'm guessing that you're wondering why she's here," he said.

Check.

"And possibly you're wondering if your former fiancée is in danger from me."

Double check.

"It happens that she is beyond my, or anyone's reach. She died fourteen years ago in a flyer collision. I had people watching her for long before that in case you tried to make contact with her, so they were on the spot quickly to get her out of the wreckage and to a hospital, but she was dead on arrival. I did not cause the accident. She was no use to me dead. Neither is Ms. Maxwell, so I hope you're not going to wreak carnage in the ship."

I was beginning to think that I was going to die since I couldn't give Oberst the secret of a weapon I didn't have. Or an anti-aging secret. If I died, what would happen to the Shadow. Would it find a new—host, pet, anchor, whatever I was to it? And maybe switch to someone else on the ship. Someone who would go back to Earth. Maybe what I had feared for five decades would happen. I had stayed away from planets because maybe if the Shadow was on a planet it would start a brood of little Shadows. And we were close to Earth . . .

I noticed that Maxwell no longer had handcuffs on, but she still had the tape over her mouth. She was working a little keypad, which must have been on a direct line to Oberst because he suddenly said, "Ms. Maxwell, are you making all this up? An invisible—well. There are plenty of other—ah, you can easily be replaced, and not pleasantly at all. If you thought being abducted was upsetting, understand that much worse can happen."

I realized what word he had almost said. She was a telepath.

"What you are sending is ridiculous," Oberst said. "What and where is his weapon?"

And words began to appear to me, as if written on the inside of my eyelids in luminous paint.

HE HAS A BOMB ON THIS SHIP. HE CAN SET IT OFF BY A SWITCH UNDER HIS DESK.

I'd heard about this, but never seen it before. Most telepaths can only receive. A few can send, making the receiver "hear" a silent voice. But others can send pictures—including pictures of words. Which was what she was doing.

I wondered if the bomb could kill the Shadow. I often wondered if *anything* could kill the Shadow. If the ship were blown up—but was the bomb nuclear or just chemical?

CHEMICAL.

Of course, she was following my thoughts. Which were not happy. A chemical bomb would destroy the ship and kill me and everyone on it—every *human* on it—but a nuke might have a better chance of destroying the Shadow.

Then I realized why they had put tape over her mouth.

THEY BROUGHT ME ABOARD UNCONSCIOUS.

Because he didn't want the crew to know— "There's a bomb on board the ship," I said, "and Oberst can set it off by a switch under his desk."

Oberst's thugs were already uneasy, and that news really stirred them up. "Is that true, Mr. Oberst?" one of them said.

"Be sensible! Why would I blow up Mr. Kelly now that I finally have him?"

BECAUSE HE DIDN'T KNOW WHAT YOU COULD DO, EVEN IMMOBILIZED. AND NOW THAT HE'S STARTING TO BELIEVE ABOUT THE SHADOW—

I had been repeating what she had sent to me aloud, as fast as she sent it, but then she stopped and I stopped.

One of the thugs in the back wasn't there any more, and little unpleasant remnants were falling to the deck. Maxwell had been looking at me, but she had caught my stare and turned around.

"Look behind you," I yelled. "You're all in danger."

They spun around with their guns aimed toward the back of the ship. Of course they saw no possible target.

Long ago, I had wondered if the Shadow knew what guns were. And if guns could hurt it. Maybe they couldn't, maybe it just didn't like having the things pointed at it. But it must have known what a gun was.

It didn't bother with its usual disappearing act. All the bodies were still there, on the deck, but in bloody pieces. Maxwell hadn't been hurt. Well, she hadn't been *physically* injured. Maybe I should have warned her to close her eyes—not because of the carnage—but I didn't expect what had happened.

I was hoping that Oberst was ready with that switch, and wishing that he had put a nuke on board, but when I looked at the screen, Oberst was gone, except for the usual human blood and confetti. Then the screen went blank.

Other things were gone. I was no longer in a cocoon, and there was no longer a transparent barrier blocking me off from the ship.

I ran forward to the control room, planning to get far away from Earth as quickly as possible, but not expecting that to do any good. Obviously, the Shadow could travel to Earth and back in a fraction of a second, as it had just demonstrated. Then I realized that it could do more than that, when I recognized the blue planet ahead of the ship. It wasn't Earth. And the Tucker space station was maybe half a kilometer from the ship. I could see where my battered old *Dutchman* was, docked at the station.

I had thought I was keeping the thing away from Earth. Some protector I had made. It could have gone there anytime, if it had known where to go. And it knew now.

I went back to see about Callie Maxwell, wondering if I ought to find some clothes first. She was sitting on the deck, starting at the bodies, looking as if she needed to cry, but couldn't, saying softly, repeatedly, "I saw it. I saw it."

In half a century, I had never seen it. It was just a shadow seen out of the corner of my eye. Even though its victims always reacted as if they had seen something coming at them, something terrifying, still I had wondered if it had any real form. I knew now that it did.

Maxwell had seen it, and she had been sending images to me when she saw it, so I saw it too. I wish I hadn't.

In the last five decades, I had accessed a lot of databases, even checking fiction, trying to see if something like the Shadow had been encountered before. One of the first things I turned up was a fictional character, from even before the Moon had been reached, called the Shadow, who could hide in darkness, or turn invisible—the text versions differed from the audio versions—but my Shadow didn't seem to have much else in common with Lamont Cranston. Then another ancient story called "The Shadow Over Innsmouth" turned up, not only pre-spaceflight, but pre-atomic, and that led me to reading other material by the same author. I also found examples of critics ridiculing him for writing stories of *things* which were not only indescribable, but so horrible that those who saw them went mad.

Mr. Lovecraft, you really knew what you were talking about. I've seen it and I wish I could go mad. Or maybe I did a long time ago . . .

The ship had a lifeboat, so I could set the ship's controls on timer to take it on a long orbit out to the edge of the system, while we left in the lifeboat. No one would find it, or the bodies on board, for a long time.

As we headed for my ship, I asked Callie, "Are you going to be all right?"

She gave me a look that would make liquid helium look warm. "I've seen it," she said again.

I wanted to keep quiet, but I had to find out what she was going to do. "We're a long way from Earth," I said. "Do you need funds to get home?"

"He was a fool," she said. She picked up that I was worried about her mental state, because next she said, "Oberst was a fool. He didn't know how good I was. How much I picked up from his thoughts. I know his secret account numbers and I.D. codes. With them, I'm a billionaire. I can get home. Even better, I can afford the memory wipe treatment. Wipe out the last few days. I hope it will work."

Hank Davis

Then she started again, saying "I saw it," a few more times, until she turned to me again and said, "I know what you're looking for, and I know where it is."

I hoped I knew what she meant, but I just said, "Where what is?"

"Oberst had people looking for another gate. They found one a week ago. It's located at—" and she read off numbers which meant nothing to her, but which I memorized. Later, I'd punch them into my ship's computer.

"Once we dock with my ship, you can go into the station," I said. Then I almost said, "Will you be all right?" but didn't because it was a stupid question. But it was also a stupid thought, and of course she had read it without my saying anything.

"Stop saying that!" she said. "Stop *thinking* it."

She wouldn't be all right ever again, unless the memory wipe treatment worked. I hoped it would.

I saw it, too.

I hoped that Oberst didn't have any more of his thugs guarding the other gate. I hoped it for their sake. It doesn't seem to want me to be hurt.

And if the gate is there, maybe it would like to go home. If "like" or "want" have any meaning to it. Even if it isn't homesick, maybe it'll follow me, as it's been doing for half a century, when I walk through the gate to whatever's on the other side.

And stay there.

((((Clark Ashton Smith))))

Here's another gem from the heyday of the pulps, originally appearing in the October, 1932 *Wonder Stories* under a title not of the author's choosing, "Master of the Asteroid." The space explorer was trapped in his wrecked ship on an asteroid which was large enough to hold a thin atmosphere and support a host of odd beings who seemed to think the crashed explorer was a god. Perhaps he should have wondered if they had mistaken him for someone—or something—else . . .

Clark Ashton Smith (1893-1961), a poet, sculptor, and painter, was also a prolific author of sf, fantasy, and horror stories, writing close to 300 short stories. He was a star contributor to the great fantasy-horror pulp, *Weird Tales*, where his stories appeared alongside those of such other luminaries as H.P. Lovecraft (with whom Smith carried on a long and voluminous correspondence), Robert E. Howard, and Seabury Quinn. He also wrote science fiction stories, including such standout classics as "The City of the Singing Flame" and its sequel, "Beyond the Singing Flame." Some of his sf tales had a horror slant, and when they appeared in Hugo Gernsback's *Wonder Stories* they were apparently a bit too intense for the editor, who often published them with cuts to make them less horrific. Thanks to William A. Dorman and Scott Connors, this is the version as Smith originally wrote it, with no cuts and all shivers intact.

THE GOD OF THE
(((((ASTEROID)))))

Clark Ashton Smith

Man's conquest of the interplanetary gulfs has been fraught with many tragedies. Vessel after vessel, like a venturous mote, has disappeared in the infinite—and has not returned. Inevitably, for the most part, the lost explorers have left no record of their fate. Their ships have flared as unknown meteors through the atmosphere of the further planets, to fall like shapeless metal cinders on a never-visited terrain; or have become the dead, frozen satellites of other worlds or moons. A few, perhaps, among the unreturning fliers, have succeeded in landing somewhere, and their crews have perished immediately, or survived for a little while amid the inconceivably hostile environment of a cosmos not designed for men.

In later years, with the progress of exploration, more than one of the early derelicts has been descried, following its solitary orbit; and the wrecks of others have been found on ultra-terrene shores. Occasionally—not often—it has been possible to reconstruct the details of the lone, remote disaster. Sometimes, in a fused and twisted hull, a log or record has been preserved intact. Among others, there is the case of the *Selenite*, the first known rocket-ship to dare the zone of the asteroids.

At the time of its disappearance, fifty years ago, in 1980, a dozen voyages had been made to Mars, and a rocket-base had been established in Syrtis Major, with a small permanent colony of terrestrials, all of whom were trained scientists as well as men of uncommon hardihood and physical stamina.

The effects of the Martian climate, and the utter alienation from familiar conditions, as might have been expected, were extremely trying and even disastrous. There was an unremitting struggle with deadly or pestiferous bacteria new to science, a perpetual assailment by dangerous radiations of soil and air and sun. The lessened gravity played its part also, in contributing to curious and profound disturbances of metabolism. The worst effects were nervous and mental. Queer, irrational animosities, manias or phobias never classified by alienists, began to develop among the personnel at the rocket-base.

Violent quarrels broke out between men who were normally controlled and urbane. The party, numbering fifteen in all, soon divided into several cliques, one against the others; and this morbid antagonism led at times to actual fighting and even bloodshed.

One of the cliques consisted of three men, Roger Colt, Phil Gershom and Edmond Beverly. These three, through banding together in a curious fashion, became intolerably antisocial toward all the others. It would seem that they must have gone close to the borderline of insanity, and were subject to actual delusions. At any rate, they conceived the idea that Mars, with its fifteen earth-men, was entirely too crowded. Voicing this idea in a most offensive and belligerent manner, they also began to hint their intention of faring even further afield in space.

Their hints were not taken seriously by the others, since a crew of three was insufficient for the proper manning of even the lightest rocket-vessel used at that time. Colt, Gershom, and Beverly had no difficulty at all in stealing the *Selenite*, the smaller of the two ships then reposing at the Syrtis Major base. Their fellow-colonists were aroused one night by the cannon-like roar of the discharging tubes, and emerged from their huts of sheet-iron in time to see the vessel departing in a fiery streak toward Jupiter.

No attempt was made to follow it; but the incident helped to sober the remaining twelve and to calm their unnatural animosities. It was believed, from certain remarks that the malcontents had let drop, that their particular objective was Ganymede or Europa, both of which were thought to possess an atmosphere suitable for human respiration. It seemed very doubtful, however, that they could pass the perilous belt of the asteroids. Apart from the difficulty of steering a course amid these innumerable, far-strewn bodies, the *Selenite* was not fuelled or provisioned for a voyage of such length. Gershom, Colt and Beverly, in their mad haste to quit the company of the others, had forgotten to calculate the actual necessities of their proposed voyage, and had wholly overlooked its dangers.

After that departing flash on the Martian skies, the *Selenite* was not seen again; and its fate remained a mystery for thirty years. Then, on tiny, remote Phocea, its dented wreck was found by the Holdane expedition to the asteroids.

Phocea, at the time of the expedition's visit, was in aphelion. Like others of the planetoids, it was discovered to possess a rare atmosphere, too thin for human breathing. Both hemispheres were covered with thin snow; and lying amid this snow, the *Selenite* was sighted by the explorers as they circled about the little world.

Much interest prevailed, for the shape of the partially bare mound was plainly recognizable and not to be confused with the surrounding rocks. Holdane ordered a landing, and several men in space-suits proceeded to examine the wreck. They soon identified it as the long-missing *Selenite*.

Peering in through one of the thick, unbreakable neo-crystal ports, they met the eyeless gaze of a human skeleton, which had fallen forward against the slanting, overhanging wall. It seemed to grin a sardonic welcome. The vessel's hull was partly buried in the stony soil, and had been crumpled and even slightly fused, though not broken, by its plunge. The manhole lid was so thoroughly jammed and soldered that it was impossible to effect an entrance without the use of a cutting-torch.

Enormous, withered, cryptogamous plants with the habit of vines, that crumbled at a touch, were clinging to the hull and the adjacent rocks. In the light snow beneath the skeleton-guarded port, a number of sharded bodies were lying, which proved to be those of tall insect forms, like giant *phasmidae*. From the posture and arrangement of their lank, pipy members, longer than those of a man, it seemed that they had walked erect. They were unimaginably grotesque, and their composition, due to the almost non-existent gravity, was fantastically porous and insubstantial. Many more bodies, of a similar type, were afterwards found on other portions of the planetoid; but no living thing was discovered. All life, it was plain, had perished in the trans-arctic winter of Phocea's aphelion.

When the *Selenite* had been entered, the party learned, from a sort of log or notebook found on the floor, that the skeleton was all that remained of Edmond Beverly. There was no trace of his two companions; but the log, on examination, proved to contain a record of their fate as well as the subsequent adventures of Beverly almost to the very moment of his own death from a doubtful, unexplained cause.

The tale was a strange and tragic one. Beverly, it would seem, had written it day by day, after the departure from Syrtis Major, in an effort to retain a semblance of morale and mental coherence amid the black alienation and disorientation of infinitude. I transcribe it herewith, omitting only the earlier passages, which were full of unimportant details and personal animadversions. The first entries were all dated, and Beverly had made an heroic attempt to measure and mark off the seasonless night of the void in terms of earthly time. But after the disastrous landing on Phocea, he had abandoned this; and the actual length of time covered by his entries can only be conjectured.

THE LOG

Sept. 10th. Mars is only a pale-red star through our rear ports; and according to my calculations we will soon approach the orbit of the nearer asteroids. Jupiter and its system of moons are seemingly as far off as ever, like beacons on the unattainable shore of immensity. More even than at first, I feel that dreadful, suffocating illusion, which accompanies ether-travel, of being perfectly stationary in a static void.

Gershom, however, complains of a disturbance of equilibrium, with much vertigo and a frequent sense of falling, as if the vessel were sinking beneath him through bottomless space at a headlong speed. The causation of such symptoms is rather obscure, since the artificial gravity regulators are in good working-order. Colt and I have not suffered from any similar disturbance. It seems to me that the sense of falling would be almost a relief from this illusion of nightmare immobility; but Gershom appears to be greatly distressed by it, and says that his hallucination is growing stronger, with fewer and briefer intervals of normality. He fears that it will become continuous.

◉◉◉◉◉◉◉

Sept. 11th. Colt has made an estimate of our fuel and provisions and thinks that with careful husbandry we will be able to reach Europa. I have been checking up on his calculations, and find that he is altogether too sanguine. According to my estimate, the fuel will give out while we are still midway in the belt of asteroids; though the food, water and compressed air would possibly take us most of the way to Europa. This discovery I must conceal from the others. It is too late to turn back. I wonder if we have all been mad, to start out on this errant voyage into cosmical immensity with no real preparation or thought of consequences. Colt, it would seem, has lost even the power of mathematical calculation: his figurings are full of the most egregious errors.

Gershom has been unable to sleep, and is not even fit to take his turn at the watch. The hallucination of falling obsesses him perpetually, and he cries out in terror, thinking that the vessel is about to crash on some dark, unknown planet to which it is being drawn by an irresistible gravitation. Eating, drinking and locomotion are very difficult for him, and he complains that he cannot even draw a full breath—that the air is snatched away from him in his precipitate descent. His condition is indeed painful and pitiable.

◉◉◉◉◉◉◉

Sept. 12th. Gershom is worse—bromide of potassium and even a heavy dose of morphine from the *Selenite's* medicine lockers, have not relieved him or enabled him to sleep. He has the look of a drowning man and seems to be on the point of strangulation. It is hard for him to speak.

Colt has become very morose and sullen, and snarls at me when I address him. I think that Gershom's plight has preyed sorely upon his nerves—as it has on mine. But my burden is heavier than Colt's: for I know the inevitable doom of our insane and ill-starred expedition. Sometimes I wish it were all over. . . . The hells of the human mind are vaster than space, darker than the night between the worlds . . . and all three of us have spent several eternities in hell. Our attempt to flee has only plunged us into a black and shoreless limbo, through which we are fated to carry still our own private perdition.

I, too, like Gershom, have been unable to sleep. But, unlike him, I am tormented by the illusion of eternal immobility. In spite of the daily calculations that assure me of our progress through the gulf, I cannot convince myself that we have moved at all. It seems to me that we hang suspended like Mohammed's coffin, remote from earth and equally remote from the stars, in an incommensurable vastness without bourn or direction. I cannot describe the awfulness of the feeling.

⁑⁑⁑

Sept. 13th. During my watch, Colt opened the medicine locker and managed to shoot himself full of morphine. When his turn came, he was in a stupor and I could do nothing to rouse him. Gershom had gotten steadily worse and seemed to be enduring a thousand deaths . . . so there was nothing for me to do but keep on with the watch as long as I could. I locked the controls, anyway, so that the vessel would continue its course without human guidance if I should fall asleep.

I don't know how long I kept awake—nor how long I slept. I was aroused by a queer hissing whose nature and cause I could not identify at first. I looked around and saw that Colt was in his hammock, still lying in a drug-induced sopor. Then I saw that Gershom was gone, and began to realize that the hissing came from the air-lock. The inner door of the lock was closed securely—but evidently someone had opened the outer manhole, and the sound was being made by the escaping air. It grew fainter and ceased as I listened.

I knew then what had happened—Gershom, unable to endure his strange hallucination any longer, had actually flung himself into space from the *Selenite*! Going to the rear ports, I saw his body, with a pale, slightly bloated face and open, bulging eyes. It was following us like a satellite, keeping an even distance of ten or twelve feet from the lee of the vessel's stern. I could have gone out in a space-suit to retrieve the body; but I felt sure that Gershom was already dead, and the effort seemed more than useless. Since there was no leakage of air from the interior, I did not even try to close the manhole.

I hope and pray that Gershom is at peace. He will float forever in cosmic space—and in that further void where the torment of human consciousness can never follow.

◦◦◦◦◦◦◦

Sept. 15th. We have kept our course somehow, though Colt is too demoralized and drug-sodden to be of much assistance. I pity him when the limited supply of morphine gives out.

Gershom's body is still following us, held by the slight power of the vessel's gravitational attraction. It seems to terrify Colt in his more lucid moments; and he complains that we are being haunted by the dead man. It's bad enough for me, too, and I wonder how much my nerves and mind will stand. Sometimes I think that I am beginning to develop the delusion that tortured Gershom and drove him to his death. An awful dizziness assails me, and I fear that I shall start to fall. But somehow I regain my equilibrium.

◦◦◦◦◦◦◦

Sept. 16th. Colt used up all the morphine, and began to show signs of intense depression and uncontrollable nervousness. His fear of the satellite corpse appeared to grow upon him like an obsession; and I could do nothing to reassure him. His terror was deepened by an eerie, superstitious belief.

"I tell you, I hear Gershom calling us," he cried. "He wants company, out there in the black, frozen emptiness; and he won't leave the vessel till one of us goes out to join him. You've got to go,

Beverly—it's either you or me—otherwise he'll follow the *Selenite* forever."

I tried to reason with him, but in vain. He turned upon me in a sudden shift of maniacal rage.

"Damn you, I'll throw you out, if you won't go any other way!" he shrieked.

Clawing and mouthing like a mad beast, he leapt toward me where I sat before the *Selenite*'s control-board. I was almost overborne by his onset, for he fought with a wild and frantic strength . . . I don't like to write down all that happened, for the mere recollection makes me sick . . . Finally he got me by the throat, with a sharp-nailed clutch that I could not loosen, and began to choke me to death. In self-defense, I had to shoot him with an automatic which I carried in my pocket. Reeling dizzily, gasping for breath, I found myself staring down at his prostrate body, from which a crimson puddle was widening on the floor.

Somehow, I managed to put on a space-suit. Dragging Colt by the ankles, I got him to the inner door of the air-lock. When I opened the door, the escaping air hurled me toward the open manhole together with the corpse; and it was hard to regain my footing and avoid being carried through into space. Colt's body, turning transversely in its movement, was jammed across the manhole; and I had to thrust it out with my hands. Then I closed the lid after it. When I returned to the ship's interior, I saw it floating, pale and bloated, beside the corpse of Gershom.

ιιιιιιιιιιι

Sept. 17th. I am alone—and yet most horribly I am pursued and companioned by the dead men. I have sought to concentrate my faculties on the hopeless problem of survival, on the exigencies of space navigation; but it is all useless. Ever I am aware of those stiff and swollen bodies, swimming in the awful silence of the void, with the white, airless sun like a leprosy of light on their upturned faces. I try to keep my eyes on the control-board—on the astronomic charts—on the log I am writing—on the stars toward which I am travelling. But a frightful and irresistible magnetism makes me turn at intervals, mechanically, helplessly, to the rearward ports. There are no words for what I feel and think—and words are as lost things along with the worlds I have left so far behind. I sink in a chaos of vertiginous horror, beyond all possibility of return.

Sept. 18th. I am entering the zone of the asteroids—those desert rocks, fragmentary and amorphous, that whirl in far-scattered array between Mars and Jupiter. Today the *Selenite* passed very close to one of them—a small body like a broken-off mountain, which heaved suddenly from the gulf with knife-sharp pinnacles and black gullies that seemed to cleave its very heart. The *Selenite* would have crashed full upon it in a few instants, if I had not reversed the power and steered in an abrupt diagonal to the right. As it was, I passed near enough for the bodies of Colt and Gershom to be caught by the gravitational pull of the planetoid; and when I looked back at the receding rock, after the vessel was out of danger, they had disappeared from sight. Finally I located them with the telescopic reflector, and saw that they were revolving in space, like infinitesimal moons, about that awful, naked asteroid. Perhaps they will float thus forever, or will drift gradually down in lessening circles, to find a tomb in one of those bleak, bottomless ravines.

Sept. 19th. I have passed several more of the asteroids—irregular fragments, little larger than meteoric stones; and all my skill of spacemanship has been taxed severely to avert collision. Because of the need for unrelaxing vigilance, I have been compelled to keep awake at all times. But sooner or later, sleep will overpower me, and the *Selenite* will crash to destruction.

After all, it matters little: the end is inevitable, and must come soon enough in any case. The store of concentrated food, the tanks of compressed oxygen, might keep me alive for many months, since there is no one but myself to consume them. But the fuel is almost gone, as I know from my former calculations. At any moment, the propulsion may cease. Then the vessel will drift idly and helplessly in this cosmic limbo, and be drawn to its doom on some asteroidal reef.

Sep. 21st (?). Everything I have expected has happened, and yet by some miracle of chance—or mischance—I am still alive.

⑴⑴⑴⑴⑴⑴

The fuel gave out yesterday (at least I think it was yesterday). But I was too close to the nadir of physical and mental exhaustion to realize clearly that the rocket-explosions had ceased. I was dead for want of sleep, and had gotten into a state beyond hope or despair. Dimly I remember setting the vessel's controls through automatic force of habit; and then I lashed myself in my hammock and fell asleep instantly.

I have no means of guessing how long I slept. Vaguely, in the gulf beyond dreams, I heard a crash as of far-off thunder, and felt a violent vibration that jarred me into dull wakefulness. A sensation of unnatural, sweltering heat began to oppress me as I struggled toward consciousness; but when I had opened my heavy eyes, I was unable to determine for some little time what had really happened.

Twisting my head so that I could peer out through one of the ports, I was startled to see, on a purple-black sky, an icy, glittering horizon of saw-edged rocks.

For an instant, I thought that the vessel was about to strike on some looming planetoid. Then, overwhelmingly, I realized *that the crash had already occurred*—that I had been awakened from my coma-like slumber by the falling of the *Selenite* upon one of those barren cosmic islets.

I was wide-awake now, and I hastened to unlash myself from the hammock. I found that the floor was pitched sharply, as if the *Selenite* had landed on a slope or had buried its nose in the alien terrain. Feeling a queer, disconcerting lightness, and barely able to re-establish my feet on the floor at each step, I made my way to the nearest port. It was plain that the artificial gravity-system of the flier had been thrown out of commission by the crash, and that I was now subject only to the feeble gravitation of the asteroid. It seemed to me that I was light and incorporeal as a cloud—that I was no more than the airy specter of my former self.

The floor and walls were strangely hot; and it came to me that the heating must have been caused by the passage of the *vessel* through some sort of atmosphere. The asteroid, then, was not wholly airless, as such bodies are commonly supposed to be; and probably it was one of the larger fragments, with a diameter of many miles—perhaps hundreds. But even this realization failed to prepare me for the weird and surprising scene upon which I gazed through the port.

The horizon of serrate peaks, like a miniature mountain-range, lay at a distance of several hundred yards. Above it, the small, intensely brilliant sun, like a fiery moon in its magnitude, was sinking with visible rapidity in the dark sky that revealed the major stars and planets.

The *Selenite* had plunged into a shallow valley, and had half-buried its prow and bottom in a soil that was formed by decomposing rock, mainly basaltic. All about were fretted ridges, guttering pillars and pinnacles; and over these, amazingly, there clambered frail, pipy, leafless vines with broad, yellow-green tendrils flat and thin as paper. Insubstantial-looking lichens, taller than a man, and having the form of flat antlers, grew in single rows and thickets along the valley beside rills of water like molten moonstone.

Between the thickets, I saw the approach of certain living creatures who rose from behind the middle rocks with the suddenness and lightness of leaping insects. They seemed to skim the ground with long, flying steps that were both easy and abrupt.

There were five of these beings, who, no doubt, had been attracted by the fall of the *Selenite* from space and were coming to inspect it. In a few moments, they neared the vessel and paused before it with the same effortless ease that had marked all their movements.

What they really were, I do not know; but for want of other analogies, I must liken them to insects. Standing perfectly erect, they towered seven feet in air. Their eyes, like faceted opals, at the end of curving protractile stalks, rose level with the port. Their unbelievably thin limbs, their stem-like bodies, comparable to those of the *phasmidae*, or "walking-sticks", were covered with grey-green shards. Their heads, triangular in shape, were flanked with immense, perforated membranes, and were fitted with mandibular mouths that seemed to grin eternally.

I think that they saw me with those weird, inexpressive eyes; for they drew nearer, pressing against the very port, till I could have touched them with my hand if the port had been open. Perhaps they too were surprised: for the thin eye-stalks seemed to lengthen as they stared; and there was a queer waving of their sharded arms, a quivering of their horny mouths, as if they were holding converse with each other. After a while they went away, vanishing swiftly beyond the near horizon.

Since then, I have examined the *Selenite* as fully as possible, to ascertain the extent of the damage. I think that the outer hull has been crumpled or even fused in places: for when I approached the manhole, clad in a space-suit, with the idea of emerging, I found that I could not open the lid. My exit from the flier has been rendered impossible, since I have no tools with which to cut the heavy metal or shatter the tough, neo-crystal ports. I am sealed in the *Selenite* as in a prison; and the prison, in due time, must also become my tomb.

Later. I shall no longer try to date this record. It is impossible, under the circumstances, to retain even an approximate sense of earthly time. The chronometers have ceased running, and their machinery has been hopelessly jarred by the vessel's fall. The diurnal periods of this planetoid are, it would seem, no more than an hour or two in duration; and the nights are equally short. Darkness swept upon the landscape like a black wing after I had finished writing my last entry; and since then, so many of these ephemeral days and nights have shuttled by, that I have now ceased to count them. My very sense of duration is becoming oddly confused. Now that I have grown somewhat used to my situation, the brief days drag with immeasurable tedium.

The beings whom I call the walking-sticks have returned to the *Selenite*, coming daily, and bringing scores and hundreds of others. It would seem that they correspond in some measure to humanity, being the dominant life-form of this little world. In most ways, they are incomprehensibly alien; but certain of their actions bear a remote kinship to those of men, and suggest similar impulses and instincts.

Evidently they are curious. They crowd around the *Selenite* in great numbers, inspecting it with their stalk-borne eyes, touching the hull and ports with their attenuated members. I believe they are trying to establish some sort of communication with me. I cannot be sure that they emit vocal sounds, since the hull of the flier is sound-proof; but I am sure that the stiff, semaphoric gestures which they repeat in a certain order before the port as soon as they catch sight of me, are fraught with conscious and definite meaning.

Also, I surmise an actual veneration in their attitude, such as would be accorded by savages to some mysterious visitant from the heavens. Each day, when they gather before the ship, they bring curious spongy fruits and porous vegetable forms which they leave like a sacrificial offering on the ground. By their gestures, they seem to implore me to accept these offerings.

Oddly enough, the fruits and vegetables always disappear during the night. They are eaten by large, luminous, flying creatures with filmy wings, that seem to be wholly nocturnal in their habits. Doubtless, however, the walking-sticks believe that I, the strange ultra-stellar god, have accepted the sacrifice.

It is all strange, unreal, immaterial. The loss of normal gravity makes me feel like a phantom; and I seem to live in a phantom world. My thoughts, my memories, my despair—all are no more than mists that waver on the verge of oblivion. And yet, by some fantastic irony, I am worshipped as a god!

Innumerable days have gone by since I made the last entry in this log. The seasons of the asteroid have changed: the days have grown briefer, the nights longer; and a bleak wintriness pervades the valley. The frail, flat vines are withering on the rocks, and the tall lichen-thickets have assumed funereal autumn hues of madder and mauve. The sun revolves in a low arc above the saw-toothed horizon, and its orb is small and pale as if it were receding into the black gulf among the stars.

The people of the asteroid appear less often, they seem fewer in number, and their sacrificial gifts are rare and scant. No longer do they bring sponge-like fruits, but only pale and porous fungi that seem to have been gathered in caverns.

They move slowly, as if the winter cold were beginning to numb them. Yesterday, three of them fell, after depositing their gifts, and lay still before the flier. They have not moved, and I feel sure that they are dead. The luminous night-flying creatures have ceased to come, and the sacrifices remain undisturbed beside their bearers.

The awfulness of my fate has closed upon me today. No more of the walking-sticks have appeared. I think that they have all died— the ephemerae of this tiny world that is bearing me with it into some Arctic limbo of the solar system. Doubtless their life-time corresponds only to its summer—to its perihelion.

Thin clouds have gathered in the dark air, and snow is falling like fine powder. I feel an unspeakable desolation—a dreariness that I cannot write. The heating-apparatus of the *Selenite* is still in good working-order; so the cold cannot reach me. But the black frost of space has fallen upon my spirit. Strange—I did not feel so utterly bereft and alone while the insect people came daily. Now that they come no more, I seem to have been overtaken by the ultimate horror of solitude, by the chill terror of an alienation beyond life. I can write no longer, for my brain and my heart fail me.

Still, it would seem, I live, after an eternity of darkness and madness in the flier, of death and winter in the world outside. During that time, I have not written in the log; and I know not what obscure impulse prompts me to resume a practice so irrational and futile.

I think it is the sun, passing in a higher and longer arc above the dead landscape, that has called me back from the utterness of despair. The snow has melted from the rocks, forming little rills and pools of water; and strange plant-buds are protruding from the sandy soil. They lift and swell visibly as I watch them. I am beyond hope, beyond life, in a weird vacuum; but I see these things as a condemned captive sees the stirring of spring from his cell. They rouse in me an emotion whose very name I had forgotten.

My food-supply is getting low, and the reserve of compressed air is even lower. I am afraid to calculate how much longer it will last. I have tried to break the neo-crystal ports with a large monkey-wrench for hammer; but the blows, owing partly to my own weightlessness, are futile as the tapping of a feather. Anyway, in all likelihood, the outside air would be too thin for human respiration.

The walking-stick people have re-appeared before the flier. I feel sure, from their lesser height, their brighter coloring, and the immature development of certain members, that they all represent a new generation. None of my former visitors have survived the winter; but somehow, the new ones seem to regard the *Selenite* and me with the same curiosity and reverence that were shown by their elders. They, too, have begun to bring gifts of insubstantial-looking fruit; and they strew filmy blossoms below the por . . . I wonder how they propagate themselves, and how knowledge is transmitted from one generation to another. . . .

·|·|·|·|·|·|·|·|·|·

The flat, lichenous vines are mounting on the rocks, are clambering over the hull of the *Selenite*. The young walking-sticks gather daily to worship me—they make those enigmatic signs which I have never understood, and they move in swift gyrations about the vessel, as in the measures of a hieratic dance. . . . I, the lost and doomed, have been the god of two generations. No doubt they will still worship me when I am dead. I think the air is almost gone—I am more light-headed than usual today, and there is a queer constriction in my throat and chest. . . .

Perhaps I am a little delirious, and have begun to imagine things; but I have just perceived an odd phenomenon, hitherto unnoted. I don't know what it is. A thin, columnar mist, moving and writhing like a serpent, with opal colors that change momently, has appeared among the rocks and is approaching the vessel. It seems like a live thing—like a vaporous entity; and somehow, it is poisonous and inimical. It glides forward, rearing above the throng of *phasmidae*, who have all prostrated themselves as if in fear. I see it more clearly now: it is half-transparent, with a web of grey threads among its changing colors; and it is putting forth a long, wavering tentacle.

It is some rare life-form, unknown to earthly science; and I cannot even surmise its nature and attributes. Perhaps it is the only one of its kind on the asteroid. No doubt it has just discovered the presence of the *Selenite*, and has been drawn by curiosity, like the walking-stick people.

The tentacle has touched the hull—it has reached the port behind which I stand, pencilling these words. The grey threads in the tentacle glow as if with sudden fire. My God—*it is coming through the neo-crystal lens—*

«««« George R.R. Martin »»»»

Pets can enrich a person's life, but this person, and his life, needed more enriching than any pet should be expected to accomplish. And the sort of pets he kept weren't the warm and fuzzy kind, but then neither was he. His new acquisition was a very exotic type of creature from another planet, with high entertainment value. Maybe he should have considered the possibility that the entertainment might become mutual . . .

If the name of George R.R. Martin is unfamiliar to you, I'll assume that you've spent the last decade or longer in the Foreign Legion, doing research in Antarctica, or were abducted as a child by aliens who just now dropped you off at the corner of Main Street and Loopy Lane. *Time* magazine selected him in 2011 as one of the "100 Most Influential People in the World." His award-winning high fantasy series, collectively titled A Song of Fire and Ice, which began with *A Game of Thrones* and has continued through four more novels, with two more planned, *owns* the *New York Times* best seller list, and has spun off art books, board games, video games, and a popular HBO TV series. He has won five Hugo Awards, two Nebula Awards, five *Locus* Awards, a Quill Award, a Bram Stoker Award, and the World Fantasy Convention's Life Achievement Award. He created (and frequently contributed to) the long-running and popular Wild Cards series, presently totaling 23 volumes. Martin has long had an interest in horror—his early Hugo-winner, "A Song for Lya," can be read as an ambiguous horror story—and wrote the novels *Fevre Dream* (described as Bram Stoker meets Mark Twain) and *The Armageddon Rag*, a horror story set in the rock music culture of the sixties and eighties. And of course, there's the story you're about to read, which won both the Hugo and Nebula Awards. But first make sure your skimmer is in working order . . .

⟪⟨⟨ SANDKINGS ⟩⟩⟫

George R.R. Martin

Simon Kress lived alone in a sprawling manor house among the dry, rocky hills fifty kilometers from the city. So, when he was called away unexpectedly on business, he had no neighbors he could conveniently impose on to take his pets. The carrion hawk was no problem; it roosted in the unused belfry and customarily fed itself anyway. The shambler Kress simply shooed outside and left to fend for itself; the little monster would gorge on slugs and birds and rockjocks. But the fish tank, stocked with genuine Earth piranha, posed a difficulty. Kress finally just threw a haunch of beef into the huge tank. The piranha could always eat each other if he were detained longer than expected. They'd done it before. It amused him.

Unfortunately, he was detained *much* longer than expected this time. When he finally returned, all the fish were dead. So was the carrion hawk. The shambler had climbed up to the belfry and eaten it. Simon Kress was vexed.

The next day he flew his skimmer to Asgard, a journey of some two hundred kilometers. Asgard was Baldur's largest city and boasted the oldest and largest starport as well. Kress liked to impress his friends with animals that were unusual, entertaining, and expensive; Asgard was the place to buy them.

This time, though, he had poor luck. Xenopets had closed its doors; t'Etherane the Petseller tried to foist another carrion hawk off on him; and Strange Waters offered nothing more exotic than piranha, glow-sharks, and spider squids. Kress had had all those; he wanted something new.

Near dusk, he found himself walking down the Rainbow Boulevard, looking for places he had not patronized before. So close to the starport, the street was lined by importers' marts. The big corporate emporiums had impressive long windows, where rare and costly alien artifacts reposed on felt cushions against dark drapes that made the interiors of the stores a mystery. Between them were the junk shops—narrow, nasty little places whose display areas were crammed with all manner of off-world bric-a-brac. Kress tried both kinds of shop, with equal dissatisfaction.

Then he came across a store that was different.

It was quite close to the port. Kress had never been there before. The shop occupied a small, single-story building of moderate size, set between a euphoria bar and a temple-brothel of the Secret Sisterhood. Down this far, the Rainbow Boulevard grew tacky. The shop itself was unusual. Arresting.

The windows were full of mist; now a pale red, now the gray of true fog, now sparkling and golden. The mist swirled and eddied and glowed faintly from within. Kress glimpsed objects in the window—machines, pieces of art, other things he could not recognize—but he could not get a good look at any of them. The mists flowed sensuously around them, displaying a bit of first one thing and then another, then cloaking all. It was intriguing.

As he watched, the mist began to form letters. One word at a time. Kress stood and read:

WO. AND. SHADE. IMPORTERS.
ARTIFACTS. ART. LIFEFORMS. AND. MISC.

The letters stopped. Through the fog, Kress saw something moving. That was enough for him, that and the word "Lifeforms" in the advertisement. He swept his walking cloak over his shoulder and entered the store.

Inside, Kress felt disoriented. The interior seemed vast, much larger than he would have guessed from the relatively modest frontage. It was dimly lit, peaceful. The ceiling was a starscape, complete with spiral nebulae, very dark and realistic, very nice. The counters all shone faintly, the better to display the merchandise within. The aisles were carpeted with ground fog. In places, it came almost to his knees and swirled about his feet as he walked.

"Can I help you?"

She seemed almost to have risen from the fog. Tall and gaunt and pale, she wore a practical gray jumpsuit and a strange little cap that rested well back on her head.

"Are you Wo or Shade?" Kress asked. "Or only sales help?"

"Jala Wo, ready to serve you," she replied. "Shade does not see customers. We have no sales help."

"You have quite a large establishment," Kress said. "Odd that I have never heard of you before."

"We have only just opened this shop on Baldur," the woman said. "We have franchises on a number of other worlds, however. What can I sell you? Art, perhaps? You have the look of a collector. We have some fine Nor T'alush crystal carvings."

"No," Simon Kress said. "I own all the crystal carvings I desire. I came to see about a pet."

"A lifeform?"

"Yes."

"Alien?"

"Of course."

"We have a mimic in stock. From Celia's World. A clever little simian. Not only will it learn to speak, but eventually it will mimic your voice, inflections, gestures, even facial expressions."

"Cute," said Kress. "And common. I have no use for either, Wo. I want something exotic. Unusual. And not cute. I detest cute animals. At the moment I own a shambler. Imported from Cotho, at no mean expense. From time to time I feed him a litter of unwanted kittens. That is what I think of *cute*. Do I make myself understood?"

Wo smiled enigmatically. "Have you ever owned an animal that worshipped you?" she asked.

Kress grinned. "Oh, now and again. But I don't require worship, Wo. Just entertainment."

"You misunderstood me," Wo said, still wearing her strange smile. "I meant worship literally."

"What are you talking about?"

"I think I have just the thing for you," Wo said. "Follow me."

She led Kress between the radiant counters and down a long, fog-shrouded aisle beneath false starlight. They passed through a wall of mist into another section of the store, and stopped before a large plastic tank. An aquarium, thought Kress.

Wo beckoned. He stepped closer and saw that he was wrong. It was a terrarium. Within lay a miniature desert about two meters square. Pale and bleached scarlet by wan red light. Rocks: basalt and quartz and granite. In each corner of the tank stood a castle.

Kress blinked, and peered, and corrected himself; actually only three castles stood. The fourth leaned; a crumbled, broken ruin. The other three were crude but intact, carved of stone and sand. Over their battlements and through their rounded porticoes, tiny creatures climbed and scrambled. Kress pressed his face against the plastic. "Insects?" he asked.

"No," Wo replied. "A much more complex lifeform. More intelligent as well. Considerably smarter than your shambler. They are called sandkings."

"Insects," Kress said, drawing back from the tank. "I don't care how complex they are." He frowned. "And kindly don't try to gull me with this talk of intelligence. These things are far too small to have anything but the most rudimentary brains."

"They share hive minds," Wo said. "Castle minds, in this case. There are only three organisms in the tank, actually. The fourth died. You see how her castle has fallen."

Kress looked back at the tank. "Hive minds, eh? Interesting." He frowned again. "Still, it is only an oversized ant farm. I'd hoped for something better."

"They fight wars."

"Wars? Hmmm." Kress looked again.

"Note the colors, if you will," Wo told him. She pointed to the creatures that swarmed over the nearest castle. One was scrabbling at the tank wall. Kress studied it. It still looked like an insect to his eyes.

Barely as long as his fingernail, six-limbed, with six tiny eyes set all around its body. A wicked set of mandibles clacked visibly, while two long, fine antennae wove patterns in the air. Antennae, mandibles, eyes, and legs were sooty black, but the dominant color was the burnt orange of its armor plating. "It's an insect," Kress repeated.

"It is not an insect," Wo insisted calmly. "The armored exo-skeleton is shed when the sandking grows larger. *If* it grows larger. In a tank this size, it won't." She took Kress by the elbow and led him around the tank to the next castle. "Look at the colors here."

He did. They were different. Here the sandkings had bright red armor; antennae, mandibles, eyes, and legs were yellow. Kress glanced across the tank. The denizens of the third live castle were off-white, with red trim. "Hmmm," he said.

"They war, as I said," Wo told him. "They even have truces and alliances. It was an alliance that destroyed the fourth castle in this tank. The blacks were getting too numerous, so the others joined forces to destroy them."

Kress remained unconvinced. "Amusing, no doubt. But insects fight wars too."

"Insects do not worship," Wo said.

"Eh?"

Wo smiled and pointed at the castle. Kress stared. A face had been carved into the wall of the highest tower. He recognized it. It was Jala Wo's face. "How . . . ?"

"I projected a hologram of my face into the tank, kept it there for a few days. The face of god, you see? I feed them; I am always close. The sandkings have a rudimentary psionic sense. Proximity telepathy. They sense me, and worship me by using my face to decorate their buildings. All the castles have them, see." They did.

On the castle, the face of Jala Wo was serene and peaceful, and very lifelike. Kress marveled at the workmanship. "How do they do it?"

"The foremost legs double as arms. They even have fingers of a sort; three small, flexible tendrils. And they cooperate well, both in building and in battle. Remember, all the mobiles of one color share a single mind."

"Tell me more," Kress said.

Wo smiled. "The maw lives in the castle. Maw is my name for her. A pun, if you will; the thing is mother and stomach both. Female, large as your fist, immobile. Actually, sandking is a bit of a misnomer. The mobiles are peasants and warriors, the real ruler is a queen. But that analogy is faulty as well. Considered as a whole, each castle is a single hermaphroditic creature."

"What do they eat?"

"The mobiles eat pap—predigested food obtained inside the castle. They get it from the maw after she has worked on it for several days. Their stomachs can't handle anything else, so if the maw dies, they soon die as well. The maw . . . the maw eats anything. You'll have no special expense there. Table scraps will do excellently."

"Live food?" Kress asked.

Wo shrugged. "Each maw eats mobiles from the other castles, yes."

"I am intrigued," he admitted. "If only they weren't so small."

"Yours can be larger. These sandkings are small because their tank is small. They seem to limit their growth to fit available space. If I moved these to a larger tank, they'd start growing again."

"Hmmmm. My piranha tank is twice this size, and vacant. It could be cleaned out, filled with sand . . ."

"Wo and Shade would take care of the installation. It would be our pleasure."

"Of course," said Kress, "I would expect four intact castles."

"Certainly," Wo said.

They began to haggle about the price.

Three days later, Jala Wo arrived at Simon Kress' estate, with dormant sandkings and a work crew to take charge of the installation. Wo's assistants were aliens unlike any Kress was familiar with—squat, broad bipeds with four arms and bulging, multifaceted eyes. Their skin was thick and leathery, twisted into horns and spines and protrusions at odd spots upon their bodies. But they were very strong, and good workers. Wo ordered them about in a musical tongue that Kress had never heard.

In a day it was done. They moved his piranha tank to the center of his spacious living room, arranged couches on either side of it for better viewing, scrubbed it clean, and filled it two-thirds of the way up with sand and rock. Then they installed a special lighting system, both to provide the dim red illumination the sandkings preferred and to project holographic images into the tank. On top they mounted a sturdy plastic cover, with a feeder mechanism built in. "This way you can feed your sandkings without removing the top of the tank," Wo explained. "You would not want to take any chances on the mobiles escaping."

The cover also included climate control devices, to condense just the right amount of moisture from the air. "You want it dry, but not too dry," Wo said.

Finally one of the four-armed workers climbed into the tank and dug deep pits in the four corners. One of his companions handed the dormant maws over to him, removing them one by one from their frosted cryonic traveling cases. They were nothing to look at. Kress decided they resembled nothing so much as a mottled, half-spoiled chunk of raw meat. With a mouth.

The alien buried them, one in each corner of the tank. Then they sealed it all up and took their leave.

"The heat will bring the maws out of dormancy," Wo said. "In less than a week, mobiles will begin to hatch and burrow to the surface. Be certain to give them plenty of food. They will need all their strength until they are well established. I would estimate that you will have castles rising in about three weeks."

"And my face? When will they carve my face?"

"Turn on the hologram after about a month," she advised him. "And be patient. If you have any questions, please call. Wo and Shade are at your service." She bowed and left.

Kress wandered back to the tank and lit a joystick. The desert was still and empty. He drummed his fingers impatiently against the plastic, and frowned.

On the fourth day, Kress thought he glimpsed motion beneath the sand, subtle subterranean stirrings.

On the fifth day, he saw his first mobile, a lone white.

On the sixth day, he counted a dozen of them, whites and reds and blacks. The oranges were tardy. He cycled through a bowl of half-decayed table scraps. The mobiles sensed it at once, rushed to it, and began to drag pieces back to their respective corners. Each color group was very organized. They did not fight. Kress was a bit disappointed, but he decided to give them time.

The oranges made their appearance on the eighth day. By then the other sandkings had begun to carry small stones and erect crude fortifications. They still did not war. At the moment they were only half the size of those he had seen at Wo and Shade's, but Kress thought they were growing rapidly.

The castles began to rise midway through the second week. Organized battalions of mobiles dragged heavy chunks of sandstone and granite to their corners, where other mobiles were pushing sand into place with mandibles and tendrils. Kress had purchased a pair of magnifying goggles so he could watch them work, wherever they might go in the tank. He wandered around and around the tall plastic walls, observing. It was fascinating. The castles were a bit plainer than Kress would have liked, but he had an idea about that. The next day he cycled through some obsidian and flakes of colored glass along with the food. Within hours, they had been incorporated into the castle walls.

The black castle was the first completed, followed by the white and red fortresses. The oranges were last, as usual. Kress took his meals into the living room and ate seated on the couch, so he could watch. He expected the first war to break out any hour now.

He was disappointed. Days passed; the castles grew taller and more grand, and Kress seldom left the tank except to attend to his sanitary needs and answer critical business calls. But the sandkings did not war. He was getting upset.

Finally, he stopped feeding them.

Two days after the table scraps had ceased to fall from their desert sky, four black mobiles surrounded an orange and dragged it back to their maw. They maimed it first, ripping off its mandibles and antennae and limbs, and carried it through the shadowed main gate of their miniature castle. It never emerged. Within an hour, more than forty orange mobiles marched across the sand and attacked the blacks' corner. They were outnumbered by the blacks that came rushing up from the depths. When the fighting was over, the attackers had been slaughtered. The dead and dying were taken down to feed the black maw.

Kress, delighted, congratulated himself on his genius.

When he put food into the tank the following day, a three-cornered battle broke out over its possession. The whites were the big winners. After that, war followed war.

Almost a month to the day after Jala Wo had delivered the sandkings, Kress turned on the hologram projector, and his face materialized in the tank. It turned, slowly, around and around so his gaze fell on all four castles equally. Kress thought it rather a good likeness—it had his impish grin, wide mouth, full cheeks. His blue eyes sparkled, his gray hair was carefully arrayed in a fashionable side sweep, his eyebrows were thin and sophisticated.

Soon enough, the sandkings set to work. Kress fed them lavishly while his image beamed down at them from their sky. Temporarily, the wars stopped. All activity was directed towards worship.

His face emerged on the castle walls.

At first all four carvings looked alike to him, but as the work continued and Kress studied the reproductions, he began to detect subtle differences in technique and execution. The reds were the most creative, using tiny flakes of slate to put the gray in his hair. The white idol seemed young and mischievous to him, while the face shaped by the blacks—although virtually the same, line for line—struck him as wise and beneficent. The orange sandkings, as ever, were last and least. The wars had not gone well for them, and their castle was sad compared to the others. The image they carved was crude and cartoonish, and they seemed to intend to leave it that way. When they stopped work on the face, Kress grew quite piqued with them, but there was really nothing he could do.

When all the sandkings had finished their Kress-faces, he turned off the hologram and decided that it was time to have a party. His friends would be impressed. He could even stage a war for them, he thought. Humming happily to himself, he began to draw up a guest list.

The party was a wild success.

Kress invited thirty people: a handful of close friends who shared his amusements, a few former lovers, and a collection of business and social rivals who could not afford to ignore his summons. He knew some of them would be discomfited and even offended by his sandkings. He counted on it. Simon Kress customarily considered his parties a failure unless at least one guest walked out in high dudgeon.

On impulse, he added Jala Wo's name to his list. "Bring Shade if you like," he added when dictating her invitation.

Her acceptance surprised him just a bit. "Shade, alas, will be unable to attend. He does not go to social functions," Wo added. "As for myself, I look forward to the chance to see how your sandkings are doing."

Kress ordered them up a sumptuous meal. And when at last the conversation had died down, and most of his guests had gotten silly on wine and joysticks, he shocked them by personally scraping their table leavings into a large bowl. "Come, all of you," he told them. "I want to introduce you to my newest pets." Carrying the bowl, he conducted them into his living room.

The sandkings lived up to his fondest expectations. He had starved them for two days in preparation, and they were in a fighting mood. While the guests ringed the tank, looking through the magnifying glasses Kress had thoughtfully provided, the sandkings waged a glorious battle over the scraps. He counted almost sixty dead mobiles when the struggle was over. The reds and whites, who had recently formed an alliance, emerged with most of the food.

"Kress, you're disgusting," Cath m'Lane told him. She had lived with him for a short time two years before, until her soppy sentimentality almost drove him mad. "I was a fool to come back here. I thought perhaps you'd changed, wanted to apologize." She had never forgiven him for the time his shambler had eaten an excessively cute puppy of which she had been fond. "Don't *ever* invite me here again,

Simon." She strode out, accompanied by her current lover and a chorus of laughter.

His other guests were full of questions.

Where did the sandkings come from? they wanted to know. "From Wo and Shade, Importers," he replied, with a polite gesture towards Jala Wo, who had remained quiet and apart through most of the evening.

Why did they decorate their castles with his likeness? "Because I am the source of all good things. Surely you know that?" That brought a round of chuckles.

Will they fight again? "Of course, but not tonight. Don't worry. There will be other parties."

Jad Rakkis, who was an amateur xenologist, began talking about other social insects and the wars they fought. "These sandkings are amusing, but nothing really. You ought to read about Terran soldier ants, for instance."

"Sandkings are not insects," Jala Wo said sharply, but Jad was off and running, and no one paid her the slightest attention. Kress smiled at her and shrugged.

Malada Blane suggested a betting pool the next time they got together to watch a war, and everyone was taken with the idea. An animated discussion about rules and odds ensued. It lasted for almost an hour. Finally the guests began to take their leave.

Jala Wo was the last to depart. "So," Kress said to her when they were alone, "it appears my sandkings are a hit."

"They are doing well," Wo said. "Already they are larger than my own."

"Yes," Kress said, "except for the oranges."

"I had noticed that," Wo replied. "They seem few in number, and their castle is shabby."

"Well, someone must lose," Kress said. "The oranges were late to emerge and get established. They have suffered for it."

"Pardon," said Wo, "but might I ask if you are feeding your sandkings sufficiently?"

Kress shrugged. "They diet from time to time. It makes them fiercer."

She frowned. "There is no need to starve them. Let them war in their own time, for their own reasons. It is their nature, and you will witness conflicts that are delightfully subtle and complex. The constant war brought on by hunger is artless and degrading."

Simon Kress repaid Wo's frown with interest. "You are in my house, Wo, and here I am the judge of what is degrading. I fed the sandkings as you advised, and they did not fight."

"You must have patience."

"No," Kress said. "I am their master and their god, after all. Why should I wait on their impulses? They did not war often enough to suit me. I corrected the situation."

"I see," said Wo. "I will discuss the matter with Shade."

"It is none of your concern, or his," Kress snapped.

"I must bid you good night, then," Wo said with resignation. But as she slipped into her coat to depart, she fixed him with a final disapproving stare. "Look to your faces, Simon Kress," she warned him. "Look to your faces."

Puzzled, he wandered back to the tank and stared at the castles after she had taken her departure. His faces were still there, as ever. Except—he snatched up his magnifying goggles and slipped them on. Even then it was hard to make out. But it seemed to him that the expression on the face of his images had changed slightly, that his smile was somehow twisted so that it seemed a touch malicious. But it was a very subtle change, if it was a change at all. Kress finally put it down to his suggestibility, and resolved not to invite Jala Wo to any more of his gatherings.

Over the next few months, Kress and about a dozen of his favorites got together weekly for what he liked to call his "war games." Now that his initial fascination with the sandkings was past, Kress spent less time around his tank and more on his business affairs and his social life, but he still enjoyed having a few friends over for a war or two. He kept the combatants sharp on a constant edge of hunger. It had severe effects on the orange sandkings, who dwindled visibly until Kress began to wonder if their maw was dead. But the others did well enough.

Sometimes at night, when he could not sleep, Kress would take a bottle of wine into the darkened living room, where the red gloom of his miniature desert was the only light. He would drink and watch for hours, alone. There was usually a fight going on somewhere, and when there was not he could easily start one by dropping in some small morsel of food.

They took to betting on the weekly battles, as Malada Blane had suggested. Kress won a good amount by betting on the whites, who had become the most powerful and numerous colony in the tank, with the grandest castle. One week he slid the corner of the tank top aside, and dropped the food close to the white castle instead of on the central battleground as usual, so that the others had to attack the whites in their stronghold to get any food at all. They tried. The whites were brilliant in defense. Kress won a hundred standards from Jad Rakkis.

Rakkis, in fact, lost heavily on the sandkings almost every week. He pretended to a vast knowledge of them and their ways, claiming that he had studied them after the first party, but he had no luck when it came to placing his bets. Kress suspected that Jad's claims were empty boasting. He had tried to study the sandkings a bit himself, in a moment of idle curiosity, tying in to the library to find out to what world his pets were native. But there was no listing for them. He wanted to get in touch with Wo and ask her about it, but he had other concerns, and the matter kept slipping his mind.

Finally, after a month in which his losses totaled more than a thousand standards, Jad Rakkis arrived at the war games carrying a small plastic case under his arm. Inside was a spiderlike thing covered with fine golden hair.

"A sand spider," Rakkis announced. "From Cathaday. I got it this afternoon from t'Etherane the Petseller. Usually they remove the poison sacs, but this one is intact. Are you game, Simon? I want my money back. I'll bet a thousand standards, sand spider against sandkings."

Kress studied the spider in its plastic prison. His sandkings had grown—they were twice as large as Wo's, as she'd predicted—but they were still dwarfed by this thing. It was venomed, and they were not.

Still, there were an awful lot of them. Besides, the endless sandking wars had begun to grow tiresome lately. The novelty of the match intrigued him. "Done," Kress said. "Jad, you are a fool. The sandkings will just keep coming until this ugly creature of yours is dead."

"You are the fool, Simon," Rakkis replied, smiling. "The Cathadayn sand spider customarily feeds on burrowers that hide in nooks and crevices and—well, watch—it will go straight into those castles, and eat the maws."

Kress scowled amid general laughter. He hadn't counted on that. "Get on with it," he said irritably. He went to freshen his drink.

The spider was too large to cycle conveniently through the food chamber. Two of the others helped Rakkis slide the tank top slightly to one side, and Malada Blane handed him up his case. He shook the spider out. It landed lightly on a miniature dune in front of the red castle, and stood confused for a moment, mouth working, legs twitching menacingly.

"Come on," Rakkis urged. They all gathered round the tank. Simon Kress found his magnifiers and slipped them on. If he was going to lose a thousand standards, at least he wanted a good view of the action.

The sandkings had seen the invader. All over the castle, activity had ceased. The small scarlet mobiles were frozen, watching.

The spider began to move toward the dark promise of the gate. On the tower above, Simon Kress' countenance stared down impassively.

At once there was a flurry of activity. The nearest red mobiles formed themselves into two wedges and streamed over the sand toward the spider. More warriors erupted from inside the castle and assembled in a triple line to guard the approach to the underground chamber where the maw lived. Scouts came scuttling over the dunes, recalled to fight.

Battle was joined.

The attacking sandkings washed over the spider. Mandibles snapped shut on legs and abdomen, and clung. Reds raced up the golden legs to the invader's back. They bit and tore. One of them found an eye, and ripped it loose with tiny yellow tendrils. Kress smiled and pointed.

But they were *small*, and they had no venom, and the spider did not stop. Its legs flicked sandkings off to either side. Its dripping jaws found others, and left them broken and stiffening. Already a dozen of the reds lay dying. The sand spider came on and on. It strode straight through the triple line of guardians before the castle. The lines closed around it, covered it, waging desperate battle. A team of sandkings had bitten off one of the spider's legs, Kress saw. Defenders leaped from atop the towers to land on the twitching, heaving mass.

Lost beneath the sandkings, the spider somehow lurched down into the darkness and vanished.

Jad Rakkis let out a long breath. He looked pale. "Wonderful," someone else said. Malada Blane chuckled deep in her throat.

"Look," said Idi Noreddian, tugging Kress by the arm.

They had been so intent on the struggle in the corner that none of them had noticed the activity elsewhere in the tank. But now the castle was still, the sands empty save for dead red mobiles, and now they saw.

Three armies were drawn up before the red castle. They stood quite still, in perfect array, rank after rank of sandkings, orange and white and black. Waiting to see what emerged from the depths.

Simon Kress smiled. "A *cordon sanitaire*," he said. "And glance at the other castles, if you will, Jad."

Rakkis did, and swore. Teams of mobiles were sealing up the gates with sand and stone. If the spider somehow survived this encounter, it would find no easy entrance at the other castles. "I should have brought four spiders," Jad Rakkis said. "Still, I've won. My spider is down there right now, eating your damned maw."

Kress did not reply. He waited. There was motion in the shadows.

All at once, red mobiles began pouring out of the gate. They took their positions on the castle, and began repairing the damage the spider had wrought. The other armies dissolved and began to retreat to their respective corners.

"Jad," said Simon Kress, "I think you are a bit confused about who is eating who."

The following week, Rakkis brought four slim silver snakes. The sandkings dispatched them without much trouble.

Next he tried a large black bird. It ate more than thirty white mobiles, and its thrashing and blundering virtually destroyed their castle, but ultimately its wings grew tired, and the sandkings attacked in force wherever it landed.

After that it was a case of insects, armored beetles not too unlike the sandkings themselves. But stupid, stupid. An allied force of oranges and blacks broke their formation, divided them, and butchered them.

Rakkis began giving Kress promissory notes.

It was around that time that Kress met Cath m'Lane again, one evening when he was dining in Asgard at his favorite restaurant. He stopped at her table briefly and told her about the war games, inviting her to join them. She flushed, then regained control of herself and grew icy. "Someone has to put a stop to you, Simon. I guess it's going to be me," she said. Kress shrugged and enjoyed a lovely meal and thought no more about her threat.

Until a week later, when a small, stout woman arrived at his door and showed him a police wristband. "We've had complaints," she said. "Do you keep a tank lull of dangerous insects, Kress?"

"Not insects," he said, furious. "Come, I'll show you."

When she had seen the sandkings, she shook her head. "This will never do. What do you know about these creatures, anyway? Do you know what world they're from? Have they been cleared by the ecological board? Do you have a license for these things? We have a report that they're carnivores, possibly dangerous. We also have a report that they are semi-sentient. Where did you get these creatures, anyway?"

"From Wo and Shade," Kress replied.

"Never heard of them," the woman said. "Probably smuggled them in, knowing our ecologists would never approve them. No, Kress, this won't do. I'm going to confiscate this tank and have it destroyed. And you're going to have to expect a few fines as well."

Kress offered her a hundred standards to forget all about him and his sandkings.

She *tsked.* "Now I'll have to add attempted bribery to the charges against you."

Not until he raised the figure to two thousand standards was she willing to be persuaded. "It's not going to be easy, you know," she said. "There are forms to be altered, records to be wiped. And getting a forged license from the ecologists will be time-consuming. Not to mention dealing with the complainant. What if she calls again?"

"Leave her to me," Kress said. "Leave her to me."

He thought about it for a while. That night he made some calls.

First he got t'Etherane the Petseller. "I want to buy a dog," he said. "A puppy."

The round-faced merchant gawked at him. "A puppy? That is not like you, Simon. Why don't you come in? I have a lovely choice."

"I want a very specific *kind* of puppy," Kress said. "Take notes. I'll describe to you what it must look like."

Afterward he punched for Idi Noreddian. "Idi," he said, "I want you out here tonight with your holo equipment. I have a notion to record a sandking battle. A present for one of my friends."

The night after they made the recording, Simon Kress stayed up late. He absorbed a controversial new drama in his sensorium, fixed himself a small snack, smoked a joystick or two, and broke out a bottle of wine. Feeling very happy with himself, he wandered into the living room, glass in hand.

The lights were out. The red glow of the terrarium made the shadows flushed and feverish. He walked over to look at his domain, curious as to how the blacks were doing in the repairs on their castle. The puppy had left it in ruins.

The restoration went well. But as Kress inspected the work through his magnifiers, he chanced to glance closely at the face. It startled him.

He drew back, blinked, took a healthy gulp of wine, and looked again.

The face on the walls was still his. But it was all wrong, all *twisted.*

His cheeks were bloated and piggish, his smile was a crooked leer. He looked impossibly malevolent.

Uneasy, he moved around the tank to inspect the other castles. They were each a bit different, but ultimately all the same.

The oranges had left out most of the fine detail, but the result still seemed monstrous, crude—a brutal mouth and mindless eyes.

The reds gave him a satanic, twitching kind of smile. His mouth did odd, unlovely things at its corners.

The whites, his favorites, had carved a cruel idiot god.

Simon Kress flung his wine across the room in rage. "You *dare*," he said under his breath. "Now you won't eat for a week, you damned . . ." His voice was shrill. "I'll teach you." He had an idea. He strode out of the room, and returned a moment later with an antique iron throwing-sword in his hand. It was a meter long, and the point was still sharp. Kress smiled, climbed up and moved the tank cover aside just enough to give him working room, opening one corner of the desert. He leaned down, and jabbed the sword at the white castle below him. He waved it back and forth, smashing towers and ramparts and walls. Sand and stone collapsed, burying the scrambling mobiles. A flick of his wrist obliterated the features of the insolent, insulting caricature the sandkings had made of his face. Then he poised the point of the sword above the dark mouth that opened down into the maw's chamber, and thrust with all his strength. He heard a soft, squishing sound, and met resistance. All of the mobiles trembled and collapsed. Satisfied, Kress pulled back.

He watched for a moment, wondering whether he'd killed the maw. The point of the throwing-sword was wet and slimy. But finally the white sandkings began to move again. Feebly, slowly, but they moved.

He was preparing to slide the cover back in place and move on to a second castle when he felt something crawling on his hand.

He screamed and dropped the sword, and brushed the sandking from his flesh. It fell to the carpet, and he ground it beneath his heel, crushing it thoroughly long after it was dead. It had crunched when he stepped on it. After that, trembling, he hurried to seal the tank up again, and rushed off to shower and inspect himself carefully. He boiled his clothing.

Later, after several fresh glasses of wine, he returned to the living room. He was a bit ashamed of the way the sandking had terrified him. But he was not about to open the tank again. From now on, the cover stayed sealed permanently. Still, he had to punish the others.

Kress decided to lubricate his mental processes with another glass of wine. As he finished it, an inspiration came to him. He went to the tank smiling, and made a few adjustments to the humidity controls.

By the time he fell asleep on the couch, his wine glass still in his hand, the sand castles were melting in the rain.

Kress woke to angry pounding on his door.

He sat up, groggy, his head throbbing. Wine hangovers were always the worst, he thought. He lurched to the entry chamber.

Cath m'Lane was outside. "You monster," she said, her face swollen and puffy and streaked by tears. "I cried all night, damn you. But no more, Simon, no more."

"Easy," he said, holding his head. "I've got a hangover."

She swore and shoved him aside and pushed her way into his house. The shambler came peering round a corner to see what the noise was. She spat at it and stalked into the living room, Kress trailing ineffectually after her.

"Hold on," he said. "Where do you . . . you can't . . ." He stopped, suddenly horrorstruck. She was carrying a heavy sledgehammer in her left hand. "No," he said.

She went directly to the sandking tank. "You like the little charmers so much, Simon? Then you can live with them."

"*Cath!*" he shrieked.

Gripping the hammer with both hands, she swung as hard as she could against the side of the tank. The sound of the impact set his head to screaming, and Kress made a low blubbering sound of despair. But the plastic held.

She swung again. This time there was a *crack,* and a network of thin lines sprang into being.

Kress threw himself at her as she drew back her hammer for a third swing. They went down flailing, and rolled. She lost her grip on the hammer and tried to throttle him, but Kress wrenched free and bit her on the arm, drawing blood. They both staggered to their feet, panting.

"You should see yourself, Simon," she said grimly. "Blood dripping from your mouth. You look like one of your pets. How do you like the taste?"

"Get out," he said. He saw the throwing-sword where it had fallen the night before, and snatched it up. "Get out," he repeated, waving the sword for emphasis. "Don't go near that tank again."

She laughed at him. "You wouldn't dare," she said. She bent to pick up her hammer.

Kress shrieked at her, and lunged. Before he quite knew what was happening, the iron blade had gone clear through her abdomen. Cath m'Lane looked at him wonderingly, and down at the sword. Kress fell back whimpering. "I didn't mean . . . I only wanted . . ."

She was transfixed, bleeding, dead, but somehow she did not fall. "You monster," she managed to say, though her mouth was full of blood. And she whirled, impossibly; the sword in her, and swung with her last strength at the tank. The tortured wall shattered, and Cath m'Lane was buried beneath an avalanche of plastic and sand and mud.

Kress made small hysterical noises and scrambled up on the couch.

Sandkings were emerging from the muck on his living room floor. They were crawling across Cath's body. A few of them ventured tentatively out across the carpet. More followed.

He watched as a column took shape, a living, writhing square of sandkings, bearing something, something slimy and featureless, a piece of raw meat big as a man's head. They began to carry it away from the tank. It pulsed.

That was when Kress broke and ran.

It was late afternoon before he found the courage to return. He had run to his skimmer and flown to the nearest city, some fifty kilometers away, almost sick with fear. But once safely away, he had found a small restaurant, put down several mugs of coffee and two anti-hangover tabs, eaten a full breakfast, and gradually regained his composure.

It had been a dreadful morning, but dwelling on that would solve nothing. He ordered more coffee and considered his situation with icy rationality.

Cath m'Lane was dead at his hand. Could he report it, plead that it had been an accident? Unlikely. He had run her through, after all, and he had already told that policer to leave her to him. He would have to get rid of the evidence, and hope that she had not told anyone where she was going this morning. That was probable. She could only have gotten his gift late last night. She said that she had cried all night, and she had been alone when she arrived. Very well; he had one body and one skimmer to dispose of.

That left the sandkings. They might prove more of a difficulty. No doubt they had all escaped by now. The thought of them around his house, in his bed and his clothes, infesting his food—it made his flesh crawl. He shuddered and overcame his revulsion. It really shouldn't be too hard to kill them, he reminded himself. He didn't have to account for every mobile. Just the four maws, that was all. He could do that. They were large, as he'd seen. He would find them and kill them.

Simon Kress went shopping before he flew back to his home. He bought a set of skinthins that would cover him from head to foot, several bags of poison pellets for rockjock control, and a spray canister of illegally strong pesticide. He also bought a magnalock towing device.

When he landed, he went about things methodically. First he hooked Cath's skimmer to his own with the magnalock. Searching it, he had his first piece of luck. The crystal chip with Idi Noreddian's holo of the sandking fight was on the front seat. He had worried about that.

When the skimmers were ready, he slipped into his skinthins and went inside for Cath's body.

It wasn't there.

He poked through the fast-drying sand carefully, but there was no doubt of it; the body was gone. Could she have dragged herself away? Unlikely, but Kress searched. A cursory inspection of his house turned up neither the body nor any sign of the sandkings. He did not have time for a more thorough investigation, not with the incriminating skimmer outside his front door. He resolved to try later.

Some seventy kilometers north of Kress' estate was a range of active volcanoes. He flew there, Cath's skimmer in tow. Above the glowering cone of the largest, he released the magnalock and watched it vanish in the lava below.

It was dusk when he returned to his house. That gave him pause. Briefly he considered flying back to the city and spending the night there. He put the thought aside. There was work to do. He wasn't safe yet.

He scattered the poison pellets around the exterior of his house. No one would find that suspicious. He'd always had a rockjock problem. When that task was completed, he primed the canister of pesticide and ventured back inside.

Kress went through the house room by room, turning on lights everywhere he went until he was surrounded by a blaze of artificial illumination. He paused to clean up in the living room, shoveling sand and plastic fragments back into the broken tank. The sandkings were all gone, as he'd feared. The castles were shrunken and distorted, slagged by the watery bombardment Kress had visited upon them, and what little remained was crumbling as it dried.

He frowned and searched on, the canister of pest spray strapped across his shoulders.

Down in his deepest wine cellar, he came upon Cath m'Lane's corpse.

It sprawled at the foot of a steep flight of stairs, the limbs twisted as if by a fall. White mobiles were swarming all over it, and as Kress watched, the body moved jerkily across the hard-packed dirt floor.

He laughed, and twisted the illumination up to maximum. In the far corner, a squat little earthen castle and a dark hole were visible between two wine racks. Kress could make out a rough outline of his face on the cellar wall.

The body shifted once again, moving a few centimeters towards the castle. Kress had a sudden vision of the white maw waiting hungrily. It might be able to get Cath's foot in its mouth, but no more. It was too absurd. He laughed again, and started down into the cellar, finger poised on the trigger of the hose that snaked down his right arm. The sandkings—hundreds of them moving as one—deserted the body and formed up battle lines, a field of white between him and their maw.

Suddenly Kress had another inspiration. He smiled and lowered his firing hand. "Cath was always hard to swallow," he said, delighted at his wit. "Especially for one your size. Here, let me give you some help. What are gods for, after all?"

He retreated upstairs, returning shortly with a cleaver. The sandkings, patient, waited and watched while Kress chopped Cath m'Lane into small, easily digestible pieces.

Simon Kress slept in his skinthins that night, the pesticide close at hand, but he did not need it. The whites, sated, remained in the cellar, and he saw no sign of the others.

In the morning he finished the clean-up of the living room. After he was through, no trace of the struggle remained except for the broken tank.

He ate a light lunch, and resumed his hunt for the missing sandkings. In full daylight, it was not too difficult. The blacks had located in his rock garden, and built a castle heavy with obsidian and quartz. The reds he founds at the bottom of his long-disused swimming pool, which had partially filled with windblown sand over the years. He saw mobiles of both colors ranging about his grounds, many of them carrying poison pellets back to their maws. Kress decided his pesticide was unnecessary. No use risking a fight when he could just let the poison do its work. Both maws should be dead by evening.

That left only the burnt-orange sandkings unaccounted for. Kress circled his estate several times, in ever-widening spirals, but found no trace of them. When he began to sweat in his skinthins—it was a hot, dry day—he decided it was not important. If they were out here, they were probably eating the poison pellets along with the reds and blacks.

He crunched several sandkings underfoot, with a certain degree of satisfaction, as he walked back to the house. Inside, he removed his skinthins, settled down to a delicious meal, and finally began to relax.

Everything was under control. Two of the maws would soon be defunct, the third was safely located where he could dispose of it after it had served his purposes, and he had no doubt that he would find the fourth. As for Cath, all trace of her visit had been obliterated.

His reverie was interrupted when his viewscreen began to blink at him. It was Jad Rakkis, calling to brag about some cannibal worms he was bringing to the war games tonight.

Kress had forgotten about that, but he recovered quickly. "Oh, Jad, my pardons. I neglected to tell you. I grew bored with all that, and got rid of the sandkings. Ugly little things. Sorry, but there'll be no party tonight."

Rakkis was indignant. "But what will I do with my worms?"

"Put them in a basket of fruit and send them to a loved one," Kress said, signing off. Quickly he began calling the others. He did not need anyone arriving at his doorstep now, with the sandkings alive and infesting the estate.

As he was calling Idi Noreddian, Kress became aware of an annoying oversight. The screen began to clear, indicating that someone had answered at the other end. Kress flicked off.

Idi arrived on schedule an hour later. She was surprised to find the party cancelled, but perfectly happy to share an evening alone with Kress. He delighted her with his story of Cath's reaction to the holo they had made together. While telling it, he managed to ascertain that she had not mentioned the prank to anyone. He nodded, satisfied, and refilled their wine glasses. Only a trickle was left. "I'll have to get a fresh bottle," he said. "Come with me to my wine cellar, and help me pick out a good vintage. You've always had a better palate than I."

She came along willingly enough, but balked at the top of the stairs when Kress opened the door and gestured for her to precede him. "Where are the lights?" she said. "And that smell—what's that peculiar smell, Simon?"

When he shoved her, she looked briefly startled. She screamed as she tumbled down the stairs. Kress closed the door and began to nail it shut with the boards and air hammer he had left for that purpose. As he was finishing, he heard Idi groan. "I'm hurt," she said.

"Simon, what is this?" Suddenly she squealed, and shortly after that, the screaming started.

It did not cease for hours. Kress went to his sensorium and dialed up a saucy comedy to blot it out of his mind.

When he was sure she was dead, Kress flew her skimmer north to the volcanoes and discarded it. The magnalock was proving a good investment.

Odd scrabbling noises were coming from beyond the wine cellar door the next morning when Kress went down to check it out. He listened for several uneasy moments, wondering if Idi Noreddian could possibly have survived, and was now scratching to get out. It seemed unlikely; it had to be the sandkings. Kress did not like the implications of that. He decided that he would keep the door sealed, at least for the moment, and went outside with a shovel to bury the red and black maws in their own castles.

He found them very much alive.

The black castle was glittering with volcanic glass, and sandkings were all over it, repairing and improving. The highest tower was up to his waist, and on it was a hideous caricature of his face. When he approached, the blacks halted in their labors, and formed up into two threatening phalanxes. Kress glanced behind him and saw others closing off his escape. Startled, he dropped the shovel and sprinted out of the trap, crushing several mobiles beneath his boots.

The red castle was creeping up the walls of the swimming pool. The maw was safely settled in a pit, surrounded by sand and concrete and battlements. The reds crept all over the bottom of the pool. Kress watched them carry a rockjock and a large lizard into the castle. He stepped back from the poolside, horrified, and felt something crunch. Looking down, he saw three mobiles climbing up his leg. He brushed them off and stamped them to death, but others were approaching quickly. They were larger than he remembered. Some were almost as big as his thumb.

He ran. By the time he reached the safety of the house, his heart was racing and he was short of breath. The door closed behind him, and Kress hurried to lock it. His house was supposed to be pest-proof. He'd be safe in here.

A stiff drink steadied his nerve. So poison doesn't faze them, he thought. He should have known. Wo had warned him that the maw could eat anything. He would have to use the pesticide. Kress took another drink for good measure, donned his skinthins, and strapped the canister to his back. He unlocked the door.

Outside, the sandkings were waiting.

Two armies confronted him, allied against the common threat. More than he could have guessed. The damned maws must be breeding like rockjocks. They were everywhere, a creeping sea of them.

Kress brought up the hose and flicked the trigger.

A gray mist washed over the nearest rank of sandkings. He moved his hand from side to side.

Where the mist fell, the sandkings twitched violently and died in sudden spasms. Kress smiled. They were no match for him. He sprayed in a wide arc before him and stepped forward confidently over a litter of black and red bodies. The armies fell back. Kress advanced, intent on cutting through them to their maws.

All at once the retreat stopped. A thousand sandkings surged toward him.

Kress had been expecting the counterattack. He stood his ground, sweeping his misty sword before him in great looping strokes. They came at him and died. A few got through; he could not spray everywhere at once. He felt them climbing up his legs, sensed their mandibles biting futilely at the reinforced plastic of his skinthins. He ignored them, and kept spraying.

Then he began to feel soft impacts on his head and shoulders.

Kress trembled and spun and looked up above him. The front of his house was alive with sandkings. Blacks and reds, hundreds of them. They were launching themselves into the air, raining down on him. They fell all around him. One landed on his faceplate, its mandibles scraping at his eyes for a terrible second before he plucked it away.

He swung up his hose and sprayed the air, sprayed the house, sprayed until the airborne sandkings were all dead and dying. The mist settled back on him, making him cough. He coughed, and kept spraying. Only when the front of the house was clean did Kress turn his attention back to the ground.

They were all around him, on him, dozens of them scurrying over his body, hundreds of others hurrying to join them. He turned the mist on them. The hose went dead. Kress heard a loud *hiss,* and the deadly fog rose in a great cloud from between his shoulders, cloaking him, choking him, making his eyes burn and blur. He felt for the hose, and his hand came away covered with dying sandkings. The hose was severed; they'd eaten it through. He was surrounded by a shroud of pesticide, blinded. He stumbled and screamed, and began to run back to the house, pulling sandkings from his body as he went.

Inside, he sealed the door and collapsed on the carpet, rolling back and forth until he was sure he had crushed them all. The canister was empty by then, hissing feebly. Kress stripped off his skinthins and showered. The hot spray scalded him and left his skin reddened and sensitive, but it made his flesh stop crawling.

He dressed in his heaviest clothing, thick workpants and leathers, after shaking them out nervously. "Damn," he kept muttering, "damn." His throat was dry. After searching the entry hall thoroughly to make certain it was clean, he allowed himself to sit and pour a drink. "Damn," he repeated. His hand shook as he poured, slopping liquor on the carpet.

The alcohol settled him, but it did not wash away the fear. He had a second drink, and went to the window furtively. Sandkings were moving across the thick plastic pane. He shuddered and retreated to his communications console. He had to get help, he thought wildly. He would punch through a call to the authorities, and policers would come out with flame throwers and . . .

Simon Kress stopped in mid-call, and groaned. He couldn't call in the police. He would have to tell them about the whites in his cellar, and they'd find the bodies there. Perhaps the maw might have finished Cath m'Lane by now, but certainly not Idi Noreddian. He hadn't even cut her up. Besides, there would be bones. No, the police could be called in only as a last resort.

He sat the console, frowning. His communications equipment filled a whole wall; from here he could reach anyone on Baldur. He had plenty of money, and his cunning—he had always prided himself on his cunning. He would handle this somehow.

He briefly considered calling Wo, but soon dismissed the idea. Wo knew too much, and she would ask questions, and he did not trust her. No, he needed someone who would do as he asked *without* questions.

His frown faded, and slowly turned into a smile. Simon Kress had contacts. He put through a call to a number he had not used in a long time.

A woman's face took shape on his viewscreen: white-haired, bland of expression, with a long hook nose. Her voice was brisk and efficient. "Simon," she said. "How is business?"

"Business is fine, Lissandra," Kress replied. "I have a job for you."

"A removal? My price has gone up since last time, Simon. It has been ten years, after all."

"You will be well paid," Kress said. "You know I'm generous. I want you for a bit of pest control."

She smiled a thin smile. "No need to use euphemisms, Simon. The call is shielded."

"No, I'm serious. I have a pest problem. Dangerous pests. Take care of them for me. No questions. Understood?"

"Understood."

"Good. You'll need . . . oh, three or four operatives. Wear heat-resistant skinthins, and equip them with flame-throwers, or lasers, something on that order. Come out to my place. You'll see the problem. Bugs, lots and lots of them. In my rock garden and the old swimming pool you'll find castles. Destroy them, kill everything inside them. Then knock on the door, and I'll show you what else needs to be done. Can you get out here quickly?"

Her face was impassive. "We'll leave within the hour."

Lissandra was true to her word. She arrived in a lean black skimmer with three operatives. Kress watched them from the safety of a second-story window. They were all faceless in dark plastic skinthins. Two of them wore portable flamethrowers, a third carried laser cannon and explosives. Lissandra carried nothing; Kress recognized her by the way she gave orders.

Their skimmer passed low overhead first, checking out the situation. The sandkings went mad. Scarlet and ebon mobiles ran everywhere, frenetic. Kress could see the castle in the rock garden from his vantage point. It stood tall as a man. Its ramparts were crawling with black defenders, and a steady stream of mobiles flowed down into its depths.

Lissandra's skimmer came down next to Kress' and the operatives vaulted out and unlimbered their weapons. They looked inhuman, deadly.

The black army drew up between them and the castle. The reds—Kress suddenly realized that he could not see the reds. He blinked. Where had they gone?

Lissandra pointed and shouted, and her two flamethrowers spread out and opened up on the black sandkings. Their weapons coughed dully and began to roar, long tongues of blue-and-scarlet fire licking out before them. Sandkings crisped and blackened and died. The operatives began to play the fire back and forth in an efficient, interlocking pattern. They advanced with careful, measured steps.

The black army burned and disintegrated, the mobiles fleeing in a thousand different directions, some back toward the castle, others toward the enemy. None reached the operatives with the flame throwers. Lissandra's people were very professional.

Then one of them stumbled.

Or seemed to stumble. Kress looked again, and saw that the ground had given way beneath the man. Tunnels, he thought with a tremor of fear—tunnels, pits, traps. The flamer was sunk in sand up to his waist, and suddenly the ground around him seemed to erupt, and he was covered with scarlet sandkings. He dropped the flamethrower and began to claw wildly at his own body. His screams were horrible to hear.

His companion hesitated, then swung and fired. A blast of flame swallowed human and sandkings both. The screaming stopped abruptly. Satisfied, the second flamer turned back to the castle and took another step forward, and recoiled as his foot broke through the ground and vanished up to the ankle. He tried to pull it back and retreat, and the sand all around him gave way. He lost his balance and stumbled, flailing, and the sandkings were everywhere, a boiling mass of them, covering him as he writhed and rolled. His flamethrower was useless and forgotten.

Kress pounded wildly on the window, shouting for attention. "The castle! Get the castle!"

Lissandra, standing back by her skimmer, heard and gestured. Her third operative sighted with the laser cannon and fired. The beam throbbed across the grounds and sliced off the top of the castle. He brought it down sharply, hacking at the sand and stone parapets. Towers fell. Kress' face disintegrated. The laser bit into the ground, searching round and about. The castle crumbled; now it was only a heap of sand. But the black mobiles continued to move. The maw was buried too deeply; they hadn't touched her.

Lissandra gave another order. Her operative discarded the laser, primed an explosive, and darted forward. He leaped over the smoking corpse of the first flamer, landed on solid ground within Kress' rock garden, and heaved. The explosive ball landed square atop the ruins of the black castle. White-hot light seared Kress' eyes, and there was a tremendous gout of sand and rock and mobiles. For a moment dust obscured everything. It was raining sandkings and pieces of sandkings.

Kress saw that the black mobiles were dead and unmoving.

"The pool," he shouted down through the window. "Get the castle in the pool."

Lissandra understood quickly; the ground was littered with motionless blacks, but the reds were pulling back hurriedly and reforming. Her operative stood uncertain, then reached down and pulled out another explosive ball. He took one step forward, but Lissandra called him and he sprinted back in her direction.

It was all so simple then. He reached the skimmer, and Lissandra took him aloft. Kress rushed to another window in another room to watch. They came swooping in just over the pool, and the operative pitched his bombs down at the red castle from the safety of the skimmer. After the fourth run, the castle was unrecognizable, and the sandkings stopped moving.

Lissandra was thorough. She had him bomb each castle several additional times. Then he used the laser cannon, crisscrossing methodically until it was certain that nothing living could remain intact beneath those small patches of ground.

Finally they came knocking at his door. Kress was grinning manically when he let them in. "Lovely," he said, "lovely."

Lissandra pulled off the mask of her skinthins. "This will cost you, Simon. Two operatives gone, not to mention the danger to my own life."

"Of course," Kress blurted. "You'll be well paid, Lissandra. Whatever you ask, just so you finish the job."

"What remains to be done?"

"You have to clean out my wine cellar," Kress said. "There's another castle down there. And you'll have to do it without explosives. I don't want my house coming down around me."

Lissandra motioned to her operative. "Go outside and get Rajk's flamethrower. It should be intact."

He returned armed, ready, silent. Kress led them down to the wine cellar.

The heavy door was still nailed shut, as he had left it. But it bulged outward slightly, as if warped by some tremendous pressure. That made Kress uneasy, as did the silence that held reign about them. He stood well away from the door as Lissandra's operative removed his nails and planks. "Is that safe in here?" he found himself muttering, pointing at the flamethrower. "I don't want a fire, either, you know."

"I have the laser," Lissandra said. "We'll use that for the kill. The flamethrower probably won't be needed. But I want it here just in case. There are worse things than fire, Simon."

He nodded.

The last plank came free of the cellar door. There was still no sound from below. Lissandra snapped an order, and her underling fell back, took up a position behind her, and leveled the flamethrower square at the door. She slipped her mask back on, hefted the laser, stepped forward, and pulled open the door.

No motion. No sound. It was dark down there.

"Is there a light?" Lissandra asked.

"Just inside the door," Kress said. "On the right-hand side. Mind the stairs, they're quite steep."

She stepped into the door, shifted the laser to her left hand, and reached up with her right, fumbling inside for the light panel. Nothing happened. "I feel it," Lissandra said, "but it doesn't seem to . . ."

Then she was screaming, and she stumbled backward. A great white sandking had clamped itself around her wrist. Blood welled through her skinthins where its mandibles had sunk in. It was fully as large as her hand.

Lissandra did a horrible little jig across the room and began to smash her hand against the nearest wall. Again and again and again. It landed with a heavy, meaty thud. Finally the sandking fell away. She whimpered and fell to her knees. "I think my fingers are broken," she said softly. The blood was still flowing freely. She had dropped the laser near the cellar door.

"I'm not going down there," her operative announced in clear firm tones.

Lissandra looked up at him. "No," she said. "Stand in the door and flame it all. Cinder it. Do you understand?"

He nodded. Simon Kress moaned. "My *house*," he said. His stomach churned. The white sandking had been so *large*. How many more were down there? "Don't," he continued. "Leave it alone. I've changed my mind. Leave it alone."

Lissandra misunderstood. She held out her hand. It was covered with blood and greenish-black ichor. "Your little friend bit clean through my glove, and you saw what it took to get it off. I don't care about your house, Simon. Whatever is down there is going to die."

Kress hardly heard her. He thought he could see movement in the shadows beyond the cellar door. He imagined a white army bursting forth, all as large as the sandking that had attacked Lissandra. He saw himself being lifted by a hundred tiny arms, and dragged down into the darkness where the maw waited hungrily. He was afraid. "Don't," he said.

They ignored him.

Kress darted forward, and his shoulder slammed into the back of Lissandra's operative just as the man was bracing to fire. He grunted and unbalanced and pitched forward into the black. Kress listened to him fall down the stairs. Afterward there were other noises—scuttlings and snaps and soft squishing sounds.

Kress swung around to face Lissandra. He was drenched in cold sweat, but a sickly kind of excitement was on him. It was almost sexual.

Lissandra's calm cold eyes regarded him through her mask. "What are you doing?" she demanded as Kress picked up the laser she had dropped. *"Simon!"*

"Making a peace," he said, giggling. "They won't hurt god, no, not so long as god is good and generous. I was cruel. Starved them. I have to make up for it now, you see."

"You're insane," Lissandra said. It was the last thing she said. Kress burned a hole in her chest big enough to put his arm through. He dragged the body across the floor and rolled it down the cellar stairs. The noises were louder—chitinous clackings and scrapings and echoes that were thick and liquid. Kress nailed up the door once again.

As he fled, he was filled with a deep sense of contentment that coated his fear like a layer of syrup. He suspected it was not his own.

He planned to leave his home, to fly to the city and take a room for a night, or perhaps for a year. Instead Kress started drinking. He was not quite sure why. He drank steadily for hours, and retched it all up violently on his living room carpet. At some point he fell asleep. When he woke, it was pitch dark in the house.

He cowered against the couch. He could hear *noises*. Things were moving in the walls. They were all around him. His hearing was extraordinarily acute. Every little creak was the footstep of a sandking. He closed his eyes and waited, expecting to feel their terrible touch, afraid to move lest he brush against one.

Kress sobbed, and was very still for a while, but nothing happened.

He opened his eyes again. He trembled. Slowly the shadows

began to soften and dissolve. Moonlight was filtering through the high windows. His eyes adjusted.

The living room was empty. Nothing there, nothing, nothing. Only his drunken fears.

Simon Kress steeled himself, and rose, and went to a light.

Nothing there. The room was quiet, deserted.

He listened. Nothing. No sound. Nothing in the walls. It had all been his imagination, his fear.

The memories of Lissandra and the thing in the cellar returned to him unbidden. Shame and anger washed over him. Why had he done that? He could have helped her burn it out, kill it. *Why* . . . he knew why. The maw had done it to him, put fear in him. Wo had said it was psionic, even when it was small. And now it was large, so large. It had feasted on Cath, and Idi, and now it had two more bodies down there. It would keep growing. And it had learned to like the taste of human flesh, he thought.

He began to shake, but he took control of himself again and stopped. It wouldn't hurt him. He was god. The whites had always been his favorites.

He remembered how he had stabbed it with his throwing-sword. That was before Cath came. Damn her anyway.

He couldn't stay here. The maw would grow hungry again. Large as it was, it wouldn't take long. Its appetite would be terrible. What would it do then? He had to get away, back to the safety of the city while it was still contained in his wine cellar. It was only plaster and hard-packed earth down there, and the mobiles could dig and tunnel. When they got free . . . Kress didn't want to think about it.

He went to his bedroom and packed. He took three bags. Just a single change of clothing, that was all he needed; the rest of the space he filled with his valuables, with jewelry and art and other things he could not bear to lose. He did not expect to return.

His shambler followed him down the stairs, staring at him from its baleful glowing eyes. It was gaunt. Kress realized that it had been ages since he had fed it. Normally it could take care of itself, but no doubt the pickings had grown lean of late. When it tried to clutch at his leg, he snarled at it and kicked it away, and it scurried off, offended.

Kress slipped outside, carrying his bags awkwardly, and shut the door behind him.

For a moment he stood pressed against the house, his heart thudding in his chest. Only a few meters between him and his skimmer. He was afraid to cross them. The moonlight was bright, and the front of his house was a scene of carnage. The bodies of Lissandra's two flamers lay where they had fallen, one twisted and burned, the other swollen beneath a mass of dead sandkings. And the mobiles, the black and red mobiles, they were all around him. It was an effort to remember that they were dead. It was almost as if they were simply waiting, as they had waited so often before.

Nonsense, Kress told himself. More drunken fears. He had seen the castles blown apart. They were dead, and the white maw was trapped in his cellar. He took several deep and deliberate breaths, and stepped forward onto the sandkings. They crunched. He ground them into the sand savagely. They did not move.

Kress smiled, and walked slowly across the battleground, listening to the sounds, the sounds of safety.

Crunch. Crackle. Crunch.

He lowered his bags to the ground and opened the door to his skimmer.

Something moved from shadow into light. A pale shape on the seat of his skimmer. It was as long as his forearm. Its mandibles clacked together softly, and it looked up at him from six small eyes set all around its body.

Kress wet his pants and backed away slowly.

There was more motion from inside the skimmer. He had left the door open. The sandking emerged and came toward him, cautiously. Others followed. They had been hiding beneath his seats, burrowed into the upholstery. But now they emerged. They formed a ragged ring around the skimmer.

Kress licked his lips, turned, and moved quickly to Lissandra's skimmer.

He stopped before he was halfway there. Things were moving inside that one too. Great maggoty things, half-seen by the light of the moon.

Kress whimpered and retreated back toward the house. Near the front door, he looked up.

He counted a dozen long white shapes creeping back and forth across the walls of the building. Four of them were clustered close together near the top of the unused belfry where the carrion hawk had once roosted. They were carving something. A face. A very recognizable face.

Simon Kress shrieked and ran back inside.

A sufficient quantity of drink brought him the easy oblivion he sought. But he woke. Despite everything, he woke. He had a terrible headache, and he smelled, and he was hungry. Oh so very hungry. He had never been so hungry.

Kress knew it was not his *own* stomach hurting.

A white sandking watched him from atop the dresser in his bedroom, its antennae moving faintly. It was as big as the one in the skimmer the night before. He tried not to shrink away. "I'll . . . I'll feed you," he said to it. "I'll feed you." His mouth was horribly dry, sandpaper dry. He licked his lips and fled from the room.

The house was full of sandkings; he had to be careful where he put his feet. They all seemed busy on errands of their own. They were making modifications in his house, burrowing into or out of his walls, carving things. Twice he saw his own likeness staring out at him from unexpected places. The faces were warped, twisted, livid with fear.

He went outside to get the bodies that had been rotting in the yard, hoping to appease the white maw's hunger. They were gone, both of them. Kress remembered how easily the mobiles could carry things many times their own weight.

It was terrible to think that the maw was *still* hungry after all of that.

When Kress re-entered the house, a column of sandkings was wending its way down the stairs. Each carried a piece of his shambler. The head seemed to look at him reproachfully as it went by.

Kress emptied his freezers, his cabinets, everything, piling all the food in the house in the center of his kitchen floor. A dozen whites waited to take it away. They avoided the frozen food, leaving it to thaw in a great puddle, but they carried off everything else.

When all the food was gone, Kress felt his own hunger pangs abate just a bit, though he had not eaten a thing. But he knew the respite would be short-lived. Soon the maw would be hungry again. He had to feed it.

Kress knew what to do. He went to his communicator. "Malada," he began casually when the first of his friends answered, "I'm having a small party tonight. I realize this is terribly short notice, but I hope you can make it. I really do."

He called Jad Rakkis next, and then the others. By the time he had finished, nine of them had accepted his invitation. Kress hoped that would be enough.

Kress met his guests outside—the mobiles had cleaned up remarkably quickly, and the grounds looked almost as they had before the battle—and walked them to his front door. He let them enter first. He did not follow.

When four of them had gone through, Kress finally worked up his courage. He closed the door behind his latest guest, ignoring the startled exclamations that soon turned into shrill gibbering, and sprinted for the skimmer the man had arrived in. He slid in safely, thumbed the startplate, and swore. It was programmed to lift only in response to its owner's thumbprint, of course.

Jad Rakkis was the next to arrive. Kress ran to his skimmer as it set down, and seized Rakkis by the arm as he was climbing out. "Get back in, quickly," he said, pushing. "Take me to the city. Hurry, Jad. *Get out of here!*"

But Rakkis only stared at him, and would not move. "Why, what's wrong, Simon? I don't understand. What about your party?'

And then it was too late, because the loose sand all around them was stirring, and the red eyes were staring at them, and the mandibles were clacking. Rakkis made a choking sound, and moved to get back in his skimmer, but a pair of mandibles snapped shut about his ankle, and suddenly he was on his knees. The sand seemed to boil with subterranean activity. Jad thrashed and cried terribly as they tore him apart. Kress could hardly bear to watch.

After that, he did not try to escape again. When it was all over, he cleaned out what remained in his liquor cabinet, and got extremely drunk. It would be the last time he would enjoy that luxury, he knew. The only alcohol remaining in the house was stored down in the wine cellar.

Kress did not touch a bite of food the entire day, but he fell asleep feeling bloated, sated at last, the awful hunger vanquished. His last thoughts before the nightmares took him were of whom he could ask out tomorrow.

Morning was hot and dry. Kress opened his eyes to see the white sandking on his dresser again. He shut them again quickly, hoping the dream would leave him. It did not, and he could not go back to sleep. Soon he found himself staring at the thing.

He stared for almost five minutes before the strangeness of it dawned on him; the sandking was not moving.

The mobiles could be preternaturally still, to be sure. He had seen them wait and watch a thousand times. But always there was some motion about them—the mandibles clacked, the legs twitched, the long fine antennae stirred and swayed.

But the sandking on his dresser was completely still.

Kress rose, holding his breath, not daring to hope. Could it be dead? Could something have killed it? He walked across the room.

The eyes were glassy and black. The creature seemed swollen, somehow, as if it were soft and rotting inside, filling up with gas that pushed outward at the plates of white armor.

Kress reached out a trembling hand and touched it.

It was warm—hot even—and growing hotter. But it did not move.

He pulled his hand back, and as he did, a segment of the sandking's white exoskeleton fell away from it. The flesh beneath was the same color, but softer-looking, swollen and feverish. And it almost seemed to throb.

Kress backed away, and ran to the door.

Three more white mobiles lay in his hall. They were all like the one in his bedroom.

He ran down the stairs, jumping over sandkings. None of them moved. The house was full of them, all dead, dying, comatose, whatever. Kress did not care what was wrong with them. Just so they could not move.

He found four of them inside his skimmer. He picked them up one by one, and threw them as far as he could. Damned monsters. He slid back in, on the ruined half-eaten seats, and thumbed the startplate.

Nothing happened.

Kress tried again, and again. Nothing. It wasn't fair. This was *his* skimmer, it ought to start, why wouldn't it lift, he didn't understand.

Finally he got out and checked, expecting the worst. He found it. The sandkings had torn apart his gravity grid. He was trapped. He was still trapped.

Grimly, Kress marched back into the house. He went to his gallery and found the antique axe that had hung next to the throwing-sword he had used on Cath m'Lane. He set to work. The sandkings did not stir even as he chopped them to pieces. But they splattered when he made the first cut, the bodies almost bursting. Inside was awful; strange half-formed organs, a viscous reddish ooze that looked almost like human blood, and the yellow ichor.

Kress destroyed twenty of them before he realized the futility of what he was doing. The mobiles were nothing, really. Besides, there were so *many* of them. He could work for a day and night and still not kill them all.

He had to go down into the wine cellar and use the axe on the maw.

Resolute, he started down. He got within sight of the door, and stopped.

It was not a door any more. The walls had been eaten away, so that the hole was twice the size it had been, and round. A pit, that was all. There was no sign that there had ever been a door nailed shut over that black abyss.

A ghastly, choking, fetid odor seemed to come from below.

And the walls were wet and bloody and covered with patches of white fungus.

And worst, it was *breathing*.

Kress stood across the room and felt the warm wind wash over him as it exhaled, and he tried not to choke, and when the wind reversed direction, he fled.

Back in the living room, he destroyed three more mobiles, and collapsed. What was *happening?* He didn't understand.

Then he remembered the only person who might understand. Kress went to his communicator again, stepping on a sandking in his haste, and prayed fervently that the device still worked.

When Jala Wo answered, he broke down and told her everything.

She let him talk without interruption, no expression save for a slight frown on her gaunt, pale face. When Kress had finished, she said only, "I ought to leave you there."

Kress began to blubber. "You can't. Help me. I'll pay . . ."

"I ought to," Wo repeated, "but I won't."

"Thank you," Kress said. "Oh, thank—"

"Quiet," said Wo. "Listen to me. This is your own doing. Keep your sandkings well, and they are courtly ritual warriors. You turned yours into something else, with starvation and torture. You were their god. You made them what they are. That maw in your cellar is sick, still suffering from the wound you gave it. It is probably insane. Its behavior is . . . unusual.

"You have to get out of there quickly. The mobiles are not dead, Kress. They are dormant. I told you the exoskeleton falls off when they grow larger. Normally, in fact, it falls off much earlier. I have never heard of sandkings growing as large as yours while still in the insectoid stage. It is another result of crippling the white maw, I would say. That does not matter.

"What matters is the metamorphosis your sandkings are now undergoing. As the maw grows, you see, *it* gets progressively more intelligent. Its psionic powers strengthen, and its mind becomes more sophisticated, more ambitious. The armored mobiles are useful enough when the maw is tiny and only semi-sentient, but now it needs better servants, bodies with more capabilities. Do you understand? The mobiles are all going to give birth to a new breed of sandking. I can't say exactly what it will look like. Each maw designs its own, to fit its perceived needs and desires. But it will be bi-ped, with four arms, and opposable thumbs. It will be able to construct and operate advanced machinery. The individual sandkings will not be sentient. But the maw will be very sentient indeed."

Simon Kress was gaping at Wo's image on the viewscreen. "Your workers," he said, with an effort. "The ones who came out here . . . who installed the tank . . ."

Jala Wo managed a faint smile. "Shade," she said.

"Shade is a sandking," Kress repeated numbly. "And you sold me a tank of . . . of . . . infants, ah . . ."

"Do not be absurd," Wo said. "A first-stage sandking is more like a sperm than an infant. The wars temper and control them in nature. Only one in a hundred reaches second stage. Only one in a thousand achieves the third and final plateau, and becomes like Shade. Adult sandkings are not sentimental about the small maws. There are too many of them, and their mobiles are pests." She sighed. "And all this talk wastes time. That white sandking is going to waken to full sentience soon. It is not going to need you any longer, and it hates you, and it will be very hungry. The transformation is taxing. The maw must eat enormous amounts both before and after. So you have to get out of there. Do you understand?"

"I *can't*," Kress said. "My skimmer is destroyed, and I can't get any of the others to start. I don't know how to reprogram them. Can you come out for me?"

"Yes," said Wo. "Shade and I will leave at once, but it is more than two hundred kilometers from Asgard to you, and there is equipment we will need to deal with the deranged sandking you've created. You cannot wait there. You have two feet. Walk. Go due east, as near as you can determine, as quickly as you can. The land out there is pretty desolate. We can find you easily with an aerial search, and you'll be safely away from the sandking. Do you understand?"

"Yes," said Simon Kress. "Yes, oh, yes."

They signed off, and he walked quickly toward the door. He was halfway there when he heard the noise—a sound halfway between a pop and a crack.

One of the sandkings had split open. Four tiny hands covered with pinkish-yellow blood came up out of the gap and began to push the dead skin aside.

Kress began to run.

He had not counted on the heat.

The hills were dry and rocky. Kress ran from the house as quickly as he could, ran until his ribs ached and his breath was coming in gasps. Then he walked, but as soon as he had recovered he began to run again. For almost an hour he ran and walked, ran and walked, beneath the fierce hot sun. He sweated freely, and wished that he had thought to bring some water. He watched the sky in hopes of seeing Wo and Shade.

He was not made for this. It was too hot, and too dry, and he was in no condition. But he kept himself going with the memory of the way the maw had breathed, and the thought of the wriggling little things that by now were surely crawling all over his house. He hoped Wo and Shade would know how to deal with them.

He had his own plans for Wo and Shade. It was all their fault, Kress had decided, and they would suffer for it. Lissandra was dead, but he knew others in her profession. He would have his revenge. He promised himself that a hundred times as he struggled and sweated his way east.

At least he hoped it was east. He was not that good at directions, and he wasn't certain which way he had run in his initial panic, but since then he had made an effort to bear due east, as Wo had suggested. When he had been running for several hours, with no sign of rescue, Kress began to grow certain that he had gone wrong.

When several more hours passed, he began to grow afraid. What if Wo and Shade could not find him? He would die out here. He hadn't eaten in two days; he was weak and frightened; his throat was raw for want of water. He couldn't keep going. The sun was sinking now, and he'd be completely lost in the dark. What was wrong? Had the sandkings eaten Wo and Shade? The fear was on him again, filling him, and with it a great thirst and a terrible hunger. But Kress kept going. He stumbled now when he tried to run, and twice he fell. The second time he scraped his hand on a rock, and it came away bloody. He sucked at it as he walked, and worried about infection.

The sun was on the horizon behind him. The ground grew a little cooler, for which Kress was grateful. He decided to walk until last light and settle in for the night. Surely he was far enough from the sandkings to be safe, and Wo and Shade would find him come morning.

When he topped the next rise, he saw the outline of a house in front of him.

It wasn't as big as his own house, but it was big enough. It was habitation, safety. Kress shouted and began to run toward it. Food and drink, he had to have nourishment, he could taste the meal now. He was aching with hunger. He ran down the hill towards the house, waving his arms and shouting to the inhabitants. The light was almost gone now, but he could still make out a half-dozen children playing in the twilight. "Hey there," he shouted. "Help, help."

They came running toward him.

Kress stopped suddenly. "No," he said, "oh, no. Oh, no." He backpedaled, slipped on the sand, got up and tried to run again. They caught him easily. They were ghastly little things with bulging eyes and dusky orange skin. He struggled, but it was useless. Small as they were, each of them had four arms, and Kress had only two.

They carried him toward the house. It was a sad, shabby house built of crumbling sand, but the door was quite large, and dark, and it breathed. That was terrible, but it was not the thing that set Simon Kress to screaming. He screamed because of the others, the little orange children who came crawling out from the castle, and watched impassive as he passed. All of them had his face.